'*Dice* has a forensic depth that is compelling, that challenges and deeply moves the reader. But what sets this novel apart is the precision and power of the writing. This is fiction that doesn't want to be journalism, it affirms the truth and nuance and possibility of imagination.'

**Christos Tsiolkas, bestselling author of *The Slap***

'*Dice* achieves what the best fiction achieves: it draws us into the story on a deeply personal level, coaxing us to consider what we would do in the same situation . . . Step by skilful step in this potent, compelling debut, Baylis exposes the flawed nature of justice. In granting us access to the sacred space of the jury room, she challenges us to confront our own preconceptions. A deeply involving and eloquent novel.'

**Catherine Chidgey, award-winning author of *Remote Sympathy***

# DICE

## CLAIRE BAYLIS

ALLEN&UNWIN
SYDNEY • MELBOURNE • AUCKLAND • LONDON

This is a work of fiction. Names, characters, places and incidents are products of the author's imagination or are used fictitiously. Any resemblance to actual events, locales or persons, living or dead, is entirely coincidental.

First published in 2023



Allen & Unwin
Cammeraygal Country
83 Alexander Street
Crows Nest NSW 2065
Australia
Phone: (61 2) 8425 0100
Email: info@allenandunwin.com
Web: www.allenandunwin.com

*Allen & Unwin acknowledges the Traditional Owners of the Country on which we live and work. We pay our respects to all Aboriginal and Torres Strait Islander Elders, past and present.*

NATIONAL LIBRARY OF AUSTRALIA

A catalogue record for this book is available from the National Library of Australia

ISBN 978 1 76106 724 2

Set in 13/17.5 pt Granjon BH Pro by Bookhouse, Sydney
Printed and bound in Australia by the Opus Group

10 9 8 7 6 5 4 3 2 1

FSC www.fsc.org MIX Paper | Supporting responsible forestry FSC® C001695

The paper in this book is FSC® certified. FSC® promotes environmentally responsible, socially beneficial and economically viable management of the world's forests.

*For Henry*
*And for Linda and Geoff*

# CHARACTERS

**THE JURY**

Jake
Dave
Bethany
Fiona
Susannah
Scott
Chantae
Kahu
Mark
Les
Eva
Hayley

**THE DEFENDANTS**

Lee
Chris
Jayden/Jayz
Travis

**THE COMPLAINANTS**

Samara
Maia
Amy

*They come from Ngongotahā and Lynmore, from Western Heights and Tarawera, from Koutu, Springfield, Glenholme and Ōwhata. In ones and twos they come to the corner where Tūtānekai Street crosses Arawa, where the white building with its coat of arms and tinted windows sits in a courtyard bordered by kōwhaiwhai-patterned benches.*

*Some are dropped off. Some catch the bus. A few, like the elderly man in the checked shirt and beige trousers, walk. A tall man with wavy hair leaves his car in the free sixty-minute parking, assuming that will be long enough. Others pass the pale unblinking gaze of the pou and drive under the Prince's Gate to the free parking in the Government Gardens, or they choose the patch of dirt where the hospice used to be, where the sulphur smell is strong. An eighteen-year-old walking that way from his Mazda, looking out for the carved warrior with the bowler hat, notices that the mere pounamu another holds is actually a lizard. He pauses, breathes.*

*Past the brick pub on the corner they come, under the huge sycamore tree that is lit at night by fairy lights. Or they cross the road by the after-hours medical centre, or from the Fat Dog cafe.*

*People mill around in the courtyard, smoking, waiting, hugging; listening to lawyers with oversized briefcases who talk in authoritative, urgent tones. Some walk fast, head down, past these people. A few recognise familiar faces. One pauses, a hand on an arm: 'You okay, whaea? What's the story?'*

*Others catch up with the person ahead:*

*'Do you know where we go?'*

*'Have you done this before?'*

*A blonde woman in heels and a linen jacket glances nervously at the waiting people, avoiding their eyes, checking the colours of their clothes, their tattoos.*

*One or two mutter swearwords. Many worry about their arrangements, sending last-minute texts, while a handful, bolstered by experience, stride towards the door; it is a mere inconvenience to them.*

*A thin man with scraggly facial hair skulks by the planter, flicking ash on the azalea.*

*Someone talks about duty, another about community service. One has dressed in a suit in the hope of being challenged; others have dressed down in the same hope. A few, like the young woman in the mint green dungarees and the man from the bank, are content—a day away from work. But if it carries on, if they are chosen . . .*

*'What's the pay, anyway?'*

*'And what about petrol?'*

*'Bus fare?'*

*'Lunch?'*

*'Child care?'*

*The self-employed, imagining aggrieved clients and directionless apprentices, consider how to persuade whoever needs persuading of the untenability of their predicament. A few have already tried this on the form; none here succeeded.*

*A woman in a loose flapping cardigan hovers by the rubbish bin, holding a takeaway coffee.*

*Another pauses by her. 'I didn't think they'd summon me at my age.'*

*The younger woman twitches a brief smile.*

*'Come on, we'll be in it together,' says the older woman.*

## CHAPTER ONE

# Jake

Jake added 'Dice Bros' to his search.

He clicked on the most recent news article about the case—it said the police had charged the boys involved in the teen sex game. Jake had lost track; he hadn't realised it had progressed that far. Four youths were facing charges for rape and sexual assaults and making a video. Jake scrolled all the way through and then clicked back to the search results.

• • •

THE FIRST JAKE heard of the Dice Bros (although not by that name) was when he was thumbing through the local newspaper as a way of putting off the mowing for a few more minutes. It was one of those summary sidebar stories, stating that police had made inquiries at two local high schools following allegations that a teen sex game had gone awry. There was a number to call if you knew more information. Jake was curious, but there was no detail and it wasn't his children's school, so, sighing, he closed the paper and headed down to the bottom section of the garden by the sleep-out, where he'd left the mower.

The mowing was part of his preparation for summer. By the time Tilly came back from her mother's he'd planned to have the deck washed and oiled, chairs scrubbed, lawns mown—a present for his wife. A shiny ordered garden. Instead, in the nearly three weeks of her absence, all he'd managed was to weed the vegetable boxes and then overcrowd them with parsley, lettuce, corn and tomato seedlings.

As Jake mowed, he thought that somehow the weekends seemed to both stretch and bulge without Tilly here to shape them. He wasn't even sure how today had drifted away. He had spent several hours flicking between the Test and the tennis while he waited for her to call. Not that she'd had anything new to report. Her mother was still in ICU in Christchurch Hospital, and Tilly was still in emergency mode—he could hear it in her voice, could tell by the odd times she was ringing. Jake had lost that sense of urgency; he was in limbo, not knowing how long his wife would be away, nor how they would manage if her mother was discharged.

The mower was heavy. The catcher must be nearly full.

He wondered what food there was for dinner. It would only be him and TJ, because Annelyse was at a sleepover. Jake had been especially glad of that when TJ had turned up with his new girlfriend, Melissa. Melissa and Annelyse were in the same year, two years below TJ, and Annelyse's shorts were as skimpy as Melissa's skirt, but it was the way Melissa's skirt swished as she sashayed past Jake on the way down to the lake that made him almost worry for TJ—you could practically see her knickers.

Perhaps, just this once, he'd send TJ and Melissa for takeaways. TJ wasn't meant to drive Melissa on his restricted licence, but he'd taken to dropping her home, and the Indian wasn't much further. Then tomorrow Jake would do a shop and wash the deck, and that reminded him that he'd left the laundry neglected in the washer all day. Tilly should be here. There was just too much stuff with the kids and work as well.

Jake shoved the lawnmower forwards, and as he did there was a cracking, splintering noise. The mower spluttered, spluttered, and stalled.

Jake swore and, pulling it back, saw he'd run over a stick, a stick with a piece of garden twine attached; the other half was probably wrapped around the mower blades. It would be one of the bows and arrows TJ made when only he and Annelyse were around. Surely they should be too old for this now. Jake searched through the long grass for the companion arrows. Recently, TJ had adopted six-inch nails as arrow tips, taping them on with duct tape, and Jake imagined one of those through his shinbone. He considered marching down to the lake; TJ should be here helping, not frolicking with his girlfriend.

There were three sharpened sticks in the long grass (and one did have a nail), two blown-apart L&P bottles from TJ's dry ice escapades, and the one decent cricket ball. The kids just didn't look after things, or clear up after themselves, even though their mother was a teacher.

He undid the catcher, scooped up the matted grass that fell out, and decided to throw this load down the bank into the reserve. As he pushed the earmuffs down to his neck he heard music—not TJ's usual thudding bass, it was more melodic. He hadn't heard TJ and Melissa come back from the lake, but clearly they were in the sleep-out now. The sleep-out where the children used to play houses with Annelyse's tea set, mixing flowers and herbs with water and eating biscuits pillaged from the kitchen, and where these days TJ and his mates experimented with alcohol. Jake had found the empty beer and RTD cans over the fence when he was spraying the wandering willie. And now TJ was in there kissing and feeling up his girlfriend. To think that Melissa had been a friend of his daughter's not that long ago; Annelyse was miles off that stuff.

Jake started whistling as he shook out the catcher, thinking he'd just make them aware he was on to them, but the music was loud, and then he caught the lyrics. Something about wanting head, tongue. And then he heard the word 'pussy'. The song paused, before the singer, practically speaking, instructed the woman to talk dirty, put her legs up, poke out her butt.

It was too much. Melissa was only fourteen. And there were the neighbours.

He would tell his son to move the song on; he wouldn't make a big deal out of it.

Jake coughed, and banged the catcher against the weatherboard planks as if to shake loose the last clumps of grass. Then he peered in through the high side window.

The late sun streaming through the French doors cast a shadow on the back wall—an upright shadow moving back and forth in the bright patch of sunlight. Jake registered that it was a single shadow: the shadow of his son, cap on. Didn't understand. Looked across to the divan, where Melissa was on her hands and knees in front of TJ, her top half bare, her surprisingly large breasts hanging. She still had the skirt around her waist and TJ, his son, was fucking her. A fourteen-year-old. Doggy-style.

Jake backed away.

IN THE KITCHEN Jake poured himself a cold water, downed it, and then opened a Croucher. He sculled half of that too. Should he have stopped them? He could hardly barge in there with the girl all naked and . . .

He went into the toilet, realising as he did that he hadn't taken off his boots—there were grass clippings all over them and his bare shins were stained green. He followed the grassy trail back through the kitchen to the sliding door and kicked the boots off, sending them bouncing down the steps. The house was a pigsty. He finished that beer. Opened another.

Had TJ used a condom? Jesus Christ, what if he got her pregnant? A fourteen-year-old. Jake went back to the cricket that he'd left on live pause and started to fast-forward at double speed. He supposed Melissa might be fifteen; Annelyse was young in her year.

TJ had been staring straight ahead. From what Jake had seen there hadn't been any connection, except at that most base level.

Jake paused the TV when the West Indies bowler threw his arms into the air. Rewound. Re-watched. The New Zealand captain had been caught out. The fielder hadn't even moved his feet, just stuck out his arm and caught it. A completely botched shot.

Jake was eighteen when he lost his virginity. He'd met Chloe at university, and they'd been on dates, and kissed, and held hands. Their first sex, most of their sex, was missionary and loving and facing each other. He remembered the first time, how he'd kept telling her how smooth her skin was and how he'd felt an overwhelming sense of gratitude—that she was touching him, that she would want to. She wasn't a virgin, and had laughed at Jake, but she'd liked him and afterwards they'd lain together, faces touching, sharing the same breath, and he'd felt so indebted to her.

With TJ there had been a casual disregard for the girl, almost a callousness. It was the way he'd gripped her hips—Jake had seen the indentations from his fingers digging into her flesh; he thought that's what he'd seen. It was probably because of the internet. They should have banned iPads and phones from the kids' bedrooms, like that TV guy said, but Tilly made the rules. She was the expert. Deputy principal at an intermediate school now. And then it occurred to Jake that if that's what TJ did, what on earth did he watch? And her, Melissa: he couldn't believe she was so loose at fifteen.

Live now, he watched the West Indies bat and he let his eyes lose focus so the men became white blurs against the vivid green pitch.

He wished he hadn't looked in the window.

Early on, one of the first times he and Tilly made love, she had placed her hand over his eyes. When he asked her why, she'd said, 'You're staring. Too intense.'

Above the noise of the TV Jake could hear TJ and Melissa coming up through the garden, loud and sparking—she swearing about something, until she saw him.

'Ooh, sorry, Jake.'

She wasn't, he thought. He couldn't look at her. Mumbled to TJ about his exam revision.

'Yeah, we're just—'

'Now, TJ.'

'Has something happened with Nana?'

'No. She's fine. Just the same.'

'What did New Zealand go for?'

Jake answered.

TJ asked about the captain.

Jake answered.

'That's crap,' said TJ. 'Hey, we're gonna make some toasties, then I'll drop Mel home. D'you want one, Dad?'

Look at him. So full of himself. Jake shook his head, keeping his eyes on the screen. Usually he'd confer with Tilly on how to handle something like this—not that there'd been anything quite like this—but he couldn't tell Tilly, not while her mother was dying, because that's what was happening. And whatever he said to TJ it wouldn't make any difference now anyway. They were doing it. TJ wasn't going to go back from that. He should tell him to use condoms, but they'd never had that kind of relationship. Tilly was responsible for the sex ed stuff.

With a creeping dread, it occurred to Jake that perhaps he should be telling Melissa's parents. Imagine that conversation. He didn't know them. Maybe he'd met her mother on the sideline at Annelyse's soccer games . . . or was that Bailey's mum?

Tilly would be the one to do it, but he couldn't tell her yet, and surely Melissa's parents should know what their daughter was up to anyway. If Annelyse had a boyfriend, he'd supervise. And then he thought, Melissa's parents might think he was supervising them right now.

• • •

SITTING OPPOSITE JAKE at the kitchen bench, Tilly was silently reading something on her phone, frowning as she scrolled down. She sighed, but didn't look up.

It was two weeks since her mother had died. Tilly had cried when she met them at Christchurch airport, again at the end of the funeral and the day they got home, but since then she seemed to have adjusted. They had packed up her mother's villa and given most of the furniture to Women's Refuge—Tilly's idea; TJ had wanted to sell it all on Trade Me for a cut. And they'd shipped home five boxes of books, linen and kitchenware, which were stored—temporarily, Jake hoped—in the garage.

Finally Tilly said, 'Have you seen this?' It was her outraged voice. 'Nothing changes.' Her tone was far from resigned. Sometimes she got fired up unnecessarily, pointlessly. It would be a council issue—the grey hair brigade getting their knickers in a twist again over some Te Arawa proposal, either that or another refugee crisis, or perhaps, with all that sighing, climate change. She leaned right over the bench, thrusting the phone between Jake's face and his cereal bowl, until he slowly lowered his spoon and took it.

She was looking at a news report headed POLICE INVESTIGATE TEEN SEX GAME. It was alleged that a group of boys calling themselves the Dice Bros had plied underage girls with alcohol and sexually assaulted them.

'Unbelievable,' said Jake. 'You'd think after all the publicity about Me Too they'd know better. I thought schools—'

'Keep reading,' said Tilly. 'It's here—in Rotorua. One boy's only year twelve.'

It took him a moment to register. Year twelve. The same year as TJ.

Jake felt the blush creep up his face, and the more he was aware of it, aware of Tilly noticing, the worse it became. The bane of his adolescence.

TJ and Melissa. Melissa was, at best, fifteen. He still hadn't told Tilly. The timing hadn't been right. She'd been down south, and then back here, but preoccupied. Grieving. He was worried she'd overreact. He didn't want a scene; he wasn't sure how TJ would respond.

Nor had Jake told his son that he'd seen him. He'd hinted. The day after, he'd reminded TJ that Melissa and Annelyse used to be friends. TJ had scoffed, 'In about year five, Dad. Melissa's a lot more mature than Annelyse. A lot.'

'I'm just saying be careful—she's much younger than you.'

'Sure.'

'How old is she anyway?'

TJ had already gone back to his phone, clicking on the Snapchat ghost icon.

Jake took the opportunity while he was engrossed. 'You need to respect her. Girls are different . . .'

TJ nodded, grunted, leaned forwards so his face filled the screen.

'TJ?'

The phone clicked. 'I'm listening.'

'You need to be sensible. Girls can feel pressured.'

'Believe me, Dad, *I'm* not pressuring Melissa.'

Jake ignored this. 'We've got a lot on at the moment, TJ.'

TJ was smirking.

'What?' asked Jake, his voice tight.

'Nothing. Just something here.' He waggled his phone.

Jake had left then; he wasn't getting anywhere, and he'd thought it would be better for them to talk once he'd touched base with Tilly.

Only he hadn't yet.

In the kitchen, Jake gave the phone back to Tilly. The news report was vague—it said the students were from three local schools. The police were still investigating; no charges had been laid at this point. The police would not comment, nor would the schools.

As Jake put his bowl in the dishwasher, he said, 'Melissa's the same age as Annelyse, isn't she?'

'We don't need to worry about that. It's hardly serious; he had a "thing" with her friend last month.' For some reason, Tilly made air quotes as she said 'thing'.

Maybe TJ had had sex with that girl too. Maybe he'd had intercourse with lots of girls.

• • •

BY THE FOLLOWING Saturday, the news reports about the Dice Bros seemed to have solidified—there were five boys and as many as six girls involved, aged between fifteen and eighteen. The boys were mainly finishing year thirteen, although one had left school and one was in TJ's year. Investigations were ongoing.

Jake skimmed through an opinion piece, and then said to Tilly tentatively, 'I suppose it's social media that drives this Dice Bros kind of behaviour?'

'It's rape culture, Jake, isn't it? Attitudes. It doesn't matter if it's on Snapchat or Facebook or at a party on a Saturday night.'

'From pornography, d'you think? I mean, have you talked to TJ?'

'He doesn't know them.'

'Oh. Good. I meant more generally, though, you know?'

'I think TJ understands about consent.'

''Course.' The image was before him again: Melissa on all fours, his son's body moving. He tried to bring to mind her face—had she been okay with it? And then he thought about her joking and swearing as they came into the house afterwards.

'He needs to be careful, though,' Jake said. 'Girls can change their mind, can't they?'

Tilly was looking at him over the top of her glasses and he nodded to her, thinking, yes, he could trust TJ's judgement.

'We need to be afraid for our daughters, not our sons, Jake,' said Tilly in her teacher tone.

CLOSE TO ELEVEN, when TJ hadn't surfaced, Jake knocked on his door, gave him a minute, then shoved it open. Picking a path through the wet towels, strewn clothes and tattered schoolbooks, he deposited a rubbish bag on the bed and told TJ he had half an hour to clean the sleep-out. TJ stretched, rolled over and then settled again, muttering about breakfast and his exams, even as he pulled his phone and headphones out from under the bed.

'Mum'll be home from yoga in an hour. I think you want to do it before then.' Jake left the room.

No doubt TJ was startled—would think him firm, but fair. Discreet even.

Jake waited. He wasn't going to clean up his son's empty cans and chippie packets. He had a vision of a used condom down the side of the divan, imagined pulling it out and finding the floor littered with them, Melissa's underwear, oh God . . .

He marched back. TJ was still lying there, smiling at the phone as he texted.

'Get up!' screamed Jake. It was Tilly who lost her temper in this house. Tilly and TJ who had shouting matches. Jake was the peacemaker. 'I want everything out of the sleep-out. All the rubbish gone and the floor swept. NOW.'

'What the . . . ?'

Regaining control of himself, Jake told TJ in a normal tone that, once he'd cleaned up, they were going to move Nana's boxes into the sleep-out, so TJ wouldn't be able to use it for a while. He considered adding that when Melissa was over, the door had to stay open.

He said, 'And you're too young for RTDs.'

• • •

THE NEXT DAY, at lunchtime, Jake came into the kitchen to find Tilly bending over, peering into the back of a drawer.

'Have you seen that mandolin thing?'

Jake thought a mandolin was a musical instrument. 'No.'

She was wearing a skirt and the material of it clung, so he could see the curves of her buttocks, the shape of her thighs. And then that song came into his head—the man speaking—poke out your butt.

Jake moved so he was right behind her, as if he were going to help her look; closer, so he was pressing against her. How could he be turned on by that song, by that line?

Tilly giggled and straightened up. 'What's got into you, tiger?'

Bending to nuzzle her ear, he laughed too, relieved to hear her happiness again.

'I thought a mandolin was something Captain Corelli played,' he said into her ear. His hand stroked, cupped her breast, fingering the button on her shirt. Tilly arched against him, her frizzy hair in his face. Then, smiling, she turned, plonked a kiss on his nose and moved back to the dishwasher.

It didn't matter—for the rest of the day, Jake knew, they'd occasionally touch or catch the other's eye, a reminder, a message. Tonight. In bed.

THAT NIGHT, IN their room, with just the lamp on, as Tilly was lifting his T-shirt over his head, kissing his neck, pressing herself against him, Jake had an appalling thought. It wasn't that he visualised Melissa's breasts. Hanging there. But imagine if he did. Imagine if he thought of her now, in this moment.

• • •

IN THE CAR, TJ was telling Jake how Melissa and his friend Liam had played a prank on one of the teachers, plastering her classroom with posters of Trump with speech bubble comments, because they knew she hated him. He talked fast, explaining some of the comments, and Jake got lost, but laughed when TJ did.

'You and Melissa still together then?'

'Yeah.'

'She's quite a bit younger.'

'She's fifteen.'

Jake nodded and refrained from pointing out it was two years and asked instead how they'd got together.

'We were playing Smash or Pass, and Liam gave me Melissa.'

'Playing what?'

'It's a game in the group chat, it's like Tap or Gap, where your mate gives you a girl and you have to say "tap" or "gap" and why.'

'So, "tap"?' Jake asked with trepidation.

TJ grinned. 'Yeah, you know, you'd do her . . .' He shrugged. 'Want to be with her.'

'And "gap"? Do you say on the group chat that you don't like them?'

'You can say it like—"just a friend" or "too young".'

'And what exactly does tap involve?'

TJ laughed. 'Chill, Dad.'

'So, you said tap to Melissa.'

'Well, not to her. About her. And someone tagged her and she said, "Let's go then."'

'Very romantic,' said Jake.

'Only don't tell Mum, 'cos it'll end up as one of those conversations.'

'Those conversations?'

'Not playing those kinds of games, respecting girls, the dangers of social media—you know, Dad.'

Jake nodded his head a fraction. He waited a while and then said, 'It's good to talk. We don't so often now with you driving yourself.'

TJ didn't answer.

'We should go biking. We haven't been for ages.'

TJ didn't answer.

'Teej?'

'Sure, Dad,' he said.

• • •

ON SATURDAY AFTERNOON Jake was having a nap when Annelyse burst in.

'Dad, quick, it's TJ—he's crying.'

Jake jumped up; he couldn't remember the last time TJ had cried.

Annelyse didn't answer his questions as they ran down the stairs—he wasn't sure if she didn't know what was going on, or if she was holding back.

The boy was curled on the window seat in the kitchen, hands over his head, his body shuddering. Jake perched next to him, asking what was wrong, looking for signs of injury, prising TJ's hands off his face. TJ started to rock, his body heaving.

Shouting, Jake asked Annelyse again, 'What happened?'

'He just came in like that.' Annelyse's voice was high and panicky.

'TJ, are you hurt?'

Why wasn't Tilly here? Why was she never here when things happened?

'Turn over. Tell me what's going on.'

TJ tried to explain. It was difficult to understand. Jake caught the name Melissa and then Liam. The slut—she must have gone off with his mate. This was what happened when kids had sex too early: they got caught up like this. TJ was hurting—real heartache.

Jake tried to imagine what Tilly would do. He poured a glass of water, ran the kitchen towel under the hot tap and wrung it out.

'Now sit up,' he said, in a voice which sounded calmer than he felt. 'Wash your face. Drink this. You can tell me anything. Annelyse, you should go.'

TJ held the towel over his face. Annelyse hovered.

'Is it . . . did Melissa . . . ?'

Sitting up, his hands dropping away with the towel, TJ made full eye contact for his confession. 'We killed a dog. It ran out in front of us. By Blue Lake.'

'How did you get to . . . ? In a car? Was anyone hurt?'

Gradually, Jake pieced it together. Two carloads of TJ's friends, both with drivers on their restricted, had driven out to Blue Lake. On the way home they'd decided to race. TJ and Melissa were in Liam's car, along with Liam's girlfriend. They'd all been egging Liam on, so that as he pulled out to overtake the other car he hadn't been able to stop in time when the dog ran out.

It took a little longer to get the full subtleties. They'd been yelling out the windows, which was what had drawn the black lab, barking and bouncing, on to the road. Yes, he did mean the part around from the lakefront where it was still fifty k's, and Liam was, for sure, speeding. The other car drove on, possibly not even realising what had happened. The owners, including their daughters, saw the whole thing.

TJ broke down again as he described the girls, the dog's injuries, and how it had died when he and the owner tried to lift it. He said the man had taken Liam's details and told him to expect the police to call. Liam was blaming TJ and Melissa for making him speed, and overtake, for attracting the dog.

Jake sat next to his son on the window seat and held him. He stroked TJ's hair, and told him it would be all right.

He didn't say it out loud, but he kept thinking, thank God his son wasn't hurt. Thank God they hadn't hit a child; thank God it was only a dog.

WHEN TILLY CAME home, Jake made TJ explain it all again.

To begin with, Tilly kept unpacking the shopping and Jake wasn't sure she'd understood, so he started filling in the details—the kids in the car calling out, the daughters seeing it all, TJ and the man lifting the dog—letting TJ correct him.

Tilly stopped moving around the kitchen.

'Oh, TJ, those poor girls. That poor family.'

Jake put his hand on her arm. 'He knows. He's really upset, Tilly.'

'I should bloody hope so.'

'Fuck, Mum, it wasn't me driving.' TJ started towards the door.

Jake wished Tilly had been there earlier to see how upset TJ had been.

'Thomas James, get back here,' she said, and her voice was hard and low.

He turned. 'What?'

She put her hands on his shoulders. 'You can't run away from something like this.'

He whined, 'Mum, I know we screwed up.'

Tilly remained absolutely still. Mother and son, eyeing each other—like animals, Jake thought.

And then TJ broke. 'I'm sorry, Mum. I'm so sorry. It was . . . the way the dog's head . . .' He started to cry again and Tilly put her arms around the boy, who was a little taller than her now. He was mumbling about the blood from the dog's eye, and seeing bone.

After a while, she started to rub his back and gently she said, 'We need to phone Liam's parents, and if the police haven't been in touch we should all go to the police station.'

'It wasn't just us in the car, you know,' said TJ, pulling away.

'Hold on,' said Jake, coming closer. 'Let's slow down. Fine to phone Liam's parents, but we need to be clear about what they could be charged with before we talk to the police.'

'Why?' said Tilly. 'They've done what they did.'

'Yes, but their futures . . . universities, jobs. We might need advice.' They had a lawyer who'd done their conveyancing and wills; Jake doubted he knew anything about criminal law.

'Imagine if it'd been a person,' said Tilly. 'A child.'

'It was a dog, Mum, please.'

'I know they've been bloody stupid,' said Jake loudly. 'Let things get out of hand. I know they could have ruined their lives. But they're just kids.' His hand sliced the air. 'Just slow down.'

No one spoke.

'It's a good idea for you two to phone Liam's parents, but I'm going to find out what the law is, okay? And we'll go from there. Just see if the guy's phoned.'

'What if Liam hasn't told his parents?' asked TJ, but they both cut him off, and that was it, thought Jake as he jogged up the stairs, they were back on the same page.

IT WAS MORE difficult than he'd anticipated to find anything about the law. There were Google results for accidents where the driver and dog were killed, for cruelty to dogs, and something about a dog being pulled behind a ute. There was an article about what to do if you hit an animal—it didn't say it was a crime. It was clear the speeding and overtaking would be careless or reckless driving, but could the police prove it?

TJ came in and told him that Liam hadn't heard from the man or the police yet.

'All right,' said Jake. 'Give me a bit longer. Thank goodness you didn't hit someone.'

'I didn't hit anything, Dad. I wasn't driving.'

'No,' said Jake. 'You were just yelling out the window, getting him to race.'

When TJ left the room, Jake thought that he did have a point. Liam was culpable, not TJ. TJ had made a mistake. He'd been irresponsible. But was it illegal? Jake couldn't even find any laws about drivers hitting animals, never mind the culpability of passengers.

For a while he stared at the Google search screen, unsure what to look up that would cover TJ's position.

Then he typed, 'Law sex with minor New Zealand'.

There were some bits of the Crimes Act—something about consent and being drunk. Further down, a paragraph said: *New Zealand statutory rape law is violated when an individual has consensual sexual contact with a person under the age of 16.*

TJ had done exactly that. Statutory rape. He could go to prison.

Jake should have told Tilly. Why hadn't he?

Statutory rape. That's what those boys had done too, wasn't it? That Dice case.

'Jesus, TJ,' Jake whispered.

He added 'Dice Bros' to his search.

There were news articles about the case. He clicked on the most recent—it said the police had charged the boys involved in the teen sex game. Jake had lost track; he hadn't realised it had progressed that far. Four youths were facing charges of sexual violation and sexual assaults and making a video. It didn't say statutory rape. Jake scrolled all the way through and then clicked back to the search results.

Words from a blog further down caught his eye. *One of rape gang had sexual intercourse with a girl aged just 13!!* Jake clicked. The screen went black except for a paragraph in red with a rant about the oldest boy, the one who'd left school, suggesting this was his modus operandi—preying on young girls—and that the police were ignoring it.

Tilly was calling. Jake clicked back to the traffic offences, then went downstairs. The man had called Liam's parents. He wanted all the kids to come to his house the next day and apologise, and eventually he wanted them to pay for a new dog. He'd witnessed how upset they'd been. He felt if they complied with his suggestions, they'd have learned their lesson; the police didn't need to be involved.

Jake listened and nodded. 'You're lucky, TJ.'

'It's called restorative justice,' said Tilly.

TJ didn't seem to be listening.

'Will you come with me?' he asked suddenly, looking at Tilly. When she nodded, TJ glanced at Jake and he nodded, even though he wasn't sure whether TJ was asking him to go too.

After TJ went to his room, Jake poured them a wine.

'They've charged those boys in that sex game case.'

'I know,' said Tilly. 'Good on them.'

'Do you think? What does sending them to prison achieve?'

TJ was having sex with a minor. She was fifteen; it was statutory rape. If TJ dumped Melissa, she could report him.

If he told Tilly, what would she do?

'Imagine if it was TJ,' he said, seeing again his son's shadow on the wall.

'It wouldn't be, though, would it?' Tilly said it with such conviction that he agreed.

Jake thought then about the weight of TJ leaning against his chest when he'd been crying, and the shape of his son's head cupped in his hand, and he thought, he would hold this burden himself. He could do that for his son.

CHAPTER TWO

# Selection

Crossing the courtyard, Jake noticed a slim brown-haired woman in a long cardigan hovering by the rubbish bin. She was holding a takeaway coffee but didn't seem to be drinking it. She looked like she might be about to throw up. As he got closer it occurred to him that she too had been summoned, and that she was afraid, not ill. He slowed. Before he'd decided whether he should reassure her, a woman in her late sixties with short grey hair approached her and Jake heard her say, 'Come on, we'll be in it together.' He waved them on through the doors ahead of him and, as he did, he smiled conspiratorially at the older woman, but she didn't notice.

HAYLEY THREW AWAY the too-milky coffee and followed the old lady.

Inside there was a security doorway to step through, like at Sydney Airport, and a bench where they checked your belongings. The lady, who'd said her name was Fiona, chatted to the security guard about how to silence her new phone while he rifled through her handbag. Hayley tuned out. She didn't have a bag. She put her phone on the bench and stepped towards the doorway as Fiona, turning back to her, said, 'Into a different world, like in Narnia. Remember Aslan's door?'

Hayley was trying to make sense of this when the bleeper sounded. The other security guard asked what she had in her pockets, and she remembered the car keys. He directed her back through.

People were watching; a queue had formed. The tall man behind her gave a sympathetic smile.

Hayley's blush deepened when the alarm went off again. The security guard motioned her to the side and she saw that Fiona, who'd hesitated, was chatting now to a blonde lady in a navy linen jacket. They set off up the stairs together.

The guard squatted and waved a hand-held scanner over Hayley's sneakers. Her hands were fists. Her cheeks burned as the machine climbed her legs. It bleeped when he reached her middle.

'I think it'll be your belt.'

She stared at the man.

'Are you wearing a belt? Can you show me, please?'

Hayley inched up her shirt so he could see the bottom of the buckle. Losing interest, he waved her on.

FIONA SAT DOWN in the second row of the jury assembly room, next to Susannah.

'No, it's my first time,' she said, looking around to see if she could spot Hayley. 'I read on the website all you need is your life experience.'

Susannah told her that she'd been summoned when her children were young, but had made excuses. 'They don't let you do that anymore—you can only defer jury service now.'

'Oh, I don't mind,' said Fiona. 'Gets me out of the house.' She explained that she didn't work; she used the word retired, although, really, resigned would be more accurate. It'd been some years ago. Irreconcilable differences with the new principal was how she'd explained it to her book group—the principal had wanted Fiona to spend the school library budget on graphic novels and literacy computer software, while Fiona argued that children needed library time to feel like Christmas: so many choices of actual physical books (not comics) and they were only allowed three—that was how you developed the love of reading. There'd been no compromise on either side. Fiona's son had suggested it was intentional on the principal's part—a way to cut the expense of a school librarian without having to pay her out. Fiona knew that he meant it wasn't her fault, but all she could think of was that term dead wood, and so she'd resigned. It was before Anton, her husband, had died, and he'd persuaded her then to let her teacher's registration lapse. She'd been reluctant, but he'd said with such absolute certainty, 'It's a waste of money—you'll never go back to it,' that she had felt compelled to give it away.

'I suppose that's why juries often end up with lots of retired people on them,' said Susannah.

Looking around at the sixty-odd people in the room, there actually wasn't a disproportionate number of older people. Fiona pointed that out.

THE JURY ASSEMBLY area reminded Hayley again of an airport. The only time she'd been on a plane was a few years ago, when Phil took her and Tyler, his son, to Sydney to watch the Warriors. They lost to the Sea Eagles, but at Manly Sea Life Sanctuary they saw grey nurse sharks and manta rays, and then they shared a KFC family meal sitting on the wall above the beach, she and Phil hot and sweaty in their jeans and new season's singlets, and the next day she had a pink band of sunburn around each armhole.

Hayley tried to think about these things and not this room, or the lady in the dark skirt with the pale grey blouse through which you could see the lace of her bra and the indentation of her navel. Hayley tried not to think about her name being on that lady's list. She looked at all the people in the rows in front of her. An old man in dark-rimmed glasses was doing the newspaper sudoku, several people were reading books, but most were on their phones. There were all these people, and there was Hayley's name on the list, and she didn't know how it got down to twelve.

She tried to remember the sun's heat on her thighs through her black jeans in Aussie, and whether the chips were crispy. There was no clarity; she hadn't practised that memory. It would be a good one for 'taste', though—the sweet and sour dip had stung her chapped lips.

What she could recall was that Tyler had found something yellow and plastic in the sand as he'd dug, and she'd imagined condoms and syringes and had started to tell him not to touch it when Phil had put his hand on her thigh. So they'd both watched as Tyler carefully extracted it, working the sand away from the edges until it lay there exposed in the sun, just a broken snorkel and mask, which he'd then picked up and taken to the bin without being told, and Hayley had stopped herself from saying, 'Go wash your hands.'

The lady in the grey blouse told them she would play a video and then randomly select some names by ballot to go into the court, from which a jury would be empanelled.

'Embalmed,' said someone and a few people laughed, but the room was filled with apprehension. Hayley could feel all the anxious thoughts of these people crowding her. Pressing against her. If she was not careful they would squeeze the air out of her chest.

The screen turned bright blue.

She could hear that her breathing had become fast and shallow, as if she were running up the quarry track. She tried to let the air flow in through her nose but had to take two big gulping breaths.

'Easy,' said the young guy sitting next to her, and he tapped her forearm, which made Hayley jump.

SITTING IN THE back row, Kahu smiled to reassure the jumpy woman next to him, and she nodded briefly, but then she made her index finger and thumb into a circle and sat with her head bowed, staring at her hand.

Kahu's mum, who was a family lawyer, had assured him that it was unlikely he would be selected. His dad had told him the statistical probability was one in five, but then he and Kahu went right through and worked out the probability of being the second person, and the third—it dropped away, so for the last place on the jury he had only a one in forty-nine chance of being picked. And then his dad started messing with him. 'We haven't considered the no-shows. Or the challenges.'

'What?'

'Those lawyer fellas can decide they don't like the look of you, and they just say, "Challenge," eh, and it's over.'

'Over?' He looked at his mum.

'Yeah, you're a reject.' His dad laughed.

'They have to do it before you sit down in the jury box,' said his mum.

'Perhaps I'll just say I'm sick—or could I tell them about training, the competition?'

'Nah,' said his dad. 'Better to get it over with and then they can't call you again for years, eh.'

'I'm not sure it's years,' said his mum. 'To be honest, I'd be surprised if you get on the jury, and if you do, it'll only be for a few days. Do you good.'

So here he was. And it was a day off work.

He'd been pleased with the broken two hundred metres he'd swum this morning, although his coach had said he hadn't pushed the third fifty enough. Tonight would be the lactate set they were doing every week, which he liked because it meant he could measure his progress, both in terms of his hundred butterfly time and the skills requirements his coach had set—for him it was no breathing last fifteen. Tomorrow he would nail that. Kahu let his eyes shut for a moment, imagining himself, head down, coming into the wall. His eyes stayed shut. He was aware and not aware of the noise of the video, of the people around him, a few latecomers arriving. It was warm in the room. Then the registrar started to talk and he jolted awake, embarrassed. Catching the eye of the nervy woman beside him, he grinned. She gave him a quick smile back this time.

WHEN SHE HAD felt the thoughts crowding her, Hayley knew what to do. Soon after she'd shifted in, she'd told Phil she was going mad, and he'd smiled and shaken his head and taken her to the GP, who'd referred her to a psychologist. So, Hayley had learned how to manage the feelings, and Phil had helped, and Tyler didn't even know. And mostly it worked.

As the others watched the video, Hayley closed her eyes and, inhaling slowly, placed the tip of the first finger of her right hand against the pad of her right thumb. She could hear the calm narrating voice on the video, the air conditioning, the boy next to her breathing slowly through his mouth, while she pictured the surface of a perfectly still lake, right at eye level. So smooth it looked viscous, like mercury. Quicksilver.

She was interrupted by the registrar lady calling out names. After a while she heard her own.

'That's me,' she said quietly.

The young guy nodded as if he'd expected that.

'Just raise your hand,' he whispered, and as she did, he said, 'You have to go into the courtroom when she's finished choosing.'

Hayley sat motionless, waiting, as if she were just like everyone else here.

All eyes were on the woman as she selected more names from a small wooden barrel.

Hayley placed her finger back against her thumb and this time she imagined a white downy feather floating on the water's surface above its own reflection, and now ripples circling outwards as she swam her steady breaststroke.

Lake Waikareiti.

She'd worked so hard at this one that, even though it was her 'sight' memory, she could hear Tyler and Phil on the shoreline unpacking the picnic she'd made for that day. That special day. Bacon, potato and egg pie; afghans without walnuts; cheese and parsley scones. And she was swimming in the smooth mercury lake, swimming towards the island with its own lake, with its own island, which she imagined as an endless repetition—like those Russian nesting dolls. Sun in her eyes. Sound of cicadas. Cheeks hot from the climb. Even here, in the jury assembly room of Rotorua's courthouse, she could feel the warmth on her face. And she imagined diving down. The cool of the deepening green water.

THERE WAS A crush of people when the selected thirty filed through the double doors into the public gallery of the courtroom. Dave ignored the people scrambling for seats and moved to the back corner and stood there with four or five others, mostly men.

'They're keen,' he muttered, and the young Māori guy standing next to him nodded while a slight girl with honey-coloured hair in a high ponytail said, 'Sitting's the new smoking anyway.'

'Ha,' Dave said, and noticed the young guy smile too.

Dave rubbed his jawline; his goatee was making him feel itchy, his Swanndri was too hot. He could think of nothing worse than being on a jury. Listening to people dobbing in some poor bugger who probably didn't deserve to be there. The pigs rarely got the real bad guys—the murderers, the pedos who made child porn or the druggies who imported kilos of meth. And then he noticed that it wasn't one poor bugger in the dock, it was four, and they were just boys.

FIONA GRUMBLED AS she directed Hayley into the row, and then someone moved, and there were two seats next to a large man with a moustache. Fiona was relieved she was not the one sitting next to him, because he was taking up part of Hayley's seat. She saw the girl shrink into herself, pulling her cardigan closed as she stared around the courtroom. The lawyers, in black robes, were sitting at tables, and in the front, at a raised bench, was the judge, who looked just like he should—glasses, grey hair and a sombre, patient expression. Fiona's eyes were drawn to the two rows of empty blue seats in a partitioned-off box.

'I knew it,' said the large man. And then, when neither Fiona nor Hayley answered, he repeated, 'I knew it.'

'What?' whispered Fiona, leaning across Hayley.

'I knew it would be this case soon as I saw the reporters.'

Fiona didn't understand.

'Look.' He pointed to her left. Fiona had to lean forwards to see past the people who were still moving around. There was a wooden barrier between them and the courtroom, and on the left side a glass window stretched from the barrier to the high ceiling. On the other side of it were guards in uniform standing either side of four youths. They were crowded behind what she knew from TV programs was the dock. The one she could see most easily was wearing a dark suit and his black hair was combed back like that All Black her grandsons liked. The two brown-haired boys in the middle were wearing shirts without ties and had short messy hair. The older one kept whispering to the smaller boy with the bad skin. The fourth one was blond, and as she watched he rubbed his finger along the top of the wooden dock as if testing for dust.

Fiona had expected prisoners to be in orange uniforms. But they weren't prisoners yet; that was what this was about.

'It's the Dice Bros,' whispered the man. 'You know?'

The name meant nothing to her, but she thought it must be a gang thing because when he said it there was a mumbling behind them. He moved closer, leaning right over Hayley; he smelled like sausage rolls.

'Those schoolboys, the sex game, remember? Last year?'

TWO ROWS BACK, Jake heard what the man said. He stared at the boys in the dock. The blond one looked the same age as TJ and could easily have been one of his friends, and the small one with the spiky hair looked even younger.

There was a commotion in front of him. He heard the older woman ask the thin one in the cardigan if she was all right, and she said she didn't feel well and then she said her hearing had gone funny.

'Are you feeling faint?' asked the older woman.

Jake looked around to see if there were any court staff nearby, and by the time he turned back, the older woman was pushing on the younger's shoulder, telling her to put her head down between her knees.

'She's shaking,' said the man sitting on the other side of her.

'She'll be all right in a minute,' said the older woman.

It was then that proceedings started, with the registrar reading out the boys' names and the charges against them—it was a lot to take in. In the silence after the last one, 'indecent assault', the judge cleared his throat. Then the prosecutor read out a list of witnesses and Jake listened carefully, wondering if any of TJ's friends could be on there, but he didn't recognise any of the names.

Finally the judge said, 'Members of the jury panel, we are now going to select the jury for this trial. Juries are a core part of our system of justice and we do rely on your help.'

'All right now?' whispered the older woman as the thin woman straightened up.

It seemed like an inevitability to Jake when his was the first name called, and then he thought Tilly would probably be pleased he was on this jury.

DAVE WATCHED AS the man called Jake stood up. He was tall with wavy hair and red cheeks. He was smiling apologetically as he looked around, until the court attendant motioned him through the wooden gate into the courtroom. The man leaned down to hear the whispered instructions, then walked quickly past the lawyers' tables towards the judge's bench, before turning into the jury box, where he sat in the front row in the seat closest to the public gallery.

'One down,' muttered Dave.

A woman with a Samoan name the registrar couldn't pronounce was challenged as soon as she stepped into the courtroom. She stopped immediately and laughed, and someone ushered her back. Dave heard a whisper: 'No surprise . . . teacher.' When the next name was called, Eva someone, the girl standing beside him made a noise like a brief suppressed laugh. She was dressed casually in jeans, Converse sneakers and a hoodie, and Dave watched with interest the progress of her bobbing ponytail through the courtroom, waiting to see if she would be challenged, but she wasn't, and as she sat down the red-faced man whispered something and they smiled. She didn't seem to mind, and the old lady who was next practically trotted past the lawyers when she was called.

Susannah, a blonde lady, was chosen, and then a man in a suit, Mark, made the walk, glancing constantly at the lawyers sitting at their desks; they didn't even look up. When he reached the corner by the judge's bench he stepped to the side, head tilting up as the judge leaned down. They conferred. The judge shook his head. The man had more to say. The judge was not agreeing. As the man moved into the jury box, Dave rolled his eyes at the young guy next to him. 'So Mark's an arse.'

An elderly man with glasses called Les was followed by another man in a suit, and this time one of the lawyers said, 'Challenge,' and that man walked back with a self-satisfied smile.

HAYLEY'S NAME WAS called. She didn't move. The registrar standing below the judge, holding the piece of card, looked around.

The lady read out Hayley's name again.

The big guy nudged her. 'Isn't that you? That old lady called you Hayley.'

Hayley was shaking.

'Best go or they can put you in jail.' He stood up then, so she had no choice.

She could feel the eyes behind her staring. The judge was watching and even some of the lawyers twisted around to look.

As she eased past the man, her back brushed his belly and she jolted forwards. In the aisle, she paused, not wanting to go through the open gateway.

The judge gave her a slight nod. Hayley tried to shake her head.

The man at the back desk in his flappy black gown stared coolly.

The judge had told them if there was a reason they couldn't serve to step aside, like the man called Mark had, and approach the bench. That's what she would do.

Hayley took a step, her hand still holding the wooden barrier. She would walk over to the judge and explain that she couldn't do this case.

As she moved through the courtroom she saw Fiona in the jury box, watching her. They were all watching her. Every single person in this room.

Those boys.

The boys accused of doing stuff to those girls.

There was no air. Hayley was panting, sweating. She just had to get to the judge, but how would she explain? With what words?

He was looking at her, encouraging her.

She passed the tables of lawyers and they didn't challenge her, and when she reached the corner where she just needed to step aside and ask the judge to be excused, she kept her head bowed and turned into the jury box. As quickly as possible, keeping her eyes down, Hayley shuffled into the back row and sat in the seat that would be hers now for the duration of the trial.

## CHAPTER THREE

# The foreperson

As they filed into the jury room, Susannah watched Mark move to the far end of the table, pull a chair right out and sit, leaning back, with one leg stretched almost straight and his elbows spread over the chair's arms. He was occupying it, occupying the whole end of the room.

So he hadn't changed.

She had known that Mark had moved back to Rotorua. When they were still living in Auckland, she and Jon had come down for her mother's birthday, and Mark had been at the restaurant they'd chosen, hosting a table of employees in celebration of the opening of his IT business. Ridiculously, she'd blushed when Mark came over, shook hands with Jon and, kissing her on the cheek, crouched down next to her chair. The whole time they'd talked she was conscious of her body's desire to simply tilt towards him. She was also hyper aware of Jon watching her as she explained that Mark had grown up in Rotorua too, but that it wasn't until university that they'd become friends.

That night she'd anticipated Jon's disparaging comments about the town, the restaurant and Mark. Instead he'd said, 'That's what we should do: move here and set up a business,' and she'd laughed. After Jon's heart scare, though, it became their way to step off the treadmill. Jon set up the mountain bike hire and cafe, and she did the books, ran the house, organised the children. They kayaked, swam and waterskied in the lake in summer and drove down to the mountain for weekend skiing in the winter. And in the eighteen months since they'd moved here, she hadn't seen Mark once. She'd assiduously made no effort to find him and had thought he must've left town. And now he was a member of this jury.

He'd been selected straight after her, so she was still flustered when his name was called. He was carrying a little more weight these days and his hair needed trimming, but he looked good in the suit. His face was tanned, which, because it was still only spring, she assumed must be a ski tan. From her seat in the jury box, she'd watched him enter the courtroom, looking at the lawyers as if he expected something, and then, when he was alongside her, he turned and smiled that same old smile that bordered on a smirk, the one that always made her stomach contract.

When they'd been sworn in and were sent out to choose a foreperson, Mark was waiting in the corridor.

'Susannah—long time,' he said, his voice low, and it went through her head momentarily that they were not meant to know each other, and then she remembered the rule was about not knowing the defendants and witnesses, not the other jurors.

'Mark Winters. How are you?' She reached for his forearm then, realising, let her hand drop away, but she felt the light press of his fingers on her back as he guided her down the corridor.

'Talk after?' he said, and she'd smiled and tried to look nonchalant.

Now, in the jury room, Susannah sat down next to the Māori boy. She was surprised he was here, but it was good to have a range of opinions. She moved her handbag under her chair, and wondered what they were meant to do with their personal belongings while they were in court. She looked around the room; there were no lockers.

Mark clearly wanted to take control, but she admired the way he waited for someone else to speak. It was the old man. He introduced himself as Les and suggested they move promptly on with electing a foreperson. Mark interrupted; he'd been on a jury before, he said, and this was an opportunity to introduce themselves, especially seeing as it was going to be a long haul—the judge had told them the trial was set down for three weeks. There was a murmur of discontent as Mark reminded them of this.

FIONA OFFERED HAYLEY a glass of water as they came into the jury room. The girl simply shook her head and sat near the door, staring at her hands.

The room was tight for twelve of them because the boardroom table took up so much space. The walls were bare, except for a whiteboard and an emergency evacuation map, but the windows right across the external wall made the room light. There was a kitchenette and in the corner, a door, standing ajar, into a cloakroom and, beyond that, the toilet. Fiona decided she wouldn't be using that toilet, and she'd sit at the far end of the room so she wouldn't hear these men passing wind and urinating.

She listened carefully as people started to introduce themselves. Susannah had a business degree; the tall man, Jake, was a regulatory services manager at the council—whatever that meant; Bethany, the plump girl, worked at a childcare centre; Scott, a jowly man with sandy-coloured hair, worked at a bank. Chantae, the stocky Māori woman in her thirties, laughed in a self-deprecating way when she said she was a dishwasher. Fiona tried to catch her eye to give her an encouraging smile. Hayley, it turned out, gardened for the council and Jake said he recognised her. Dave, with the untidy goatee, just said the word 'forestry'. He kept moving around in his chair as if he had ants in his pants, as Fiona used to say about the children at school.

It was obvious that Mark, in his forties and wearing a suit, wanted to be foreman. He owned some sort of computer business. Fiona wondered about Les, though; he was a retired scientist, and then it occurred to her that perhaps she should put her hand up. You didn't have to be an expert, the judge had said—it was more the role of a chairperson, and she was, informally, the chair of her book group.

BETHANY WAS STARING out of the windows at the brightness of the light blue sky above the rooftops and the slow-moving clouds. Today, the clouds weren't white; they were almost the colour of vanilla custard.

She watched the blue sky shapes compress and morph as the clouds converged, but after a while she realised it was an optical illusion and only the big cloud was moving.

WHEN LES ASKED, 'So, who is willing to be foreperson?', Susannah was surprised that it was the boy, Kahu, who answered.

'What about you, matua?'

Susannah liked his politeness. He was good-looking, although his hair could have done with a brush. He was muscly, she could see from his forearms; they were not a boy's arms at all. His face, though, was still a boy's, and his eagerness too.

Eva, who'd told them she was a physiotherapist specialising in brain injuries, agreed with the boy, and Susannah heard herself make a small affirmative noise. She glanced quickly at Mark then; he was staring at the pencils and paper in the middle of the table.

Les said firmly, 'No. I'm not the right candidate. I tend to be more . . . individually focused.'

The fat girl in the green dungarees let out a snorty laugh; Susannah had no idea why.

'What about you, in the suit?' said Dave, waving towards the head of the table.

'Yes, Mark would be good,' said Susannah, not looking at him.

For a moment no one spoke, then Jake said, 'Sounds good.' His teeth were quite crooked, but he had nice eyes.

Scott said, 'Yeah, sure,' and there were a few other murmurs of agreement. Susannah felt vindicated.

FIONA NOTICED THAT while the others were talking about him, Mark had tipped back on his chair as if he was a child.

'If that's what people want, I'd—'

Fiona interrupted. 'Actually,' she said in a shaky voice, '*I'm* prepared to give it a go.'

Chantae, the dishwasher, said, 'So you're up for it, Mr Suit Guy?' and, at the same time, the boy said, 'That'd be good, matua.' It made Fiona think that they must know each other.

With a nod towards Mark, Chantae added, 'It'd be your kinda thing, wouldn't it?' She wore an amused expression, and Fiona wasn't sure if it was genuine or not.

'We could have a vote if there are two candidates,' Les said.

'Look, I don't mind who does it, but I think it would be better if we could agree at this stage,' said Jake.

'Mark would be good,' repeated Susannah. 'And the sooner we go back, the sooner we finish.'

And that seemed to be it. Only Les had taken Fiona's offer seriously, and the others wanted the man just because he was in a suit. Fiona swallowed a few mouthfuls of water, then followed the others back into court. Her face was hot as they quietly rearranged themselves so they were sitting in the order they'd been selected, except for Mark, who now sat in the front row, in the seat closest to the judge.

The charges were put to the defendants then, and each boy pleaded not guilty to each charge. Then the judge turned towards the jury box.

'Members of the jury, it is your duty to decide whether the defendants are guilty or not guilty of these charges. To do this you must listen to the evidence and give your verdict according to it.'

Glancing down, Fiona found that her hands were trembling.

## CHAPTER FOUR

# The opening

'Ladies and gentlemen of the jury, as His Honour has explained, my name is Mr Evans and I am the prosecutor, acting on behalf of the Crown.'

The man was small, and younger than Eva had expected; she knew it was a stereotype, but she'd thought the prosecutor would have more gravitas.

'This case is about these four young men, who, led by Lee on the far left, made up a sex game. They called themselves "the Dice Bros" because the game involved throwing a dice to determine what sexual act they had to perform and with which particular girl. The Crown alleges that they took this game so far that they proceeded even when some girls were not consenting. The result is that these young men are charged with indecent assault, making an intimate visual recording, and sexual violation by forced oral sex and by rape.'

The prosecutor paused and, looking at his notes, gave a small shake of his head.

Eva felt there was a mismatch between what was happening here in the courtroom and what had happened out there in the real world with these teenagers. She felt like she was watching a play, but then there was another audience too—the people in the public gallery watching them, the jury—so did that make her part of the play?

'Over the course of the next few weeks you will become familiar with all the people involved in this trial. For now, I want to introduce the defendants, the young men who are alleged to have committed these crimes.' He gestured across the courtroom as he said each boy's full name. On the pad she had been given, Eva made a note of the boys' first names with a word or two of description.

Lee, the blond boy, wore a black suit that might have been bought for a school ball, but his navy-striped tie looked borrowed from his father. Eva swept her eyes over the full public gallery. She couldn't immediately identify his parents, and the prosecutor was moving on.

The next boy, Travis, had grown up a few houses down from Lee, the prosecutor told them, and the two of them became friends with the other boys through rowing. Travis was the cox. It was easy to see; he was narrow-shouldered and skinny. His light brown hair was spiked up like the oldest boy's and his blue shirt was tucked in and buttoned to the top. Travis had a rash of teenage acne across his face, and Eva doubted he even shaved yet.

Next to him, the prosecutor pointed out Chris, who looked the oldest by far, with a six o'clock shadow on his cheeks. His grey eyes were deep-set, and he was wearing a navy shirt that was tight around the muscles of his arms and across his barrel chest. Even as the prosecutor told them that it was Chris who had 'upped the ante' when he joined the game, the boy started whispering to Travis, who, with a small smile, nodded back; Eva felt a surge of irritation.

The last defendant, Jayden, was generally known by his nickname, Jayz, the prosecutor told them. Eva found her eyes drawn back to him because he sat tall in the dock, eyebrows slightly arched, wide, dark brown eyes staring steadily at the base of the jury box. Clear skin, clean-shaven, shortish dark hair brushed back. He, too, wore a suit, with a light blue tie. Jayz was the only defendant who looked Māori, and this felt like a relief to Eva; presumably she could be assured there was no racial motivation to these charges. She looked along the row of jurors, wondering if any would prejudge him. It was too early to tell, and anyway they had to find a way to fulfil their duty. She had felt the responsibility settle on them as a group, as a jury, when they were sworn in, and the judge's opening remarks had only reinforced it.

'At the time of these alleged offences, Chris was nineteen and the others eighteen,' the prosecutor said.

They were ordinary guys, Eva thought. Why would they have made up a game like this? Then she reminded herself that she didn't yet know if even that much was true.

'There were six girls, and the defendants assigned each of them a number on the dice. The Crown alleges that three of these girls—Samara, Maia and Amy—were indecently assaulted or sexually violated by the defendants, so they are called the complainants. The other girls consented to everything, and that is why they are not complainants.'

Eva felt confident; the prosecutor was making it easily comprehensible.

'Now, I do not represent the complainants. I act on behalf of the Crown. That is the way our justice system works. However, each of my learned colleagues here represents one of these defendants, and that's why, today, our courtroom is so full of lawyers!' He smiled and Eva smiled back.

SCOTT SAT IN the back row of the jury box, with Kahu and then Dave to his right and Bethany on his left. Bethany was doodling while the prosecutor spoke. The jurors in the front row were all making notes, but he, Kahu and Dave hadn't written anything down.

The prosecutor said, 'As His Honour instructed, if you have read or seen media reports about this case, you must put that out of your heads, and you should not now follow any reporting of this trial.'

Scott had read about the case nearly a year ago when the boys were first charged. He'd found the reporting to be annoyingly scant on the details of the game. He'd discussed it with his wife, and from the summary the prosecutor had given their guesses had been on the right track.

'Anything you've read or heard in the media is totally . . . irrelevant . . . to you.' The prosecutor punctuated his words with deliberate taps of his hand against the desk lectern. 'The only thing you should base your decisions on is the evidence that is tested in this court.'

Scott saw Mark nod to the prosecutor as if to say he could trust him to do his duty. Mark was so keen; not that Scott resented being here, especially now he knew the bank would still pay him. He shifted in his seat and his arm momentarily touched Bethany's. She moved over to give him more room.

'LADIES AND GENTLEMEN, each of you brings your own common sense, experience and knowledge of the world to the task of judging the facts of this case. Because—that's right—*you* are the judges of the facts.'

The prosecutor paused. Chantae sighed. The jury was important, she understood that, but how was her experience relevant? What knowledge could she possibly bring?

She was still panicking, trying to work out how they could make jury service work, and for three weeks. In the break between the judge's talk and the prosecutor's, Chantae had tried to call Mike, but he'd only just started at his new job and didn't pick up. She texted Slo-mo to meet the boys after school, then she messaged her boss at MexTex. His reply was blunt: *I'm not paying you if you're not here.* She wasn't due to work again until Wednesday, but she called Chef anyway, and he said he'd sort one of the kitchen hands to cover her shift until she got there after court. When Mike called her back she listed what she'd arranged and then, running straight on so he didn't get stressed out, she suggested Slo-mo could cover her house-cleaning jobs on Tuesdays too. Slo-mo, Mike's aunty, had come to stay with them while she got her life straightened out; that'd been six months ago now.

'No way,' said Mike. 'She'll mess up.'

'Then I'll have to tell my ladies I can't go, but if it's three weeks that's nearly three hundred bucks. Cash. If Slo-mo does it, it could be, like, rent.'

Mike told her Slo-mo wouldn't clean properly and she'd lose the work. Chantae knew better than to argue right then; she'd talk him round tonight.

'. . . and we trust you to do this impartially and without prejudice.'

The prosecutor looked slowly along the two rows of the jury box, making eye contact with each juror, and it embarrassed Chantae because he was separating them out, making them each responsible for this impartiality, but she'd missed his point.

'Some evidence might make you upset or angry. You must put aside those personal feelings and listen carefully, so that, as a jury, you can decide whether the prosecution has led the evidence to prove, beyond a reasonable doubt, the facts alleged by the Crown. Because it is *not* up to the defendants to prove their innocence.'

This she knew—innocent until proven guilty. They all knew that. Chantae nodded.

'The Crown alleges that the defendants played the Dice Game four times, and that in specific instances for each of the complainants they did . . . not . . . care . . . that the girls were not consenting. In fact, the Crown alleges that they *forced* sexual acts on two of their victims, having given them alcohol or drugs. Two girls were only *sixteen* at the time—that is two full years younger than most of the defendants.'

The prosecutor explained then that the jury would be expected to give separate verdicts for each defendant on each charge. 'All the charges arise from the Dice Game, the game the boys invented to *encourage* each other to perform these sex acts. The Crown alleges these were not separate, isolated incidents, but, rather, that the defendants all *encouraged* and *assisted* each other to have sexual relations with some girls as part of the game *even if they did not consent*. This is important, because the Crown is alleging that even when one of these defendants was not the person actually performing the illegal act, they were still a *party* to it and are thus culpable for that act.'

Chantae shook her head. She didn't get it. She looked along the row of faces, wondering if the others understood. To her left, Hayley had written a few notes, and to her right, Bethany was drawing what looked like clouds. Chantae leaned forwards. In the front row, Jake and Eva were both writing and, further along, the old man was scrawling notes very fast. Chantae wasn't sure what she should write down. She noticed Mark staring eagerly at the prosecutor, willing him to give some acknowledgement; it didn't mean he'd understood, though.

'Each round of the Dice Game was centred on one of four events. The first round took place at Travis's eighteenth birthday drinks, the second at an outdoor concert at Blue Lake, the third at a barbecue at Lee's house and the last at a sixteenth birthday party. I will now explain who the witnesses are, and outline what they will tell you happened in each round of the Dice Game as the defendants' behaviour got more and more out of control.'

The prosecutor paused and sipped his water. He was building the tension, and looking at the way all the jurors were sitting up expectantly, Chantae thought he was clever as.

CHAPTER FIVE

# Dave

They heard from the first witness on Tuesday morning. His name was Caleb, and he was meant to be the good guy—the one who'd pulled out of the game when he realised where it was heading—but Dave felt his answers were deliberately vague. It wasn't helped by the prosecutor's questioning, which was like the slow, low quartering of a hawk hunting.

'Caleb, who made up the Dice Game?'

'Lee. Mainly, yeah.'

'Did he tell you where he got the idea from?'

'Mm, not sure.'

'Did he make it up or copy it from something?'

'Not sure.'

'Where were you when Lee first suggested it?'

'Like, the Dice Game?'

Maybe he wasn't all there, thought Dave.

'Yes.'

'On the bus going to a rowing camp.'

'Can you tell us what happened?'

'Er, we were playing Smash or Pass, and then Lee says he's got this idea to mix it up, eh. He said we'd shake a dice and do something to the chick we shook.'

'So did you all agree to play the game then, Caleb?'

'Nah, not then.'

'So, when exactly?'

'Um, Lee set up a group chat called Dice Bros, and if you wanted to be in it, you had to play.'

'So, this was on Facebook?'

The boy laughed. 'Nah, Snapchat.'

Dave tilted his neck to the right until he could feel the tightness all the way from the top of his shoulder to the base of his skull. He didn't use Snapchat. He had an Instagram account and a Facebook page, but he wasn't much into them. He wanted the prosecutor to crack on, or even better he wanted to be able to ask the boy his own questions—he'd be like a kārearea, a falcon, and cut straight to the chase.

The lawyer asked the judge for permission to have a booklet of messages entered into evidence, then the court attendant gave each juror a copy. The prosecutor asked Caleb to read out the first message from Lee.

'It said, *Wanna be a Dice Bro, gotta risk the throw. You in?*'

The booklet was thick, and as Dave leafed through it Fiona twisted around and frowned at him.

The prosecutor asked Caleb to explain how the game worked.

'So, it was me, Jayz, Travis and Lee, and we agreed the first round was gonna be at Travis's eighteenth birthday drinks. We chose six girls, eh, and we gave each girl a number, and whatever number you shook first was who you had to do stuff with, and then you shook again for what you had to do.'

'All right. So, how did you agree on those particular girls?'

'We all made suggestions—so I chose Kasey. Tia and Samara are always around, so they were kinda obvious. And, um, Sacha's in a pair with Samara at rowing. I think Travis was into her.'

'All right, and the other two?'

Caleb shrugged. 'Amy and Maia were a bit of a joke because we knew they were down bad for Lee and Jayz. They're a couple of years below us, and kinda nerdy, you know? So, like, fresh blood, eh.' The boy shifted, then added, 'Not in that way.' He dropped his head and Dave wasn't surprised to see him turn his body further away from the dock.

'Was there discussion about how old Sacha, Amy and Maia were?'

Caleb shrugged.

The judge told him he had to answer.

'Think so.'

'What was said, Caleb?'

'Well, they were all year eleven, and we knew Sacha and Amy were fifteen—so they kinda said something about them being underage. But, I mean, Amy was sixteen before any of the bad stuff happened.' His voice had developed a pleading tone.

'All right, thank you, Caleb. Can you carry on explaining the game, please?'

'Yeah, I just wanna say I didn't agree with those younger girls being in it. I thought it should all be about chicks we liked, you know?' He looked at the jury, and Dave noticed Fiona gave him a little nod as if he was talking directly to her.

'Anyways,' said the boy, 'you had to do the challenge you shook and then you had to send a message to the girl saying, like, *You been diced*, and if you didn't manage the challenge then you had to buy a sixpack for anyone who did. So Travis was out of pocket straight away, eh.' The boy almost laughed and the boys in the dock smirked, except for Lee—he kept his expression neutral, but Dave could see the tension in his jaw.

'We'll come to that,' said the prosecutor sharply.

'Lee's fuming,' Dave whispered to Kahu.

'Caleb is narking, though, isn't he?' Kahu whispered back, then the judge glanced at them, so they fell silent.

'When Lee suggested the game, did he tell you where he got the idea from?'

'Maybe a book of his dad's?' Caleb said it slowly as if it was a question. 'About a guy who threw a dice.'

'All right.'

Dave thought the prosecutor seemed relieved then, although Dave didn't understand why they were back covering the same ground.

'Was it this book, *The Dice Man*?' The prosecutor held up a worn paperback.

'Think so.'

'Did he read out the blurb on the back, about how the man was going to rape his neighbour if he threw a one on a dice?'

'Maybe.' Caleb shrugged.

The prosecutor read the blurb out loud.

'And when you heard that, about how the dice dictated your behaviour, what did that make you feel about your responsibility for your actions?'

'Dunno.'

'All right. How did *you* feel about the game, Caleb?'

The boy shrugged again. 'Was a laugh.'

'Pardon?' There was a hardness to the prosecutor's voice then, a warning.

'I mean, to begin with . . . not when they did stuff the girls didn't want. But that wasn't me. I'd pulled out by then.'

Dave inspected the boy's face—his expression seemed genuine. The whole thing felt petty, as if the prosecutor and police were just trying to make a point because of all the PC bullshit that went on these days. It was insane the amount of money this must be costing. The investigation. All these lawyers. Dave shifted position; he wanted to stand up. There weren't even any windows in the courtroom.

'Let's turn to what actually happened in the first round. Can you explain to the jury what the different numbers meant?'

One of the defence lawyers started shuffling around, fiddling with what Dave realised was his hearing aid. Dave watched him remove the battery.

'That round, if you shook a one you had to kiss the girl,' Caleb was saying, while the lawyer started rummaging through his briefcase. 'Two was a feel.'

'A feel? Of . . . ?'

'Yeah, her . . . um, arse, and three was her, er, tits.'

'All right, and four?'

'You had to get the chick to send a pic and then you shared it.'

'Caleb, can you tell us a bit more about the pic, the selfie?'

'Nah, not really.'

'I mean the idea. Did the girl have to be wearing anything specific?'

'Nah, that was the point—she had to be naked.'

Dave noticed Caleb glance then at the boys in the dock. Lee, stony-faced, was deliberately not looking at him. The others didn't seem particularly worried, though.

In front of Dave, Mark and Les were writing down the numbers and what each meant. Five was to get the girl to give them a blow job, and six was to have sex. Kahu had written it down too. When Fiona finished writing, Dave saw her look around and he realised she was checking to see who in the back row was taking notes. He saw her look disapprovingly at his blank pad and Scott's. Then she twisted right around so she could check on Bethany, who sat directly behind her. Dave snorted; Bethany had drawn a dice.

SHORTLY AFTER THIS, the jury was sent out of the room because, the judge explained, he and the lawyers needed to discuss something legal without them being present. On the way to the jury room, Dave quietly said to Kahu, 'You write stuff down for the both of us, eh?' and the boy didn't question him, just nodded.

Dave could write; he wasn't thick. It just took him longer, and he knew he wouldn't be able to keep up if they kept talking; it was better if he just listened. At school, weirdly, it'd mattered less as he got older—then he did more of the practical subjects and the teachers seemed to accept it, but when he was little the obsession with reading and writing made school a bit rubbish for him. Although, if he thought about his small rural primary school, it wasn't even the classroom stuff he remembered; it was the sandpit, the cold shallow swimming pool and, most of all, the neighbouring reserve. They played there before and after school and sometimes at lunchtime. They dammed the stream, made camps in the undergrowth, and when a big tree fell down after a storm the girls filled the bowl where its roots had been with a carpet of flax, while the boys climbed the wall of the tree roots still clumped with soil and manned the defences. The best day, though, was when his stepdad brought in a ute-load of seedlings. The boys dug in a row of kōwhai at the front of the playing field, while the girls planted flax along the fence line. It was the only time Dave could remember either of his parents ever being at the school, and the only time he was appointed a leader, his stepdad having told the teacher that Dave knew what he was doing and could teach the others.

BACK IN THE courtroom, in response to the tedious circular questioning of the prosecutor, Caleb told them that the first time they played the game, at Travis's drinks, Lee had to kiss Sacha, which Caleb saw him do, Travis was meant to have sex with Maia and he hadn't even tried, and Jayz had successfully felt up Samara's breasts and her arse. Caleb explained that he hadn't rolled the dice that round. He'd told the boys he'd only play if he got Kasey, so Lee and Jayz said in that case he had to go straight for the six and have sex with her. Caleb confirmed again that Chris was not yet involved, and the judge reminded the jury that there were no charges relating to this first round of the game.

For a moment Dave was confused. Then he remembered it was all about consent. The game itself wasn't illegal, it depended on whether the girl agreed. He shut his eyes; if everything the guy had talked about so far was legal, what was the point? And then, even though there were no charges for it, the prosecutor asked Caleb about Kasey. Dave was sure he had some quarry in mind, but he still didn't come at it directly and Caleb mumbled now—more embarrassed to be talking about this than he had about the details of the game.

'Yeah, um, we'd hooked up before.'

'Can you explain that phrase? I'm sorry—we're out of touch with the lingo, some of us.' The prosecutor looked at Les and then Fiona, with just the hint of a smile. Fiona leaned forwards on her elbows. She was like a golden retriever, Dave thought.

'Hooking up means you get with the person—you know, kissing and stuff. Could be sex, but not with me and Kasey.'

'All right, so prior to playing the Dice Game you'd fooled around with Kasey. What changed the night of the sixth of October?'

Caleb started to shrug, then said, 'That was Travis's eighteenth, eh?'

'I understand so. That is the night I'm asking about.'

'Um . . .'

It would be embarrassing to have to talk about it in front of them and the lawyers and judge and all the people watching, and from what the prosecutor had said, it was going to get much worse. Dave wondered why the girls had even brought it up; he'd have thought they'd prefer to keep what had happened private.

'Did you go to the party with the intention of having sexual intercourse with Kasey?'

'I was gonna try my best.'

'So, why suddenly that night, when you'd just been "hooking up" before?'

'Oh, because of the Dice Game. Because that was what the boys told me to do. In a way I had the easiest score. I knew Kasey was keen, and I wasn't gonna lose to those boys, eh.'

Unintentionally he glanced at them, and Jayz raised his head a fraction and stared.

Looking away, Caleb said, 'I made sure Kasey was into it, though.'

'So you told Kasey about the Dice Game? When exactly?'

'In the hammock in Travis's garden. I told her before anything happened.'

'Before anything happened,' repeated the prosecutor, and he made a point of turning towards the defendants.

One of the defence lawyers was frowning, while the others seemed to be deliberately not reacting; they kept writing their notes. Dave supposed they were working out what questions to ask Caleb; they were all going to cross-examine him. How long would this take? There were a lot of witnesses; they'd read out their names at the start to make sure none of the jurors knew them. Dave yawned.

'What exactly did you tell Kasey?'

'I told her we were playing this game, and I'd . . . *chosen her*, and I was meant to . . . have sex, but that I couldn't see it happening.'

'You couldn't?'

'Well, I could . . . like, I was hoping, right?' He smiled then, forgetting himself, and Dave thought he'd be funny in a normal context. 'I wasn't gonna say that to her, though. I didn't want her thinking I was, like, expecting . . .'

'Assuming, yes, okay. And so what happened?'

'Yeah, well, she took off her T-shirt and said, she'd see, or we'd see.'

Chris and Travis were whispering.

'And then we . . . in the hammock.'

'So, with this consensual sex, Caleb, which happened that night because of the Dice Game, did the others encourage or help you in any way?'

'Yeah, they were hyping me up before, especially after Lee and Jayz had done their challenges. And Lee persuaded some guys who were hanging round the garden to go out the front so it felt private for Kasey, you know?'

'And that was when she agreed to have sex?'

'It was tricky, though, there's those holes . . .'

Scott laughed, and Dave did too.

Caleb grinned. 'Holes in the hammock, I mean. It was one of those rope ones, eh. My knees . . .'

There was more laughter, and from at least one of the defence lawyers. Dave heard Susannah make a huffy sound.

Caleb glanced at the defendants; he still wanted their approval, Dave thought.

AT MORNING TEA, while Dave ate his biscuit, the old guy, Les, who was going back over his notes, said, 'Caleb mentioned a game they were playing before the Dice Game, "Smash or Pass". Does anyone know what that is?' He looked at Kahu.

It was Jake who answered. 'I think my son's mentioned it. It means they would say whether they wanted to be with a girl or pass.'

'So "smash" is how they describe being with a girl,' said Eva.

'Yuck,' said Susannah.

'Does your son play that? Do they all?' Fiona sounded shocked. She looked at Kahu. 'Have you heard of it?'

Chantae broke in: 'That's not relevant, is it?' More tentatively she added, 'I don't even think that game's relevant to the trial.'

Fiona sighed, then smiled and said Chantae was right. Then she suggested they make a chart on the whiteboard so they could record which boy shook which girl and what they were meant to do.

'And whether they actually did it,' said Jake.

'Isn't that what the whole trial's about?' asked Dave. It was enough to be listening in the courtroom; did they really need to analyse it all while they were on a break?

'And we need to record whether the other boys are charged as a party too, because that's the complicated thing,' said Fiona. 'At least, I think so.'

Jake started to agree, but Mark said absently, 'What the numbers meant changed the next time they played it, so we're better off waiting.'

'Well, all the more—'

Fiona was interrupted by a knock, and the court crier came in with the box he kept their phones in and they all scrambled to get theirs back.

'We can write that up as well,' said Fiona loudly.

Mark didn't answer; he was putting his phone in his jacket pocket. It amused Dave that it was a black denim jacket. So he'd only worn the suit the first day because he wanted to be foreman.

'Don't you think, Les?' said Fiona. 'Don't you think that would be an idea?'

'Just a second.' Les was writing on his notepad in small, tight handwriting.

'I'm going outside,' said Dave.

'Yes, I could do with some fresh air,' said Mark.

'I meant for a smoke,' said Dave, but Mark still followed him, along with Bethany and Chantae, who were the other smokers.

IN THE NEXT session, Caleb explained that Jayz had told Chris about the game and he'd wanted to play in round two.

'Chris told us the first numbers were too easy—for pussies, he said. So he took kissing out and after some banter he decided throwing a one should be going down on the girl.'

'So, one became performing oral sex on the girl . . . and two?'

'Yeah, Chris made it, like, getting your finger up there, in the girl's, er, vagina.'

'So, two was digital penetration. And the escalation of those numbers, that was why you stopped . . . sorry, um, how did that escalation make you feel about the game, Caleb?'

'I didn't stop playing because Chris changed what the numbers stood for,' said Caleb, and Dave noticed the prosecutor's sudden sharp expression, and he realised that the lawyer didn't know what Caleb was going to say.

'It was because Chris said we had to do it *whatever*. And he made it for eyebrows.'

'Let's just pause there a moment, Caleb. "For eyebrows"—can you explain that term?'

'It meant if you didn't do it, the boys shaved your eyebrows, or at least shaved slits in them. They did it to Travis a few times, eh, 'cos he couldn't score.'

'And did Chris explain what he meant by you having to do it "whatever"?'

'Well, when Travis said he hadn't even tried to have sex with Maia at his drinks because he knew there was no way it would happen, Chris said that wasn't good enough. He said in the next round we just had to get the job done. Travis argued that there was no way Maia or Sacha would ever do anything with him. And Kasey was there, and she said he was right, but Chris said there were ways and means. He said we were the Dice Bros, a team, and we had to make it happen, and if necessary we'd get the girls out of it to make it easier.'

'What did you understand by the phrase "out of it"?'

'Drunk, I s'pose. Drunk or high.'

'All right, thank you, Caleb. So how did that make you feel about the game?'

'Well, I wasn't going to force Kasey to do anything, so I said I was out.'

WHEN THE JUDGE asked the jury to leave the courtroom again, Dave asked the court crier how long it would be. The guy just smiled and said, 'How long's a piece of string?' Then he reminded them that they had to stay in the jury room, ready for when they were called back in.

Dave grumbled, but the others seemed relieved; there was the atmosphere of a class unexpectedly without a teacher.

Kahu joked about taking a quick nap, and Fiona asked why he would need one.

'I'm a swimmer, whaea, been up since five.'

'Really, why?'

'Training starts at six and we need to be pool deck by five forty-five.'

'Why so early?' asked Jake.

'Because we have to be out of there by eight for school or work.'

'Why not just train after work?' asked Fiona.

Kahu laughed, and Dave thought he was a genuine guy.

'I do that too. I train four till six thirty in the afternoon as well.'

There were murmurs of astonishment, a few guffaws.

Dave found it hard to process. 'Four and a half hours a day? For fun?'

Kahu shrugged. 'And dryland three nights a week and Saturday mornings. Sunday's a rest day.'

'Should bloody think so,' said Mark.

'Unless there's a competition.'

'Oh my God,' said Susannah, as Dave said, 'Shit,' but he apologised when he saw Fiona look at him. She gave a quick smile.

'You going to the Olympics?' asked Chantae.

Dave expected Kahu to laugh, but he didn't; he said his dream right now was the Commonwealth Games. He told them he'd been training seriously since he was twelve, which was very late to begin.

Fiona asked him how old he was.

'Eighteen.'

'It's young, isn't it, to be on a jury—to have this level of responsibility?' said Les.

Dave respected Les, but he wished he hadn't brought them back to the trial, especially when Jake said, 'So what are people thinking?'

'I just don't see how this is gonna help anyone,' said Kahu. 'How does it make anything right?'

'They have to be held responsible if they did it,' said Susannah.

Mark interrupted: 'We can't be discussing verdicts at this stage.'

'No, of course not.' Susannah blushed.

'In fact, can I just make it clear, as your foreman, we will only discuss verdicts when we're all together in the deliberation, after we've heard all the evidence. Okay?'

A few people murmured agreement.

'Yes, boss,' said Dave, and Kahu grinned.

'What I don't get,' said Chantae, 'is how come Caleb's not charged, when he played the game too? Didn't some of them get charged for things the others did? So why not Caleb?'

Dave noticed that she, along with several others, looked at Les then, even though Mark jumped in with an answer. 'Obviously he's made a deal.'

Dave's eyes flicked back to Les—he should have been foreman.

Scott said Caleb hadn't done anything that Kasey didn't want, so how could they charge him?

Clearly Scott didn't understand how the party charges worked; Dave was surprised, Scott was a money man, you'd think he'd get it.

'I can't get my head around how come Caleb would dob in his mates,' Kahu said to Dave, but before Dave could answer Mark cut him off.

'Like I said, he's made a deal. He gets off being charged because he turns the others in. Otherwise, he'd be charged as a party too.'

'I think Caleb wasn't charged because he stopped playing the game before the bad stuff happened,' Fiona said, and Les nodded.

That was when the court crier came in to say the judge was ready for them.

WHEN THEY WERE sent out again less than an hour later, everyone was frustrated. Dave listened as they discussed how crucial the jury was as the judge of the facts, but how they were convinced now that facts were being kept from them. Les and Mark said it was obvious that the judge and the lawyers were discussing what Caleb was and wasn't allowed to say. Staring out of the window at the elder trees between the buildings, Dave noticed for the first time that from where he was sitting he could glimpse the hills of Whakarewarewa Forest on the horizon.

'I think there's other girls they're not telling us about,' said Jake. 'I saw something on the internet before they were charged.'

'We can't discuss prior publicity,' said Les, as Scott said, 'Maybe Caleb's not so innocent after all.'

Dave couldn't believe how pedantic it all seemed.

BACK IN COURT, the defence lawyers took it in turns to question Caleb. Dave thought that each cross-examination was like stopping, rewinding and replaying a movie, only when you replayed it, the storyline had changed, sometimes only in a minor way but sometimes more significantly. It made his head hurt, but he kind of admired the woman who was Lee's lawyer; she was definitely a falcon.

'Caleb, did you watch a TV show called *Skins*?'

'Yeah.' He laughed. 'Yeah, we watched that.'

'Can you explain about the dice in that program?'

'Um, a character . . . it was the homo, er, the gay one, he did this thing where he shook a dice to decide what to do. He wrote a list and it had things on it like kiss someone or steal something.'

Dave had no idea what this was about.

'Can I put it to you that you watched that TV show, and then you boys came up with the Dice Game together?'

'Er, I can't remember exactly.'

'Why not? Were you, perhaps, having a few coldies? Or a smoke?'

'Beers? Nah . . . maybe a smoke.'

She dived then. 'Caleb, you don't mean cigarettes, do you?'

The boy looked around. 'No,' he said slowly.

'Was Lee smoking the dope?'

'Doubt it; he doesn't usually.'

'So, while you were high and discussing the Dice Game, was that when you guys made up that line: *Wanna be a Dice Bros, gotta risk the throw*?'

'Yeah, nah, I think it was made up while we were watching.'

'So, you helped?'

'Not sure.'

'So when you helped invent the game, did you intend to hurt the girls? To do anything non-consensual?'

'No, it was just a joke.'

'Just boys being boys?'

'Yes.'

'Thank you, Caleb.'

WHILE THEY WERE waiting for their phones so they could go for lunch, Fiona said that the prosecutor had been clear that the game was Lee's idea and came from the book. Mark said that'd all changed—they'd obviously come up with it together. Les said he wasn't sure the evidence had gone quite that far.

'Surely they know? I mean, it actually was someone's idea, wasn't it? Factually.' Dave could hear the hairline cracks in Fiona's voice, and he understood: all the different charges, the number of witnesses and the different versions of their evidence—it was going to be overwhelming enough without disagreements over these kinds of basic facts.

Mark started talking about credibility and proof, but Dave tuned out. He felt more dead than after a full day at work. It was as if sitting for the last day and a half had brought out years of stored-up muscle fatigue. It didn't help that he'd been called out last night with the Rural Fire Brigade just after 2 am to an overturned ute that had brought down a tree. The driver was taken away in an ambulance and one of the cops had given Dave a ride home to fetch his chainsaw. It'd taken nearly an hour to clear the road.

As he walked down the stairs with Eva, Dave asked, 'What was it you said yesterday about sitting?'

She smiled. 'Sitting's the new smoking.'

'Ha, well, now I do both.'

'Do they let you smoke when you're out in the forest, or do they worry about fires?' She sounded interested, not judgemental.

'Funny you ask,' he said. 'I am a firefighter.'

'Oh? I thought you worked in forestry?'

'I do. But I do fire service for the timber company when they need me. And the volunteer Rural Fire Brigade.'

They were crossing the gated car park now, where the jurors were allowed during breaks.

'The bushfires are getting worse, aren't they, with climate change?' asked Eva.

'Mm, maybe.' Dave knew what his stepdad would say—bloody greenies scaremongering. 'The fire seasons overseas are definitely longer.'

Dave's stepdad was an old-school Forest Service guy; he liked to talk about his big stand against the greenies at Whirinaki, back before Dave was born, when they used to fell the huge native podocarps—tōtara, rimu, kahikatea and mataī. He'd tell stories about the forestry workers barricading the road while the despised greenies tied themselves to the treetops.

Recently, Dave had gone into that forest on a pig-hunting trip, and his mate had taken him up to an ephemeral lagoon where there were all these fifty-metre-tall kahikatea standing in the water. There was no one there. The only sound the croaking of frogs. It was like something out of *Lord of the Rings*. Overawed, Dave had thought: thank Christ for the greenies.

As they came out of the gate by the pub, Eva said, 'I'm looking forward to a drink at the end of this. At least we get a break on Thursday.' The judge had told them there would be no court that day because he had to go to a funeral.

'I wish they'd just get on with it, instead of all these stops and starts,' said Dave. 'I was meant to be going to the States, but they won't give me a deployment date now because of the trial.' He glanced at her. 'That's why I was shitty yesterday.' Dave had sworn when he was selected. He was grateful that the judge had simply ignored it.

'A deployment?'

'Meant to be going to California to help fight their wildfires. I've been to Canada, and to Aussie a bunch of times. Never over there.'

'Wow, that's impressive. And you wanted to go?'

'Yeah. Yeah, I did.'

Eva nodded. 'Well, I'm sorry.'

THAT AFTERNOON, CALEB'S girlfriend, Kasey, testified. She had long, straight black hair and long, pink-painted fingernails which she repeatedly flicked against her thumbnail. Dave found it annoyingly distracting.

'Caleb only agreed to play if he got me, and anyways he never thought the younger girls should be—'

The prosecutor interrupted: 'Kasey, please tell us only what Caleb said while you were there with him, not what you think he thought. Now, I want to go back to the texts Caleb sent you after the first round of the Dice Game.'

'Yeah. You know, the game was just kinda an excuse for us—it wasn't like with Maia and Amy, eh?'

'Thank you, Kasey, but please let's focus only on you. Members of the jury, if you can turn to page four of the text booklet. Kasey, please read out the texts printed there.'

'Oh. Okay. So the first one, he said, *All good babe? Sending txt for game now like I told u*, and the other one just says, *Done and Diced!!* That was the one they had to send.'

'Now, you were there when they were shaking for the second round. Can you tell us what happened?'

'Well, Lee was mad I was there, but the others were chill. So Jayz shook the pics—he had to get Amy to send him nudes. And Lee had to have sex with Samara. I think Chris shook Samara as well, and Travis shook Sacha, and they were both meant to feel, um, put their finger in the girl's . . . pussy, and I guess that's why Chris went after Samara in the lake.'

Both Chris's lawyer and the prosecutor interrupted her, and this time it was the judge who said she had to restrict herself to only answering the questions.

Dave blew his breath out; it was all so roundabout. Why didn't they just let her tell her story?

The prosecutor asked what Chris had said about the boys having to do what they shook—clearly he wanted her to back up Caleb.

'Well, when it was Caleb's turn, Chris said he had to shake the dice this time. And Caleb said, "All good," thinking Chris just meant shake for what he had to do with me, and we were okay with that. It was a laugh, and I knew I could say no if I wanted. But Chris insisted that Caleb would have to shake for a girl too. And Chris said I was up for grabs. That's when Caleb said he was out of the game.'

'Oh, er . . . all right.' The prosecutor looked confused for a moment, then he asked how the others had reacted when Caleb wanted to pull out.

'They were pretty heated, eh, called him names, told him to leave the Snapchat group. But they do respect Caleb, eh. Except for Chris.' Kasey looked straight at the jury; she wanted them to believe her, but it was more than that—when she was talking about Caleb she was proud, and when she was narking on the others she was almost self-righteous. Caleb hadn't been like that, Dave thought—he'd been kind of whakamā.

DAVE WAS THE first to leave at the end of the day, along with Hayley. As they walked down the stairs, he said, 'You're hating it too, aren't you?'

'Yep.'

'So what're you up to now?'

'I need to go for a run in the Redwoods.'

'I can relate to that—just maybe not the running part.'

She gave him a tentative smile.

DRIVING HOME, DAVE thought about Les, the old geezer, who'd still been writing notes when he left. Good on him, but Dave's head was full of sludge and he wasn't even sure which bits they definitely knew. They hadn't heard about any of the charges yet, so as Chantae, the short woman, had said as they were packing up: 'If Caleb did nothing wrong and nothing bad happened to Kasey, what was the point of today?'

Les had answered her, 'I believe the prosecutor was establishing the existence of the Dice Game, and explaining its rules. And we'll have to see, but I think the messages Caleb read to us about round two are important.'

Caleb hadn't left the Dice Bros group straight away, so he'd received a message exchange which the prosecutor had asked him to read out. He'd read slowly: 'So Lee said, *Chris u have the hardest challenge this time but i reckon u can persuade Samara if u put your mind to it—haha*. And then Chris replied, *No persuasion needed I'll just do it. I told u Dice Bros aren't pussies.* And Lee said, *Lol, go Chris.* And both Jayz and Travis gave him a green thumbs-up.'

Dave felt pretty sure the whole case was overblown—kids messaging and throwing dice. It shouldn't even be in court, costing all this money and stuffing up his life and however many other people's, but there was one part of Caleb's testimony that had stuck with him. Before the prosecutor had finished he'd asked Caleb about a phone call he'd received from Travis on the last night that the others had played the Dice Game. Caleb looked shaken as he recounted it.

'Travis was drunk and hyped up. He kept saying he should have pulled the pin when I did. I asked what'd happened and he told me they'd gone to some girl's sixteenth birthday party—I couldn't even get my head round that. He started crying and saying, "They didn't stop." I asked, who? He said Jayz and Chris, and he told me it was with Amy. He wouldn't tell me what happened, though. I went over the next morning and Chris was there and Travis just kept saying it was all good.'

From the expression of shock on Travis's face, Dave thought that Caleb's testimony was true.

Caleb had paused and the prosecutor seemed to have finished, but then the boy had turned to look directly at the judge and said, 'I don't know what happened to Amy, sir, but I know that whatever Travis saw totally freaked him out.'

It had made Dave wonder what exactly those guys had done.

## CHAPTER SIX
# Bethany

Bethany twirled the end of her plait around and around her index finger until Chantae, who was squeezed next to her in the jury box, glared. Bethany tried a smile, but Chantae simply pushed her lips firmly together and turned back to watch the screen. She acted all serious and important, even though she wasn't that much older than Bethany.

The girl who was being questioned, Samara, wasn't here in the courtroom like Caleb and Kasey had been, because she was one of the girls that the sex stuff had happened to. They called her a complainant, which Bethany thought wasn't fair because it was bad to complain. The first girl, Kasey, had become Caleb's girlfriend because of the Dice Game, so she wasn't complaining, although Caleb wasn't as good-looking as Jayz or Lee.

Samara was in a room by herself, so it was her image on the screen they were watching, and the judge, who was watching on his own screen, had told all the spectators to leave. There was a plant in the room next to Samara, and Bethany was sitting right forwards, trying to work out if it was plastic or not, when Scott, who sat next to her, leaned close and whispered, 'Can't see past your big boobs, Bethany.'

Bethany lurched back in her seat, folding her arms around her chest, her face so hot she must be as red as a tomato. Had Scott really said that? She couldn't look at him.

He couldn't have said it; she must have misheard.

Samara had already described how she'd danced with Jayz at Travis's eighteenth drinks, and how, even though there'd never been anything between them before, he'd stroked her bum and her breast—and then sent her a text saying: *Diced*.

Now Samara was talking about how the night before the Blue Lake concert she'd had sex with Lee in his car. She said she'd liked Lee; they'd had a bit of a thing going.

Bethany wondered if she could get her chewing gum out of her pocket without the registrar noticing. The registrar was scary, like one of those teachers who'd read out your test answer because it was dumb, or who'd call you out in class because you were eating chippies. Bethany's favourite person here was the old guy, Anaru, who looked after the jury. He smiled when he took their phones away, and he smiled even more when he brought them back, but the judge said he was a crier. Sometimes Anaru sat in the courtroom at the table with the two Les said were reporters—an older lady and a man who, today, was wearing a shirt with a dotty pattern which reminded Bethany of those magic pictures where if you let your eyes go blurry you could see hidden animals in the dots.

She'd mentioned that to Susannah and the old lady, Fiona, at morning tea, and Susannah said she needed to keep her concentration and Fiona told her to look for the hidden animals in the evidence, which made Bethany laugh.

In the courtroom, the prosecutor, who was sitting at the desk facing a monitor, talking into the microphone, said, 'And this was consensual—you wanted to have sex with Lee?'

'I hadn't planned to . . . but yes,' said Samara.

'Did Lee mention the Dice Game?'

'No . . . but my friend Kasey told me that Caleb told her . . .'

'Sorry, Samara, you can't tell us about what other people heard; we have to be careful because that's not evidence. Now, after the sex, did you receive a text from Lee?'

'Yes. It just said, *Diced*. I didn't get what it meant till later.'

'Samara, what was hanging from the rear-vision mirror in Lee's car?'

'Um, some fluffy black dice.'

Bethany liked the sound of those dice; maybe she could buy some for her sister, Carly. She shifted so she could ease the gum packet out of her jeans pocket. Susannah twisted around.

'Need the loo,' Bethany whispered.

Susannah put her finger to her lips. Yesterday and today Susannah had mainly chatted to other people, but she'd been nice on Monday when, in the jury room at the end of the day, Bethany had started crying. Bethany wasn't quite sure why she'd cried. Fiona and Susannah had sat her down, one either side of her, while everyone else went home, except for Les. Bethany was doing what her mum called egg-beating, letting one worry lead on to another and another. She was worried she wouldn't understand the trial, and she didn't like all the talking about sex, but she told them she was worried her boss would be cross. Les had looked up from his notes and said, 'I'll give you more privacy,' and when he left, Bethany had cried harder, and told them that Ricky would be grumpy she'd been selected because he hadn't even wanted her to turn up. Susannah asked who Ricky was and Bethany was sniffing and sobbing and needed to blow her nose, so when Fiona asked if Ricky was her boyfriend, she just nodded because it was easier.

'Well, you had to come,' Fiona said. 'It's the law.'

'And otherwise you'd be fined, and that would cost more,' said Susannah.

Bethany explained that Ricky didn't have a job, and then she'd told a little fib—that it was her pay that covered their rent—and they'd both been nice to her after that.

Now, Samara was describing a concert at Blue Lake with a whole lot of kids where she'd had a few drinks and swum in the lake. Samara said they'd been on the raft, and he'd kept trying to lie next to her and she didn't like him. Bethany was confused—a minute ago she'd said she was into Lee, had done stuff with him in the car.

'What did Chris do next?'

'Well, um, Chris said I looked hot and he wanted to be with me. I was lying on the edge of the raft, so I just rolled off and started swimming back.'

As Bethany ripped open the chewing gum packet, one pellet flicked onto the floor. She could see it, white and shiny, by Scott's shoe.

'When I could stand, I was wading in and Chris was following me. He's kinda sketchy. I didn't trust him, and I didn't want Lee seeing him all over me.'

Bethany shifted her bottom over and reached down to pick up the gum, and as she did Scott moved his foot so the toe of his pointy black shoe rested on her hand. He didn't tread down, he just held her hand there, firm. Bethany squirmed to look up at him. He grinned. It made his cheeks look too big for his face. Then he moved his foot and she scooped up the gum and sat up. The judge was looking at her. She pretended not to notice, straightening, and making out like she was listening really hard.

'. . . just tell us in your own words.'

Bethany pretended to cough and popped the gum in her mouth.

Samara said, 'Chris came in, like running up behind me in the water, and said, "Hot tits!" and I turned round, probably to tell him again to eff off, but he'd . . . my bikini top came undone, because he'd pulled the tie . . . he'd undone it . . . everyone could see.'

'What did you do then?'

'I put my hands over my breasts, like, to cover them. I was so embarrassed . . .'

Bethany didn't think she looked embarrassed; she wasn't blushing like she would have been.

'So, Chris had undone your top, and when you put your hands over your breasts what did he do, Samara?'

'It was a trick. I . . . he . . .'

'Just take your time.'

'He pulled down my bikini bottoms and, like, stuck his fingers right between my legs. I didn't want . . . I just had to get away as fast as I could . . .'

Bethany started because Scott's fingers had brushed hers. Then she realised he wanted the gum. He took the packet and fiddled with the wrapper without even trying to hide it, keeping his eyes fixed on the screen. The prosecutor was asking the girl to describe where Chris had touched her.

'Um, not inside my vagina. Like, just on my pubes. That doesn't make it okay.'

Scott handed back the packet; Bethany shifted closer to Chantae.

The judge said, 'Samara, it's about the charge—members of the jury, that's why the charge is an indecent assault, not the more serious—'

'It was serious,' interrupted Samara. 'And then he sent the "Diced" text and I found out it was all part of their stupid dumb game.'

THERE WAS A weird seat-swapping then. The prosecutor moved and the lady lawyer went and sat at the table with the monitor. She said, 'Samara, I have only a few questions. On the night before the concert at Blue Lake, can you confirm that you had sex with Lee in his car, and that you wanted to?'

'Yes.'

'And prior to that night, you and Lee had hooked up several times—is that correct?'

'Yes.'

'Before you had sex that night, you were aware of the Dice Game, weren't you?'

'Um . . . I'd heard of it. I didn't know he'd hooked up with me as part of the game.'

'I put it to you that you were pleased that Lee was interested, and you were hoping to end up in a relationship with him, correct?'

'I s'pose, yes.'

'At the time you and Chris were in the lake—and I make no judgement on what exactly happened in the lake—Lee was not present, was he?'

'I just told you what happened.'

The girl sounded sulky, Bethany thought.

The lawyer's tone became impatient. 'Answer the question, please. Was Lee in the lake, or on the beach, or anywhere in sight at the time you allege Chris touched you?'

'No.'

Les, the old man, coughed.

'Lee didn't shout anything, did he?'

'What? I just said he wasn't there.'

'And Lee didn't laugh, did he?'

'He wasn't there.'

'So, Lee didn't make any gestures at all to encourage Chris to do that?'

'He wasn't even there.'

The girl was cross, and Bethany could understand—the lady wasn't listening.

'That's all, thank you, Your Honour.' The lawyer stood up with a strange smirky smile and made a big deal out of gathering her black robe around her, and then the younger guy with the glasses sat in the seat, and said he acted for Jayden, which was Jayz's real name. He asked the same kinds of questions about Jayz, and the girl said she hadn't minded when he felt her up at Travis's drinks or when he kissed her at a barbecue a few weeks later. She did say Jayz had sent a second 'Diced' message after the barbecue, and the lawyer looked grumpy and made her repeat that she had wanted to kiss him.

If it was Chris who grabbed Samara in the lake, Bethany didn't get why it mattered if she'd kissed Jayz at a party. But it was quite bad if she'd done things with Jayz *and* Chris *and* Lee. Bethany sat forwards again, wondering why the girl on the screen was so popular.

AFTER LUNCH, ANARU said they had to wait—the judge and lawyers were discussing legal matters. Each morning- and afternoon-tea time so far Bethany had gone downstairs to smoke with Dave and Chantae, even though normally she only smoked one cigarette a day with Ricky. Both lunchtimes they had all gone their own separate ways. On Monday, Bethany ate a ham roll and chippies by the new playground at the library, and on Tuesday she'd taken a pie and a Snickers there. But when there were delays in court they had to stay in the jury room, and without their phones, people talked about the trial, which Bethany didn't like.

That morning was different, though. Mark was being funny, teasing Kahu about getting up early.

Then Chantae said Les must get up at 5 am to make his sandwiches because they had so many fillings, and Les played right along. Jake, Susannah and Mark discussed their children, and still they were waiting. Jake asked Eva if she had children, and she didn't, and Scott's were preschoolers and his wife stayed home with them. He didn't use their names, he called his boy his 'little man' and the baby his 'princess', and Bethany imagined the four-year-old dressed up in a suit and tie and the baby in a bassinet with one of those plastic tiaras on her head, and she had to stop herself from laughing. Then Chantae told how one day she'd come home to find her boys playing rugby on the empty section next to their house. 'Totally starkers except for their rugby socks and boots.' They'd all laughed at that, so Bethany, of her own accord, told them how every morning Hunter lined up all the books right across the floor and even up the table leg and over the table, and some of the jurors had forgotten she worked at the childcare centre, so they asked questions, and Bethany talked. When Eva asked about her family, though, she went quiet. Susannah answered for her, 'She lives with her boyfriend, and comes from Te Puke.'

Bethany wished now she'd never told Susannah and Fiona that Ricky was her boyfriend. Ricky was her sister Carly's boyfriend. Bethany had moved in after her mum shifted to Hamilton with her new man. They'd put a bed in the alcove in the sitting room, because it was a one-bedroom place, and she'd bought a divider from The Warehouse so she could go to bed when they watched their fast, noisy TV shows. That's what Carly and Ricky were like. Carly worked at a gym, and had tried to get Bethany interested when she first moved in. Ricky didn't work, but he never just chilled. He always wanted to do something or go somewhere—his mates', or the gym, or the pub, or he'd take Carly into the bedroom, or play loud, aggressive rap that talked about bitches and used the n-word as he stomped around the flat, or at the very least he'd want to watch one of his running, fighting, shouting, doing-it programs. Ricky and Carly liked the dragon lady one, and the cowboy one with the mannequins that came to life. Bethany went to bed then—she didn't like watching people hurt each other, and she didn't want to watch sex stuff with her big sister and Ricky. She liked that they were there, though, on the other side of the divider. She'd smooth out her fleecy blanket and her stripy duvet, fluff up her pillows, and then she'd flick through Instagram or play Two Dots.

At night, Bethany sometimes woke and heard them—Carly's huffing and pleading and Ricky's groaning noise at the end that made him sound . . . less, somehow. Other times she'd just hear his dry, raspy snores, or he'd be grinding his teeth. It reminded her of a film they'd watched when she first moved in, where people started eating each other, bones and gristle—it still came back to her when she heard Ricky's teeth grating and gnashing.

THAT CONVERSATION IN the jury room made a difference, Bethany found. When they were called back in, Mark held the door open and gave a salute as she went past, and Susannah offered her a quick, thin-lipped smile before she sat down. When the judge thanked them for their patience, Bethany felt proud that she was here, part of this group, and she saw Mark nod to Les and Susannah, and she knew they felt it too.

It was the lawyer with the hearing aid who moved into the seat in front of the microphone then, and he asked Samara lots of questions but he told a different story.

'So, Samara, you were on the raft in the Blue Lake and Chris and Travis were there?'

'Yes.'

'And you were all laughing and having a good time?'

'Was all right, until I got sick of Chris.'

'I put it to you that you were on the raft having a good time, flirting and laughing with Chris and some other boys, and you'd had a few drinks . . .'

'I wasn't drunk—I left 'cos Chris wouldn't leave me alone.'

'You didn't want Lee to see you with Chris?'

'I thought Chris was sketchy.'

'You'd been joking around—you were all friends, weren't you?'

'He doesn't get to take my top off.'

'You were joking and chasing each other?'

'I wasn't chasing him. I was trying to get away.'

'So it got a bit out of hand. It was a joke, though—you weren't *afraid*?'

'I wasn't afraid. But I didn't like it.'

'Boys and girls splash each other and chase each other. In fact, hadn't there been an incident earlier when some of the boys pulled down Travis's shorts on the raft?'

'Think so.'

'You were there, weren't you? You saw?'

'Yes.'

'So, there was an incident like I just described?'

'It wasn't a big deal. They did stuff like that to Travis. He's their cox, he gets a bit of shit—sorry, I mean . . . you know, 'cos he's small and, like, a good laugh.'

'And you're a good laugh too, aren't you?'

'Pardon?'

'The other kids like you?'

'Think so.'

'You can take a joke, like Travis? They'd think you were up for a bit of a laugh?'

'Mm.'

'We need a yes or a no, Samara, please.' He sounded like a school principal.

'Yes.' Samara wasn't looking at the camera anymore.

'So, they'd have thought you were up for a bit of fun, because you're all friends, aren't you?'

Bethany could feel her heart beating faster as she recognised the cajoling, tricking tone the lawyer was using.

'And you'd had a few RTDs before the swim?'

'Only about two.'

'So, you were intoxicated enough that your inhibitions were lowered?'

'What?'

'You were relaxed, and you liked lying next to Chris?'

'No.'

'You moved onto your side; he was behind you, wasn't he?'

'No.'

The lawyer's voice was firm and reassuring, and his questions seemed to run together, and Bethany could imagine the girl lying on the raft in a blue bikini, next to Chris.

'I put it to you, Samara, that you were deliberately lying provocatively close to Chris, weren't you? . . . You said, "Come and get me," and rolled into the water, didn't you? . . . You checked he was following you, didn't you?'

The girl kept saying no, and the lawyer kept telling the story as if she hadn't even spoken, and her answers got quieter and quieter.

'When you stood up you undid your bikini top . . . You put your hands on your breasts . . . You were tipsy, and you put your hands on your breasts, and said, "Come and get me, Chris" . . . When he was behind you, you rubbed your buttocks against him . . . You said, "I'm wet, feel me" . . . And he said, "Not here with all these people," didn't he?'

On the screen, the girl, who was crying silently now, said, 'I would never say that . . .' Her voice was very small.

The judge said, 'Samara, I understand it's difficult, but if you can speak up, please.'

Bethany drew a triangle on her pad, pushing hard into the paper.

The lawyer said, 'I put it to you, Samara, there was no assault—you asked Chris to touch you, and he refused.'

'He did touch me.'

'I put it to you that the only person who touched your breasts was you.'

'He pulled down my bikini bottoms and touched me.'

'If that had happened, you would have shouted out and pushed him away, wouldn't you? No one saw a struggle, did they?'

'No, but . . .' Her voice trailed off.

'You were in a safe place with people all around, and yet you didn't call for help, did you, Samara?'

'I was embarrassed.'

'Yes. You were.'

Bethany looked up; his tone had changed.

The girl was nodding.

'You were embarrassed that he'd rejected you, weren't you, Samara?'

'Chris? No.'

'That's why you didn't tell your friends that day, because it was all a story you made up and you weren't attacked at all, were you?'

'Not *attacked*, but Chris did touch me.'

'Samara, in your version of the story, what did you do after he'd moved away?'

'I did up my top and pulled up my bottoms.'

'In that order?'

'What? Um . . . I'm not sure. Then I went and put my clothes on.'

'So, you weren't upset, were you? And you didn't call for help, you just calmly got changed—into what, Samara?'

'Not sure.'

'Well, from the photos—members of the jury, you have these on page two of your photo booklet—we can see you put on your sundress. Is that right?'

'I guess.'

'So, you claim someone indecently assaulted you, and yet you didn't scream or tell anyone, you just changed into this very short, strappy dress, and carried on partying; it beggars belief really, Samara, doesn't it?'

'I'd only brought the sundress, and I didn't tell anyone because I was freaked out.'

'You weren't so "freaked out" that it stopped you chatting up Lee, though, were you?'

'That was later.'

'Were you worried that Lee had heard about you flirting with Chris? That wouldn't help you become his girlfriend, would it?'

'Chris shouldn't have—'

The lawyer interrupted her. 'If we just stick to the questions, Samara. So, I put it to you, you were annoyed the flirty stuff went too far and you were embarrassed when Chris turned your propositioning down, so you went back to flirting with Lee, correct?'

The girl seemed confused but then said firmly, 'I was freaked out and angry because Chris undid my top and pulled my bottoms down and felt me up, and then when Kasey told me that Caleb said it was part of—'

'I'll have to stop you there, Samara. That's not evidence if you heard something from someone else. In court we don't listen to rumours. So, you're a good-time girl, and you—'

The judge interrupted. 'Mr Daniels . . .'

'Sorry, Your Honour. I put it to you, you were having a good time at the lake, but you were disappointed when Chris and Lee turned you down, and when you heard the chatter about these allegations, you made up a story about Chris when actually—'

The girl spoke up, trying to deny what the lawyer was saying, but the judge told her she had to wait for the question.

'—you'd taken your own top off and asked him to touch you, and when he refused you were cross, so you jumped on the bandwagon—'

'That's a very long question, Mr Daniels,' said the judge.

'I can answer it,' said Samara, from the monitor. 'It's not true.'

'I understand that Maia and Amy are your friends, but these are serious allegations and colluding to get revenge is just not on, Samara, is it?'

Bethany didn't like that lawyer, nor did she like the expression on the oldest boy's face—he thought he was winning.

THEY HAD FINISHED early that afternoon because they were ready to move on to the next girl—Maia—but the judge said because they had tomorrow off, they would start hearing her testimony on Friday. When they got back to the jury room Mark said that before they left he wanted to have a quick discussion about the charges relating to Samara.

'We can do that, can't we, Les?' Mark said. 'Seeing as we're all here, and we've heard her testimony?'

Les said of course, as long as they kept an open mind.

Mark said there were clearly two sides to this one; it was a 'he-said, she-said' situation, so they had to work out whether there was any proof.

'Beyond a reasonable doubt,' said Jake.

'We have to decide if we believe her,' said Eva.

Scott said it didn't matter, it was hardly criminal behaviour—kids playing in a lake—and Mark agreed it did seem to be overkill.

Dave said he believed Chris had undone her top, but he thought the stuff about feeling her up seemed unlikely, especially because she didn't scream; she'd just carried on partying.

'Why would she make it up?' asked Chantae.

'Who knows?' said Mark. 'Girls do, though, don't they? And remember Samara was happy for Jayz to have a feel at Travis's party.'

Eva said that was completely irrelevant, and Chantae agreed.

Dave pointed out that she'd also bonked Lee in the car.

'She is quite slutty,' said Scott slowly, and everyone went quiet.

'I think we can avoid that kind of terminology,' Les said.

Then Susannah reminded them that Samara had been all over Jayz at the barbecue.

'So?' said Kahu, shrugging. 'Samara got around. It's not uncommon.'

Les said that, actually, according to Samara, over a two-month period she'd been with two blokes consensually, and perhaps in today's context that wasn't 'getting around'.

'Yeah, it's up to her,' said Chantae, in her full-on tone.

Hayley stood up then. She walked around the table towards the door.

'You can't leave when we're all discussing this,' said Susannah.

'You okay, Hayley?' asked Dave.

Hayley muttered something and went into the bathroom.

'At the end of the day,' said Jake, 'while these boys were bloody stupid, we have to be careful—this could ruin their whole lives.'

Quietly Bethany got up from her seat. No one asked her what she was doing.

'What about the girls?' said Chantae. 'What about *their* lives?'

As Bethany opened the bathroom door, she heard Jake stuttering, 'I didn't mean to detract . . . I was just looking at it from the boys' perspective. I mean, it's all a tragedy, isn't it?'

Hayley wasn't in the toilet cubicle; she was sitting on the floor below the hand dryer, her back against the wall. Her eyes were shut, but she opened them, saw it was Bethany, and shut them again.

Bethany crouched down. 'You okay?'

Hayley didn't open her eyes; she gave a small nod. Bethany sat cross-legged next to her. After a while, she whispered, 'I don't like them arguing either.'

Hayley didn't answer.

'And Chantae can be scary as, if you say the wrong thing, but you don't always know what the wrong thing is,' said Bethany. 'Least I don't.' Because she was looking straight ahead at the curve of the pipe under the sink, Bethany hadn't noticed Hayley reach for her, so she jumped when Hayley patted her leg.

• • •

BETHANY ROCKED THE baby. Rocked the baby. Rocked the baby. Her torso swaying back and forth.

Bethany liked the baby.

She would like her own baby. She'd need a boyfriend to have a baby.

If she had a baby she wouldn't have to go to work; she could stay at home.

Her sister and Ricky would kick her out if she had a baby. Then she'd have to go to work with the baby, to pay for rent, or she'd have to move back home to Te Puke, but her mum wasn't there anymore.

The baby scrambled with his knees against her tummy as if he was trying to crawl up her. Bethany rubbed his back—just upwards, not both ways.

'Thank God you're back,' said the girl she was working with, as she scraped orange mush from a toddler's lips.

'I'm not really. I'm just here for today. The judge has a funeral. I'll be away for two more weeks—it's an important trial.' Bethany straightened as she spoke.

The girl was too busy to notice; the baby did, though, and, stretched against her, he relaxed, eyes closing.

When Bethany finally put the baby down, her boss, Amanda, told her to go through to the big kids' room. The light in there was subdued by the thin purple curtains with yellow stars and moons. Twelve green vinyl mattresses were lined up on the floor, three rows of four, each with a child in a sleeping sheet, curled fetus-like, stretched out or spread-eagled. Bethany tiptoed in. The rain music was playing faintly. She could smell the lunchtime baked beans and, even though she didn't like baked beans, today they smelled good.

'Hi, Bef'nee,' Hunter whispered, his eyes still bleary. Glad of the excuse, she kneeled and stroked his hair.

'Beffy's back,' called Ella, scrambling out of her sleeping sheet. Katie was quicker and clambered over Hunter, arms tightening around Bethany's neck.

Now Ella was there, and next thing Nikau was reaching to hug her. Bethany, laughing, loosened Katie's arms, while Hunter wormed his way under her elbow. Bethany wobbled, and that gave the children the idea that she might fall, so they pushed, laughing and shouting, and some of the others joined in, and Bethany rolled onto her side and they were all trying to sit on her, or lie on her, and everyone was giggling. Sam, who had his usual white tutu over his tracksuit trousers, sat down on her head, and she had to call out to him through the mesh skirt to get up.

Amanda came in. 'E tū tamariki.' She hustled the children off to get ready for the karakia before afternoon tea.

'Bethany, you're not one of them,' she said. Today, though, there was a lightness to her exasperation, and on the mat she asked Bethany to lead the karakia. Bethany chose the traditional one, not the one about Jesus Christ but about Tāne and Tangaroa, and the gift of food from the sacred forests and cultivated gardens. She wasn't sure if Amanda's frown was because of her pronunciation or because she hadn't chosen the Christian one. Either way, today it didn't matter; Bethany put her arms around Katie and squeezed.

At afternoon tea there was a cake for Patrick's birthday and after they'd sung Happy Birthday, the older children sang, 'Welcome back to you, welcome back to you, welcome back, dear Beffy, welcome back to you.' They sang it fast, over and over, so the words muddled together, and Bethany smiled and smiled.

AT THE END of the day, Bethany sat on the beanbag in the sunroom with Hunter snuggled under one dimpled arm and his baby sister curled up in the other, asleep now. This was the only time of day that the sun came in through the side windows, through the hands the children had cut out from transparent plastic and blu-tacked to the glass—purple, orange and yellow—patching her pale skin with their colours.

Ella and Sam were dancing and prancing around the beanbag, and the light—magenta and orange and lemon-coloured—shone on to Bethany as she watched the children skip and spin, as Hunter cuddled between her soft arm and her bosoms; that's what her grandmother called them and the word seemed right for this moment. This moment, with Elaine singing and playing the ukulele, and only these four children left here in the sunroom, waiting for their parents, who would work the last minutes of this sunlit afternoon and then rush through the traffic to get to the centre before Amanda charged them the late fee. And usually Bethany would bitch with the other workers about the cheek of these parents, but today she didn't care. She didn't want today to end. She loved it here with the sunlight in her eyes, snuggled with the baby in the crook of her arm, while Ella and Sam giggled and pushed, boogied and swayed, jiggled and bopped. While Elaine strummed and sang, her short grey hair fluffed up because she was hot and sweaty in the sunroom. And Elaine kept singing, and Sam kept swaying, and Hunter shuffled closer, and Bethany could smell the sourness of her sweat when he pushed her arm higher so he could snuggle in tighter, while the baby slept, and her skin was dappled with the handprints of light from the windows—magenta, orange and lemon.

NORMALLY, WHEN BETHANY got home from work, she cooked herself dinner, nothing flash—noodles with ham, peas and corn (the green and yellow to make it look appetising), or mince in taco shells with fresh tomato and lettuce. Today, though, she'd bought herself a frozen butter chicken as a treat, and some dip to share with Ricky. Ricky and Carly ate separately to her because Carly wasn't home from the gym till after seven, so Ricky ate a bit of Bethany's dinner too. He didn't like Carly knowing that, though. When Carly was home, Ricky would sometimes push his finger into Bethany's thigh, holding it there, inspecting the dent it made; the depth of the dent. Commenting. He didn't like her softness, but it wasn't like Ricky worked out for his angular bony body with its hard small bulges of muscle, not like Carly did. It was just the way he was—all amped up. That was mostly how he was with Bethany too—prickly, cross and stubborn. But for the hour and a half before Carly came home, he was different.

'How d'ya make this? It's good,' said Ricky, taking another pita chip.

'You brush them with oil and bake them.'

He wasn't listening; he was scooping up a great globule of dip.

'See, I'll list the stuff on Trade Me. Phone cases, screen protectors . . . that kinda shit.' He shoved the pita chip into his mouth, and took another before he'd even swallowed, dipped, then, waving it towards her, dripping pale green blobs on the table, he added triumphantly, 'But the stuff won't be here.'

Bethany stared. 'Will you want curry? I could do two packets of rice.'

'Nah,' he said, as she'd known he would. He got up, scraping the chair back. At the sink he washed his hands and wiped his T-shirt with the dishcloth where he'd dribbled. 'See, that's the beauty.'

Bethany watched him pace across the room and latch the window open before taking a cigarette from the packet he kept on the windowsill.

'I don't have to pay the postage.' He put the unlit cigarette in his mouth.

'How not?'

He spun round. ''Cos they'll buy it off Trade Me, right?'

She nodded, wishing now she'd bought a Coke.

'And then I'll buy it off the China site that does free shipping, right, and get them to send it straight to the person, so I keep the postage money and I don't have to store boxes of crap here in this box.' Ricky looked around the flat, and she followed his gaze. The bedroom door was wide open, the double bed taking up almost the whole room; at the far end of the living room was the bathroom and, next to it, the alcove with the divider where Bethany slept.

Now Ricky started shoving dishes into the sink, then he threw away the pita pocket bag and the lid of the dip, even though Bethany hadn't meant to eat it all. 'No boxes in this box,' he muttered, and it reminded her of a song her mum used to sing about ticky-tacky houses and them being like boxes, only she couldn't remember how it went, except there were lots of different-coloured houses and they were all the same, except they weren't the same because they were different colours.

Ricky was whining about the size of the flat, and how his mate paid less rent for a two-bedroom place, and while he whined, he was making out like he was tidying when really he was just piling stuff on the table or by the couch. Carly liked the flat tidy when she came home.

Bethany watched, nodding if Ricky looked at her; he didn't much. It was one of her things, watching people—like when Carly zipped around the kitchen unpacking the shopping, reaching up to this cupboard, bending down to the freezer, emptying fruit into the bowl. Sometimes Carly caught her looking and told her to get off her fat arse and help. Bethany even liked watching Ricky strutting and smoking and anguishing. It made her wonder how he cared so much about stuff. Her favourite, though, was watching the children, even the babies sleeping—she liked it when they started and their hands flashed out, fingers splayed like the cut-out hands on the window.

In court, it wasn't so interesting, especially when the judge cleared the public seats. She liked watching the boys. She was allowed. Bethany had decided she liked Jayz the best, with his huge brown eyes. He wasn't all bone and angles, with pimples, and grey under his eyes, like Ricky. She liked Jayz's thick hair and the way his chin was wide, not thin and pointy like Ricky's. Sometimes Jayz watched them too, especially when the jurors wrote stuff down, and when she noticed him looking she drew long wavy lines on her pad so he would think she was noting something important.

Otherwise she didn't take notes in court. She couldn't imagine how people chose what to write, all those questions and answers. Chantae wrote screeds in round loopy letters and all the pages looked the same—not like those business guys, Les and Mark: they had headings and boxes, and Les had stars and arrows too. Scott hadn't even touched his pad, not the whole time.

Often Bethany found the time in court was like when Ricky was telling her some story, but now and then it faded more than that, like the soundtrack of TV programs through the divider, and occasionally it went right out of focus and was like the noise from the washing machine in the cupboard in the bathroom.

'What is this anyways?' said Ricky. He was eating the dip again.

Bethany sighed. 'Feta and spinach.'

'Spinach? Fuckin' A, you're getting like your sister.'

They both knew that wasn't true. Carly made protein salads with quinoa and chickpeas, and chicken with bean sprouts and mango. Ricky ate it all and didn't complain, but every night he ate part of Bethany's dinner.

'You get paid for today, eh? Properly, I mean—not like the shit pay you get on the jury.'

'Yeah,' she said, and then added, 'It'll be over in another two weeks,' and she was surprised to feel sad about that.

'What I don't get,' said Ricky, who'd stopped moving, who was facing her, standing close, 'is why they'd want you—that's what I don't get.'

'What?'

'The jury people—what would they want you for? You're not gonna know what the fuck, are you?'

'What d'you mean?'

'When it comes to making the decision—I mean what the fuck will *you* say? What the fuck do you know, like?'

Bethany was quiet. When he was belligerent like this it was best just to agree. Her silence now, though, wasn't only because he was being mean, but because it hadn't occurred to her that she would be asked to participate.

That she would have to deliberate.

Decide.

After a while Bethany realised that Ricky had gone into his room; he'd shut the door although he continued talking—some story about his mate—and she wasn't listening, and then he was back, in her face, buzzing now.

'Fuck, man, I've got it. Vaping gear. This is it, Bethy, could make a fortune.'

'What?'

'That's what I could sell.'

A minute later he was sitting right next to her, with AliExpress open on his phone, flicking rapidly through vaping accessories.

And it was a good idea so far as she could see. Since Ricky had failed the drug test at the sawmill, he hadn't had a proper job, and Carly earned the money. That was why they'd let Bethany move in. Sometimes she wanted to remind Ricky about that, especially when he got shitty on weekends about her always being there. But where was she supposed to go?

And even though Bethany kind of knew that Carly would come home and pour cold water all over his scheme, she was glad they were by themselves now, when he was all buzzy about it, and she pointed to the Joyetech electronic cigarettes that came in red and gold and blue, and said, 'I like those ones.'

• • •

THE NEXT MORNING, as Bethany rode the bus into town, she thought about what Ricky had said, and about how they were going to hear Maia today, and she wasn't sure she wanted to go back. Back to that chilly courtroom where she needed her hoodie on, and then it was too hot in the jury room and she had to take it off and she kept forgetting to use deodorant. And everyone else knew how the trial fitted together. It was like being back at school.

As she crossed the courtyard—there weren't many people waiting outside this morning—Bethany thought about playing netball at intermediate school and how the teacher had told her to follow the ball with her eyes the whole time, and she thought from now on she'd picture the questions and answers like netball passes, and that made her smile, imagining the back and forth. That way she'd be ready for when they had to decide.

FIRST UP, THE prosecutor showed a video of Maia being interviewed by a lady police officer. The lady asked Maia about Amy and Jayz, and Bethany liked that part. Maia told how she and Amy had snapchatted Lee and Jayz, and waited for them outside their school. It was like a love story—Travis's birthday drinks where Jayz had first kissed Amy, and the Blue Lake concert where he'd lain on the grass next to them. And then at the last party, the sixteenth, how Travis had come to tell Amy that Jayz wanted to talk to her in the garden.

Jayz had chosen Amy. That had never happened to Bethany. She'd never been chosen. No boy had ever touched her like that. And she'd always be just her, and she'd have to stay living with Carly and Ricky or move near to her mum's new home, because she'd always be by herself, and how would she ever have a baby?

The policewoman asked Maia about the night she got trashed at the barbecue. Bethany thought if she was Samara she would've hated what happened and she wouldn't have told anyone who hadn't already seen, but with Maia it was different. Maia didn't know what happened, so it didn't seem so bad.

Then the prosecutor said they were going to play the video that had been found on Travis's phone and Bethany hoped it would have the bits of Amy and Jayz dancing. The screen came on, and there was a shaky picture of someone climbing some stairs with a turquoise-coloured carpet. They stopped the video then, and talked about the sound, and then it started again and this time she could hear music and people's voices. Then she saw the back of someone, maybe Jayz, opening a white-painted door for the person filming. He kind of threw the door open and stepped to the side so they could see into the room. At first Bethany didn't understand, and then she realised what Chris was doing.

Bethany's eyes flicked to the judge. He was watching his screen.

The lawyers were watching too. And Chantae. On the other side of Bethany, Scott was sitting forwards, staring intently.

On the screen, the camera zoomed in; Bethany looked away.

She looked up at the coat of arms on the wall above the judge.

She could hear the noise of the music and the boys laughing on the video, but she kept her eyes on the boats on the shield on the wall, and she thought about the song Elaine sang about the ships a-sailing by, and there was a sheep on the shield, and she wondered why it was arched up, and there was a warrior with his cloak and feathers in his hair, and a lady in a white dress, and the dress made her think of Sam's tutu and of him twirling around and the safe safe feeling of yesterday in the sunroom with Elaine singing and Hunter and the baby and the light from the cut-out hands coming through the window and making patterns on her pale skin—magenta and orange and lemon-coloured.

# CHAPTER SEVEN
# Fiona

This girl, Maia, looked younger than sixteen. She had a round, soft face and was wearing a black-and-white dress with a small bow at the front. Fiona thought someone must have told her to wear it, to make her look girlish and innocent—her parents, perhaps, or the prosecutor. There was a stark contrast between the dress and her posture. In the little room, Maia sat collapsed in on herself, her shoulders curved forwards and her forearms crossed over her rather sizeable breasts.

After a few introductory questions, the prosecutor explained that he would show a video of Maia being interviewed by a level-two police interviewer. Fiona presumed that meant the officer was trained in talking to sexual assault victims.

The screen was split now so they could see Maia in the room via the audiovisual link, but they could also see her in a baggy blue sweatshirt with stringy-looking hair at what must be a police station, nearly a year ago.

In the video Maia's answers were mostly brief and reluctant. She admitted that it was she and Amy who had initiated contact with Lee and Jayz on Snapchat, and, in a voice devoid of emotion, she described how pleased and surprised they'd been when Lee invited them to Travis's eighteenth drinks. She spoke more freely as she described them dancing and how Jayz had kissed Amy, and then she fell back to half-sentences and one-word answers when the questions focused on her.

Yesterday, when they'd had the day off, Fiona had made herself a chart of what she knew about the game so far. It would be easier if it was on the whiteboard so everyone could see it and check it, but Mark had refused and Fiona didn't want an overt confrontation. She suspected, though, that if she was finding it hard to keep it all straight, some of the other jurors would definitely be struggling. There were no charges for the first round of the game and none of the boys had shaken Maia in the second round at Blue Lake. She would remind the others of that when they had a break. Fiona flicked back to her notes as the girl talked; the third round took place at Lee's barbecue, and this had led to the sexual violation charge concerning Maia. According to the group chat messages, Chris had shaken a one, which by then meant he had to perform oral sex on Maia, and Travis had shaken a four, so he had to get a nude photo of her.

Maia said she'd never drunk alcohol before Lee's barbecue. She explained that her parents were strict and religious, and then admitted having arranged a sleepover that night so they wouldn't know she was going to Lee's or that she was drinking. The policewoman asked her what she remembered about being in the bedroom and she described it as mere flashes of consciousness, as if she were surfacing from underwater.

After they'd finished watching the police interview, the prosecutor asked Maia more questions. While Maia explained that Lee, Chris and Jayz had given her drinks and compliments all evening, Fiona watched the boys. At one point, she caught Lee looking back at her and she could see him trying to relax his expression, to make his face seem open; Fiona looked away.

Maia said she remembered stumbling into the kitchen to get a glass of water and Lee and Chris laughing. She remembered the smell of the burgers making her nauseous. She remembered Chris telling her she was drunk and her saying she was going outside. She remembered Lee holding her by the arm and saying she'd feel better if she lay down and how much she had wanted to be at home then in her own bed.

When she said she could vaguely remember Chris and Jayz, one either side, almost carrying her up the stairs, Fiona saw Chris shake his head, but she also saw Travis bow his. Then Maia said she couldn't remember much else until she woke the next morning at her friend's, and how she'd been dressed but had no undies on.

She was obviously very upset by what had happened, or what she'd pieced together. However, there were significant gaps in her testimony and Fiona worried that if the alcohol had affected her recollections so strongly, how could they, as jurors, rely on them? But then the prosecutor said, 'Can you explain to the court how, if you were as drunk as you've described, you know what they did to you?'

For the first time Maia looked directly at the camera. 'Because of Travis's video.'

THE CAMERA WAS not held steady. It was following Jayz up the stairs, and at the top he opened a bedroom door. The music became louder then, and there was another sound, boys making noises. Affirming noises. Through the open door you could see the back of a brown-haired head between a girl's thighs. You could see her skirt hitched above her soft belly. Then the boy lifted his head. It was one of the defendants, Chris. The oldest one. He turned and grinned at the camera—or, Fiona supposed, it was probably a phone—and stuck out his tongue and waggled it, then gave that gang sign she'd banned in her school library: fingers in a fist, with his thumb and little finger stretched out, hand swivelling. There'd been no evidence of any gang associations. Then someone shoved the camera closer and for a second they could see between Maia's legs, although the centre of the image had been blurred out. Fiona looked away, and then back. The picture flashed up over the girl; her eyes were shut, head to one side, and a guy's voice said angrily, 'Fuck, Travis.' Then another voice said something about 'turn'. Maia's mouth seemed to open, and her eyes too for a moment before they shut again.

AFTER THE VIDEO, there was an adjournment because Maia, in the little room somewhere here in the courthouse, was too upset to continue, and Fiona, too, was grateful for the break. By the time the prosecutor turned off the camera, Maia was bent over with her hands covering her face as someone sitting in the room passed her tissue after tissue. Fiona ached for the girl in a shocked, disorientated way—so this was social media. Did girls actually understand how dangerous it was? Before he'd played it, the prosecutor had warned them the video was graphic, and she and Susannah had exchanged a grimace, but the video was not merely graphic, it was an invasion, and what made it worse was that Maia had to see it again, here in court, and the prosecutor had told her that she had to watch it—and, worse still, she had to watch it knowing the jurors were watching it too, the judge and lawyers, and worst of all, those boys who'd made it, who had violated her. Maia could not see them, but she would know in her room that they were watching it again, watching them violate her again, and all of this knowledge made Fiona livid.

WHEN THEY CAME back in, Maia was composed. She answered the prosecutor's questions as quickly as possible without looking at the camera.

'Can you please confirm that the girl in the video was you?'

'Yes.'

'Maia, have you seen this video before?'

'Yes.' Her voice was flat. 'The police showed it to me after they found it on Travis's phone.'

'Did you give your permission for this video to be taken?'

'No.'

'Do you remember the video being taken?'

'No.'

'Do you remember the events depicted in the video?'

'Just flashes of it. I remember the orange curtains . . . the sound of the guys. I knew they were there. I remember not being able to move . . . stay awake.'

'Were you consenting to the oral sex being performed on you by Chris?'

'No. Mostly I wasn't conscious. I was very drunk.'

This was all vital to the question of consent. Fiona looked around, wondering if the others, especially Bethany, were taking this in, and as she did she noticed that Dave's eyes were shut and his head was tipped forwards so his chin was almost resting on his chest. Kahu, the Māori boy who sat next to him, didn't seem to have noticed, but Scott, on his other side, raised his eyebrows at Fiona. Dave started then and looked around guiltily. Quickly, Fiona twisted back to face the court.

BEFORE LUNCH, WHILE people chatted, waiting for their phones, Fiona said quietly to Scott and Jake, 'Did you see? He was asleep.' She nodded towards Dave, in his scruffy fleece, who was standing looking out the window, his back to them.

Jake shook his head. Scott stared at her.

'It's not right,' she said. 'We all have to listen to the evidence. I've noticed he doesn't make notes or concentrate properly.'

'You should have a word.'

She thought Scott was mocking her, but he nodded and said, 'Seriously.'

WHEN FIONA CAME out onto the pavement, she saw Dave halfway across Arawa Street. She walked fast, and when he went into a cafe she followed and stood looking at the food in the glass-fronted cabinets.

Dave had two brown paper bags on the counter and was paying, so she hurriedly chose a wedge of bacon and egg pie, noticing only as she slipped it into the bag that the yolk had that slight greenish tinge.

Dave went outside and sat at one of the plastic tables.

When Fiona had paid, she paused at his table as if she'd just seen him. 'Oh, hello, it's Dave, isn't it?'

He was rifling in one of his bags and looked up with a blank expression.

'How are you finding the trial?' she asked.

'Tiring.'

'Yes. It is hard to concentrate and get it all down, isn't—'

'What would you know?'

She was surprised by his dismissive tone. 'Sorry, I didn't mean . . . I was agreeing—it is tiring, listening, isn't it?'

The grease from the bacon and egg pie had made the outside of the bag shiny, and she held it away from her body; she didn't want to mark her top. She considered explaining how long it had been since she'd had to concentrate like this, but she didn't want him to think that was because of her age. This wasn't at all the conversation she'd intended.

'Anyway, I'd better run.' She waved vaguely as if she had somewhere to be.

'Best run then,' he said neutrally. His beard was patchy and had some ginger in it, even though his hair was brown.

'Yes, well, it's important, jury duty. That's all I wanted to say.'

'Don't know what you're on about.' He sounded bored.

'Just, we *all* have to listen to *all* the evidence. We are dealing with people's lives.'

He stared and then muttered, 'Whatever.'

She detested that particular response.

'See you back there.' She gave a small smile.

As she turned, she heard him mumble, 'Can't wait,' but then in a louder voice he said, 'We won't hear *all* of it, you know?'

Fiona was aware that the Asian man inside the cafe was watching them impassively; he could probably hear every word through the window.

She turned back. 'All I'm saying is it's our duty to listen. We need to hear both sides.'

He gave a short laugh. 'No chance those boys'll front up.'

'Excuse me?'

'We won't hear from them.' He screwed up the first paper bag, then pulled a caramel slice out of the other. 'Might see their police interviews—they wouldn't even have known to ask for lawyers then, prob'ly.'

'The police would read them their rights,' Fiona protested.

'Yeah?' He took a bite and, with his mouth full, said, 'Wouldn't know what a "solicitor" was if it bit them on the bum.'

'Yes, well, I'd better . . .'

'Run?' he said. 'Yeah, nice talking to you, Fiona.'

She walked quickly towards the intersection. He'd known who she was the whole time. She felt shaky. Probably just needed food; the bacon and egg pie didn't appeal at all now. She threw it in the rubbish bin on the corner and walked fast towards her favourite cafe.

Dave seemed to know a lot about being arrested. Surely they wouldn't let criminals sit on a jury?

She wasn't afraid of him. She'd always been willing to mix with people from different walks of life. Only a few weeks ago she'd helped two Mongrel Mob members follow the instructions to log on to the internet at the library so they could look at the Maketū chapter's Facebook page. Some of her friends would have run a mile. No, she wasn't afraid, but nor had she made any difference; she wasn't sure he'd understood her point at all.

FIONA WENT BACK to the courthouse early, thinking she would draw the chart on the board while the others were gone. She wouldn't even need to say she'd done it. When she got back to the jury room, though, Susannah and Jake were already making hot drinks, and Les, whom she liked very much even though he was too focused on the trial to chat, was reading over the transcript of Caleb's evidence. Surprisingly, Chantae, the Māori woman, was sitting next to him, writing notes. Les had a packet of highlighter pens open by his pad and, as Fiona hung up her jacket, she watched Chantae lean across and take one without asking and then highlight something on her notepad.

At the sink, Susannah was complaining that there was only instant coffee; Fiona agreed, and then suggested that Mark wasn't very helpful, but Susannah immediately shut her down, saying, 'We need someone firm,' and Jake just nodded.

Fiona took her tea and sat down on the other side of Les. She'd noticed that he, too, had listed all the dice numbers and what Caleb had told them the boys had shaken for the first three rounds of the game before he had left the group chat. So far there was no clear evidence about the fourth round. There was a whiteboard pen attached by a magnet to the board. Fiona didn't get up. She felt almost as exhausted by the other jurors as she did by the evidence; she was glad it was Friday.

BACK IN COURT, it was still Maia in the separate room and still the prosecutor asking the questions. Fiona hadn't realised that there was another charge which involved Maia. In the last round of the game she'd apparently been at her friend Emma's sixteenth when the boys had turned up unexpectedly. Maia explained that when she saw them she'd effectively hidden on the back deck and asked Amy to go with her.

'Can you explain why you did that?' the prosecutor asked.

'I was afraid of them. Of why they were there.'

'Can you tell us in your own words what happened?'

'Travis and Lee found us. Travis said Jayz was looking for Amy. I tried to get her to stay, but she wanted to see Jayz. So I just sat on the beanbag and I planned to stay there by myself until I was picked up at eleven. Then Lee asked if he could sit with me.'

'What did you say?'

'I shrugged and he sat down and then he put his arm around me and kissed me.'

'Did you want him to do that, Maia?'

'No. I didn't want any of them near me. I'd got the "Diced" message after the barbecue but I hadn't seen the video then. I didn't know what it meant.'

'Did you respond to the kiss?'

'No.'

'Did you say anything to him?'

'Nothing.'

'And then what happened?'

'He put his hand on my leg and he just kept going.' There was no emotion or tension in her voice as she spoke, which made her sound like a bad actor reading poorly written lines. 'I sort of shoved his hand away, but he put it back, and then pushed up right under my skirt and into my undies and I ran away.'

Fiona supposed the girl's lack of emotion was shock. She hoped they'd hear from a psychologist who would explain all this.

AT AFTERNOON TEA, while they ate their one allocated biscuit, Fiona said, 'I think we need to be clear about this party business.'

'Which party?' asked Mark in a resigned tone.

'No, I mean the boys being charged as parties. So, say with this indecent assault by Lee on Maia, are all the others charged as a party to it and on what basis?'

Several people started to talk. Mark said the last incident didn't seem to amount to anything. Scott thought it was a trumped-up charge. Susannah said boys always tried it on.

Fiona had the same feeling she used to have when she was losing control of a class—a rising urge to shout, to which she knew better than to succumb. Finally, in what she intended to be a firm tone she said, 'Quiet, please,' but she heard a tremble in her voice. It did seem to startle the others, though, so she boxed on. 'I'm not talking about that specific charge—I was using it as an example. What I mean is, do we understand how the party charges work?'

Chantae said, 'Don't think I do. Can we convict the boys for stuff they weren't even there for, just 'cos they played the game?'

'It doesn't seem right,' said Jake forcefully. 'Even if they were there at the time, outside, or even in the room, if they didn't do anything, they shouldn't be liable. Obviously, it's different if they held a girl down, or took off her clothes—then they're like a getaway driver.'

Les said, 'Whether we agree or not, we have to apply the law, and as I understand it, the Crown argument is that by playing the Dice Game the boys drew moral courage from each other as well as rewards—like the beer if they did it—but also that they gave specific instances of encouragement or assistance to help facilitate the actions.'

Chantae said, 'Once more in plain English, Les,' and Les nodded sympathetically, and said, 'To be a party to a crime, the law says you must help or encourage the main person to do the crime. So, if we accept that Jayz helped Chris get Maia up the stairs so Chris could force oral sex on her, that could count as assisting.'

'Right,' said Eva. 'And Jayz and Travis basically cheering while he did that, and while he was chasing Samara in the lake, is encouraging. The prosecutor gave that example, remember, about robbing a dairy. The person standing outside keeping watch is a party to the robbery, and so is the person who goes in with the main robber but doesn't hold a gun or demand the money.'

'Now, one thing I'm confused about,' said Les, 'is do they have to both "encourage" *and* "assist", or is it just one or the other?'

Everyone looked around, passing the responsibility to answer between themselves, no one holding it, until their eyes came to rest on Mark.

'Yeah. I'd wondered about that myself.'

If her son were here, Fiona thought, he'd call Mark out as a 'bullshitter'.

'I suppose it's like that walking stick case,' said Les.

'That the one where the old age pensioners got done, matua?' asked Kahu, giggling, which set off Bethany.

But Fiona could recall that case. 'Yes, all those boys got convicted even though only one was holding the walking stick.'

'There was an appeal . . .' said Les.

Some people were still joking around. Mark said he might have been overseas.

'What's this?' Susannah asked.

'Some schoolboys inserted a walking stick with Deep Heat on it up the anus of a boy who was very inebriated,' said Les.

'Oh my God,' said Jake.

'That's right,' said Fiona.

'How fucked is that?' said Dave.

'Exactly,' said Scott.

'Seriously?' said Chantae.

'I definitely must have been overseas,' said Mark.

'I think they all encouraged him to do it, and I believe some of them might have removed the boy's trousers,' said Les.

'So, it's like this case,' said Fiona.

'It's different,' said Jake. 'They knew it was illegal from the beginning.'

'The thing is there would have been different levels of charges,' said Mark. 'They wouldn't all have been done for the, er . . . penetration—the sexual violation.'

'I believe they were,' said Les.

'Yes,' said Fiona.

'It'd be different charges,' repeated Mark.

'I would think so,' said Susannah.

'Isn't that the point of being a party to an offence—that it is the same charge?' Fiona could hear that her voice was too loud. 'Like that little girl who was killed, the one who was left in the dog kennel?'

'We got given a talk about that . . .' Kahu looked serious now.

'Yes,' said Fiona. 'All those people living in that house were convicted as parties to murder, even though the mum and the other girl weren't there at the time.'

'No,' said Les firmly. 'Actually, you're incorrect, Fiona. The mother was convicted of manslaughter because she didn't take the girl to the doctor . . .'

He started to go through each defendant in that case. Fiona wasn't listening. She got up, aware as she did that they'd all be looking at her. She lurched for the toilet door. Inside, she went through the cloakroom to the cubicle, shut the door, put down the lid of the toilet, and sat. She could feel tears in her eyes, even though she knew it was an overreaction; she hadn't expected Les to speak to her like that. She'd thought he would back her up, especially against Mark—after all, Mark had dismissed what Les said too. And Mark had refused to ask the judge the questions Les had wanted him to yesterday. She really couldn't stand the man, and frankly Susannah needed to stop being such a lackey.

There was shuffling in the jury room. Someone else must be waiting. She flushed the toilet and washed her hands. She didn't hurry, and when she opened the door, the room was empty. She could hear them right down the corridor. They must have been called back in. Panicked, she hurried after them.

FIONA FOUND THE cross-examinations exceedingly challenging. It was like those books where you saw the same events from different characters' perspectives, but here it was all Maia's perspective, only different versions of Maia's perspective, versions that were aimed at catching her out, at manipulating her. And how were you meant to take notes about that?

Lee's lawyer, who Fiona thought a thoroughly unpleasant woman, asked questions only about the indecent assault charge, her tone verging on sarcasm.

'So, Maia, was Emma's sixteenth just a week after the barbecue?'

'Yes.'

'And you went along happily to this party even though you're claiming to have been violated the week earlier, is that correct?'

'I didn't want to go. My parents made me.'

'These are the parents you describe as strict and religious, though?'

'Yes . . . Emma's family are church friends.'

'You had a crush on Lee, is that correct?'

'Earlier, yes. After the barbecue I was scared of them all.'

'You testified that at the time of Emma's party you hadn't seen the video?'

'No, I hadn't. The police showed it to me after Amy reported—'

The lawyer interrupted and asked, in a cajoling, singsong tone, 'So if you were unconscious at the barbecue, as you claimed, and couldn't remember what they supposedly did to you, why would you be scared of the boys?'

'I knew something had happened. I wasn't sure what exactly.'

'Because you were drunk, not unconscious?'

'I was drunk and mostly unconscious.'

'Mostly. All right, and so at Emma's party, when Lee came and asked if he could sit with you, you didn't object, did you?'

'No.'

'That's not the actions of someone who's scared, is it?'

'I couldn't.'

'And when he kissed you, did you say, "Please don't do that, Lee"?'

'No.'

'No. Did you push him away?'

'No.'

'No. And when he put his hand on your leg, did you shout for help?'

'I took his hand off.'

'That was teasing, though, wasn't it, because when he put it back, you didn't object, did you? Just like you didn't object when he kissed you or when he put his arm around you.'

'I felt like I couldn't move.'

'Just like you said you felt at the barbecue—but you weren't drunk at the sixteenth, were you?'

'I haven't drunk since the barbecue. I don't plan to.'

'All right, very virtuous. You did move, though, didn't you? You left when you'd had enough, didn't you?'

'Because I got so scared.'

'When you left, did Lee follow you? Chase you? Force you to the ground?'

'No.'

'So, for want of a better expression, you "hooked up" with Lee, and then you drew a line and he respected it—is that right?'

'No. I didn't do anything.'

'So you didn't do anything to let Lee know his advances weren't welcome—is that correct, Maia?'

Watching the girl on the screen, as the lawyer repeatedly leaned in to the microphone to ask her prodding, unscrupulous questions, Fiona had the same feeling as in the jury room: she wanted to shout.

• • •

THE SKY WAS only just starting to lighten when Fiona woke, thinking about the case and the conversation in the jury room at afternoon tea. When she was going through menopause, she used to do this all the time, replaying conversations from work meetings, or with her son, worrying over comments or what she'd failed to say. Back then, she used to discuss it with Anton when he woke up, until he told her it was like she was lying in wait for him each morning.

Fiona would have liked to call her son immediately, but she knew it was too early for a weekend morning. She thought then about Kahu getting up at five to swim. He didn't fall asleep during the trial like Dave. He was taking responsibility, and he was only eighteen.

At eight o'clock she phoned.

'Andrew, hello, I need some help. Do you remember that walking stick case?'

'Mum? It's Saturday. The boys have got cricket.'

'Of course. I need to work something out for the jury. Some years ago, a group of boys were drunk at a party and assaulted another boy with a walking stick—do you remember? Were they all convicted of sexual violation?'

Andrew did his fake outraged laugh then. 'Not something I keep in my head, Mum.'

She tried to explain, but he interrupted: 'Google it.'

She thought he was trying to fob her off. 'It wouldn't be there now; it was years ago.'

'It'll be there, Mum. Nothing goes. It's all there forever. Look, I need to get the boys sorted or we'll be late. If you can't find it, I'll help you tomorrow.'

The computer had been Anton's, and Fiona used it mainly for word processing and email. Today when she turned it on there was a worrying red shield at the bottom which she thought was to do with computer viruses from the internet. She decided it would be all right as long as she was quick. She typed in the city and 'walking stick sexual assault' and Andrew was right: in between an advert for a sexual assault shelter and an article about an OAP who seemed to be a paedophile were two newspaper reports and, on the next page, the sentencing decision. Les was correct—their sentences varied, but the boys in that case were all convicted as parties to sexual violation; the focus seemed to be on their common intention, though, not on whether they had encouraged the crime.

• • •

FIONA ARRIVED AT the courthouse early on the second Monday of the trial. Les was the only one there. He had a cup of tea already, but for once no papers in front of him. Fiona answered his greeting, and then pulled the mustard-yellow cardboard folder out of her bag and slid it, quite hard, across the table.

'Confirms everything,' she said, her tone matter-of-fact.

Les put his hand on the folder but he didn't open it; he just held it there under his palm.

'What's this, Fiona?' he asked.

'I found the case we were discussing. I printed off the sentencing and the law . . .'

'Stop.' He held up his other hand.

'What is it?'

Bethany came in. Her plaits were already as untidy as Pippi Longstocking's. 'Jeez, youse get here early.'

Neither of them responded.

'Les?' asked Fiona.

'We'll just wait for everyone.' His tone was almost reassuring, but Fiona's brain was scrambling. Her son had suggested she look the case up and she had, and Les had been right, and she'd printed it off. And she'd also found the relevant part of the Crimes Act about being a party to a crime, although it was still confusing. She'd thought he'd help her make sense of it, but instead he seemed annoyed. Perhaps he didn't want to have an argument with Mark.

The others were arriving—Susannah, Jake and Eva.

Les was too humble—he didn't want to draw attention to the fact that he was right.

No, it was more than that. She'd done something wrong. It was an 'error of judgement', as Anton used to say.

They were all here now. Mark was asking what was going on.

Fiona was tempted to put her fingers over her face so the others couldn't see her, but it would look dramatic.

As soon as Les spoke, everyone fell silent. 'Fiona has made a mistake. She's printed off some material pertaining to the issues we were discussing on Friday.'

'It's from the internet, it shows—'

'Fiona!'

She was shocked; Les had shouted.

Nobody spoke.

Mark rubbed his forehead. 'What should we . . . er, Les, what's the best . . . ?'

'I think, Mr Foreman, that you'd better ask the court crier to—'

'You don't need to do that,' interrupted Fiona, and she leaned over the table towards the folder. Les kept his hand on it, moving it fractionally closer to himself. He wasn't going to give it back.

'Mark, you need to ask Anaru to take a message to the judge.'

'Not the judge . . .' said Fiona. She felt nauseous.

She could hear some of the others whispering.

'The correct procedure is to inform the judge.'

'Too right,' said Scott.

Jake said, 'Can't Fiona just agree not to talk about it?'

'Yes,' said Eva.

'No, we'd risk a mistrial,' said Les. 'If we follow the correct procedure, I think we can still avoid that.'

'We could just throw it away,' said Hayley in a low voice, and Dave agreed.

Everyone started to talk. Fiona stood up.

'All right,' said Mark. 'I'll find Anaru. You keep the folder secure.'

'Secure,' said Chantae, as Mark opened the door. 'Yeah, you'll fight us off if we make a move for it, won't you, Sandwich-man?'

'It's not a joking matter, Chantae,' said Les.

Fiona reached the toilet door as Kahu came in. She hadn't even realised he wasn't there already.

He looked around.

Everyone just stared back.

He grinned. 'What's the story?'

Fiona gave him a wan smile.

'Something going down?' he asked.

As she closed the toilet door, Fiona heard Chantae say, 'Grey Hair screwed up.'

'MRS ANDERSEN, I'M going to ask you some questions so we can understand exactly what happened this morning in the jury room.'

'Yes, sir.'

Fiona's voice sounded thin and insubstantial in the courtroom. Her eyes flicked over to the empty jury box. Somehow, in the course of just over an hour, she had become an individual participant in this trial, not just part of the jury. Never had she wished so strongly to be elsewhere, anywhere other than here in the witness stand. Except, of course, in the emergency department when they couldn't resuscitate Anton. She had the same sense now of reality being fragmented, as if the interconnecting tissue between the significant moments had been cut away.

'I will need you to speak up,' the judge said.

'Yes, sir.'

This time her voice was too loud, and she imagined the lawyers smugly catching each other's eyes.

'These are serious questions. This goes to the fair administration of justice. Do you remember how in my opening remarks I stressed that the jury must make its decision based solely on the evidence you hear in this courtroom?'

'Yes, sir, but it wasn't evidence.'

This was all a misunderstanding, and again Fiona felt she couldn't connect this moment back to the moment in the jury room when she had passed Les the folder.

'Mrs Andersen, this is a matter which could cause me to abort the trial.' His tone was exasperated, and recognising this made her all the more desperate. 'That would not only be expensive and time-consuming, it would also mean considerable stress to the witnesses we've already heard from who would have to testify again in a later trial. Do you understand?'

'Yes, sir. I'm sorry. I didn't mean—'

'We'll come to that.' After a pause, the judge added, 'I'm sure your intentions were good.'

'They were, sir.'

'Mrs Andersen, I could find you in contempt of court, which would mean a fine or even potentially a term of imprisonment. Now, I do not think that will be necessary here. What I do need, though, is for you to answer each question in total honesty, so that

I can gauge the impact of your behaviour on the other members of the jury. Did any of the other jurors read this material?'

'No, sir.'

'Did you tell them what you had found out in your "research"?'

'No, I didn't get the chance.'

'Mrs Andersen, do you recall in my opening remarks my instructions about the internet and personal research?'

'Yes, sir. You said we shouldn't follow any publicity about the trial.'

'Or make inquiries of your own. I specifically asked you to focus solely on the evidence that has been tested in this court.'

'Yes, sir.'

'And yet you chose to ignore me?'

'I wanted to help. There were some misunderstandings . . . Your Honour,' she added, remembering that this was what the lawyers said.

'Mrs Andersen, it is not your place . . .'

Fiona understood that she had behaved wrongly. She understood that the judge needed to tell her off, but she also had a peculiar feeling in her chest, as if inside her there was an abundance of energy. Her heart was racing ahead, and she placed one hand on her chest and the other on her ribs beneath her breast, and taking her heart in her two hands she interrupted the judge and told him that the jury didn't understand the concept of being a party to a crime, and that some of them, at least one, had no idea what was going on, and another had even fallen asleep during court and all she'd wanted to do was ensure there was justice for these girls, and the boys, because in all honesty she wasn't sure the process was capable of delivering that.

The judge let her speak and then, with a glance at the prosecutor—and Fiona saw the glint of amusement in his eyes—he told her that this was not unusual; that it was, perhaps, an inevitability of the jury system.

'However,' he said, 'on most juries there are plenty of jurors like yourself who are extremely assiduous and diligent, and it is these jurors who, if you like, carry the others. And, Mrs Andersen, it is for me as judge to instruct the jury on the law. That is my role, as I explained. In that way the jury is all presented with the same information about the law, and it is the *correct* information that pertains to this *particular* case.'

Fiona gave in then; she had made her point and he his. She waited for him to have the last word before sending her back to the others with her tail between her legs. Instead, the judge said, 'Unfortunately, this jury is going to have to do without your industriousness, Mrs Andersen. I'm afraid you have brought that upon yourself. You have conducted research into matters relating to this trial and, to ensure this does not taint the jury, I must now dismiss you.'

CHAPTER EIGHT

# Susannah

Everyone was quiet when the court crier took Fiona through to the courtroom to explain her actions. He had told them he would come back for Mark who, as foreman, would need to be questioned too.

'What will happen?' asked Bethany in what Susannah thought was a particularly childlike voice.

'I think we've avoided the trial being aborted, but I imagine Fiona will be dismissed,' said Les.

'I didn't realise that,' said Mark.

'Well, you both rushed our response,' said Eva, who sat on the other side of Fiona in court. Susannah hadn't spoken to Eva much.

'It just feels unnecessarily harsh.' Eva's tone was calmly assertive.

'Sadly, Fiona forced us into the situation, Eva,' said Les. 'We had to avoid a mistrial. We couldn't put the witnesses through that.'

'I suppose that's true,' Eva conceded.

'I think you both did the right thing,' said Susannah, looking from Les to Mark. Mark seemed shaken now, but after a few moments he gave her a nod and then, without explanation, he stood up and started writing the boys' names across the top of the whiteboard—the four defendants and Caleb—and down the side the names of the girls: Kasey, Samara and Maia, whom they'd heard from, and the next complainant, Amy. He put an asterisk by Kasey and explained that was because she was just a witness, not a complainant. Les told him the name of the fifth girl, Sacha, and that she was down to testify after Amy, and then Eva pointed out that there were meant to be six girls because of the numbers on the dice. None of them could recall the name of the sixth girl. Jake said he'd read stuff in the news back when it first happened about a much younger girl, but Mark said the prosecutor hadn't mentioned that and Les shut Jake down and Jake apologised. Mark drew arrows for which boys had done what to which girls, and then he was summoned into the courtroom.

WHEN MARK RETURNED, he looked stressed. He collected Fiona's jacket and bag and handed them to the court crier. Then he told them court would resume in fifteen minutes. And that was it, Fiona was gone.

'Why don't we go straight back in?' said Dave. 'We've just had a break.'

'Well, I haven't, and nor have the lawyers or the judge,' said Mark.

'Everything takes so friggin' long,' said Dave, and he stood up.

Les gently suggested they change Mark's chart on the whiteboard so they could see what happened for each round of the game. 'If people feel that would be helpful?'

Susannah noticed that he looked straight at Chantae then, and she agreed and so did Kahu, so obviously they were both struggling.

In a resigned voice, Mark said, 'Do what you want, Les. But if we're going to discuss the case we all have to stay here. All right, Dave?'

So Les wiped off the girls' names and wrote, *1. Travis's drinks*, and he put ticks under Lee, Jayz and Caleb's names, because everything was consensual, and a cross under Travis because he hadn't done anything. Then he wrote, *2. Blue Lake*, and he reminded them that Lee had consensual sex with Samara in that round, and that Travis had shaken Sacha but hadn't done anything, so he put a cross. He reiterated what the prosecutor had said about Jayz persuading Amy to send the nude photo, which Jayz had admitted to, but there were no charges for that. Susannah wasn't sure if that meant he'd pleaded guilty, but she didn't ask. Then Les wrote, *Indecent assault Samara?* under Chris's name, and reminded them that was the incident in the lake. He had written, *3. BBQ*, and put *forced oral* under Chris and *video* under Travis when they were called back in.

As Mark led the way down the corridor, Susannah said, 'You're doing a good job.'

IN THE COURTROOM, it took Susannah a few minutes to convince Eva and Jake to move over so there wasn't a gap where Fiona had been. The judge waited until they were sorted and then thanked the jury for their diligence in upholding the rules.

'I am aware that Fiona was a valuable member of your number; it is unfortunate that she needed to be discharged, but there was no other option available. It is imperative now that the rest of you act with integrity, and consider only the evidence tested in this court.'

Susannah was surprised the judge regarded Fiona so highly.

Jayz's lawyer started his cross-examination of Maia. Strangely, Susannah thought, his questions focused mainly on how Maia and Amy had waited outside the boys' school, and how they'd followed Jayz and Lee on social media. He asked Maia more about Amy's behaviour towards Jayz at Travis's drinks and the Blue Lake concert than he did about the allegation that Jayz had helped Maia up the stairs at the barbecue. And what Maia described seemed nothing more than typical girlhood crushes.

Susannah remembered her own versions of these crushes—the blond schoolboy who sauntered past her every afternoon while she waited for her lift home in the quiet green shade of a horse chestnut tree. The curly-haired first-five on the rugby team who gave serious, frowning pep talks in the drizzle on Saturday mornings. And, unimaginatively, the lead guitarist of the boys' school band. Even now, she could re-create a shadowy version of him flicking back his hair from his big doe eyes as he pulled up the neck of the guitar in a show-off riff. What came back to her then, with an almost frightening clarity, was the intensity of her desire at fifteen. She recalled walking home with her friend from one of his gigs and, when the blackness of the night obliterated her friend's features, saying, 'I'd do anything to be with him—I should've just climbed into his van.' It made Susannah think that if, back then, there had been some instantaneous way of contacting that boy, a way that, initially at least, did not require her to speak to him but through which she'd been able to offer herself up, she would have done it. She would have messaged or texted or sent a photo of some body part as a lure. It was no wonder these girls had got themselves into trouble; Susannah didn't blame them.

Her own crushes had sometimes turned into long-term obsessions, and the weirdest thing was that Mark Winters had been one of these. She'd spent countless hours thinking about him, talking about him, imagining him. Scheming to be where he was, she'd taken business courses at varsity, worked out where on campus he ate lunch, and cruised parties or pubs with friends. And now he was the foreman of this trial.

Susannah had supported Mark's election as foreman, convinced he'd be fair and clever, but she'd woken that first night thinking that she couldn't recall a single conversation that justified her faith in him. Instead, what came back was a memory, nearly twenty years old, of bumping into him on an Auckland street above Albert Park in the spring sunshine, maybe in third-year uni. He was with guys she didn't know—Islanders, they'd looked like—and she had just returned from travelling in Lombok, and was tanned and skinny. They hadn't hugged, even though she hadn't seen him all summer (so it couldn't have been spring). He'd come up very close to her, asking about her trip while his fingers jangled the silver bangles on her arm. She'd invited him to some drinks for a mutual friend and he'd promised to come, but hadn't shown up.

In court, since that first morning, Susannah had avoided being alone with Mark. At the end of the first day she'd stayed behind with Fiona, ostensibly to soothe Bethany, and each lunchtime since she'd hurried off, citing mysterious errands or appointments.

She wasn't sure she wanted to know the details of Mark's current life. She preferred to keep him in the past. And in her head.

IT WAS 1997, and it was her move. They were standing a foot apart, Susannah holding a glass of red wine at a provocative angle, centimetres from his chest. They were motionless. It was like one of those movies—eyes locked, neither smiling, and anyone could recognise the sexual tension between them. The guy who'd been patiently chatting her up for weeks at the pub was glancing around.

She'd only met Mark Winters that night. They were at a student party in an old villa, crowded into the kitchen, and, with a taunting smile, he'd made some smart-arse comment so she'd threatened to pour the wine down his light blue chambray shirt. She was drunk and had to concentrate to hold the glass steady.

'Go on,' he said.

She tipped the glass so the wine lapped at the rim. This was the moment. A romantic movie moment.

'What will you do?' she asked.

'Do it and you'll find out.'

He hadn't smiled, and Susannah had no idea what would happen if she poured the wine—would he grab her and kiss her like he was meant to, or slap her and tell her she was a silly bitch? She hesitated, made a joke, sipped the wine.

IN COURT, CHRIS'S lawyer was asking the questions now, and Maia confirmed that she was not alleging her drink had been spiked; that, yes, the boys, too, were drunk; and, yes, she had spoken to Chris in the kitchen.

'And you kissed him in the kitchen, didn't you?'

Maia looked confused, and then she said, 'No.'

'So you didn't kiss him until you were upstairs?'

The girl frowned. 'I didn't kiss him. I didn't do anything.'

'And upstairs you discussed having sex and he said you were too young, correct?'

'What? No.'

'And then you asked him to go down on you, didn't you?'

'I wouldn't, I didn't.'

Susannah remembered then that Maia was looking not at an image of the whole court, but at just the lawyer. At the start of the trial, the judge had explained that it was standard practice to use the AVL, the audiovisual link, to make the complainants more comfortable, but when Susannah had discussed it with Jon the night after Samara's testimony, they'd both agreed that it would make it easier for the girls to lie—being alone in that little room instead of facing the jury and the defendants like the other witnesses. It didn't seem fair to the boys.

• • •

ALONE IN THE sunroom that afternoon, looking across the lake at Tarawera, which was glowing a mauve-brown, Susannah sipped her rosé, listened to a tui outside in the japonica, and remembered Lucas's teacher, in about year four, ripping up his picture of purple mountains. 'I want real,' she'd said. When Lucas had told the story at dinner, Charlotte, who was only about six at the time, had said, 'When we're at Granny's I've seen Mount Tarawera go purple when the sun sets.' And she was right.

It was so peaceful. Jon was mountain-biking as usual on a Monday, but for once he'd deigned to pick up the kids from rock climbing and rep waterpolo practice on his way home. The cleaner had been through this morning, and, before she came home, Susannah had bought all the trappings to reassure Jon that everything was under control, because he hadn't wanted her to do jury service. She had a lasagne from Capers heating in the oven, had replaced the flowers on the hall table, and had thrown away the picked-at grapes from the weekend and refilled the fruit bowl. She could unwind—she wasn't used to concentrating all day. She couldn't see, though, how they were meant to reconcile the evidence.

In cross-examination Maia had said she'd agreed to go up the stairs with Jayz and Chris. She'd said that was the last thing she remembered and didn't know what had happened until the police had shown her the video, but surely if Maia's story was true and she'd been assaulted she wouldn't have gone to her friend's sixteenth the week after, even if her parents had wanted her to. And she'd claimed she'd stayed on the deck with Lee at the sixteenth because she was afraid of him, but also that she'd left because she was afraid. It just didn't add up.

Susannah wouldn't even have recognised Maia in the video if the girl hadn't confirmed it was her. She was pretty sure Maia had a navel piercing, which didn't seem consistent with her presentation as being all innocent and naive. Maia hadn't been asked by any of the lawyers if she was a virgin or what sexual experience she had, which Susannah thought would have been useful to know. Susannah knew what sixteen-year-olds were like, though; she followed her nieces, with their piercings and cleavage, on Instagram, and her friends had shown her school ball photos of their daughters wearing dresses that were extraordinarily low-cut and had slits up to their hips.

Once, after a ball in first year, a whole group of them had ended up at Mark's flat and he'd made some excuse to take off his shirt right there in the living room, his torso muscular and smooth. They'd stayed up all night, and the next day she remembered being in the back of a car with him and another guy, and she couldn't think, now, where they had been going. Susannah was between them, her body pressed against Mark's, his hand resting casually on her thigh, for hours. Nothing had come of it, though.

Susannah refilled her wine. If she thought about the nature of her relationship with Jon, it was largely defined by a simple accumulation of time. It was hard to identify any key moments of significance, although she supposed there was his elaborate proposal on the yacht in Auckland Harbour, and the surprise trip to Melbourne for her thirtieth. There was also the first time she'd understood the slow fuse of his temper, when he'd erupted in the car over a comment she'd made to another couple hours earlier. And afterwards he'd told her she couldn't ever leave him—he wouldn't be able to go on. That was what he'd said, and it had seemed uncharacteristically, and disappointingly, reliant.

And today, at least, his comment from last night seemed significant, even though he would think it innocuous. They'd been discussing the children. How Lucas biked and played rep waterpolo, waterskied and read books about inventions and evolution, whereas Charlotte was different. Because of Jon's rule about participating in sport, they'd tried her with tennis and netball, soccer, swimming, and now even rock climbing, without success. According to her teacher, she had some mild variant of dyslexia.

She wasn't into music or theatre either, or art. Charlotte just was—she watched TV, played on the computer and lay around snacking if she had the chance. Last night, Susannah had said to Jon that she wished they could find Charlotte's passion, her 'thing', and Jon had looked at her in a blank way and said, 'Maybe she doesn't have one—you don't.' Susannah told him that was offensive—she was a mum, had a business degree, biked, skied, waterskied, and she was creative, which had made Jon laugh out loud. Not a malicious laugh; he'd genuinely thought she was joking. But she *was* a creator—the interior of this house, the themed children's parties, even their sophisticated dinners.

But what she'd thought afterwards, when she was lying awake, was that perhaps Jon was right. Perhaps she no longer felt passion in her life. She thought back to the years of imagining and replaying scenes in her head like movies, her and Mark Winters, the schoolboy guitarist and all the others. She'd felt nothing like that for years.

Weirdly, though, in this last week as a juror, her imagination had been peopled by those girls—those girls talking, dancing, flirting with the boys. After Maia had described the first time Jayz flirted with Amy at Travis's drinks, before he'd even shaken her on their idiotic dice, Susannah had imagined it all in that semiconscious free flow of images when she woke in the night.

She visualised Maia and Amy in those short ruched dresses her nieces wore, dancing in Travis's living room. Amy dancing like Susannah's friend used to—eyes shut, hips swaying, arms raised, feeling the music. Once, when Susannah's friend was dancing like that, a guy had called her a cocktease, and Susannah remembered that she'd merely laughed half-heartedly in response.

Susannah imagined Jayz seeing Amy swaying, losing herself to the music, between the pushed-back vinyl couches and the TV. She saw Amy catching him looking, and Jayz raising his head fractionally in a nod, smirking—the kind of smirk that made your stomach contract. Then he pulled the girl he was dancing with closer, draping himself over her, while all the time he kept his eyes on Amy. And Amy, hesitantly, smiled back. Jayz slid his hand down the girl's back, over her skirt and back up her bare thigh, under her skirt now, and all the time he was watching Amy, who was blushing. Maia had said so.

The girl, wriggling, reached around to straighten her skirt, while Jayz laughed into the curve of her ear. He took her hand in his, his fingers pushing between hers, while his other hand ran back up her leg, so high this time that Amy could see her undies.

Susannah could imagine Amy seeing the girl's undies. It would make Amy feel weird.

Imagining it, Susannah felt weird.

And when the song finished, Amy would move away and make herself not look back at Jayz.

Later, according to Maia, when they were in the hall, the group of them came past—Lee, Sacha, Samara, Tia, Caleb, Kasey and Jayz. And Susannah realised then that the girl Jayz had danced with wasn't the girl her imagination had supplied, who looked African American, as if she'd stepped out of one of Lucas's hip-hop videos; the girl was Samara. The Samara whom Susannah had seen in court last week.

Susannah could imagine Jayz coming up close in the crush of people and taking Amy's phone out of her hand.

'Hey,' Amy said, mock angry.

Maia said he'd held up a single finger to Amy, so they'd both leaned in to see that he was adding himself as a contact.

Giving her back the phone, Jayz stepped closer, so Amy shifted against the wall. From the doorway, Caleb and Lee were calling to him. And Maia was disappointed that Lee was leaving, while Jayz had apparently stroked the side of Amy's face, lifted a strand of her hair and tucked it behind her ear. 'Double D, baby,' he'd whispered, and through her top he'd twanged the front of her bra. 'Send me a photo of what's under here.' In court, Maia had explained that it was a reference to the lyrics of a song.

Then Jayz had taken Amy's face in his big hands and kissed her.

Susannah imagined his tongue pushing hard into Amy's mouth. It was not pleasant, not how Amy had imagined that kiss, but her tummy would turn over as if it was. He was pulled away then by Samara, and as he went out the door, Maia said she heard him laughing, protesting, calling her 'babe', saying, 'It's all right, I'm coming with you, babe. Oh, we're coming, babe.'

Susannah supposed it was Amy's first real kiss.

SUSANNAH'S FIRST KISS was when she was fourteen, at a beach bonfire on a family holiday in Tahiti, with a seventeen-year-old French boy—there was both kudos and fear associated with his age and nationality. The weird oversizedness of his face close up, just before their lips met. The worry about how to tilt her head, and then the slight knock of her teeth against his. His tongue at first a shock, but soon she was tentatively responding, and then he'd drawn her away from the circle around the bonfire, the circle which included her older sister, over to the boulders underneath the coconut trees, and there, still kissing her, he'd fumbled undone the buttons of her pale cotton shirt with its tiny embroidered lavender flowers, and pushed his hand into her bra, her shiny-white lacy bra that was one of her three first bras, bought only a few months previously. Susannah could remember all this. She could remember her sense of panic wrestling with the imperative not to embarrass herself, or him. She hadn't liked his hand there, had not wanted it, but she certainly hadn't asked him to stop.

It had not been the first kiss that Susannah had longed for, and planned, and had always imagined happening *to* her. But nor had the first kisser in her head been seventeen and French.

THAT NIGHT, SUSANNAH woke, sweating, heart pounding, desperately shoving off the duvet. Would a boy really go down on a girl as Maia was claiming, unless she was a willing participant? Unless she was going to do stuff to him? Surely there must be more between her and Chris. More that had happened.

On her back, staring into the blackness and trying to slow her breathing, Susannah waited for the cool air of the bedroom to soothe her, but then she remembered she had forgotten to phone back the orthodontist, and she'd promised Jon she'd talk to Charlotte's teacher again. Fully awake now, Susannah reached for her phone; it was three twenty-three. She put in her earphones and flicked on her meditation app with the volume low enough not to disturb Jon. Before she had taken her three deep breaths she was worrying about whether she should tell Jon what Mark had said that afternoon about investment funds, which meant she might have done their tax wrong, and what if Lucas grew up to be like those boys with allegations against them. She and

Jon needed to talk to him about girls, and drinking, and girls drinking, and being so, so careful that nothing could ever be misconstrued. But how could Lucas protect himself? When she thought about the last incident Maia had described, which the prosecution said was Lee acting on his fourth shake of the dice, feeling Maia up at her friend's sixteenth, Susannah felt the police had simply gone too far. Lee and Maia had been sitting on a beanbag on the deck, they'd kissed and touched, and eventually he'd stroked her leg, and for that he was up on indecent assault charges, and the other boys too, as parties. For goodness' sake, that's what boys did—they tried it on. They always had done.

THE RUMPUS ROOM in the house she grew up in. Her first boyfriend, who'd asked her out when they were on a school tramping trip a few months after the Tahiti holiday. They were lying on the couch and he was kissing her, kissing her. She liked him. He was not the boy she'd written about in her diary for two years, but she liked him. He was only a year older and not much taller, but she did like him, although he didn't give her tummy butterflies when he touched her, which perhaps would have made the difference. Instead, when he undid the zip of her jeans and struggled his hand inside—inside, not outside her knickers—she didn't like it. Felt guilty, ashamed, and most of all scared. It was not what she wanted at all. But not once did she say out loud: 'Stop. Get your bloody hands out of my knickers.' She didn't once say: 'I don't like that. I'm not ready for that. Slow down, pal.' These were the phrases she must teach Charlotte for when she was older. At primary school, her children were taught to say, 'Stop it, I don't like it,' when other kids pushed, shoved, bullied—but never had she discussed those words in any sexual context. All she'd told the children was not to get in cars with strangers, and that, except for doctors, grown-ups weren't allowed to touch their bodies.

On the couch Susannah had tried to move away. Her boyfriend had whispered, 'No, stay,' and squeezed her wrist so she went quiet, letting him kiss her as she lay stiff and still. It wasn't just that she didn't know how to tell him to stop, she thought, it was as if she hadn't known she was allowed to. It was only weeks later, when a friend's older sister said, 'Ooh, careful, he's dirty,' that she felt she could legitimately break up with him.

ALL THIS WAS natural, though. Boys tried it on; girls worked out how to manage them. And these boys were no different. They weren't criminals.

The meditation app had finished. Susannah was meant to be asleep. Needed to sleep. She indulged herself then, allowing herself to think about Mark. Not the Mark who sat two along in court, but Mark in his twenties. The Mark who had whispered into the curves and folds of her ear, who had brushed her lips with his.

• • •

IN COURT, MAIA'S parents were testifying. They didn't add much. They hadn't known that Maia had gone to the barbecue. They said she had been withdrawn and spent a lot of time alone in her bedroom all that week, and that was why they'd arranged for Amy to take her to Emma's sixteenth.

The friend that Maia had stayed with the night of the barbecue testified too. She said that at the end of the barbecue she'd found Maia in the bedroom upstairs, under the covers, and she hadn't noticed her being in any state of undress. The girl and her boyfriend had helped Maia to the car and he'd driven them back to her house. Maia was definitely very drunk. It was hard to tell if she was upset. In the night, the friend had heard Maia get up and vomit; in the morning she'd left by the time the girl woke up. Maia had not mentioned the barbecue again.

Chris's lawyer, who Susannah thought was the most experienced, had tried to get mileage out of the conversation in the car, but the girl was vague, unsurprisingly. It was a year since it'd all happened—that was the thing they had to remember. Susannah couldn't understand why the police and the justice system moved so slowly. For these friends and parents, even for the boys, how could they remember a year later the details of nights they hadn't thought held any significance?

AS THEY LEFT the courtroom at lunchtime, Mark caught up with Susannah in the corridor, stopping her with his hand on her arm, so she turned back to face him.

'Come for lunch?'

Her eyebrows lifted, but she didn't answer.

'Susannah? Just across the road?'

'Okay.'

While they waited for their phones in the jury room, Jake said, 'Maia and Amy are only the year above my daughter.'

No one answered, so Susannah said, 'My kids are a bit younger.' And then she felt she hadn't valued what he'd said, and she liked Jake, so she added, 'Do you feel there but for the grace of God . . . ?'

Jake stared at her. 'Not at all. Annelyse doesn't drink and hasn't had a boyfriend.'

'Just wait,' said Les. 'One minute they're reading horse books and plaiting their friend's hair, and the next they're mixing with all sorts and don't even seem to be the same person.'

For a moment no one spoke. Susannah smiled at Mark. Jake started to talk about his son, but Susannah was distracted then, remembering a night she'd completely forgotten. She'd been at the university Commerce Ball in the old bank building, perhaps in third year. It was one of the nights when she and Mark had been flirting, when it'd seemed like this would be the night. They'd danced a slow dance, her hands straying across his back, and in her ear he'd told her how good it felt, then he'd suddenly excused himself. She assumed he'd gone to the toilet, so she bought them both a drink. When he didn't come back, she undertook a wobbly circuit of the room, until someone told her he'd left.

She went after him, ignoring how desperate it looked, pushing open the huge oak doors and slipping into the street. It was early morning by then and there was no traffic, no one around; the pavement was lit a dull amber from the streetlights. He was gone, and the city was silent. She tottered down the steps, unsure how she'd get home; she walked around the corner not even considering what the point was, and there he was, his back to her, facing a woman, their shoulders brushing the sandstone wall of the building. They were kissing, and in the orange light she saw that his hand was cupping the burgundy shot-silk of the woman's breast, and hers was on his back where Susannah's hand had been, but under his shirt, touching his skin.

Susannah had gone back inside, drank her drink and his, made small talk and even kissed Mark goodbye when he came inside with, apparently, his girlfriend.

In the jury room, while Mark waited at the door, Susannah asked Jake to join them for lunch, and she ignored both Bethany's eager glance and Mark's reproachful look.

SITTING IN THE back section of the Fat Dog cafe, Susannah stretched and yawned, pushing back her blonde hair. She wished now she'd worn it up—the drizzle this morning had made it frizz. They were idly talking about names.

'She was called Le-Leigh—L, E, dash, L, E, I, G, H—but it was pronounced Ledashleigh—you pronounced the dash,' said Jake.

'No way,' said Susannah, laughing.

Mark said, 'Well, even Mahi or Whare are bad enough. What you're saying is, "Come here, Work," or, "It's bedtime, House."'

When Jake didn't answer, Susannah said, 'There's a girl in Charlotte's class called Desire.'

'Sounds like a stripper,' said Mark.

Idly, Susannah watched two men in suits greeting a table of three others. They looked familiar and then she realised who they were; it was the lack of robes that had confused her.

'Look.' She nodded towards them. 'The lawyers.'

The prosecutor, who was standing, flanked by his assistant, was telling a story, complete with hand gestures. One of the defence lawyers was staring up at him, his mouth open, while the other two were cracking up. The assistant lawyer seemed to have heard it all before. The waitress came over with a paper bag and two takeaway coffees—they all seemed to know her.

'That's weird,' said Mark.

'Should they be talking like that?'

'Should we be here together?' It took both Susannah and Mark a moment to register what Jake meant.

'We can have lunch—we just can't discuss the evidence,' said Mark, his tone impatient.

The prosecutor was leaving now. Jake looked at his watch and said they should head back too. Susannah went off to the toilet, where the quotes from children's books that were written on the wall had been half-concealed by white panels. She thought about Fiona then—she'd have been disappointed not to see the trial through. Disappointed to have been thrust back into her lonely, empty retirement.

Back at the table, Mark was saying, 'I can't believe they got themselves into this mess.'

All the lawyers had left now. Jake didn't answer.

'The girls?' Susannah asked.

Jake picked up his phone and stood up.

'If they hadn't been so drunk . . .' she said.

Jake mumbled that teenagers did dumb stuff.

'I'm not sure I buy this whole prosecution story,' said Mark. 'They'd have us believe those boys planned everything; the more likely story is they're popular, good-looking boys, and the girls were into it, until they weren't.'

'We'd best go,' said Susannah, and then she added, 'The girls are young and inexperienced.'

'And they were definitely hammered,' said Mark.

As they were weaving their way out through the cafe tables, Mark said, 'We've all done things when we're drunk that perhaps we shouldn't have.' He was behind her, and Jake in front. Mark had said it quietly. To her. She wondered if it was some form of apology, but out on the street, while they were waiting between the parked cars to cross back over to the court building, he said, 'The thing is, there shouldn't be criminal charges for this. You know, the parents should deal with it.'

'It's not always easy for parents,' said Jake.

'That's no reason for it to be criminal, though.'

'No, agreed; I didn't mean that.'

And Jake and Mark jogged across the road between two cars and didn't even look back to see if she was following.

AT THE ENTRANCE to the courthouse, they met up with Scott, who asked how their lunch was, and Mark said he should have come too. Scott told them he'd had to pop in to work, so Jake asked what exactly he did, and it made Susannah realise that they'd all barely spoken to him.

'Mortgages and business loans mainly. I manage a team.'

As they climbed the stairs, Susannah mentioned that she had been finding it hard to sleep since she'd been selected.

Scott said, 'You're telling me.'

Mark said, 'Well, we're nearly done. Amy this afternoon.'

'Yep, we're getting to it now,' said Scott.

AMY IN THE little room watched the Amy on the right-hand side of the screen being interviewed by the police, a year earlier.

'Travis found Maia and me on the back deck, and he said Jayz wanted to talk to me, so I followed him. Jayz and Chris were sitting inside the trampoline. One of those ones with the net round it.'

As if she were talking to a child, the police interviewer asked, 'What happened next, Amy?'

'I was drunk, so I found it hard to get in.' Amy made a small noise, like a 'ha'. 'Travis tried to push my butt, and I told him not to, so Jayz helped me.'

'What happened then?'

'Jayz pulled me over next to him. He put his arm round me.'

'How did you feel about that?'

'I was pleased; I really liked him then.'

'What did Travis do?'

'He came in too, and then Chris zipped up the door in the net.'

'What did Chris do then?'

In court, the prosecutor was looking through his notes.

'He sat next to me on the other side.'

'So you were between Travis and Jayz?'

'No—Chris and Jayz.'

'So where was Travis?'

'Opposite us—we were sitting in one curve of the tramp and he was at the other end.'

The prosecutor paused the tape. 'Members of the jury, on page seventeen of the photo booklet there's a photo of the trampoline and a diagram of the garden layout in relation to the house.' He turned the tape back on and the interviewer asked, 'Amy, where were the other people who were at Emma's party?'

'Well, like I said, I left Maia on the back deck with Lee, because I thought she liked him and I didn't know what they'd done to her then, and the others were in the garage and out the front. There was a fire pit out there.'

'All right, so you were alone with the older boys on the trampoline. Did you mind that you were the only girl there?'

'No.' Amy's voice was almost a whisper then as she said she'd liked it, had felt special. 'I wanted to hang out with them. I thought they were cool. I was flattered because they said they'd crashed the party to see Maia and me. And I really liked Jayz.'

'So, what happened next?'

'Chris put his hand on my leg in a sort of jokey way and told me I was a good sort. He told me they all liked me because I wasn't uptight. He kept saying that, and stroking my leg. I didn't say anything 'cos I wanted to be with Jayz.'

'Can you keep telling us in your own words, Amy?'

'We were drinking, and . . . Chris had these pills—mollies. I'd never taken anything like that and I didn't want to, but they kept telling me I should.'

'Who told you?'

'All three. They were going on about it, and I felt like I'd look kinda dorky if I didn't. I asked what it was, and Chris told me it was something to make me chilled. They all took one with the vodka cruisers, so I did too. I didn't want to seem young.'

'And then?'

'Jayz kissed me. I . . .' The girl stopped talking and shook her head. It was hard to see her expression on the screen.

'Amy?'

'I feel bad.'

'Okay, Amy, just take your time.'

Susannah felt for the girl, but in an abstract way. Like if she were on a TV show.

'Amy, are you all right to go on?' the interviewer prompted.

The girl didn't answer.

'Amy, did you kiss Jayz back?'

'Yes.'

'What happened next?'

'Chris asked me if I liked it . . . I said yes. Then he asked Jayz if I was a good kisser and he said, "Not bad." Then Chris asked . . .' She paused, then in a rush said, 'Chris asked if he could see how good a kisser I was, and I didn't really get what he meant, so I looked at Jayz and he sort of nodded, so I let Chris kiss me.'

'Sorry, Amy, I just need to be clear—did you agree to Chris kissing you?'

'I sort of felt like I had to, but . . . yeah, I did.'

'And then?'

'Chris said I needed practice, and Jayz said he could sort that out, and then he kept kissing me and for a while it was all good. It was just me and him kissing and hugging. And I couldn't really believe it.'

'You couldn't believe . . . ?'

'I thought I was lucky.' Her voice was expressionless, like when Charlotte read books out loud.

'All right, and what were Chris and Travis doing at that time?'

'Um, they were both still there, talking and playing music, and Chris . . . yeah, I think he had his hand on my leg. I remember because it seemed weird.'

'So, did you . . . it seemed weird?'

'Well, yes, but I wanted to be with Jayz, and I was high, and it all kinda felt okay then—that was why it was weird.'

'And you remember this even though you were high?'

'I remember it all.'

'Even though you'd been drinking too?'

'I remember.'

'Did you feel like there was a risk then? Were you worried?'

'No . . . I never imagined . . .' Amy just stopped talking.

The interviewer sat with it, but Amy didn't say any more. Susannah shook her head.

'Can you tell me what happened next?'

'Chris gave me another drink and then he asked Jayz if I'd gotten better. And Jayz said definitely. I know this sounds really dumb, but I was pleased, so when Chris said he wanted to see if it was true, I . . . kissed him again.'

'And Travis?'

'No. Chris suggested it, because he said I'd got so good. But I said no, and they just made a joke about Travis being a loser. Then Chris told us all to lie down and look at the stars and we did.'

'So, at that point you were lying on your back, between Jayz and Chris?'

'Yes, and by then I was feeling weirder—sort of spacey and happy. But it was okay. Jayz and I were kissing and stuff.'

'Stuff?'

'I think he had a bit of a feel; it was okay.'

Susannah noticed that word—it was all 'okay'; none of it was good.

'Can you explain where he felt?'

'My breasts, my, like . . . body, my legs.'

'And then what happened?'

'Um, I was quite out of it. I remember feeling Chris against my back kind of, er, pushing against me.'

'So, you were lying on your side?'

'Yes, I was facing Jayz, and we were kissing.'

'And Chris was lying behind you?'

'Yes, and then this thing happened . . . So, Chris undid my bra and straight away Jayz had his hands there and that freaked me out.' She spoke quickly, her voice rising.

'You mean he touched your bare breasts?'

'Yes. But it was the way . . . I can't explain.'

'Can you—'

Amy interrupted. 'It was like they both were doing it together; like they'd planned it. I got scared then, but I didn't want them to think I was immature, so I just sort of pushed Chris away. I think I laughed.'

Susannah thought the planned bit was too convenient for the prosecutor's case—someone must have told her to say that.

'And did Chris move away?'

'For a bit.'

It all seemed unbelievable to Susannah. What had Amy been thinking, getting into the trampoline with three older guys? Or letting Jayz and Chris kiss her while Travis watched? Or taking drugs with them? It was so dumb, and so obviously going to go horribly wrong. She just couldn't believe Amy was so naive.

It became harder to hear Amy the longer the interview went on, even though the police lady asked her again and again to speak up. Then, in a burst, looking at the floor, she said, 'Chris was holding my arms. He told Jayz to take off my jeans.' She paused. 'Jayz, he . . . um, he . . . they . . .'

She paused again, then looked straight at the camera and without crying she said, 'He raped me. And then Chris did. And then when Travis was going to, someone called out . . . and they left me there.'

Her eyes, still looking directly at the camera, were unfocused now. 'Then Jayz came back and drove me home.'

Amy appeared to be calm.

'All right,' said the prosecutor, stopping the interview tape. 'Let's just pause there.'

# CHAPTER NINE
# Scott

'Let's just pause there,' said the prosecutor.

The girl in the room looked relieved, but then the lawyer looped back and asked her question after question. Did she object when Jayz took down her undies? She told him not to, and she tried to stop him, but Chris and Jayz held her arms. Did she struggle while Jayz raped her? She tried to, but Chris held her and Jayz was on top of her. And when Chris raped her? She couldn't. There was no point. Did she shout for help? There was no one around. It was a party, though—she and Maia had both testified there were over thirty people? The party was in the basement and garage, and the trampoline was on the little patch of lawn below the main deck on the other side of the house. The prosecutor referred them to the map again.

Scott looked over at the boys. Jayz was looking down. Lee and Chris were staring at the screen. Travis looked like he might blub.

Last night Scott had found a girl online who looked like Maia. She was Hispanic probably, not Māori, and a bit younger, but she had similar hair, rounded cheeks and large brown breasts. It would be easy to find a girl who looked like Amy with her blondish-brown straight hair. And a gang-bang one. Scott shifted in his seat. Bethany glanced at him with a vapid smile.

The prosecutor was still going. When she said they raped her, could she please describe the physical act that happened, in relation to Jayz first? He put his penis inside her vagina. Did she consent to that? No. What did Chris do? The same, and she wasn't consenting. What did Travis do? Nothing. Did he in any way penetrate her genitalia, with his penis or his fingers? No. She heard him moving around; she thought he was unzipping his trousers when someone called out. Who called out? She didn't know; she thought it was Lee. She wasn't sure. And just to clarify, did she have injuries from when Jayz and Chris held her down? They hurt her arm, but it hurt more when they raped her.

Scott leaned against big boob Bethany.

'Now we're talking,' he whispered, and the smell of her sweat made him harder.

## CHAPTER TEN

# Chantae

They began to cross-examine Amy on Wednesday morning. Chantae knew each defence lawyer would take a turn, and each would put the best spin on it they could for their boy.

'Did Lee ask you to go to the trampoline?' 'Was Lee on the trampoline at any time?' 'Did Travis kiss you?' 'Did Travis hold you down?' 'At any time did Travis touch your genitalia?' All these questions were designed to be answered in the negative to make the jury doubt her.

And then there were the other ones, the statements disguised as questions that started with 'I put it to you . . .' Chantae had noticed these throughout the trial. All the defendants' lawyers used them, but especially Chris's lawyer, and she dreaded his turn with Amy. She knew that the questions posed by Travis's and Lee's lawyers in the morning would be innocuous by comparison.

'I put it to you that you had barely any interaction with Lee throughout this whole time period, true?'

'That's not true. He gave Maia and me drinks at the barbecue and we talked then. And snapped.'

'Can I put it to you that you knew about the Dice Game and were flattered to be part of it?'

'I didn't know about it until after Emma's sixteenth.'

'I put it to you that is not true, because you received a "Diced" message from Jayz after you sent him the nude photos of yourself, correct?'

'I didn't understand it.'

'I put it to you that at the barbecue you invited the boys to Emma's sixteenth, didn't you?'

'I . . . Jayz asked what I was doing that weekend and I told him.'

'Can I put it to you that it was you who asked Travis where Jayz was when you were on the back deck at Emma's sixteenth?'

'That's not true. Travis told me Jayz wanted to talk to me. He took me down there.'

'I put it to you that it was too dark to see if Travis was undoing his trousers, wasn't it?'

'I'm not sure.'

'I put it to you that while you were engaged with Jayz and Chris in sexual foreplay, Travis left the trampoline, correct?'

'I heard him at the end. They spoke to him.'

AT LUNCHTIME WHEN Chantae had settled herself opposite Les and pulled over one of the folders of transcripts and turned back in her notes to the last page with highlighting, she said to Sandwich-man, 'I reckon when those lawyers say, "I put it to you," they just mean they're gonna make up their own story of what happened.'

'Well, you're not far off the mark, Chantae,' said Les. 'If their client is going to say something different happened to what the complainant alleges, they have to "put it" to her.'

'So we can already guess what Jayz and Chris are gonna say—that she wanted it?' Chantae knew her tone was scathing, so she wasn't surprised when Les reminded her that she had to keep an open mind until she'd heard all the evidence.

THERE HAD BEEN a week of lunchtimes like this, her and Les reading over the court transcripts while they ate. It seemed longer than that, because somehow time stretched during this trial, it stretched all the way between the edges of each day—from the moment she walked in through security until they left by the side gate, or even, some days, all the way until Mouse dropped her home after work and she crept into the house, snuck past Slo-mo, Mike's aunty, dead to the world on her mattress in the living room, kissed her sleeping sons in their bunks, and climbed, with aching feet and back and mind, into bed next to Mike.

The lunchtimes had started on the third day of the trial, when Chantae had waited until everyone had left the jury room except for Sandwich-man, who was sitting writing his notes.

'Excuse me?'

'Chantae, isn't it?'

She felt bad then, that he knew her name. She thought he was called Les, but since the first day she and Mike had called him Sandwich-man. The jury had been told they weren't allowed to discuss the trial with their families, so instead each evening Chantae told Mike about the other jurors—Kahu the swimmer; Flaky Jake; Jumpstart Hayley, who was so nervy; and Daycare Bethany, who'd blubbed. She told Mike that Grey Hair and

Susannah were like the ladies she cleaned for, all super-groomed, and ironed, and how protective they were of their handbags, especially if they were sitting near Kahu or Dave. And how Susannah wore a jacket even in the boiling-hot jury room, and her handbag matched her shoes, which had heels, so she clearly had a sitting-down job, and Chantae thought she'd call her Glitz. And there was Bankman Scott with his saggy face, and Mr Mana-Big Man, the Pākehā dude who'd pretended not to want to be foreman, but who'd been stoked to end up as it.

It was Sandwich-man they'd joked about on Messenger, because Chantae had told Mike about the fancy sandwiches the old fella brought in—the filling thicker than the bread, and how he ate them still wrapped up tight in baking paper, taking little bites and then pushing the paper down a fraction more. The first day, from what she could see, his filling had been lettuce, salami, cheese, egg and yellow pickled cauliflower. When Mike asked her on Tuesday, Chantae had made up the filling because she wasn't waiting round to see—*Mouldy vomit cheese and cold fish fingers in garlic bread.*

In the jury room on that first Wednesday, Sandwich-man had pushed a strand of something pale grey back into the sandwich with his index finger.

'What is that stuff?' she'd asked him. It smelled weird.

'Sauerkraut, white anchovies, baba ganoush and spinach. A multicultural mix. One of my favourites.'

Chantae laughed. 'That's even better than I thought,' she said, which made him smile.

'Want to try?'

'Nah, thanks. I'll go get something in a minute. It's fermented, isn't it—sauerkraut?'

'Very good for your intestinal flora.'

She liked that he didn't talk down to her.

She said, 'Can I ask you a question about Caleb's girlfriend?'

'Kasey? We can't talk about the testimony unless all the jurors are together.'

'It's not about what she said—it's more about the way she said it.'

He nodded, and carefully wrapped the white shiny paper back over the triangles of bread. 'Fire away.'

'Did you think . . . I mean, I felt like with Kasey, and sometimes with Samara too, like the lawyer keeps stopping them, eh? As if they knew what they're gonna say. I mean, isn't that cheating?'

'I understand what you're saying.' He rested his elbows on the table, his fingers interlinked, lips against them. Chantae liked his humility. He'd turned down being foreperson, but he just quietly got on with the mahi—like now, he was organising his notes.

'It's that thing about the truth, and nothing but the whole truth,' she said, slowly. 'I think Kasey said what happened, but she wasn't getting to say everything. Like about the other girls.'

'I suspect when they stop the witnesses, it's because of hearsay,' said Les. 'Gossip. So Kasey, for example, can only testify to what happened when she was there, not what someone else told her—that's the rules.'

Chantae nodded. 'I suppose we just have to use what we get.'

'And that's an assessment for the whole jury.' Les's tone was thoughtful—he wasn't telling her off. 'We'll need to decide if we believe the girls, and what the defendants believed too.'

'Well, it happened or it didn't—it shouldn't matter what they believe.'

'Unfortunately, it appears from the prosecutor's opening statement that it might not be as simple as that. But we'll have to wait for the judge to instruct us on the law—that's his role.'

Chantae shook her head. 'I don't think I should be here, eh.'

'They don't mind us staying in here.'

'No, I mean I don't think I'm qualified right to do this. Be a juror. Like, you understand it all and swot up—look at you.' She shrugged. 'I'm struggling.'

Sandwich-man smiled sympathetically, and she could see that was how the lines on his face had come into being. 'I think the fact you're struggling means you should be here. It's the willingness to engage. I'm not sure all the jury have that same dedication.'

They sat in silence then, until Les asked her if she had children.

'Boys. Five and eight.' He seemed genuinely interested, so she added, 'They're pretty full-on.' She meant they fought and laughed and fell over, and banged into each other, and made so much mess in every room, even just brushing their teeth—afterwards there'd be toothpaste smeared on the basin and the tap, towels knocked off the rail, toilet unflushed, race cars dodging droplets of pee on the floor. 'What about you?'

'A daughter, Kaye,' he said. 'She's grown up, of course. Lives in Wellington.'

'Only the one?'

He nodded, and just when she thought he'd lost interest in the conversation, he said, 'We tried for another, but it wasn't to be.'

'Oh.' She was surprised he was inclined to tell her something so personal.

'What does your husband do, Chantae? Oh, not that I'm assuming—'

She interrupted because he looked embarrassed. 'Mike's just started at WorkSafe.'

Les looked as if he was thinking hard, and then he said, 'And you must be busy with the boys. Do you work as well?'

''Course.' After a moment, she added, 'At MexTex. Just a dishwasher.'

'Oh, yes. I imagine that must be the busiest job in the whole place?' He was watching her.

She shrugged. 'Maybe.' There were times when Chef and Mouse were busiest, but most nights they'd be outside having a smoke while she was still at it—scraping, stacking, hosing, pulling out one steaming tray of crockery, pushing over the next. Unpacking hot plates, restacking them on the metal shelves, emptying the soaking silverware, or tackling the greasy oven trays with baked-on cheese and taco sauce. Imagining it, Chantae saw herself in one of those sped-up videos, where her constant movement became jerky and comical. 'There's some quiet bits,' she said.

He smiled. 'So jury service is a walk in the park for you.'

She looked at him carefully. 'It's hard concentrating all day. Haven't done that since school.'

He nodded. Chantae was pleased that he hadn't tried to fix the problem or make it her that was the problem.

'And there's a lot to take in, like what they're saying, but, you know, whether we can trust it too. And how it all matches up.'

'Yes. That's exactly what I'm trying to do now, see.' He showed her the page of his notepad. He wrote only on the right side of the page, and now he was making notes and drawing stars and arrows in the left column. Then he explained his colour-coded highlighting system for the transcript.

After a while he asked where she'd grown up, and she told him about moving from Rotorua to Whakatāne and back again. And that made her think about surfing at West End and the Heads, and how much she'd like to be there right now. She didn't explain that to Les, nor about all the shifting. After her mum passed on, Chantae and her dad lived with Koro. And then for a while she lived with Koro and her dad didn't. And then her dad moved in with Carol, who already had two little girls, so Chantae went to stay there too. Back then, Chantae had got on well with Carol, but when she was older, she realised her stepmum had used her as a babysitter, nappy-changer, dogsbody. At nine and ten Chantae spent her afternoons and weekends looking after her stepsisters, and she'd wanted to. If she imagined herself back then, all she saw was her eagerness to be appreciated, to be indispensable, and that's what'd happened. When her dad moved out, he left Chantae there, because Carol needed her.

Chantae had asked Les about his English accent that lunchtime and he'd talked about emigrating as a young man with his wife. And then he'd insisted she eat the other half of his sandwich, and it was good, once you got used to the different tastes. When Jumpstart came in, and Les explained they were sharing his lunch because he'd talked so much that Chantae hadn't had time to get any, Hayley brought out her 'keto' bar and cut it into three, and it'd felt like one of the good days at work when the owner wasn't in and they all sat together eating their staff meal while Mouse and Chef riffed off each other.

EVEN THOUGH IT was Amy who was being cross-examined today, the pages of transcript that Anaru had brought them this morning were Maia's evidence. The transcripts were always a few days behind, so at any time Chantae had two different parts of the trial in her head simultaneously. Chantae flicked through Maia's interview with the police officer. She'd given mostly short, shaky answers. Chantae remembered, though, how she'd started to cry when she got to the part about the barbecue. She'd only been describing who was there, but she had all these tears on her face and then her body started to shudder and her voice broke as if someone was fiddling with the car radio; it'd made Chantae catch her breath.

After the adjournment, Maia was different. She'd answered as quickly as she could, hadn't cried and her voice wasn't broken up, but it was like everything she said had been put through a colander and all the feeling had drained away so that all that was left was a collection of the things they'd done to her.

Pausing in her reading, Chantae looked up and saw from the high window behind her a shaft of sunlight and, within it, dust motes floating as if they could exist only within this beam of light, when really, she thought, they must be all around her in the room. Everywhere in the air.

If these boys had done this stuff, was it any different to what happened at drunken parties all the time? Chantae knew women to whom so much worse had happened in their own homes. And what about all the stuff that happened to children—the violence as well as the sexual abuse?

The prosecutor had started by asking about Maia's whānau and the church she went to. Chantae figured it was meant to make them think she was a good girl. Chantae knew that church. When they'd moved back from Whakatāne, Carol, her stepmum, had joined it and she'd made Chantae go too. Later, when Carol found out about Mike, she banned Chantae because our God didn't save hoes like her apparently—not that Carol had ever married Chantae's dad or the dude in Whakatāne. Shortly after that, Chantae moved in with Mike's whānau, but once she started working at Pak'nSave she'd put fifty bucks in Carol's handbag every time she went to visit, up until her stepsisters told her Carol used it as her church tithe.

Last year Carol had got married to a church dude in that old theatre church. Now, in the jury room, Chantae imagined herself back there. Her and Mike in the semi-darkness, sitting in the tiers of seats, looking up at Carol in her bouffy white dress, while the woman pastor told the congregation, who were more like an audience, how the couple had been celibate since joining the church, but all that would change tonight, and the guests, even the children, had laughed and clapped and cheered. And when Chantae could picture Carol and her groom onstage, like little figures on the top of a wedding cake, she tried to imagine the faces around her in the congregation, because this girl, Maia, with the moon-shaped face, would most likely have been there too, perhaps even wearing that same girly dress.

Chantae's eyes were resting on Les. His head was bent so far over she could see his scalp through his thinning hair—it was pink and grey, mottled. There was a small scab above his left ear. He looked up and pushed the folder across the table towards her with his right index finger on the page, and it took her a moment to realise he was pointing. She glanced at him, startled, and he nodded.

'No *talking* about the evidence when we're not all here. Understand?'

'Yes.'

He tapped the page again, and Chantae read Maia's words from the police interview describing what she remembered from the bedroom; Chantae had asked Les about it yesterday.

> 'It was like in a movie when someone's drowning, they're under the water, floating, and it's slow motion . . . it was like I was outside that floating body. I couldn't move my arms or legs . . . I couldn't hear what was happening. And then every so often I would burst through . . . back to being there, desperately trying to stay conscious, trying to tell him to leave me alone, but they'd just push me back down and I'd sink under the surface and the noises would be muffled . . . and I couldn't move.'

Chantae felt a catch in her throat as she read the words. She wrote the page number on her notepad.

The first days in court, Chantae had found it hard to sit still. For an hour or so it was like watching TV, but then she'd start to fidget and think about things she had to do at home or for the boys or what she needed from the Four Square. After she'd talked to Les a few times and listened to him explain how he was analysing the evidence, she saw that it wasn't like watching TV shows, not if you were doing it properly. They, the jurors, were part of it. They had to watch the witnesses as they spoke, to see their reactions and the way their voices, their confidence even, fluctuated. You had to be careful not to take everything at face value. As Les said, the prosecutor had to prove the stuff. It had to be strong enough to be beyond a doubt, and all the time the defence lawyers were trying to tear down what the prosecutor was building up—this castle in the air. Wasn't that what people said? All these scraps of words had to be built into something concrete and strong that would be left even after the defence lawyers had come in with their sharp pointy questions and tried to splinter it away.

Turning the pages to Maia's cross-examination, Chantae could see one now—a pointy question: *Maia, you went upstairs with Chris because you wanted to be somewhere more private, didn't you?*

She could imagine the shards flying.

*And when you were in the bedroom, giggling and kissing, you took off your panties, didn't you?*

Even reading the question in the transcript—and it didn't tell her which lawyer had asked it—Chantae could remember the look of shock on the girl's face at the accusation that she'd taken off her own undies.

But what if she had gone up the stairs to be with Chris? Had been flattered that he, a nineteen-year-old, was interested in her? Back at school Chantae had liked it that Mike was older. And Maia had been drunk. Perhaps it had all gone further than she'd expected, but she had gone into a bedroom with him; she must have thought something was going to happen.

Chantae pushed her folder towards Les and pointed with her finger to a question where the lawyer said Maia had lain on the bed, kissing Chris, and then pushed his head down between her legs, hadn't she?

Les pointed to the 'A' under that question; Maia's answer was *No.* And then he tapped below the next question, and the answer was no, and again and again, and the only time Maia hadn't said no, while the lawyer had been chip, chipping away, was when she'd been sobbing, and it said the court addressed the witness.

Chantae remembered the judge asking if she needed a break, and she'd shaken her head and said, 'It didn't happen like that.'

'Remember,' said Les, and his voice was reassuring, 'and I'll say it again when the others come back, it is the witnesses' answers that are the evidence, not the questions.'

She turned back a page and saw it now—the pattern. If she looked at Maia's answers it was like a force field around this castle the prosecution had built.

Les shifted awkwardly in his seat.

'You all right?' she asked.

'Yes, I twinged my back cleaning my daughter's room last night. She's coming to stay next week.'

'Can I get you something?'

'No, no.'

They fell back to reading, and Chantae, appreciating the silence in the room and the companionship, said, 'This is so different from my usual day.'

'I can believe that—a bit quieter?'

'It's not just the quietness. Or the sitting.'

'For me it's all the people,' said Les. 'At home there's mostly just Sylvie and me.'

Chantae nodded. 'Usually I have people round me most of the time, but not much time to talk. And no mind space. That's what it is for me—the thinking. It's like this dream I sometimes have, where I find our house has another room I didn't even know about.'

THAT AFTERNOON, CHANTAE noticed the similarities between the assertions Jayz's lawyer put to Amy and those that Chris's lawyer made.

'You helped Jayz and Chris undress you on the trampoline, didn't you?'

'No one was holding your wrists, Amy, were they?'

'I put it to you that you wanted to have sexual intercourse with Jayz, didn't you?'

Until the propositions culminated in a variation of the same theme:

'I put it to you that you had been drinking alcohol and taking drugs, and in that state you had a consensual sexual encounter with Jayz and Chris, and you woke the next day regretting your intoxicated actions, so you made up these allegations, didn't you?'

But it was Jayz's lawyer this time who was more detailed. He went right back to the beginning, asking Amy about her crush on Jayz, and how pleased she was when he kissed her at Travis's drinks, which was nothing to do with the game. He asked about her sending the nude photo to Jayz and her flirtatious behaviour on the trampoline. Chantae understood he was building a case that Amy had wanted to have sex with Jayz—but as if she'd want to have sex at a party with two other guys watching.

While Chantae listened to Amy's answers, she was struck by the degree to which the girl had thought everything was happening on her own terms, and how gradually she'd realised control had slipped away, until it was a wave crashing down on her, leaving her flailing in the whitewater.

Chantae had been a surfer in one incarnation of her life. Before being a juror. Before being a dishwasher, or a mum, or a supermarket shelf stocker. Before being the rebellious teenager who'd slept with her boyfriend, who ended up as her baby daddy and life love.

Before Carol had seen the light, but after Chantae's dad had moved on, Carol had shifted them in with a dude in Whakatāne who had no regular work, and she'd let the reins go loose on the girls, so Chantae had become a surfer. Not a surfie chick with cut-off denim shorts and ankle bracelets who sat on the pale grey sand waiting for boys with long hair and sun-darkened skin, but a stocky, athletic thirteen-year-old in a spring wetsuit on a crappy board lent to her by the old guy who did the rentals, in exchange for covering for him when he wanted to go for coffee, or a smoothie, or a joint.

Perhaps it was reading Maia's words earlier that had made Chantae think about surfing, about her wipe-outs—when she would be paddling for a wave and, looking back over her shoulder, would realise it was way too big for her to make the drop. And she'd hesitate, and in that second of indecision she'd lose any chance of engaging the inside rail and bottom-turning up along the face. Instead, she'd plummet into a nosedive. Arse over kite.

So what Chantae was listening for, as she followed this version of Amy's story, was the moment when, in realising the force of what she'd set in motion, the urgency of these boys' desire and her powerlessness to resist, Amy had faltered, and in doing so had allowed all control to pass to them. Chantae thought perhaps it was the moment when, according to Amy, Chris had said, 'You can't leave, we've only just got going,' and she had stayed. Or was it earlier, when she'd let them take off her bra, even though she thought it seemed planned?

IN THE LAST session of the day, it was still Jayz's lawyer homing in on Amy, and he was asking for more and more detail. Chantae felt her own cheeks blazing and she had to force herself to keep watching the girl on the screen.

'When Jayden was touching you, were you aroused?'

'Um . . .'

'Were you "into it", Amy?'

'To begin with.'

'And your vagina was lubricated?'

'Pardon?'

'You were wet?'

'Um, not sure. I didn't want his, um . . .'

'Sorry, but you will have to speak up, Amy.'

'I didn't want his penis in me.'

'All right, so you understand what an orgasm is, don't you, Amy?'

'Uh-huh.'

'Can you tell the court, please, did you have an orgasm that night on the trampoline?'

'Oh.' The girl looked almost as if the question were a physical blow. She literally moved back in the seat. Chantae couldn't believe the lawyer had asked that. Then Amy's answer was all over the place, and Chantae was completely thrown. 'I . . . don't . . . not then.'

The lawyer tried the question in different words a second time, but the judge suggested they move on.

Later, in re-examining Amy, the prosecutor came back to that point in an attempt to undo the damage.

'Amy, did you consent to intercourse on the trampoline with Jayz or with Chris?'

'No.'

'Amy, I'm sorry to ask this, but did you like having intercourse with Jayz or Chris?'

'No!'

'And, Amy, can you be really clear for us—when Jayz was having intercourse with you, did you experience sexual pleasure?'

'No.'

'And when Chris was having intercourse with you, did you experience sexual pleasure?'

'No—it was rape. I didn't want to do that. I didn't want them inside me. I didn't ever want Chris or Travis to even be there.'

'And, Amy, if it'd just been you and Jayz, would you have wanted to have intercourse with him?'

'Not like that. I've only had sex with one boy, and that was my boyfriend after months of being together.'

'And finally, in what ways did you show those boys you didn't want to have sex?'

Suddenly, Chantae felt Daycare pressing her elbow into her arm. 'See? He's doing it again,' Bethany whispered, nodding towards Chris's lawyer, who'd taken out his hearing aid. This was what Grey Hair and Glitz had been all excited about early in the trial, before Grey Hair was dismissed. They thought they'd invented electricity because they'd realised Chris's lawyer used his hearing aid to distract the jury. Chantae shook her head, irritated, because Daycare had just made her miss Amy's answer.

'And earlier, with Chris, you said you'd stopped struggling—why was that?'

'It was too late. I felt like . . . like I couldn't move. I can't explain . . . it was like they were doing it to my body and I wasn't there anymore.'

• • •

THAT NIGHT, CHANTAE was leaning over the sink in the MexTex kitchen, thinking how much her lower back hurt, and how she was hungry but sick of burritos, and she wondered what Sandwich-man had for dinner, and whether his wife cooked weird combinations too. She took her phone out and messaged the boys in case they were still playing on the tablet, because some nights Mike and Slo-mo got into something on Netflix and forgot to tell them it was bedtime. She replied to her two friends who had little kids, because this was the time they messaged her, once their bubbas were down. Then she checked her littlest stepsister's messages, but she was in one of her full-on moods so it was better not to reply, and anyway the boys had said goodnight and that they'd had fish and chips for tea, which irritated Chantae because Slo-mo had said she'd make tacos. Usually Chantae made dinner before work, something Slo-mo could heat up easily—maccy cheese, spag bol, boil-up or butter chicken—but now, with the trial, there wasn't time in the mornings.

Chantae noticed Chef watching her then, so she put away her phone and scraped the remnants of the refried beans and pulled-pork enchiladas off the last plates, and thought how a week ago she hadn't even known most of the trial words—defendant, complainant, counsel—even though she watched *CSI*. But the trial wasn't like those shows; sometimes she didn't even know why the lawyers were asking stuff.

Amy was just sixteen when it had all happened, and Jayz was eighteen. They were the same ages she and Mike were when they first got together, back when he used to drive her up to the top of the road and along to the car park by the stadium, where they'd climb into the back of the car and he'd make her come before he even entered her. Afterwards, in the summer, Mike would wind down all the car windows and they'd lie naked under his sleeping bag looking out at the dark hills and the stars, and one time a cop had come and told them to move on, and another time Mike had sung her that Beach Boys song, 'Wouldn't It Be Nice', and Chantae hadn't even known the song, but she'd thought it would be nice. And mainly it was. And for sure it would be, once Slo-mo left, and they'd saved enough for a house deposit.

For over a week Chantae had noticed the trial creeping into her head, even at breakfast with the boys, but she was surprised to find herself thinking about it at work. Usually, here, the doing took up all her mind space, and that was part of why she liked her job. Tonight, though, as she stacked the plates with one hand, hosing them off with the power spray in the other, she tried to imagine the evidence like one of the boys' jigsaws, so she could work out if there were bits missing. Then she thought, of course there were—how could they give you all the pieces? And you wouldn't want to hear them all anyway; there'd be loads of sky bits or sea bits, which were boring. It was the bits of, like, the racing cars or the diggers that you needed. You had to work out if they were giving you all those bits.

• • •

THE NEXT MORNING, Sandwich-man helped all the jurors fit the jigsaw together. Mr Mana had written a chart on the whiteboard the morning Grey Hair stuffed up, and he'd drawn arrows between the names—which boys had done stuff with which girls; it hadn't seemed very respectful. Chantae wasn't going to complain, but Sandwich-man had. In a quiet voice, he asked if they could 'erase the arrows'—that's how he'd put it—'until they heard it directly from the witnesses and complainants', and Brain-box Eva agreed, and Mr Mana, sighing away, had rubbed the arrows out.

Then Les had suggested they change the chart so they could see what'd happened for each round of the game, but he'd only got as far as round three before they were called back in. Since then the chart had remained unfinished on the board, but at morning tea that Thursday, he persuaded Mark that he should complete it. So Sandwich-man stood there with the whiteboard marker like a schoolteacher and said, 'Remember the big question in round three was what happened with Maia at the barbecue? Now, my understanding is that Chris is not denying the oral sex, but we'll hear that from him shortly—'

'Well, he can't, can he?' said Scott. 'It's there on film.'

'—so it's about whether she consented to that, and to Travis taking the video.'

'So what did Jayz and Lee have to do that round?' asked Flaky Jake.

Chantae flicked back through her notes. 'Jayz had to kiss Samara, and she said they kissed at the barbecue, and he sent her a "Diced" message afterwards.'

Les nodded and Chantae thought she was on top of this, but then none of them could remember what Lee had to do and with whom.

Les said they'd better move on, and that in round four the issue was what happened to Amy on the trampoline, but also in that round they mustn't forget this one, and he wrote, *Indecent assault Maia*, and said that was the allegation against Lee on the beanbag at Emma's sixteenth. Les was fitting it all together, but Chantae was glad when Anaru called them back into court—sometimes even Les treated it like a maths problem.

THURSDAY WAS TAKEN up with peripheral witnesses. Sacha, the fifth girl, testified after Amy. Her voice was thin and high-pitched, but she was believable. She said Lee kissed her at Travis's drinks and she'd felt bad because she knew Samara liked him, but that Samara was with Jayz that night. Sacha said she'd hoped she might get with Lee properly, but when she'd sent him a snap the next day, he'd replied, *You been diced*. They'd entered that message into evidence and made Sacha read it out. Chantae understood it was all proof that the game existed and that the boys did what they shook.

The prosecutor asked Sacha some questions about Travis at the Blue Lake concert, and she testified that he'd paddled around after her on a blow-up unicorn, but that nothing had happened. Chantae didn't understand the relevance until Les reminded them in the break that in round two Travis had shaken Sacha and digital penetration. Chantae was pretty sure that meant a finger up, but no way was she going to ask.

They also heard from Amy and Maia's friend Emma. Emma testified that, although she hadn't invited those boys to her sixteenth, she was flattered when they turned up. She said they hadn't really mixed, though. They heard briefly from Amy's parents, and the teacher in whose lesson Amy had collapsed into tears. A statement from a scientist was read that there was stuff from Jayz and Chris on Amy's clothes, but because she hadn't told anyone for several days, a doctor explained, there was no DNA evidence from inside Amy. The doctor said there were no internal injuries, but that wasn't uncommon with rape. Finally they heard from two police officers before the prosecutor said, 'That concludes the Crown case, so please Your Honour.'

IT WAS SANDWICH-MAN who suggested they go for a walk, because it was sunny and they'd finished earlier than expected, and Chantae agreed because she wasn't due at work for nearly two hours. Walking, not looking at each other, the conversation took a weirdly personal bent.

'It's easy, isn't it, for life to become reduced?' said Les. 'For me, because Sylvie's not well and I'm retired, I don't see many people. This has been a reminder.'

'To go out more?'

'That stimulation's important; new people and situations. Do you read, Chantae?'

'Read?'

'Fiction? Essays?'

She laughed. 'Not so much.' She occasionally read crime fiction or chick lit, stuff she could read in a few days, skipping over the boring bits.

'Oh.'

He sounded so disappointed that she tried to think of some consoling fact, a book she could offer up, but he'd already moved on.

'Being on the jury has been like travelling. It takes you out of your life enough to let you re-evaluate it.'

He walked faster than she'd expected. Chantae had to take a little skippy step every so often to keep up; it made her breathless.

'Do you travel much? To see your daughter?' she asked.

'Sylvie isn't up to it now. We used to. Not to see Kaye, but after she left home we travelled in Asia a lot—Vietnam, Cambodia, Indonesia.'

Chantae nodded; she had nothing to say about those countries.

'For you,' he asked slowly, 'does the trial make you think . . . I mean, you're smart, Chantae. How long will you stay being a dishwasher?'

She shrugged away a ripple of irritation. 'I'm not a chef and I'm not the right shape for waitressing, according to my boss, so a while I'd think.'

'What does that even mean, "the right shape"?' Les shook his head.

Chantae laughed. 'Anyway, pays no better. Boss likes me, knows I can handle myself. He hates I won't do Tuesdays, but I need some afternoons with the boys.'

'I know this sounds like an interview question, but where do you see yourself in the future?'

'In a house,' Chantae said immediately, even though she'd never been asked a question like that before.

'Pardon?'

'We want to own our own house.'

'Oh, I meant work.'

'Work's the way to get the house.'

He was nodding, but she knew he didn't get it.

They were walking along the lakefront, past the playground.

'That's why I clean houses on my days off. Why Mike retrained.'

'That's a good goal, Chantae.'

She looked at him; another ripple of irritation.

'Don't limit yourself, though. You have real potential.'

'Potential?'

'You're very attuned to what's going on in the courtroom.'

'Think I should be a lawyer, Les?'

'Well, that would take—' He broke off, because he'd noticed the expression on her face. 'You could.'

She laughed. 'No. I couldn't.'

After they'd walked a bit further, Les told her that what they actually deserved this afternoon, having made it through the whole prosecution case, was a wine, and then he changed it to a drink, because he probably realised she wouldn't drink wine, and she didn't. What Chantae really wanted was a Woody, but when he directed her along to Brew Bar and insisted it was his treat, she wasn't sure if that was the right thing, so she just asked for a beer. She sat outside waiting, thinking about the black cans in the fridge hidden from Slo-mo behind the apples and the bag of carrots.

It turned out this was a fancy beer place, and Les had ordered two sets of four different beers, each in a wooden rack.

'Holy shit, Les. We having a party?'

He told her he hadn't had a clue which craft beer to order, so the barman had suggested this. Les was child-like in his excitement, and that made her laugh.

'He saw you coming. Thought you were a tourist.'

She wondered how much the beers had cost, and then decided he could afford it and she should enjoy herself.

She sipped the lightest beer. 'It's funny how things happen. I'd never of thought we'd become friends.' Really, Chantae thought, if you'd lined up every member of that jury on the first day and she'd had to go along and pick, like at school for a team, she'd have picked Les last—he was old, had glasses and wore those jerseys that Mike called David Bain jerseys, only they looked different on him. Then she thought, nah, she'd have picked Mr Mana last.

'Did you think I'd stick to Fiona?' Les asked, and that led to a conversation about Grey Hair being sent home, and Chantae said she kind of wished she could leave too.

'No. We need to keep all the smart ones.'

Chantae didn't answer; she looked up at the pitched glass-and-wood roof of Eat Street, and at all the restaurants with their tables out, and the black fence opposite them with the plants growing out of it.

'You're coping, aren't you?' he said. 'I know the content's disturbing.'

'It's tiring, especially on workdays.'

'You're not working during the trial?' He seemed genuinely shocked.

'I don't work Mondays and Tuesdays.'

'Goodness,' said Les, and his frown was disapproving, and that made her irritation settle inside her—why would he think they could afford for her not to work?

'Maybe I should print something off of the internet so I can get kicked off too.'

Les was almost cross when he answered. He told her that if anyone else did anything wrong, it would be a mistrial, because they couldn't go below eleven jurors.

'Great, then we'd all get to go home.'

'And everything those girls have gone through would be for nothing. I'm not pre-judging, we have to hear the defence side, but the girls shouldn't have to go through that again.'

Mortified, Chantae said, 'You're right. I didn't think about that.'

He changed the subject and asked her which jurors she thought were paying the closest attention, and Chantae said, 'Well, not the Googlies, even though Mark should be.'

'The what?'

'The Googlies—you know, Mark and Susannah, who've got their little thing going.'

Sandwich-man laughed. 'I thought a googly was a leg spin bowled out the back of your hand.'

Chantae just smiled because she had no idea what he was talking about.

After a while she said, 'Bunch of turkeys,' and that made him laugh, which gave her the giggles—that, and the beer, and the improbability of it all.

'So, who else has got a nickname?'

'Most people,' she said, walking right into it. And then quickly, to cover, she reeled off a few—Glitz, who was also a Googly, Flaky Jake and Daycare. 'Mark's a Googly, but he's also, like, Mr Big Man.' Mr Mana, she called him at home.

Les seemed to find it hilarious. 'Go on, tell me the rest.'

'Well, it's not everyone. Um, Jumpstart, Ika, Rush . . .'

'Hayley—I heard you call her that before. Ika is fish, so Kahu. Who's Rush?'

'Dave—he always wants to be outta there.'

'Yes.' He laughed. 'Eva?'

'Brain-box, 'cos of her work, but 'cos she's smart too, eh?'

Les nodded and finally asked, 'So come on, what's mine?'

When she told him, he didn't smile, he said, 'Of course, yes,' as if it was something deep he had to think about, and then he said, 'All right. Challenge accepted. I'll bring you a different sandwich every day, but you have to promise to eat it no matter what I put in it.'

She laughed, but she also felt a welling up of tears that she had to blink away; she couldn't remember when someone had last offered to look after her. 'I wasn't asking . . .'

'Every last bite.'

LATER, AS CHANTAE stood up to leave, wondering how well she would cope at work with the beers on board, she said, 'I'll see you tomorrow, Sandwich-man?'

'Yes. Now we hear the other side. The defendants' version. Tomorrow Jayz testifies.'

Chantae thought about Jayz's lawyer and the way he'd questioned Amy, and even though it seemed exhausting to go through all the events again, she thought it would be good to hear that boy's account, prompted by the detailed questions from his lawyer and then the prosecutor, because that was only fair.

## CHAPTER ELEVEN
# Kahu

On Friday Kahu had a later morning training than usual because it was a competition weekend, so he went straight to court from the pool, picking up a pie and a smoothie on the way and eating them in the courtyard outside. Today the defence were to begin and Kahu was eager to hear the boys explain it all in their own words.

In the jury room, everyone seemed on edge; they were like swimmers when they arrived at a competition but before they'd warmed up, Kahu thought. The complacency that had built up in the past week, the sense that they knew the drill, was gone. So when Anaru came in and told them there would be a delay in starting, Kahu had to laugh. He should have known that would happen; trials sure weren't like in the movies.

While they were waiting, Les asked if Kahu could help him decipher some of the messages between Amy and Jayz that were reproduced in the transcript. When he agreed, Les asked the others to listen, because technically they were discussing evidence, even though there were no charges relating to it.

Les showed him the pages. 'The transcript just uses a Q or an A. Here, Q is the prosecutor, and it's Amy answering the questions.'

Kahu nodded; he remembered the prosecutor making Amy read out the exchange of Instagram DMs about the pics. Even on the AVL screen, Kahu had seen the booklet tremble in the girl's hands. Now Kahu read it silently sitting next to Les and then explained the abbreviations.

Q: Please read out the exchange, Amy.
A: Okay: *Amy: Hey wyd.*

'That's "What're you doing?"' Kahu explained.

Les wrote it down in the margin of the transcript.

*Jayz: nm waiting for u to send pics*
*Amy: lmao*
*Jayz: Nah fr I want photo of u*
Then there's a photo I sent of my head and shoulders.

'Okay,' said Kahu. 'So Jayz says, "Not much, waiting for you to send the pictures," and then Amy says, um, "Laughing my arse off"—sorry, matua. Then Jayz says, "Nah, for real, I want a photo of you."'

Les nodded and they read on.

Jayz liked the photo and then messaged, *But want one like I asked for*, and I just sent back question marks.

*Jayz: Show me something I can keep lookin at*
*Amy: My face*
*Jayz: Yea and?*
*Amy: sos I'm kinda shy, ngl*

Kahu said, 'So she says, "Sorry, I'm kinda shy, not going to lie."' Les looked confused, so Kahu added, 'It's just an expression.' Dave was grinning.

*Jayz: I won't show anyone. Promise. I like u*
*Amy: tbh I like u 2*

Kahu pointed at the page. 'That's "to be honest". Another expression.'

*Amy: What u gonna send me?*
Then Jayz sent a photo of himself with no top on. So I sent back some love hearts. Then he said, *Your go*, so I sent a photo of me in my bikini top and he sent back a thumbs-up and said, *Pretty gd. Makes me horny, ngl.* And I sent back a blush emoji.

Kahu could remember how humiliating it had seemed to make Amy read it all out loud when they could see it on the page. There were all these court rules that were unnecessary, that further harmed these girls' mana.

The prosecutor asked if she could read another exchange from a day later.

A: S'pose. *Jayz: Can't stop looking at that photo.* And I sent a happy face emoji.

*Jayz: Can't stop thinking about whats under ur bikini. Show me. Plz. Want to go to sleep thinking about u*
*Amy: I'm scared ngl*
*Jayz: Don't be. Trust me*
*Amy: I do like u. Really really*
*Amy: That sounded dumb*
*Jayz: Nah. Pic plz.*
*Jayz: I won't show. I swear*
*Amy: 4yeo will snap but I'm not showing my face*
*Jayz: Sweet as*

'What does this mean, Kahu?' asked Les, pointing.

'"For your eyes only", matua.' Kahu stretched his legs. His quads were sore from last night's dryland, and he wanted to be able to loosen up, but he needed to stay focused, his parents had stressed that enough.

Les pointed back to the transcript.

Q: Amy, can you clarify when you said not sending your face?
A: I sent a nude from my neck to the top of my jeans.
Q: Now, Amy, if you can turn to page twelve. The photo there, and we have blocked out your breasts, is that the one you sent Jayz on Snapchat?
A: Yes.
Q: All right, can you keep going?
A: So now we're on Snapchat. *Jayz: Fuckkk that's hot.*
*Amy: Jayz, why tf you ss??*
*Jayz: Chill you're alg it's just for me until I get real thing.*
And I didn't reply.

Q: Thanks, Amy. So, ladies and gentlemen, that photo was posted by Jayz to the Dice Bros Snapchat group—and it was sent with the message that you can see there, saying, *Round 2 √ bring on round 3.*

Kahu remembered that by then Amy had been sitting in the little room with her head bowed and her hair curtaining her face.

'Now,' said Les, '*tf you ss*?'

Kahu coughed. Everyone was listening but no one else answered. 'Um, she says, "Why the f-word you screenshot?" Sorry, matua.'

Les nodded. 'Thank you. Kahu, why didn't she just text the photo?'

'They weren't texting,' said Kahu. 'They were messaging on Instagram. But Amy said she thought if she sent it on Snapchat it would disappear.'

'Why?'

Kahu started to answer, but Susannah jumped in. 'My son's got Snapchat. We checked it out. The photos go once you open them, and you're notified if someone screenshots it.'

Then Les asked about screenshots and Facebook and Instagram and group chats and who could see what, until Mark interrupted, 'So, this sexting . . . ? I mean, Kahu, just so we get a sense, how common is that among your . . . cohort?'

And they all looked at him.

IN COURT, JAYZ'S lawyer stood up and said his client elected not to call evidence. There was a wave of noise from the people in the public gallery. In front of him, Kahu saw Mark turn to Les. The judge called for silence and then Chris's lawyer stood up and he, too, said his client elected not to call evidence. Kahu thought it meant they wouldn't be calling other witnesses, but then he realised that couldn't be right or they would have heard from Jayz before Chris's lawyer stood up.

Kahu muttered to Dave, 'So Jayz and Chris aren't gonna defend themselves?'

'Know they're better to keep their mouths shut,' said Dave.

Kahu felt cheated—how could they judge properly without hearing from the boys? It meant the only time they'd heard any of them speak was in the brief police interviews with Jayz that the prosecutor had shown. A police officer had told them that Chris, Lee and Travis, as was their right, had not answered any of the police questions, and then he'd played two short video interviews with Jayz.

In the first, Jayz said he'd heard of the Dice Game, but it had nothing to do with him. He'd sounded scared, but defensive too. He'd agreed that he'd kissed and touched Amy on the trampoline, but said that she'd liked it and had been touching him too. When asked if they had intercourse he said, 'No, there were other people there.' He claimed not to remember who—people came and went—but he said he'd lent Amy his hoodie and that he drove her home. He claimed he'd thought they had a 'thing'.

In the second interview, he had a lawyer and was wearing a shirt with a collar rather than the T-shirt he'd had on in the first interview. This time he admitted playing the Dice Game but said everything that happened was 'consensual by both parties'. Kahu didn't think that sounded like Jayz's own words. In that interview he agreed he'd had sex with Amy, but said he couldn't remember if anyone else was there or what happened afterwards.

Watching the videos, Kahu had thought he was glad swimming meant he didn't go to many parties.

'So what now?' Kahu whispered to Dave in court.

Dave shrugged. 'I knew they'd do this. Let's see if Travis or Lee have the balls to talk.'

It was Travis's lawyer's turn, but the judge sent the jury out for an early morning tea. They'd only been in court for a matter of minutes.

At first, the jurors were frustrated, then they tried to guess what was going on, but pretty soon they drifted—people made hot drinks, and conversations started. Kahu jiggled his leg—all this sitting around—and then he heard Mark say to Jake and Susannah, 'We'd planned to go to Raglan, but we cancelled. Bit of a shame—I love it there, it's my tūrangawaewae.'

Kahu looked straight at Mark then. He noticed that Eva was listening too; he liked the way Eva was noho ngū—she was friendly, but she spoke only when she had something to say, she didn't push herself on the others.

Jake asked if Mark was from Raglan.

'No.' Mark's eyes shifted from Jake to Kahu and back again. 'I meant that other sense of the word. You know, it's special to me . . .'

'Where are you from, Kahu?' Jake suddenly asked.

'No konei.'

'Your whānau? Where do you whakapapa . . . you know?'

Kahu supposed Jake was trying to be friendly. 'Around here,' he repeated. There was a silence; everyone was listening. Kahu sat with it.

Then Jake said, 'I went to Mokoia Intermediate and Lakes High.'

Kahu nodded—they were schools with lots of kids from Ngāti Pikiao and Ngāti Whakaue.

'What're you up to this weekend, Ika?' asked Chantae, and Kahu was grateful for the distraction.

'Swimming up and down the black line?' said Susannah with a laugh.

'Nah. Big competition.'

'Here?'

He shook his head. 'Hamilton.'

'Why's it a big one?' asked Mark.

'Lots of people, but big for me because I'm trying to qualify for . . . a team.'

'Yeah? What team's that then?' asked Mark.

'New Zealand team to the Junior Pan Pacs.' And because they exclaimed, he added, 'It's in Hawaii.'

They were all listening now, although it was still Mark asking the questions. The words suggested he was interested, but his tone didn't.

'And you stand a chance?'

'I'm point four off the hundred.'

'The hundred?'

'Fly.'

Silence.

'Butterfly—that's my thing. I'm best at sprints—the fifty, but the hundred too. I swim the two hundred sometimes, but it's too far.' He gave a self-deprecating laugh. No one spoke—they must have thought he was boasting—but then Mark started again and this time his tone was genuine.

'Slow down. So, when you say the fifty—we're talking metres, right? And, when you say you're point four off?'

'I'm four-tenths of a second off the hundred-metre butterfly qualifying time.'

Susannah said it all sounded like double-dutch. Chantae said, 'Isn't that close enough?' and Bethany said, 'You're quick,' even though he hadn't told her his time.

Eva said, 'That's nothing. It's like—bah,' and she lunged her hands forwards.

'They won't take me, though, unless I have the time. Even if I miss by one one-hundredth.'

'How quick are you?' asked Mark.

'My best time's fifty-six seconds ninety-three; I need to go under a fifty-six fifty-four. I'd be all good if there was a fifty-metre race, but there isn't one.'

'Because?'

'Fifty fly's not an Olympic event.'

Mark nodded. 'Sounds pretty friggin' fast to me.'

Chantae said, 'That's less than a second, eh?' at the same time as Dave said, 'You'll get it, mate.'

Kahu shrugged. 'Hopefully. But I did that time at Opens—the top New Zealand competition. It *was* a while ago and I've been lifting, but on the other hand I've been here at the trial missing some training sessions. I'm on a taper, but I just dunno.' He shrugged again, and then smiled briefly at Chantae.

'Well, there's always next year,' said Susannah, taking her cup to the sink.

'No, whaea, there's not.' He'd liked talking about it, but now he wished they'd get called back in. He jiggled his leg again. His coach had told him they'd go over his splits tonight and make sure his underwater work was sharp enough.

It was Les who asked in his calm manner, 'Why isn't there next year, Kahu?'

'I'm too old, matua. This is my last chance for an age group team. I'm nineteen soon.'

'Nineteen,' said Susannah, from the sink, and it sounded like she was taking the piss.

'Well, good luck,' said Mark, and there was a chorus of agreement, and even though his coach stressed to them that it was not luck but their actions that were responsible for their outcomes, Kahu felt grateful.

Eva asked him how he'd started swimming competitively, and because the others were talking among themselves now, Kahu told her about the golden ticket he'd won at interschool and how he'd thought it meant he'd get chocolate.

When he was in year eight his kura had arranged for a guy from the swimming club to help the top swimmers get ready for the interschool competition. Kahu could swim freestyle and backstroke, but the Pākehā dude had changed the way Kahu lay in the water so he was long and flat and at the surface, and then the guy had hopped in and shown them all four strokes while they stood on the side and shivered and hollered and shoved each other, until they were allowed to finish with a manu bombing competition. The next day Kahu asked the guy to teach him butterfly, and the guy gave him fins and got him going, and the more excited he got, the harder Kahu tried.

When Kahu won the novice butterfly, and came third in the competitive freestyle, the dude gave him the golden ticket for the swimming club. They offered him a place in their junior competitive squad straight off and taught him breaststroke, but Kahu was a flyer.

From the beginning, Kahu stayed in after training to practise his dives and tumble turns, to challenge himself at lung busters, and to lie on the bottom blowing bubble rings, but all the squad were better than him, and they were mostly Pākehā, and none went to his kura or knew his friends, so Kahu said he wanted to stop. His parents told him then what became their stock story whenever he or his brother didn't want to be pushed out of their comfort zone—how neither of them had had the opportunity to grow up speaking te reo Māori. How his mum was the first of her whānau to go to university, and how stink she'd felt to begin with, both in lectures, where there were so few brown faces, and at the Māori law study sessions on the marae, because she didn't know tikanga or te reo. They told Kahu he wouldn't even be at his kura now if it weren't for his mum persevering and finding her place, and they said he had to swim through to the end of the year, because he had the ability, and should see if he could find his tūranga within the swimming club.

That kōrero made a difference, and so had the Pākehā dude's encouragement, but the crucial push was when Kahu overheard the dad of the best flyer in the squad talking to another parent. He said Kahu had started swimming too late: 'Ten thousand hours and all that. It's a shame; they just don't get the opportunities. He does well now because he's bigger, but he won't stick at it. They never do.' It took Kahu over a year to beat that man's son, but once he beat him, that was it—he never let that kid win again.

And Kahu had carved out a place for himself. In the hours of training, from diving in off ice-encrusted blocks on midwinter mornings when it was dark for the first hour, through to long summer evenings, and the regular competitions—crammed into vans, cabins or motel units, and poolside—he'd become one of the swim team. Now, he'd won national medals, competed in Australia, was a junior coach, taught water safety in te reo Māori, and was comfortable mixing with teachers, parents and officials.

STILL THEY WEREN'T called back in.

Out of the blue, Susannah asked Kahu if he knew Jayz; she'd barely spoken to him directly until now.

'What d'you mean?'

Chantae let out an exaggerated guffaw.

'I was just wondering,' said Susannah, raising her thin eyebrows, but her cheeks went pink.

Before Kahu could answer, Chantae cut him off. 'She wants to know if he's one of your cuzzie-bros.'

'Cuzzie-bros,' said Kahu slowly, keeping his eyes on Chantae.

Quickly Mark said, 'She meant because you're the same age.'

'And Rotorua's a small place,' agreed Jake. 'My son's the same year . . .'

'He'd have had to declare it if he did,' said Chantae, and now her voice had an edge to it, bright and sharp, daring them to continue.

'No,' said Kahu, turning to Susannah. 'I don't know any of the defendants. They weren't at my school.'

'Which school was that?' asked Jake.

Kahu told them and they nodded, but didn't know what to say. It was Sandwich-man again who broke the silence. 'That's the kura with the exchange to Guatemala, isn't it?'

Kahu smiled. 'Yes, matua. I went last year, to Antigua.'

'What's this? What did you do?' It was as if Mark had walked in halfway through the conversation.

'I went to Guatemala for two months. We learn Spanish right through school, and then we go and stay with a Guatemalan family and study at a language institute.'

There were murmurs and exclamations.

It was Mark who asked, 'How do *you guys* pay for that?'

Chantae muttered, 'With money,' at the same time as Kahu said, 'We fundraise for years—that's a big part of it.'

Mark laughed then. 'God, I know all about that. My daughters dance—they're forever bringing home sausage rolls and chocolate bars. Don't ya hate that? They sell two bars to the neighbours then we end up buying the rest. Drives Maggie nuts.'

Kahu's kura picked up litter after events at the stadium, ran a stall at the night market and washed cars. While the others talked on about sausage sizzles and chocolate sales, Eva asked Kahu about Guatemala, and he answered willingly. It became the longest conversation he'd had with any of them. He was telling her about their trip to Tikal—the ruined Mayan city with its grey stone temples rising out of the jungle, the carved stelae and the sacrificial altars with the grooves for the human blood to run away—when they were called back in.

TRAVIS WAS ASKED to stand in the dock and the registrar said, 'Travis, you are charged with making an intimate visual recording in the form of a video of Maia. How do you plead?'

And Travis said, 'Guilty.'

Kahu felt adrenalin course through him. He looked at Dave. The trial seemed to have suddenly clicked into a sharper focus.

The judge said, 'Members of the jury, I must caution you that just because Travis has pleaded guilty to this charge, it does not indicate that he is guilty of any other charge.'

Dave whispered, ''Course it doesn't,' and Kahu wasn't sure if he was being sarcastic.

Then Travis went to the witness stand and was sworn in, his face bright red and pimply, and the lawyer started to ask him questions.

Kahu sat forwards, muscles tensed. Often in court he'd found it hard to fight the heaviness of his eyelids, but now he stared at Travis, who, since Maia had testified, had spent most of the time with his head down. He was here in the courtroom, not in that other room like the girls, and it was better having him here. Kahu looked across at the other boys. On the first day, Jayz had made eye contact with Kahu, and Kahu had looked away, embarrassed. From then on, both Jayz and Chris would periodically stare at Kahu, and after a few days Kahu had occasionally raised his head just a fraction in return. Lee never caught his eye; he was so up himself he looked straight through the jury. Now, though, all three boys had their eyes fixed on Travis, and Travis was pointedly looking only at his lawyer, and Kahu realised the others were scared of what he was going to say.

'He's gonna nark,' Kahu whispered to Dave.

Travis's lawyer asked questions to emphasise that Travis was the year below the others and had known Lee all his life.

'Can you describe the nature of your relationship with Lee?'

'We're mates.'

Dave breathed into Kahu's ear, 'Not any-fuckin'-more.'

'Would you say it's an equal friendship, Travis?'

'Um, we're good friends, but Lee's, like, the leader, the one who decides what we're doing. He's a good laugh, and clever.'

'Does he ever get you into trouble?'

'Sometimes.'

'Does he party much?'

'Sometimes.'

'And does he have many girlfriends?'

'Not girlfriends as such, but he gets with girls. Lots.'

'Travis, why did you decide to host the drinks for your eighteenth birthday?'

'Lee told me to. He knew my mum was going to my cousin's wedding, and she's never away, so he said we should.'

'Did you want to?'

'Nah, not really. My birthday was a couple of weeks later anyways.'

'All right. Now, Travis, did you help make up the Dice Game?'

'No, it was Lee's idea, but Chris kinda made it badder.'

'In what way?'

'He made it worse stuff. He'd heard about the game from some boys at rowing and he wanted in. He made it so if you didn't do what you shook, they shaved off part of your eyebrow.'

'And they did that to you?'

'Few times.' He tried a short laugh, but it just sounded as if he was hurt.

'And you let them?'

'No choice.'

'What do you mean?'

'Well, you had to . . .' The boy shrugged. He glanced at the dock, but then he dropped his head again and muttered, 'You can't not let them, that's the deal.'

For as long as he could remember, Kahu had known not to tell tales. He'd heard that from his whānau, his teachers, the older boys at the marae, his swimming coach. At school you don't be a tattle, telltale, a rat. At swimming you don't police whether other athletes are doing the set right—you just keep yourself honest. With friends, you don't dob people in and you don't nark.

Kahu remembered clearly the first time that word, 'nark', came into his consciousness. He and his brother, Īhaka, were walking to Whaea Sandy's, who looked after them some days after school while his mum finished work. They were sharing a dollar bag of Jet Planes—the gummy lollies huge and cumbersome in their mouths. At the pylon they stopped as usual to gaze up, dribbling a little as they bickered about how they'd climb it, and how awesome the view would be. Further on, there was a pair of sneakers hanging over the powerline, a kōwhai tree dripping flowers as bright as their yellow jet planes, and on the corner two little kids were scraping handfuls of mud from the bottom of a puddle in a rutted driveway and painting the wheel of a parked car with it. Kahu and Īhaka had cracked up at that. At the next intersection they saw the pale blue weatherboard house. Both boys stopped, because it had been vandalised since they'd last been here, and it took Kahu a moment to decipher the word that was spray-painted in black on the front wall, and in smaller letters on the side. NARK, it said in spiky capitals. The curtains were shut, but they could hear the TV. Swallowing the purple globule in his mouth, Kahu had grabbed his brother's sleeve, pulling him to a run, until they were sprinting down the road away from the house, away from the Nark.

ONCE TRAVIS GOT going, he testified differently from the other witnesses—he spoke fast and the lawyer interrupted far less, because Travis just spilled it all out. He kept his eyes averted from the other boys, but when he looked at the jury, he seemed eager, and periodically, Kahu thought, he tried specifically to catch Kahu's eye. Kahu dropped his gaze to his notepad.

Travis said, 'When Chris wanted to make the numbers tougher, it was me that suggested going down on the girl. I thought that would never happen unless she was really into a guy, so someone else would crap out as well as me.'

'So Chris ramped it up?'

'Yeah. He'd left school and, like, he always took things further—like, we'd buy beers and he'd bring vodka, or he'd get us to crash some party with older guys we didn't know. It was him who suggested the game was too tame. I just kinda knew it was the end of my eyebrows.'

Dave and Scott laughed when he said that, and Travis looked around gratefully, drinking it in, but then Kahu saw him glance at the other boys and none of them were laughing, and Kahu thought he'd forgotten, for a moment, what he was doing.

Kahu remembered then sitting cross-legged, aged nine or ten, listening to an important kaumātua; the formalities were over and now he was telling them what he was there to say—a girl had been killed, a toddler, and it was time to draw a line in the sand. He told them they all had a responsibility, and he turned slowly so Kahu felt the power of his stare. When he was older, Kahu thought, he would hold an audience captivated like this, and he listened to the rhythms of the man's voice, his pauses and his throat-clearing. Kahu wanted to do what the kaumātua told them but then the man said, 'We've got to learn to nark.'

Travis said, 'Before the barbecue, when Chris shook Maia and the oral sex one and I shook her and the pics one, I said to Chris that it looked like we were going to be shouting the beers and losing our eyebrows, and Chris said, "No fuckin' way, mate—us bros just need to get her pissed." And Jayz and Lee were like, "Yeah, bro."'

'Travis, how did you feel about the game generally?'

'Uncomfortable. Out of my depth. But I didn't think I'd ever get lucky anyway, and I never thought they were gonna force anyone.'

'Can you tell us what happened at the barbecue?'

'I wasn't really with the others much and then Jayz told me to come upstairs and to put my phone on video. I didn't know what they were doing, but I guess I wanted to be one of the boys—I didn't want them to think I was gay or something. So I kinda went along with it.'

'What did you think they were doing upstairs, Travis?'

'I didn't even know they had Maia, and I for sure didn't know how drunk she was until I heard her testify. Honest. Jayz told me to start recording and kinda burst the door open. She was lying on the bed; I couldn't see her face. Chris was already doing it, and Maia didn't tell me not to video, and I was drunk, so I just kinda went along . . . I'm sorry . . . sorry.' He broke down, but the lawyer kept going.

'Did you offer Maia any drinks that night?'

It took Travis a while to answer through his tears. 'No.'

'Did you offer her any drugs?'

'No.'

'Did you ask her to go upstairs?'

'I didn't know she was up there.' He was pleading now.

'Did you take any of Maia's clothes off?'

'I didn't touch her.' He sounded horrified.

'Did you speak, while you were videoing?'

'No.'

'And can you please tell the jury in your own words what was happening in the bedroom?'

He caught his breath. 'Um, Chris was having oral sex with Maia. At the time, I thought they were together, like she was into it, and Jayz had set me up to video because that's what I'd shaken, but now I know I was wrong.'

'What did Chris say to you?'

'Um, I didn't hear.'

'Did he say something about "turn"?'

'Oh, he said, "Turn it on."'

'So, Travis, did you help or encourage Chris in that sexual act in any way, whether or not it was consensual?'

'No, I didn't.'

BACK IN THE jury room while they waited for Anaru to bring their phones, Les asked Kahu how common oral sex was among people his age. Kahu muttered, 'I dunno, matua.' He could feel the heat of embarrassment rising up from his chest.

'We can't expect Kahu to represent all teenagers,' said Eva.

'Obviously you don't need to answer anything, Kahu,' said Mark. 'But we are here as members of the community to bring our life experience. That's the point, Eva. Remember, the judge said that.'

'I still don't think it's fair—' said Eva.

'Kahu can talk for himself,' said Chantae.

Kahu shrugged; he was used to being called on at the kura and the swimming club and at youth leadership events, but this was worse. This was mortifying, and he felt implicated by their questions. 'I can't say what other people do,' he told them.

Instead of his confidence growing over the course of the trial, Kahu felt as if his frustration with the process and with some of the other jurors was festering to the point where he felt the shadows falling on him. In part, it was the evidence, the hours on top of training, the sitting still, the lack of peers, the distraught girls and the responsibility for deciding the future of boys his own age, but it was also these incessant questions.

'Of course,' said Les. 'Can I just ask, though, would girls this age who were not sexually active wax their pubic hair? Because Scott mentioned that he thought Maia's . . .'

Kahu didn't have to answer; Chantae, Eva and Susannah were all up in arms.

IN COURT, THE prosecutor said, 'Travis, are you asking the jury to believe that you thought Maia was conscious and consenting to Chris having oral sex with her?'

'I wasn't there at the beginning.'

'But you thought she was consenting, even though you and Jayz were watching, cheering and videoing?'

'I s'pose.'

'When you went in there with your phone on record, did Maia look at you, or acknowledge you in any way?'

'No.'

'And did you find that odd?'

'Um, to be honest I was, er, shocked. I didn't know what to do. I'd never seen . . .' Travis shrugged.

'But you went in, with your phone on video, you pointed it at Maia's genitalia, and you kept recording even after Chris had spoken, so you weren't all that shocked, were you?'

Travis didn't answer.

'Were you?'

'I'm . . . I don't . . .'

'Travis?'

The words erupted out of him. 'I was in automatic. I didn't know what to do. I just did what Chris and Jayz told me. Honestly, if I'd known she was coma'd, I wouldn't have . . . I thought she was drunk, but not that drunk. That's why I've pleaded guilty to the videoing now.' He looked at the judge. 'I'm sorry.'

'Travis, on the video Chris says, "Your turn, Travis." So I put it to you that you were a fully participating member of this sexual violation, and you were going to do it too.'

'No!' The boy's voice became panicked. 'I didn't know what was happening. I didn't do anything. I didn't touch her.'

'But you did know what was going to happen, didn't you, Travis? Because you'd all thrown the dice and discussed how to achieve the challenge by getting her drunk?'

'We hadn't. We'd agreed what we were trying to do, but we hadn't ever agreed anything was gonna be forced . . . It was all meant to be if the girls wanted it, eh.'

The prosecutor slowed his voice. 'So, Travis, are you telling the jury that you thought Maia, who told us herself she's a virgin, would want a boy three years older than her to have oral sex with her, while she was so drunk that she was, for all intents and purposes, unconscious, in front of two other boys, one of whom was videoing it?'

Kahu blew his breath out.

• • •

KAHU WOKE ON Sunday nauseous and desperate to leave. He felt only marginally better after the team manager forced him to eat some toast. He'd screwed up his life yesterday; it was as simple as that. The hundred-metre butterfly, his only realistic shot at the New Zealand team, had been a disaster. He'd scraped into the final, and then placed fifth, adding four seconds to his best time. His stroke rate had been way off and he'd felt like he was in one of the dreams he used to have before kapa haka competitions in year ten, when he knew he'd missed too many practices because of swimming. In the dreams his movements were wooden and his timing was out, while the others, in perfect synchronisation, made their hands wiri, chanted and stamped, and he'd still been trying to catch up when they'd finished their pūkana.

Today was the two-hundred-metre fly—the race he always struggled with. This year he hadn't gone to university or taken a proper job, so he could maintain his training load. Through school, he'd half-arsed his commitments to be at swimming. He'd barely partied with his mates because he was an athlete. He'd broken it off with Pania because she'd been so down on him prioritising weekend competitions. And because he'd stayed in Rotorua to keep swimming, he'd ended up on the trial. Tomorrow, the other jurors would ask him what had happened; he should never have mentioned it. Now he'd have to admit failure, and then go back into that courtroom and listen to the final arguments, and this week they would have to decide if the boys were guilty. And his mum had told him that while he had to listen to the other jurors, *he* had to speak up too, and *he* had to believe the decision was right.

He wanted a way out of this. All of it.

He'd felt trapped like this once before. Auckland Airport gate lounge. A year ago. Sitting with his mates and his brother on their way to Guatemala. Everyone talking fast and loud, even Īhaka, who was more than a year younger than him, but Kahu had suddenly wanted to jump up and go back the wrong way down the moving walkway, back past the passport people and the security guards with their doorways, and out into that public part of the airport where all the whānau had gathered to see them off. He wanted to go into the dark Auckland night and get on the bus back to Rotorua, back to his house and his school and his swimming club, and just be himself, not the confident, lucky, Spanish-speaking Māori world traveller they wanted him to be.

His brother hadn't understood what it would be like—that there'd be times travelling when they had to face things alone, like when the soldiers had taken them off the bus from Guatemala City to Tikal, and had singled out Kahu and Matua Tai, and made them put their hands up against the side of the bus, and a young soldier had searched Kahu, aggressively patting down his body, while his gun, strapped across his back, pointed at the ground. Kahu had been alone then, even though Matua was just metres from him.

Just like he'd been alone the night four of them snuck out late to drink cerveza in the plaza, and they'd been stopped by three Guatemalans and one had a gun, and the men asked for their money. Īhaka had panicked and run, skittering the wrong way down the avenida, while Kahu, horrified, had been shouting to the men, 'I've got the money. Hermano, he's my brother. I've got his money.' And when he and the other boys had handed over their cash, the men had asked contemptuously, 'Americano?'

They'd replied hopefully, 'No, Nueva Zelanda,' but the men had simply shrugged and walked away.

And Kahu was alone now, on the pool deck with his team, before the two-hundred butterfly—his last chance to qualify. His last chance to make the swimming mean something. In his head he could hear his dad's 'Step up, son,' even though he knew his dad thought it was time to choose between university or the building apprenticeship. And he could hear his coach's 'Push on,' so he nodded at the race plan, even though, after yesterday, neither of them believed it.

In marshalling, Kahu put on his headphones and played his pre-race song with the volume turned up as high as he could bear. But behind the blocks, as soon as he turned off the music, he felt the thoughts rushing back. As he undid his tracksuit, he heard his coach yesterday saying he'd let him down, let himself down, and his teammates—that he had the ability, the training to do this; all he had to do was focus. Instead, as Kahu stood stretching his arms to their full wingspan, his mind spun away and he remembered the time some of his mates' mates had knocked over a dog and how they blabbed to their parents but it had all worked out. He remembered his own desperation the night in Antigua, when they got back to the hostel after the mugging, and Īhaka wasn't there, and the oldest boy, who'd been hit in the ribs by the men, told them if they ratted he'd kick their heads in. Kahu had tried to argue that they had to get help to find Īhaka; he was Kahu's responsibility—his parents had put that on him. He'd tried to reason with the others and he'd been going to wake Matua, he had been, when Īhaka slumped in through the door, sobbing and shaking, making Kahu cry too, and then none of them had ever mentioned it again. And

Kahu thought of Travis spilling out what they'd done to that girl, and he remembered the black spiky letters on the house, and the kaumātua telling them to learn to nark, and the wildness of Travis's expression as he'd pleaded with the jury at the end of the cross-examination—'I didn't know what to do . . . I was scared of what was going to happen with Amy. That's why I left. I wasn't there when they did stuff to her, honest.'

The whistle blew. Kahu climbed onto the block, corrected his stance, tensed, and as he dived he was beyond caring, beyond reasoning, beyond considering pacing or the length of the race—he just went for it, pushing almost as hard as in the hundred, pushing because he wanted to stop thinking. He wanted the physical to take over. He was eighteen, only eighteen, he didn't want to take this on—whether those boys should go to jail. Whether those girls had been violated. Whether he'd wasted all those hours of his life swimming. And he kicked harder, feeling his abs strain as he worked his legs both down and up, and he thought, he would fight. Like the hammerhead.

He was out near the front at the hundred, and as he turned in a tight streamline, three body kicks off the wall, needing oxygen, he, Kahu the person, was obliterated. There was nothing but the physical. He broke the surface stroking twice, still not letting himself breathe, and then the desperate suck of air, the undulation of his body through the clear water—at that moment he didn't even process the stillness of the pool in front of him. The absolute burn in his lungs took over every thought, even the pain in his arms, in his core, his quads, his shins, his ankles. But he was still breathing one in two. The intensity of his pull, deep and narrow, punctuated by the moments of recovery, wide and shallow, over and over, and the burst of sound as he raised his head to breathe, and each time he could hear the booming call of his coach, 'Go, go, go,' recognisable above the other noise.

Turning for the last fifty, he managed two body kicks and a pull before, gasping, he raised his head again. There was now a repressed excitement in his coach's tone, and Kahu felt as if the energy was a stream flowing through his body, and he wasn't letting his hips drop as usually happened in the last twenty-five, he was still planing, and he could hear his team shouting, which made him put his head down before the flags and stroke straight into the wall, crashing two-handed against the timing pad, gulping air, chest heaving, realising he'd won. His team were yelling, 'Way to go, Kahu! Shot, Kahu!' and he looked up at the scoreboard as he heard the announcer say that the age group title was his, and: 'Unofficially, that time will earn Kahurangi a place on the New Zealand team to the Junior Pan Pacs in Hawaii.'

## CHAPTER TWELVE
# Mark

'Amy said, "Don't," but then she was laughing, so the boys carried on,' said Travis.

'You claim you left the trampoline then—can you explain why?' asked the prosecutor.

The boy shook his head.

'Something made you leave, Travis?'

'Um, I kinda liked Amy . . . I suppose I was gutted she was with them and not me.'

'And when you say she was "with" them, was Amy dressed when you left?'

'I . . . I couldn't really see.'

'Emma testified that there were lights on the deck, so you could see, couldn't you?'

Mark thought it was interesting watching the prosecutor in this cross-examination role. There was a toughness he hadn't expected, but it was not the ruthlessness of Chris's lawyer.

Travis said, 'I was down the other end of the tramp, playing music, and I was out of it. I didn't know what was going on.'

'So you didn't know what was going on, yet you chose to leave?'

'Yes.'

'And did you phone Caleb that night?'

'Er, I'm not sure.'

'Caleb testified that you phoned him because you were upset; were you upset?'

'I was drunk and high.'

'Caleb testified that you said Jayz and Chris "didn't stop"—did you say that?'

'I don't remember.'

Mark sighed. They were making no progress and there was so much repetition; it was no wonder the justice system cost taxpayers so much. He wasn't sure this process of examination, cross-examination and re-examination was right. He understood the aim was to test the truth, but wouldn't a judge by himself get through the trial in half the time?

Mark hadn't taken many notes during the trial. They had the transcripts and Les knew them back to front, even though the folders were already thick. Now, as it was a Friday afternoon, Mark hadn't added anything to his page since the session started, when he'd written a reminder to contact Brayden, his 2IC, over the weekend. Looking at it, he suspected that his uneasy feeling about Brayden had been provoked by an article—'Seven Signs Someone is About to Resign'—that he'd flicked through on his Facebook feed last night.

Brayden was the head of tech at Mark's IT company; Mark was clients, marketing, accounts and staff management. Brayden had been with him since the beginning—they were a good team, and consequently they had Bay-wide contracts. But since the first Thursday of the trial he'd had a sense of disquiet. The judge had a funeral that day and Mark went into work midmorning, imagining he'd freewheel, touch base with his employees, see what arose. This kind of approach was one reason the business was so successful—Mark had read articles about the work ethos at Google and Apple.

He'd mostly left Brayden to it during the trial, because his brain was mashed after hours of listening, and unpicking and reordering the evidence, but he was excited to see him that day. Mark was the only one with an actual office, but Brayden had a corner, ring-fenced by a desk and a printer on a side table, so Mark sat on the couch by the wall and asked Brayden questions. It was like drawing blood. Brayden had been short with him and, now Mark thought about it in court, almost disrespectful.

'Baby keeping you awake?' Mark had asked finally, and was so disconcerted by Brayden's expression that he was afraid something dreadful had happened. 'He's all right?'

'Fine.'

Mark let out a reflex laugh.

'Anyways . . .' Brayden said, turning back to his screen.

Without thinking, Mark stood up, but then, not prepared to be summarily dismissed, he hovered by Brayden's desk, lifting a family photo, before turning a pile of papers to face himself. Brayden frowned. With the beard he was currently sporting, Mark found it hard to take him seriously. Mark flicked through the papers. The top ones were invoices, then there was a printed sheet advertising an IT company he'd never heard of, with a clever logo. Mark glanced down the bullet points of services provided.

Brayden stood up, leaned over the desk, and took the flyer off him. 'I was checking out what else we could offer.' He stared at Mark.

It felt like Brayden was accusing him of something. 'Great. Any inspiration?' Mark tried not to slip into a mocking tone.

'Not sure. Let me do it in my own time, all right?'

Mark shrugged, and then Brayden had said apologetically, 'Look, I'll talk to you as soon as the trial's over. Okay?'

'Fine, Brayden, whatever.' And Mark had been annoyed with himself that he'd sounded like his nine-year-old daughter, but the whole incident ticked at least two of the points on the list of pre-quitting behaviours in the article.

While the prosecutor finished questioning Travis, Mark jotted down what he remembered of the list:

*1. Negative change in attitude.*

*2. Shows dissatisfaction with boss.*

*3. Leaves earlier.*

Brayden never left work early, Mark had to give him that. Although, in the last few months he hadn't been going in on the weekends, so he was behind the eight ball at the Monday morning meetings, when not long ago he'd been the one suggesting the plays.

*4. Won't commit to long-term plans.*

A few weeks ago, Brayden had turned down Mark's invitation to join him on an expenses-paid trip to an IT conference in Auckland, because he 'was a parent now'. Mark had laughed. 'It's three days, mate!'

And another thing—Mark had developed a client form early on, with a space for notes about potential future work for the client with optimal timelines. Recently, though, he'd noticed there was often little written in this box, and Brayden was one of the worst offenders. Mark was suspicious of anything that undermined his systems. The business had grown quickly, and even when there'd been new start-ups in town, they hadn't dented his market share. Mark wasn't stupid—he knew his business did well because he had good technicians, but it was also because of his innovative, client-focused systems.

In court, the prosecutor was flicking through his notes as if he couldn't remember what to ask.

*5. Not a team player.*

Nah, Brayden got on well with the team, especially Rachel and Max. Sometimes, when Mark heard them banging on about software development or data security issues, he barely had a clue what they were talking about. The march of technology had proven too much for him, but that was what Brayden was for.

At the end of the day, it was a shame if Brayden was going to quit (he probably wanted to shift closer to his family now they'd had the baby), but it was life. The best thing would be to promote Rachel or Max—they knew his systems and the firm culture. Then Mark thought, with excitement now, perhaps he could restructure and save some money—did he even need a 2IC? He scribbled some options on the notepad. Ironically, the person he wanted to discuss them with was Brayden.

• • •

WHEN MAGGIE DROPPED the girls off on Saturday morning she finally asked how the trial was going—it'd taken her two weeks.

'It's tough—very complex, and I'm the foreman, so . . .'

''Course you are.'

'What's that supposed to mean?'

'Nothing. Listen, Ruby's been feeling sick . . .'

'The others chose me.'

'Did they?'

'I didn't volunteer.'

'I think she's okay . . .'

'It was because I was wearing a suit.'

'A suit?' She laughed. 'Why were you?'

Mark grinned. 'My lawyer said it would make the lawyers challenge me.'

And then they both said, 'Didn't work,' at the same time, and he didn't mention that his lawyer had actually said, 'You'll either be challenged, or you'll end up as foreman.'

IT WAS THE lack of noise and motion that struck Mark the most after Maggie and the girls moved out. When he got home from work, or woke in the mornings, there was a quiet stillness. He understood he was meant to feel this as a loss, but instead it felt like space. An openness. Since they'd had the girls, Mark had felt like he was trudging up a craggy mountain range. Sure, sometimes he'd drop down into ravines or valleys, but he'd always have to climb again to find a way forward. After Maggie and the girls left, Mark had truly felt he'd come out into the rolling countryside of the Waikato—pleasant undulations, but no slog.

Even the crazy weekends with the girls, three a month, weren't a trudge. He'd decided early on that he would be a yes-dad. He let the girls get out more and more toys—Lego and playhouses, dress-ups, cuddly toys and dolls—so they became princesses riding hobbyhorse ponies between fairy castles and toy towns, or pop stars performing for a cuddly-toy audience at a train station. They would build sheet forts with mattresses and Christmas lights for the three of them to sleep in, and when they got bored with the muddle of toys, he'd drive them to the playground or crazy golf and then to Lady Janes for ice cream, the girls still dressed in tutus, boob tubes, high heels or gumboots.

Mark could remember his surprise during those first sole-parent weekends at how elongated the days seemed. Back when they were all together, he was constantly fighting the slip of time on weekends. It would be four o'clock on Saturday and he'd only have mown the front lawn or read one work document because of the continual interruptions. Sometimes back then he'd tell Maggie he had to go to work, just to take a breather. Now, he was stoked on a Sunday to find it was only eleven and they still had five more hours. Now he never tried to do anything else when the girls were there. He didn't even make them clear up. He did it all on a Sunday night (despite Maggie's protestations that the girls should help), because picking up the toys, folding the dress-ups back into the suitcase and the sheets back into the laundry cupboard was a process of adjustment. It allowed him to become Mark the adult again. Mark the boss. Mark the Tinder-catch.

He knew his parenting was playing into all the clichés, and at first Maggie was furious when he returned the girls exhausted and whiny, but recently they seemed to have settled into an unspoken truce. He hoped she was glad of the break, but feared she was just too preoccupied with her new man. He chose not to establish which was true.

Mark had never meant to hurt Maggie, and he wasn't entirely sure how he had hurt her. Sometimes he thought it was all a miscommunication, and sometimes he thought that she exaggerated stuff, and sometimes, when he was having a drink with his mates, he thought she was a mad bitch. But he'd rather take her drama over that of any of the women he'd met on the internet. And there had been some drama. About four months ago, Maggie had announced that the new man wanted her and the girls to move to Napier. Mark had flatly refused, telling her he'd tie her and her money up in the Family Court for years. He said he'd go for joint custody, knowing she wouldn't cope with only three days a week with the girls, and she'd rolled, just like that, and never mentioned it again. Sure, he'd played hardball—but he couldn't lose his kids.

• • •

ON MONDAY MORNING, it was Lee's turn to testify, and Mark was pleased that finally they would get a real insight into the boys' version of events, because Chris and Jayz had offered nothing, and Travis's testimony had been utterly self-serving.

Lee was wearing his usual suit, but today his hair was carefully styled, and he wore an expression meant to convey that this was all a dreadful mistake. His lawyer was the woman, and she started off asking introductory questions in a stern voice to make them trust her impartiality. Probably that was why the boy's family had hired a female.

Then, suddenly, she cut to it. 'Did you make up the Dice Game, Lee?'

'As a group we came up with it.'

'Where did you get the dice idea from?'

'A TV show. My rowing partner Jayden and I were comparing hook-ups as a joke, and I thought of using the dice to make it a competition.'

Mark wasn't sure how Lee's approach would go down with some of the women jurors or with Les, but Mark thought good on him; he wasn't sugar-coating it.

'So had you read'—she looked down at her notes, as if checking the title—'the *Dice Man* book?'

'No-o-o?' Lee drew the word out so it sounded as if he wasn't sure what she was talking about. Mark wondered if they'd practised all this.

'But apparently your father had a copy?'

'Yes. Apparently.'

'My learned friend, the prosecutor, believes that book to be your inspiration?'

'Absolutely not.'

'All right, so the prosecution got that part wrong.'

She hesitated, waiting for them to make the inference that this was only one part of what was wrong with the prosecution's version. Mark got all this, but wondered if he might need to explain it to some of the others.

'So, Lee, what exactly was *your* idea?'

'It was all to do with Samara . . .' The boy grimaced. 'I know it's, um . . . kinda tacky—disrespectful, I mean—but, yeah, Jayz—Jayden—and I made a competition to see who could hook up with her, and I thought of using the dice to decide what we had to do. *Try* to do. And, well, one day when we were hanging out with Caleb and Travis, Caleb said we should choose six girls and shake for them and for what we were *trying* to do.'

Mark had to admire the way he'd chosen to drop Caleb in it. Caleb couldn't deny it; he wasn't here to hear it and he'd already testified.

'Did you imagine then that you would play the game for over a month?'

'God, no. No way. But actually, can I say, when Chris came on board he was more dodgy about it. I mean, us boys, we've known each other since we were little kids, like at primary school, but, you know, Chris is older—he was always more edgy, like Travis said.'

Holy shit, Lee was going for it. So that was the call; they were all going to pass the buck. Mark supposed it was inevitable that the lawyers would identify a fall guy, but he wasn't sure about the strategy—if one went down, wouldn't they all?

'How do you feel now, Lee, about playing the game?'

'I dunno, it got outta control. Like, not from me, but—'

She interrupted him sharply; clearly he'd gone off script. 'Lee, only answer about yourself.'

'Sorry. I mean, I felt bad, it wasn't respectful, but *I* didn't do anything . . . illegal.'

'So just to clarify, did you *ever* do *anything* with a girl that was not consensual?'

'Absolutely not. I wouldn't.'

He was a good performer. It was not that Mark didn't believe him, but he could see that Lee was, essentially, performing—but, then, so were the lawyers and the judge. Mark was about to add the girls to the list, but that didn't feel quite right.

'Did you intend that the Dice Game would *ever* involve anything *non*-consensual?'

''Course not. Never. I mean, no way. As I say, I'm ashamed I thought it up, and it wasn't respectful, I get that. But it was just a jokey competition. Notches on the belt or whatever. The whole point was you had to get consent . . . show how popular you were. If anyone was forced, that would have been against the whole, er, rules of the game.'

'Thank you, Lee. So, in the first round you shook . . .?'

'Sacha. I shook a one; I had to kiss her, and she's testified, hasn't she, that she wanted to? And she's young, so I'd never have done anything more anyways, whatever I shook. And, you know, Caleb and Kasey got together because of the game—it gave Caleb the push, like.'

'The impetus?'

'Exactly. And that's all I ever intended.'

'So, Lee, what would you have done if Sacha hadn't been interested?'

'I knew she was, but I'd have walked away. I mean, what else? God, you don't think I'd . . .' He broke off. The lawyer started to ask another question, but the boy interrupted. 'I do okay with girls, you know. If she wasn't keen, I'd have found someone else or not bothered—doesn't worry me.' He was almost angry, and it did seem genuine.

'The prosecution might argue that the Dice Game made you boys keep pushing when a girl didn't want to go as far as you did. What would you say about that?'

'I'm not a rapist. Look at me. I get girls. I slept with Samara, and hooked up with Tia, so when Maia—'

'Actually, Lee, can we slow down.' She wanted to keep control of him. 'We need the jury to be clear.'

'Sure, sorry, I just want them to understand.'

The lawyer confirmed with Lee that in round two he and Samara had had consensual sex.

'Now, a photo of Amy's breasts was shared on your Snapchat group by Jayden. Is that right?'

'Yes. And Jayden did get Amy to agree—no one forced her to send the pic. No one was there when she sent it.'

'Did Jayden discuss sharing the photo?'

'No. Jayz showed me and said something like, "Mission accomplished." He had to tell me it was Amy because her face wasn't on it.' He was talking fast; it was compelling. 'And I didn't do anything when he shared it, and I'm sorry to Amy, but, you know . . .' He shrugged. 'My bad. I'm not the police.'

'All right, so the first charge against you is being a party to Chris indecently assaulting Samara by feeling her up in the lake . . .'

'Look, I wasn't even there.' His voice was filled with upset outrage. 'I heard about it, but I was hanging out up by the cars. I can't, like, supervise Chris.'

'Did you encourage him to feel up Samara?'

'No way. I'd just slept with her. I wanted to get with her again; why would I help Chris?'

'All right. Lee, do you need to take a break?'

'No, I think I'm okay. It just all feels . . . so unfair.'

Mark sighed. He felt Les turn towards him, but he didn't make eye contact. At the same time, in the row behind him, he heard Chantae's sceptical, 'Ha.'

THE JURY ROOM was hot, so Mark followed the smokers downstairs. Kahu and Scott had come down too; the boy stood a little apart from the others, jogging around on the balls of his feet, swinging his arms as if he was doing backstroke and then butterfly. Mark leaned against the gate, out of arm's reach, and said, 'So, what d'you do as well as this swimming of yours? D'you work?'

'I teach swimming in schools, and work some night shifts at a supermarket.'

'Hell, that wouldn't pay well, would it?' said Scott.

'Nah, but I need work that fits round training. I live at home, but I have to pay for coaching fees and . . . er . . . competitions.'

'Doesn't the swimming organisation pay for trips?' said Mark.

Kahu shook his head. 'Mainly user pays. Some of my whānau help me out.'

'You need to get sponsors,' said Scott.

'You seem like a smart kid,' said Mark. 'Did you finish school?'

'Yes.' He didn't elaborate.

'D'you like computers?'

The boy laughed. 'Sure.'

'Well, leave it with me.'

'What?'

'I might have something . . . we'll see, hey.' And then Mark felt it would be awkward to stay, so he went back inside. Climbing the stairs, he remembered that the boy had been competing on the weekend, but he was distracted when he entered the jury room and heard Susannah telling Jake that she'd been at university with Mark.

'What did you study?' asked Jake.

'Commerce.'

Susannah looked embarrassed that he'd caught her talking about him. Eva and Hayley seemed to be listening. Les was cross-referencing the transcript with his notes.

'I didn't actually finish,' said Mark as he sat down.

It was a throwaway comment, but Susannah pounced. 'What? Your degree?'

Mark laughed. 'It's no big deal.'

'I'm sure you finished,' she said, as Mark spoke over her: 'I stuffed around in third year, failed some papers.' He shrugged. 'I moved on, set up a business.'

'Yeah, me too—I started at the council straight after school,' said Jake, while Susannah said something again about not knowing that, as if she should. It was the same overfamiliarity Mark had noticed the first day, when she'd asked about Maggie as if she knew her. 'She's fine,' Mark had said. 'Same as ever—being a mum and working part-time at the garden centre.' And then Susannah had asked about his girls.

Now, when he looked at her, she blushed. She had very straight, white teeth these days. Mark didn't remember them being like that; not that they were bad back at uni, just not as good. As she leaned across the table to reach for the water carafe, he could see the shape of her breasts under the blue and white stripes of her cotton top. She poured herself some water, then offered Jake some.

Mark had once kissed Susannah. Or, rather, she'd kissed him.

It was after uni. At a bar in Auckland that was his regular, but he'd never seen her there before. He'd watched her coming towards him without registering who she was, and it was only when she gave a shy sideways smile that he'd realised and caught her arm. She was wearing a light silver halter-neck top, and he remembered staring at the bones of her shoulders and the way the pleats of material fanned out over her breasts. He could see the definition of the muscles on her arms. When she walked away to join her sister and friends, who were on a hens' night apparently, it was clear she wasn't wearing a bra, because the cut of the top left her back almost bare.

Later, when Mark was sitting at the bar with the guy he ran his events management company with, she'd tapped him on the shoulder. By now she was drunk, and Mark was too, and he'd popped a pill to give the night an extra shine. Susannah had been friendly, standing there in her slinky top, her legs long in tight black trousers. Mark was sitting on a bar stool, and he'd spoken softly to draw her closer. Gradually, on the pretext that she couldn't hear what he was saying over the band, she'd moved between his legs, leaning to speak into his ear, her hand resting periodically on his jeaned thigh. He told her she'd changed, and she asked how.

'You're hotter than you were at uni . . . and more flirty.'

'Charming,' she'd said with fake indignation and a gentle shove of her hand on his chest. Leaving her hand there, she'd stretched her fingers out over his pecs, while she said into his ear, 'Sadly, it's all too late.'

'What d'you mean?' He stroked her back, intending to draw her hips against him, but then he restrained himself, deliberately dropping his hand away.

'I'm engaged,' she said. When he didn't react, she added, 'You've missed the boat.'

He smiled. 'Missed the boat?'

'Yep, it's set sail. Without you.'

He shrugged. 'What can I do?'

'We should have had an affair.'

'Yep,' he agreed, and just to see her reaction, he traced the line of her top from the high neck curving down across the front of her shoulder. She breathed in as he touched her, and he could see her drunkenly concentrating, not allowing the breath to come out as a sigh. 'Yeah, I missed the boat,' he said, debating whether to brush against her breast, but he didn't want to frighten her off. 'I see that now,' he whispered.

She was standing right between his friggin' legs, centimetres from his crotch. He shifted a little on the stool.

'So, who is this guy? Where is he?' He pretended to gaze around the bar.

'Jon. You won't know him; he's a bit older.'

'An older man?' It was the wrong question; he shouldn't have brought the fiancé into the conversation—now she was talking about his job in telecommunications. Mark said nothing, he just kept watching her, eyes narrowed.

They were interrupted by the band members. Mark introduced Susannah, and then, deliberately ignoring her, he chatted about their set, and potential work for them, which was really BS. When Susannah moved away, Mark pretended not to notice.

He made certain, though, that he caught her watching him from across the room. And then it became a game—him catching her looking, her him. He considered sending her a drink but knew if he alerted her friends it'd all be over. Before he'd worked anything out, she came with her sister to say goodbye. Chatted, her leg blatantly pressed against his. Told him they were going clubbing, mentioned the one down the road several times. When her sister turned away, she said softly, 'I want to kiss you goodbye.' And she looked straight at him. 'Properly.'

'Tell them you'll meet them there.'

She looked blank.

'Tell them you want to catch up with me, and you'll meet them in fifteen minutes.'

She did, but the sister argued until Mark said, 'I'll make sure she gets there safely.'

He thought her sister wanted to call them out, but she just said, 'Look after her. She's a bit drunk.'

'I can tell.' He'd smiled reassuringly, and Susannah had squeezed his arm. 'Mark's an old friend. One of the best.'

They'd both watched the group leave, giggling, chatting and stumbling, and then Mark had brought her round between his legs again, and said, 'Now what shall I do with you?'

* * *

MARK HAD ARRANGED to meet Brayden at work after court, but when he retrieved his phone from Anaru there were four missed calls from Maggie and a series of texts telling him to call. Mark phoned in a panic, imagining her car wrecked and twisted, the girls bleeding.

'Oh, thank God,' said Maggie.

'What's happened?'

'I'm going to have to drop the girls. Ruby's sick, so I can't use the babysitter and we've got the ceremony tonight.'

She was rattling on with arrangements, while he was scrolling through his mind, thinking, ceremony, what ceremony? She couldn't be getting married; she was still married to him. Finally, he asked.

'The Local Hero Awards—I'm getting the medal tonight for the school garden project.' Inevitably her tone was exasperated, but he could have sworn she'd never mentioned this.

''Course. Congratulations.' His voice was hollow. 'Won't you want someone there?' And even before he'd finished asking, he knew the answer.

BEGRUDGINGLY, IT SEEMED, Brayden agreed to meet at Mark's house instead of the office. Maggie arrived first. She hadn't explained how ill Ruby was; the girl groaned as Maggie carried her in from the car.

'What's wrong with her? Hadn't you better stay?'

Maggie put the girl into his arms—Ruby's face was pale, her smile brave.

'Ruby-tube,' he whispered.

'Tummy—she vomited,' said Maggie. 'It seems to have settled.'

Mark hurriedly put her down on the couch; he didn't want a tummy bug—imagine that in court.

'Shouldn't you stay?' he repeated.

'She's got to keep drinking, but don't give her any food. There's Pamol in the bag, but she's . . . Lizzie, don't just dump it.'

'Hey, Busy Lizzie.' His younger daughter hugged him fleetingly, then bolted up the stairs, leaving her bag in the hall. In the living room Ruby groaned. Mark wasn't sure if it was put on. Maggie hovered, but he could see she was itching to leave. He called to Lizzie to bring down Ruby's duvet and pillow.

He tried again as Maggie kissed her goodbye. 'Shouldn't she be with her mum when she's this sick?'

'She's with her dad. You wouldn't want me to miss this.'

Maggie didn't look at him as she left. He watched her trot across the lawn, her high heels sinking into the grass so her gait was staccato.

'What about tomorrow?' he called.

She opened the passenger door; so *he* was in the car.

Mark called out, 'I've got court. I can't be late. If it was work, I could take the day off, but . . .'

She turned. 'How does that saying go? Yeah, right.'

'Maggie, I'm the foreman.'

'I'll be here by eight.'

The house was quiet. Ruby, curled on the couch, seemed to be asleep. Mark put his hand on her forehead—maybe she was hot. Her skinny arms were clutching her tummy, and when he tried to move them to spread the duvet out, she groaned and tightened her hold.

BY THE TIME Brayden arrived, Mark had given Lizzie fish fingers and two-minute noodles. It wasn't the weekend, so he didn't have any fruit except a squashy kiwifruit that she turned down. He'd sent her off to have a shower, draw him a picture, and get PJ'd. When he said it, it sounded so ordered, but when he opened the door for Brayden he could hear her crashing about upstairs, 'dancing' to a hip-hop song.

In the hall Brayden made a comment about thinking kids were at least twelve before they listened to music like that. Mark didn't reply.

'Hey, Rubes,' Brayden said; Mark told her he'd carry her upstairs.

'I don't want to move,' she whined.

'She okay?'

'Just a tummy thing . . . can we sit in the kitchen instead?'

'For sure,' said Brayden, sounding relieved.

'Ruby, Daddy'll be in the kitchen—just call.'

'It hurts.'

'Where, honey?'

'Here.' She put her hand below her navel.

Mark tried to feel her tummy, but she flinched.

'She's pretty sore,' said Brayden.

'Yeah, it's in the middle, though, so it's not appendicitis. I s'pose it's a bug.'

'Look, I can't stay long. I'll be outta your hair.'

Before Mark joined Brayden, he took Ruby's temperature and left the spoonful of the Pamol on the table when she refused it, and then he texted Maggie.

*How high temp is too high?*

Her response was immediate. *Look it up.*

'Fuck.'

'All right?' asked Brayden.

'Sure, mate.' He got them a beer, which Brayden tried to turn down, but Mark had already taken the cap off.

'I can't stay,' said Brayden.

'So you keep saying.'

They talked generally, and then Mark launched in. 'I've been noticing stuff. I'm wondering if you're happy at work?'

Brayden seemed almost to laugh.

Mark could hear the girls arguing. 'Lizzie, come away,' he called.

'I think we should do this another time,' said Brayden.

'No. Let's sort it now.'

'You've got a lot on—and the trial.'

'Come on, mate, we've always been upfront—what's the story?'

'I'm leaving,' said Brayden.

'I knew it!'

'Are you going, Brayds?' said Lizzie, who was magically by the fridge now.

Mark was tempted to tell Brayden about the list and how he'd worked it out.

Brayden said, 'Yeah, poppet, I am, but I need to talk to Daddy about it, okay?'

'Yes, Lizzie, can you—'

'What can I eat?'

'I dunno. Just grab something and go sit with your sister. But keep away from her.'

'These?' Lizzie held up the bag of lollies he kept in the fridge for bribes.

'Okay, whatever.' He waved his hand.

'You shouldn't leave, Brayds.'

'Yeah,' said Mark, checking his phone. 'Lizzie's right. We're a team, you and me. So what is it? You wanting to shift back to Hamilton?'

Brayden didn't answer. He was scratching at the label on the beer bottle.

'I know it's hard with a new baby and all, mate, but we can sort it. I can do more.'

'Mark, you don't do anything. We do it all. You just faff around drinking coffee or beer while we work our arses off.'

Mark laughed. It was laughable. He wasn't going to get drawn in.

'You know less about computers than Sean, and he's been there three months.'

'I focus on the other stuff, Brayden. The staff. The clients.'

Brayden shook his head.

Back to the drama. Always back to the drama.

'Dad?' Lizzie called from the living room.

'You don't even know my baby's name, do you?'

'What the hell . . .'

'It didn't even occur to you not to expect me in on the weekends, or to take some of the workload. And then I realised—you can't, because you can't do the work.'

'I . . . you didn't . . .'

'You're a Neanderthal.' Brayden stood up.

Mark was pretty sure he'd pronounced the word wrong.

'No wonder Maggie had enough.'

'Go fuck yourself,' said Mark.

Brayden looked shocked.

Quietly, as Lizzie called out again, Mark said, 'Just get out. And tomorrow you'd best pack your things.'

Brayden leaned across the counter, his weight on his splayed fingers, but then he sat back down on the stool and told Mark he'd work out his notice.

'No,' said Mark, calm now. 'I think you've made your position clear.' He stood up, intending to check on the children, and as he did, he told Brayden how disappointed he was.

'Actually,' said Brayden, 'I haven't made my position clear yet.' He was fumbling in his pocket. He unfolded a glossy page.

Mark sighed. The friggin' drama. He took the sheet. A company name Mark didn't know. He kept his face expressionless and shrugged. 'So you've already got a new job.'

'We incorporated it yesterday. Rachel, Max and me. They're all coming—not Sean, we didn't offer him anything. Or Stuart, because he's useless—one of yours.'

Now Mark recognised the clever logo from the day at the office.

'I'm sorry, I was gonna wait till after the trial,' said Brayden. 'But you don't get it. We are your business, and you railroad us . . .'

'Brayden.' Mark kept his voice calm, quiet even. 'You don't know anything about growing a business or working with clients. You'll be eaten up. You were just an IT grad before you met me.'

'That was four years ago, mate—you're so far behind with technology, because you haven't bothered—'

Mark felt a whirring sensation. 'You can't do this,' he interrupted, grappling for the term. 'No competition. Contract. It's not legal . . .' And then he got it together. 'You've obviously never heard of a non-compete clause. This is the kind of thing I mean: you're a computer nerd—and a good one, for sure—but you've got no business acumen.' He blustered on, knowing he had to go hard to put the fear of God into Brayden. 'You'll owe me damages for breach of contract. You'll be on friggin' gardening leave for months. No one'll know who the hell you are.'

While he talked, Brayden was putting on his coat. Finally, when Mark's tirade had run out, Brayden said evenly, 'You didn't put a non-compete clause in our contracts—we had our lawyer check. You didn't bother, Mark.'

When Brayden had gone, Mark went back to the kitchen. He poured away Brayden's untouched beer and finished his own. He could feel panic rising. He needed to talk to someone. He opened the fridge, but slammed it shut again. He went into the hall to go to the girls, but then went back to the kitchen and sat down. He swore to himself, and swore again as he heard Lizzie call. He was trying to think who to phone—not Maggie, nor his brother, he didn't want to worry his mum. Mark had friends, but he could see it was essential word didn't get out. Susannah—she had faith in him. He'd have liked to call her, but he couldn't, could he?

And then Lizzie was there crying, and pulling him, because Ruby had tried to get up to vomit and had collapsed on the floor.

• • •

MARK WAS IMPRESSED by how compassionate the court registrar was when he phoned in the morning. She even suggested that perhaps he shouldn't come in at all that day. Mark insisted he'd be fine if he could just have an extra hour.

The appendectomy had been routine. Mark's mum had picked up Lizzie from the hospital, and by the time Maggie finally returned his call after he'd texted, *In ED*, Ruby was already in surgery.

Thankfully Maggie came alone, and they sat together by the children's ward and waited, and when it took longer than Mark had been told to expect, he went up to the desk and they phoned through to check, and Ruby was already in Recovery. After Maggie cried, Mark tried to wipe the smeared mascara off her face, but it was difficult, and she had to go to the toilets to wash it off. When she came back, he apologised for being a dick when she'd wanted to move to Napier, and Maggie, tearing up again, laughed and said, 'You always know when to turn on the charm, Mark.' And he'd squeezed her hand.

In the jury room they were all waiting for him, and while Anaru went to inform the judge that he'd arrived, everyone asked questions and patted his shoulder, and Susannah made him a coffee.

'So, what did I miss?' he asked, taking his seat at the head of the table.

'They don't carry on without you,' said Les. 'We all have to hear all the evidence.'

''Course,' said Mark. 'Sorry, I'm a bit tired. Once I'm in there I'll be fine.' And again, there was a murmuring of commiseration and respect.

Anaru came back and said the judge was ready, so Mark stretched and finished his coffee and said, 'All right, let's get this show on the road.' And he heard Hayley repeat the word 'show' but he was already out in the corridor.

IN COURT, LEE'S lawyer was re-examining him. 'There's just a few points I want to pick up on. Lee, can you remind the jury who you shook in the third round of the game?'

'I shook Tia. I had to make out with her and like the others she knew about the Dice Game, and we did hook up, and she'll tell you she was keen.'

'Thank you, Lee. Your Honour, members of the jury, we will be calling Tia shortly. Now, for that round, again, you face no charges—'

'Objection, Your Honour. The defendant is alleged to have—'

'Ms March?'

'Sorry, Your Honour. I may not have expressed that—'

Mark yawned.

'All right, Lee, you face charges *as a party* again. So, it is alleged that you *aided* or *encouraged* the sexual violation of Maia by forced oral sex and the making of the video . . .'

'It's not true. I said, I wasn't even there.'

'Can we just clarify for the jury, you were at the barbecue. Did you see Maia there?'

'Yes.'

'There's an allegation from the prosecution that you gave her some alcoholic drinks?'

'I had a bottle of vodka and a bottle of lemonade. I poured lots of people a drink.'

'Can you tell the court who else?'

'I don't remember everyone, but Jayden and Chris, definitely Tia, maybe Maia . . .'

'All right. And, Lee, when you poured Maia the drink, did she appear very inebriated?'

He looked confused.

'Was she very drunk?'

'No, she seemed fine. Maybe more chatty.'

'Lee, did you see Maia again after that?'

'I saw her talking to Chris in the kitchen, and I saw her leave with some girl I didn't know.'

'And to be clear, did you go upstairs with your friends?'

'No, absolutely not. I was downstairs with Tia, she'll tell you—'

The lawyer interrupted. 'Lee, did you know they were upstairs with Maia?'

'No.'

'Did you encourage them to do anything with Maia?'

'No, absolutely not.'

'Did you know Chris had shaken a one for Maia?'

'Yes, but I didn't think he stood a chance. Especially doing that—the oral . . . She's pretty young and innocent, and he's older and can be a bit'—he paused and looked across at Chris—'sleazy.' Mark glanced back at Chris, who was smirking—how stupid was he?

'I just laughed when he shook it. I think I even said, "No way." And you know, that proves it, doesn't it? I wouldn't have said that if I thought she'd be forced.'

Mark didn't believe Lee came up with that argument alone.

'Lee, did you see the video of Chris with Maia?'

'No. I mean, only here, in court. Chris said he ate her out, but I didn't believe him—or rather I didn't before the video.'

Mark remembered someone calling these types 'urgers'—the ones who keep their own nose clean but who provoke the mischief. But the thing was, Lee had kept his nose clean.

'All right, thank you, Lee. And, finally, a couple more questions about the last time the game was played. This was at the sixteenth birthday party. First, do you know who shook Amy?'

'Nah, I'm not sure. Really, the game was falling apart . . .' He trailed off. Then he looked over at Travis, and Mark was surprised to see the level of hostility on his face. 'I know Travis shook Amy. A six. For sex.'

Mark was sure the lawyer looked surprised. 'Lee, did you know anything about Amy being on the trampoline with Jayden, Chris and Travis?'

'No. Absolutely not.'

'Did you encourage them, or help them get Amy outside?'

'No, absolutely not. As I said, that night I was talking to Maia.'

'And were you the person who called out to those boys on the trampoline?'

'No, absolutely not.'

There was a danger that the repeated phrase undermined his credibility, thought Mark.

'I didn't know where any of them were. What they were doing.' His tone had slipped into pleading, and Mark understood—the sentences these boys were facing if they, the jury, found them guilty were crazy.

'All right, I think that covers off Amy. Lee, can you explain in your own words how you felt about shaking Maia that night.'

'Yep, I wasn't keen—she's not my type, and she's . . . young. Not actually, but the way she is, you know. I think she's religious. Part of the reason we chose her was for the challenge. I'd barely even spoken to her. I knew nothing was gonna happen.'

'All right, so earlier you made it clear that the, er, digital penetration didn't happen. What did occur?'

'Well, she was on the back deck by herself. I offered her a drink and she shook her head. I asked if I could sit down, and she said yes. I sat next to her on the beanbag, one of those big ones, so we weren't even touching. She wanted to go home and I offered her a ride, but she said she was waiting for Amy. We just chatted, and she loosened up. After a bit, I put my arm round her, but she didn't do anything, so, when she didn't seem keen . . . um, to be honest I was bored, so I left.'

'Did you kiss her?'

'I might've tried, but I didn't, like, push it. I mean, I texted Samara and hooked up with her again later that night. I wasn't bothered about Maia. Samara was sending me flirty messages, so she wasn't shitty anymore. She'd actually been *joking* about the Dice Game when we saw each other at training earlier. That's the thing'—Lee's tone intensified as he continued—'all these girls knew about the game, that it was just a joke. This whole thing's out of hand. It was a joke and these girls have made it into a witch-hunt. I feel like Samara's turned just because I didn't want to be her boyfriend. It's revenge.'

'All right, Lee.' The lawyer was good; she made it seem like she was shutting him down, but in fact she'd let it run. 'So, coming back to Maia, how did you know she wasn't interested? Did she say something?'

'No, nothing. But they don't, do they? Girls? That's why it's so hard for us. She wasn't responding, so I left. I didn't do anything. She was just sitting there. If she'd said something like "Go away," I'd have gone sooner, but it was just the same old—you know, that's how boys know if girls are into them, isn't it? We try it on, and if a girl's not into it, we give it away. Or I do. I don't need to force myself on anyone. I get with plenty of girls.'

Mark thought about Susannah then. Susannah in her twenties on the street in Auckland outside the pub. He remembered her coming up close and trying to kiss him. He'd pulled away, making her work for it, and then they had kissed. Passionately. And as she'd murmured, 'I shouldn't be doing this, I'm married,' he'd kissed her again, gently, teasingly, and said, 'Not yet you're not.' But after a while he'd spun her around and, walking behind her, pushing her along by her shoulders, he'd taken her all the way to the door of the nightclub, while she'd been laughing and trying to get free, wanting still to be with him. By the bouncer she'd stopped, and he'd known she would go inside then and carry on with her life.

He'd turned her to face him. Kissed her hard. And then he'd just walked away.

Nothing had really happened, but when he thought about it now, it was one of the sexiest moments of his life.

## CHAPTER THIRTEEN

# Les

Les finished spraying the ferns and sat down in the wicker chair. He said, 'After she finished with Lee, his lawyer called Tia. Now, she's the sixth girl, the one we'd all forgotten about. She's a rower and a friend of the boys. Only Lee ever shook her and that was in the third round, at the barbecue. He had to kiss her.

'I don't think you'd have liked her much, her manner. You wouldn't have thought her genuine. For example, she said she thought it was funny when Lee sent her the "Diced" message after they kissed, and I didn't believe that. I think any girl would find that humiliating.'

Les looked at his watch. 'Kaye will be here shortly, Sylvie. So we'll eat a little later tonight.' He didn't get up yet. He was still going over the end of the day in his head. He thought about the girl, Tia, whose hair from her scalp to her cheekbones was dark brown but from there to her shoulders was blonde, as if she'd dipped the bottom section into a pot of peroxide. He'd thought girls didn't want it to be obvious that their hair was dyed.

At the end of his cross-examination the prosecutor had asked Tia if she'd felt coerced by Lee. He had to explain the word as forced, but then she'd looked straight at the jury and said, ''Course not, I can look after myself. Anyway, those boys are my friends. They wouldn't hurt me; they're not like that.'

LES FELT THE tip of the pin bone with his finger and then used the tweezers to pull it out of the salmon's translucent orange flesh. On either side, white lines of fat stretched in a V-shape like the contours on an ordnance survey map. It was Tuesday evening and his daughter had arrived from Wellington, and even though it was well after six, Kaye had left Sylvie on the couch in front of the television and she'd poured him a glass of the riesling she'd brought with her. Usually by now he would be feeding Sylvie while watching the news. And normally Les didn't drink wine, especially sweeter wines. But these were the kinds of things that happened when Kaye came to visit.

'It annoys me when the shop doesn't do that for you,' said Kaye, watching him remove the salmon bones.

'I'm making the fillets with the parmesan and lemon crust. I believe you liked it last time.' He glanced at her. 'Unless you were being polite?'

She grimaced. 'Sorry, Dad, I don't remember.' She topped up their glasses. 'Couldn't we take the bones out when it's cooked?'

Les didn't answer.

Last time Kaye had visited, Les had picked up her mobile phone when he was wiping the bench and a message from her friend Anna had been there on the screen even though he hadn't pressed any buttons: *Keep Patience Hat firmly ensconced at all times.*

'Parmesan and lemon sounds good, though.'

'It's a question of angle.' It might be easier if he skinned the fish, but he'd read it was better to cook it with the skin on. 'Damn it,' he said, as he snapped a bone.

'Dad. We can pick them out.'

Les dug down with the tweezers, trying to find the remains of the snapped bone. 'It's not worth the risk with your mum.' Using the sharp-tipped knife, he cut the fillet, but he still couldn't see the bone.

Kaye muttered something.

He wouldn't drink any more wine until he'd finished. He slit the fish again and, with this second cut, found the bone and pulled it out. He pushed the fillet back together and traced the smooth flesh with his index finger, searching for any telltale catch.

'How is she?'

'We've discussed brain plasticity before?' He glanced up. 'One of the jury, a very intelligent girl'—he caught her look—'woman, Eva, works with people who've had brain injuries and strokes.'

'Did you discuss Mum?'

'No, that wouldn't be appropriate. But she told me that researchers are developing a new approach using virtual reality headsets with paraplegics to make them believe they can move their legs. They're rewiring their brains, Kaye.'

'And Mum?'

'Oh, too late now; remember the doctors said after two years we get back as much as we're going to.'

'It must be lonely for you, Dad?'

'I see Josie, and a very nice physiotherapist. Josie's been so helpful during the trial. We're running a bit of a scam, she and I—she put in for annual leave, so she doesn't have to do her other patients, and I'm paying her under the table. They're paid such rubbish, you know, home care workers.'

Kaye smiled, and then, with a soft sigh, asked if he was coping with the trial.

'I am.' He started on the second fillet. 'If it wasn't for the subject matter, I'd be completely content—it's good to get out and use my mind for something worthwhile.'

'And the subject matter?'

'It's upsetting. But less so for me than for some. I can't talk about it, of course. We're not allowed to discuss the evidence with anyone but the other jurors.' He suspected he was rattling that Patience Hat of hers now, but it couldn't be helped.

'Will it be in the newspaper? I could just look it up online and then you wouldn't be telling me.'

'We're not allowed to follow the media coverage either.'

'Golly, Dad, do you think everyone's so diligent?'

'I hope so—we've lost one already. I do worry about the lack of focus; some people aren't taking notes, for example.'

'Maybe they can't . . . you know, educationally. What d'you mean you've lost one?'

'No, it's not those people. It's people who should know better.'

'Lost one?'

Les paused then and counted the bones in the two piles he'd made.

'Dad?'

'It's even. I've got them all.'

She laughed. 'It's like pick-up sticks.'

It was very pleasant having her here. He did wish she lived closer.

'It's tidier than it used to be,' she observed.

'Well, there's only me to make a mess. Effectively. Sylvie did have a lot of hobbies, didn't she?'

They both glanced over at Sylvie's hunched body, and then with a brusqueness he took the breadcrumbs out of the larder, the parmesan from the fridge, and handed Kaye the kitchen scissors. 'Italian parsley, please. In the bed by the carport.'

When she came back in, Kaye started to unpack the dishwasher and he refrained from telling her she shouldn't, but it meant he had to keep watch as he mixed the melted butter with the other ingredients.

'No, second drawer under the hob. White mugs on the shelf by the glasses. I'll finish it off,' he said, losing track of her movements as he carefully spooned the mixture onto each fillet, spreading it out right to the edges and then scraping up the crumbs that had fallen onto the baking tray. When he turned back, she was putting the cheese grater in the pan cupboard.

'No. I won't find it there, Kaye. I won't know where it is.' He was aware that both his tone and volume were not properly regulated. After a minute, he said, 'It belongs in the bottom drawer, at the front, next to the rolling pin.'

He watched his daughter carefully stand the cheese grater in the drawer. Then she came over and put her arms around him, stroking his back and not speaking.

She was the only person who touched him now.

• • •

SYLVIE HAD OFTEN talked about aches and pains—arthritis in her knees, menstrual cramps, and allergies on the days when the deck was lightly coated with pine pollen, the same yellow-green colour as the crusts of the sulphurous pools. When Sylvie was pregnant it was heartburn, and later in life an aching back. So when she'd said her arm felt peculiar, he hadn't engaged, and even when he watched her brush her teeth with her left hand he hadn't interrupted his morning routine long enough to actually process it. She'd mentioned sweeping out the front porch and pruning the camellias the day before, so he'd lazily attributed it to that; he'd found over the years that, providing he acknowledged her complaint, there was no discernible benefit to dwelling on it—soon enough it would be a different symptom.

Privately, he considered that she had unrealistic expectations of the human body. Sylvie believed the norm should be pain-free contentment. But why would she expect such a complicated organism as a human to work perfectly at all times? And who was even to say that a stomach-ache or a runny nose wasn't the best biological management plan for a flawed environment?

And so, he had gone to work.

And so, he had come home.

And so, he had found her.

Six years ago.

When he remembered it, there was, obviously, the disquiet of walking into the silent dark house when the television should have been on and Sylvie should have been dishing up, so that by 6 pm they would be at the dinner table ready for the news. Les always watched the headlines; they were the table of contents, so to speak. He preferred to know the map of the whole before he focused on the particulars. That was why the court process suited him, or at least the prosecution case had. The prosecutor had clearly outlined the basis of his case; he'd explained who would testify and to what. And Les could see that not only had he established the existence of the Dice Game and the substance of the girls' stories, but he had also, where possible, pre-empted the defence arguments. Les had been irritated that the defendants had not outlined their arguments at the beginning too, so they all knew precisely what was being contested, but he understood they wanted to keep their powder dry. However, it was reassuring that soon each lawyer would muster their best version of the truth in their closing statement, before the judge would summarise it all, including the rules they must obey. And then they, the jury, would weigh the opposing evidence. Yes, the adversarial structure suited him perfectly.

Les was an infrequent reader of novels; he dealt in facts, while always acknowledging the limitations of human knowledge—he understood that truth could depend on perspective, and even on time and place. When he did read novels, he preferred to have read the blurb on the back, as well as a review or two, so he knew beforehand to what purpose the book was dedicated. Kaye's friend, Anna, believed this to be a heresy. She believed him to be cheating the fictional world. But wasn't fiction cheating the natural world anyway by attempting to present a narrative order?

So that day there was the quietness of the house. It was September and they were still habitually lighting the wood burner, so the coldness, too, was alarming. Les knew immediately that something was amiss, and he'd imagined the most obvious scenario—the return of the headaches. Calling out, he'd hung up his Gore-Tex jacket, changed into his slippers, and walked down the corridor expecting to find Sylvie lying in a darkened room. She was on the floor in the bedroom. Unconscious but breathing.

While holding his wife's hand, Les had timed the ambulance. It hadn't occurred to him that this was inappropriate until Kaye pointed it out the next day, when he told her that it'd taken the ambulance twenty-nine minutes, even though when he timed the drive to the hospital it took him just over seven.

In reality, of course, it was not the twenty-nine minutes that mattered, but the ten hours and five minutes that Les was out of the house. Everything he read subsequently reinforced the necessity of prompt medical attention due to the short window of opportunity to use tissue plasminogen activators to attempt to bust up the clot. And so, when he thought about the tragedy, there was always the horror of that arrival home, but the real horror was the unreliability of his apparently normal workday. While he'd walked the thirty-two minutes from Glenholme to the New Zealand Forest Research Institute—or Scion, as it was now called—Sylvie had unpacked the dishwasher and repacked it with the breakfast dishes, relying perhaps on her left hand. While he'd crossed the bridge over Waka stream and discussed the receptionist's daughter's science fair project, his wife had begun to feel increasingly unwell. During his morning team meeting, she'd perhaps taken herself into the bedroom to look in the mirror because her face felt strange. He wondered if she'd noticed the downward drag of the right side of her mouth and her right eye, or whether the suddenness with which that had most likely occurred, according to the doctors, meant she would already have been unconscious. The disfiguration was permanent. He and his daughter had surmised that Sylvie was heading for the phone but passed out before she could reach it. Sylvie would certainly have been unconscious by the time he was eating the German lemon cake that Gina had brought in for Tamashini's birthday. The cake with the lemon drizzle icing was the only blip in an otherwise entirely unremarkable workday.

As a younger man, Les had approached life as if there was a ledger and he had to keep the 'what he'd contributed' column well ahead of the 'ways he'd let himself down' column. After Sylvie's stroke, he chose not to examine his life like that anymore; there was no point in endless self-admonishment. But when Kaye and Anna had suggested putting Sylvie in a home, Les would not even entertain the idea. He understood, though, that in close relationships there were certain conversations that were preoccupations, and this was Kaye's main one, so it was no surprise that she brought it up again in the morning.

He hadn't expected her to get up so early. She was, and always had been, a night owl and a late riser, unlike himself, but like Sylvie. He wondered if that was genetically predetermined. She found him before eight, spreading the roasted red pepper paste over two large ciabatta rolls he'd bought the day before.

'Morning.'

'Morning. How did you sleep, Kaye?'

'So-so—always takes me a few nights.'

'Missing your friend, I suppose. Anna's welcome, you know; I never did mind.'

'I'm not sure you were thrilled. Anyway, we've all come to accept the situation. Even Mum, now.' She laughed.

'Kaye!' But he liked to hear her joke. 'Sylvie hoped for grandchildren, especially because it was so difficult to conceive you.' He said it matter-of-factly, but there was a silence afterwards, and he thought perhaps he'd hurt her.

'Lunch looks highly impressive.'

'Did you want one? I can make you one.' He'd started to flake the leftover salmon onto the red pepper paste.

'I presumed you were—'

'Oh, no, it's for—'

'Dad, I'm kidding; I've a lunch meeting, anyway. So, who is it for?'

'It's . . . a joke, I suppose. One of the jurors . . . she's interested in my culinary skills.'

Les squeezed lemon onto the salmon then ground pepper on top before placing spinach and kale leaves over it. 'Cream cheese, or excessive?'

'You've got quite a lot in there.'

'Part of the joke.'

'You seem to be enjoying the juror thing.'

'Kaye, it's a multiple sexual violation case!'

'Sorry, stupid thing to . . . Oh my God, Dad, it's not that dice one?'

'Kaye.'

'God, I assumed if it was that one you'd have told me.'

'I said I can't talk about it.'

For some time she didn't answer, but as he cut the rolls in half, she said, 'Maybe you should put cream cheese in there, Dad—if that's part of the joke.'

Kaye poured herself some of the muesli that Les toasted these days. There were roles you took on, and roles you gave away. He didn't shower his wife; Josie did. She would be here shortly to do just that. Les had done it once, in the hospital. The nurse had helped him undress Sylvie, and then left them in the cubicle. Sylvie was sitting, and he couldn't remember now if she was in a wheelchair or on a seat, but her head—in fact, her whole torso—was slumped. There was not the slightest reaction to the water, or to his touch. He'd washed her hair and body with the bright pink liquid soap, keeping his eyes fixed on the patch of skin he was washing, and not letting the skin attach itself to a limb, the limb to a body, to the body of his wife. And when he'd finally pushed aside the yellowed shower curtain, he'd known he did not ever want to do that again.

He could cope with her toileting and nappies. He brushed her teeth. Cut her food and fed it to her spoonful by spoonful. And he read to her.

When she first came home, he started back at the picture books they used to read to Kaye. He read about Max in his wolf suit making mischief and how the forest grew and the private boat tumbled by. Extraordinary that your brain could retain all those words, the rhythm, the cadence, even though, until then, he hadn't picked up that book for forty-odd years. He'd never thought about it before, but it was about the power of story, of words. Of labels. His mother calling him 'Wild Thing' had made a whole world grow in the boy's bedroom.

How powerful were these lawyers' words? Their labels—'rapist', 'predator', 'schoolboy', 'leader', 'virgin'? Never mind the lawyers' questions, at least for the jurors who couldn't see them for what they were—fragments of the story they were advocating.

'I put it to you, Amy, that if your story was true and you had been raped by two predators, you would have run into the party and screamed for help the moment your attackers left, wouldn't you?' 'Why did you not immediately wake your parents when you arrived in the safety of your own home, Amy, so they could call the police?' 'Lee, I put it to you that you orchestrated the Dice

Game and encouraged your friends to sexually assault and even to rape, to fulfil what they had shaken on the dice, didn't you?'

Les had noticed that the trial was intruding more and more into his everyday thinking. It was difficult not to be constantly preoccupied with it.

'I thought your mother might respond,' he said, and it was only when Kaye looked confused that he realised he hadn't told her any of his train of thought. 'It was such a happy time that I thought reading her your picture books might trigger something. I found I could almost recite the words I hadn't seen for years.'

'Like with songs—the other day I played an Oasis song I hadn't heard for twenty years and I could sing every word. In tune. In time.'

'I envisaged that we'd start with the picture books and progress; I'd read her back to adulthood. Like teaching someone to walk again, I'd teach her to think again.'

'By reading her stories. That's lovely.'

'Well, the thought might have been.' He turned away from her and chose two mandarins from the fruit bowl. 'Now I just read aloud whatever I'm reading.'

'Really?'

'Not much fiction, I'm afraid. Anna would be disappointed. More often the *Herald* or the *Listener*, but recently an article on mycological herbaria and medical mycology.'

She laughed, and then he did too, shaking his head. 'Kaye, there is no discernible difference between her reactions to medical mycology or *Where the Wild Things Are*.'

He packed the rolls side by side in his old lunchbox, along with the mandarins.

'Your friend?' his daughter asked.

'Very nice . . . young woman.' He smiled at Kaye. 'Chantae. A young mum, happily married. Māori. She's a dishwasher, but she's really surprisingly astute. It's been a revelation.'

'Dad, you need to get out more.'

'Such a waste.'

'Dad, I'm serious. It's time to put Mum into care and get on with your life.'

Les didn't answer. He rinsed the cloth under the hot tap, squirted on some dishwashing liquid and wiped the benches. Then he washed out the cloth again, more dishwashing liquid, hot water, squeezed it out and folded it in half over the tap.

'It's lovely to have you to stay, Kaye. And I do mean it about Anna—please bring her next time. But let's not go over unproductive ground.'

'No, Dad, I think we should seriously look at options. I've made a list.'

'Kaye. Please.'

• • •

PALMS ON HIS thighs, sitting with his spine long and chin tucked in, Les listened and, for the first time since the trial began, he didn't take notes. They would be given copies of these closing submissions with the transcript of the judge's summing-up, and they were not like the evidence, which flowed and ebbed, meandered and then rushed; these statements were, for the most part, logical and ordered, albeit utterly partisan. On the paper versions he could pull apart these speeches paragraph by paragraph—he almost relished the thought. For now, though, he wanted to fully experience each narrative.

The most fascinating closings were by Chris's and Jayz's lawyers because, while they had vigorously cross-examined almost every witness, they'd led no evidence of their own. This was the first time the jury had heard a coherent version of their take on events.

Jayz's lawyer was Māori, which was interesting in that he was the only Māori defendant. Les wondered if the lawyer was a relative, and then thought Chantae would tell him that was one of his 'dodgy' comments. He didn't take umbrage when she said that; he tried instead to grapple with the substance of her criticism.

Throughout the case this lawyer's aim had been to confuse matters, to disrupt any clear story that might be forming. His cross-examination modus had been obfuscation. He'd constantly introduced irrelevancies—asking Maia what Jayz had said to Amy at Travis's party before he'd even shaken her on the dice, or asking Lee to recount seeing Jayz at Blue Lake kissing a girl who had nothing to do with the Dice Game. Les understood this as a strategy, and he knew that some jurors, like Chantae, would see through this, but for others, Les suspected, the muddied water would prove distracting.

In the closing, though, the lawyer was different. He started with a basic outline. At the time of these events, Amy was an immature girl who had a huge crush on Jayden. And yes, Jayden was a bit of a lad. He perhaps took advantage of the situation because he liked her, but he was just a schoolboy.

'Look at him—he's not a rapist,' the lawyer said, pointing, and Jayz, sitting up, wore a nonchalant expression, which Les considered practised. 'I think you'll agree he is a good-looking boy. He doesn't need to force himself on girls, by any stretch of the imagination.' The man seemed almost proud of this.

'And girls do things for him they might not for other boys. Amy sent him a nude photo, and then, while drunk and high, engaged in a consensual threesome on the trampoline, and she later regretted these actions. When rumours got out at school, she made up the story of forced sex to absolve herself. And before she knew it, she was in the midst of the hysteria about the Dice Game.'

And then the lawyer filled in the shape with more and more details shined up for the jury, all carefully selected to blend in.

'The Dice Game was a boyish prank which Jayden had no part in making up. Its sole purpose was to see which boys could get girls *to consent*, and so far as my client is aware it never led to any non-consensual activity.

'Amy pursued Jayden. Amy and Maia essentially stalked these boys on Instagram and Snapchat. At the first party it was Amy who kept looking at Jayden when he was with Samara; you heard that from Maia. It was Amy who first texted Jayden—remember, he put his number in her phone, leaving it up to her to make the first move *if she wanted*. And that was nothing to do with the Dice Game—Jayden had not even shaken Amy then. After the Blue Lake concert, it was Amy who persuaded Jayden to send the first nude photo—this was a consensual sexual relationship to which the game was incidental.'

The lawyer claimed that at the barbecue, when Jayz went to get Travis, he merely meant them to interrupt Maia and Chris, who were engaged in consensual sexual activity. It was Travis who turned on the video. Jayz never touched Maia in the bedroom.

When it came to the night on the trampoline, the lawyer told them there was no evidence Jayz had shaken Amy or a six, and he went through the events in detail, building up a pattern of consent and mutual sexual satisfaction, even as he turned to the intercourse.

'When Jayden and Chris undressed her, Amy laughed—does that sound like a victim of rape? There was no screaming or shouting. She said she struggled, but the doctor told you she had no injuries on her body except for a small bruise on her upper arm which, you will remember, the doctor admitted could as easily have been caused by her knocking against a door handle. Use your common sense: if Amy had been struggling against these two boys, she would have been covered in bruises. If they'd forcibly undressed and raped her, her body would have been subjected to dreadful injuries, but the doctor told you there was no evidence that the incident was not entirely consensual. And that is exactly what happened: Amy and Jayz had a mutually sexually satisfying consensual experience. It might not be to your taste, members of the jury, but this is not a morality contest.

'Now, after their consensual sex, Jayden believed the sex between Amy and Chris was also consensual. Amy didn't scream or ask for his help, because, of course, he would have acted had he heard her protest. And, remember, Jayden offered Amy a ride home—is that the action of a violent rapist? And, ladies and gentlemen of the jury, Amy agreed. Amy got in the car. She let him drive her home. And she got into the back of the car because she wanted to have sex again. I put this to Amy and she denied it, but she is here having made allegations of rape, so she can hardly admit that.

'She did, however, admit she wore Jayden's hoodie home. She did admit that at home she sneaked in the back door. And she did admit that she went to bed without alerting her parents to *any* distressing situation, never mind multiple rapes. Now, members of the jury, do these actions sound like those of a girl who's been brutally gang-raped? Or are these actually the actions of a girl who has a big crush and is hoping to start a relationship with an older boy?

'Amy was perfectly happy until three days later at school—three days! Now, two things happened that day. A boy asked Amy if it was true that she'd had sex with two guys at the sixteenth party, and, secondly, Jayden sent a "Diced" message with Amy's photo. Now, Jayden realises that message was humiliating and upsetting. But that does not justify Amy making up these serious allegations.

'I can't tell you her motivation for fabricating this story, and Jayden does not have to prove why she would do that. Perhaps it was revenge when she realised he wasn't interested in a relationship—that is sometimes why girls make up these kinds of false allegations. Or it may have been as simple as regretting her intoxicated actions. Perhaps, giving Amy the absolute benefit of the doubt, she convinced herself of this story the next day, because otherwise she would have had to admit to herself that she was the kind of person who would participate in drunken, high, group sex on a trampoline. But that does not, in any shape or form, mean that she was not consenting that night, or that Jayden knew she was not.

'Now, Jayden admits that when the police first spoke to him, he lied and said he did not have sex with Amy. He admits that. He was concerned because they'd all indulged in Chris's MDMA. Jayden had never taken drugs before. He'd never been questioned by the police. As His Honour will explain to you, people lie for many reasons, and it certainly does not mean they are guilty of rape. Jayden did not tell the truth, because he was afraid he would be charged for having taken ecstasy. In the next police interview, as you saw, once he understood what he was being charged with, Jayden admitted that he'd had consensual sex with Amy. So please do not hold that against my client.

'My learned friend, the prosecutor, suggested that Amy must be telling the truth, because why else would she put herself through this whole court process? But remember, Amy had no idea what this process involved. When she made up this allegation to her teacher, she didn't know where it would lead. Before Amy knew it, her parents were involved, the police had been called, Maia was questioned. Samara jumped on board. There was no opportunity to say, "Stop, I made a mistake. I exaggerated. I lied." The investigation train was running down the tracks, and there was no way for these girls to stop it.

'I feel sorry for them, actually. They have been subjected to a horrendous process. But please remember, so have the boys, and it is their future that this trial determines. Look at this young man, Jayden. He was a schoolboy at the time. A young leader. Now his whole life is on hold. He is not some sexual predator. I am confident, members of the jury, that when you assess the evidence, you will agree that the prosecution has certainly not proved these charges *beyond a reasonable doubt*. You cannot convict Jayden of rape on the basis of a story made up by an intoxicated, jilted sixteen-year-old girl. Where is the evidence? Where are the injuries?'

CHRIS'S LAWYER SPOKE more briefly. His argument was simple. Everything Chris did was consensual. In the lake with Samara, it was simply kids mucking around and she had been flirting with him. There was no assault—she undid her top and Chris certainly did not put his hands inside her bikini bottoms. Samara had felt rejected by Chris and that was why she had joined these allegations.

At the barbecue, Maia and Chris kissed in the kitchen and Maia suggested they went upstairs. Jayz and Chris were simply joking around pretending to carry her. In the bedroom, Maia said she wanted to lose her virginity to Chris, but he felt she was too young, so they agreed together on oral sex. Yes, she was drunk, but the fact that they discussed intercourse and agreed on oral sex instead showed she was not so drunk. Intoxicated consent is still consent. As soon as Chris realised Travis was videoing, Chris told him to turn it off. Yes, Chris laughed, but that was because he thought he was winning the Dice Game *because* Maia was consenting. And Maia kept her eyes shut only because she was embarrassed.

With Amy, the kissing was consensual—like she said. The touching was consensual—like she said. And so was the sex. Chris certainly, and reasonably, believed it to be so. He would of course have stopped immediately if he'd thought otherwise.

The lawyer told the jurors to use their common sense. He said if Chris was a sexual predator, would he really have taken Maia upstairs at a barbecue where people could hear her if she screamed—or would he, rather, have taken her outside to some deserted place? And similarly, if he was a violent rapist would he have chosen a trampoline in a garden at a party with his friends right there—or would he have lured Amy away to some isolated spot in the bushes?

Finally, the lawyer reminded the jury of the seriousness of the charges, and that they could only convict if they were sure beyond a reasonable doubt. And how could the jury be sure that Maia didn't go upstairs voluntarily to have oral sex with Chris? How could they be sure that Amy was not consenting to sex when she was kissing him, touching him, laughing and certainly not objecting? And if those actions were not showing her consent, how could Chris be expected to know that?

• • •

ALTHOUGH THE SUN had fallen below the line of next door's roof, the sunroom was still stuffy. Kaye wasn't back, so after Josie had left, Les sat in the wicker chair with a glass of Kaye's riesling and proceeded to recount the day to Sylvie, as he had every day since the trial began. It cemented things in his mind. Clarified them. Often, he found links or inconsistencies which he hadn't noticed during the day. When this happened, he would note down the points and take the paper in with him the next morning. Early on, he'd insisted on showing Mark these notes, so, as foreman, he could be confident there was no impropriety, but Mark waved him away, even after the Fiona incident, which was concerning.

'The very best thing today was that the judge told us he'd prepared a "question trail", which breaks down each charge into factual questions for us to answer. He said he'd step us through it tomorrow. He even described it as "a map of the legal requirements"; it will be a lifesaver for keeping people focused.

'The prosecutor did a good job in his closing, Sylvie. I think he made it coherent for most people. Not Bethany and Dave, perhaps. Scott, I'm never sure about; he says so little. There's a few like that—Eva, and Hayley—she's a funny fish.

'The most startling thing is the legal test for rape. Interestingly, there can be penetration to which a girl did not consent but which is not rape if the perpetrator believes on reasonable grounds she was consenting. Prior to today, I'd have simplistically said rape was non-consensual intercourse. It does put the onus on the victim to make it clear she's not consenting.'

Leaving his wine on the bamboo table, Les picked up the spray bottle and started to mist the ferns.

'Sending the photos was foolish behaviour from Amy, but not an invitation, of course, although there will be some on the jury who'll believe it has a strong bearing. I just hope we can keep all our personal responses separate so that we can objectively . . .'

As Les turned he realised Kaye was standing at the doorway. She was motionless. Listening. She didn't speak, and nor did he. Finally, Les nodded curtly, and then suggested she pour herself a wine.

He thought, while she may have heard him, he hadn't actually told her about the case.

She would, however, believe he had just proved the degree to which he considered his wife an automaton.

## CHAPTER FOURTEEN

# Eva

It wasn't until the Wednesday of the third week when they heard the closing submissions that the full complexity of the case began to hit Eva. The prosecutor started by reinforcing that it was for the Crown to prove guilt beyond a reasonable doubt before they could convict.

'In a multi-charge, multiple complainant case like this, there will be some inconsistencies in evidence and some areas where people's memories are not entirely clear, and that's understandable. However, I do believe you have the grounds for a conviction on each offence for each defendant.' The prosecutor looked slowly along the front row of jurors. 'These girls have provided you with a detailed description of each incident to the best of their ability. They were credible in their accounts. You have seen their police interviews and heard them testify, and you have seen the boys' messages and the video that Travis took.'

Then he worked his way through the testimonies of the three complainants, weaving it all together, presenting it to the jury as a cohesive whole, tying it all back to the Dice Game. For Eva, it was the first time it had come together like that. She'd understood the chronology of the events, but she could now imagine the strands of evidence woven together into a shape. Sure, some strands simply stopped or stuck out at an angle, but overall there was a clear pattern bound by the central tenets: the defendants had invented the Dice Game; they'd become increasingly intent on fulfilling the challenges that they threw on the dice, whether or not the girls were consenting; and they'd encouraged and helped each other to do this.

The prosecutor reminded them then of an exchange of messages on the Snapchat group just before the sixteenth party that he had made Lee read out when he cross-examined him:

*Lee: For this round, we need to divide the girls to conquer*
*Chris: alg I'll bring molly*
*Jayz: Then I'm a sure bet*
*Chris: I'll follow along behind u and then Travis*
*Lee: I'm not letting you pussies win*
*Jayz: Nah we're the Dice Bros—100% success for round 4 is the goal*

The prosecutor reiterated that the other defendants gave the last message a green thumbs-up. He said the exchange showed the defendants encouraging and helping each other to set the girls up—a plan they carried out, pushing Amy to drink and get high on the molly—the ecstasy—and isolating them from each other. He gave other examples: Lee and Chris providing Maia with drink after drink at the barbecue; Jayz and Chris practically carrying a very inebriated Maia upstairs; Jayz and Travis shouting encouragement to Chris in the lake; and Chris and Jayz helping each other undress Amy and holding her down on the trampoline. Ultimately, he said, they had not cared that the girls were not consenting—Chris knew Samara wasn't consenting when he stuck his hand into her bikini bottoms in the lake; all of them knew Maia was incapable of consenting at the barbecue; and by the last night they were so out of control that Lee had forced himself on Maia, pushing his hand into her underwear, while Jayz and Chris had forcibly had non-consensual sexual intercourse with Amy while Travis watched.

AFTER MORNING TEA, Eva was ready for the defence closings to present an alternative version based around consent, and Lee's lawyer reiterated that the Dice Game was about persuading girls *to consent*. She argued that Lee had not encouraged or helped any of the others to carry out non-consensual sexual acts, but then she said Lee had no knowledge of the presence or absence of consent because he wasn't there when any of those acts occurred.

Lee's lawyer was hanging the other boys out to dry, Eva realised. She kept stressing that refrain—Lee was not even there. She told them that Lee's pattern of behaviour was about consent and restraint: he and Sacha kissed at Travis's drinks and that was all; Samara agreed she'd initiated consensual sex with Lee before the Blue Lake concert; and the night the alleged sexual violation of Maia occurred, Lee was with Tia, as she had testified, in a completely consensual encounter.

Tia had claimed that all the girls knew about the Dice Game, because everyone was talking about it, although when the prosecutor cross-examined her, she admitted she'd never actually spoken to either Maia or Amy. She said she thought it was funny when Lee sent her the 'Diced' message after they'd hooked up, that she wasn't like Amy, upset because Jayz didn't want to be her boyfriend—and then the jury was told to disregard that.

It was clear from her testimony that Tia trusted the boys, or at least believed she did. Eva wondered then if that was a false distinction—trust was a belief. Yet, in the circumstances, Eva struggled to see how Tia's trust could have any genuine basis. But if that meant she thought the girl was ignoring some deeper misgivings, then that made her very uncomfortable; it felt dangerously close to accusing Tia of not knowing her own mind.

Now the lawyer was talking about the last night, at the sixteenth, when Lee was charged for his own behaviour, not as a party to the others' actions.

'On that final night, while whatever was happening with Amy, and I make no assessment of that, Lee was "chatting up" Maia. This attempt to "make out" with her was merely Lee being opportunistic—the girl was sitting alone, and Lee joined her on the beanbag. They talked; Lee put his arm around her. Maia seemed happy to be with him and consequently, knowing she'd been obsessed with him for months, he started to kiss her. The whole encounter was a normal interaction between a boy and a girl still learning about sexual boundaries. Just like any other red-blooded adolescent male, Lee was keen, but Maia drew a line as to what behaviour she was comfortable with, just as adolescent girls do the world over, and Lee respected that line and stopped.'

Eva recalled feeling sickened by Lee's lawyer's cross-examination of Maia, but then she remembered the prosecutor re-questioning Maia, cajoling her gently into saying a little more.

'Was the sixteenth the first time you'd seen the defendants since the barbecue?'

'Yes.'

'Did you know they were going to be at Emma's sixteenth party?'

'No. I thought it would be mainly girls, and a couple of boys from our year. Emma didn't even know those boys.'

'Would you have gone to the party if you'd realised?'

'No. No way. I only went because my parents were worried I'd become unsociable.'

'Had you become unsociable?'

'I guess. Since the barbecue . . .' Her voice had dropped then and the judge had to ask her to speak up. 'I didn't know what they'd done to me . . . I felt bad I'd got so drunk . . . so I hadn't been doing anything.'

'What do you mean, Maia?'

'I'd come home from school and lie in bed. Some days I cried and couldn't go to school. So my parents wanted me to go to Emma's, and Amy promised to look after me. Then she went off to see Jayz.' The girl had sounded bitter and lost then, but after a moment she started to cry noisily, and in between sobs she said, 'I should've told Amy not to go . . . I should have told her Jayz was dangerous.'

When she'd calmed down, the prosecutor asked, 'Were you drinking that night, Maia?'

'No. I'm never going to again.'

'So when you were alone and Lee sat down, how did you feel?'

'Scared. I just sat there . . . I couldn't . . .' She shook her head.

'Sorry, Maia, but you told us that earlier you were interested in Lee, so were you pleased he was paying you attention at that point?'

'No, I was terrified.'

'Did you kiss him?'

'No.' She paused. 'I've never kissed a boy. I've never done anything with a boy.'

'All right. So, Maia, you testified that you sat in silence the whole time he was trying to kiss and touch you, and you didn't respond, so what made you leave?'

'Because he put his hand under my skirt . . . and kinda rubbed . . . inside my undies.'

Eva remembered thinking that when Lee joined her Maia was too afraid to move or speak, but by the end, she was too afraid to stay.

In her closing, though, Lee's lawyer argued that Lee realised now he'd misinterpreted Maia's signals, but that he had not touched under her skirt and would never force himself on anyone.

'Lee doesn't need to do that. I think the evidence has shown that he's a popular young man. Remember, he was Head of House at his school. Universally acknowledged as responsible and polite.

'And that's relevant because, most significantly of all, at the point at which Maia objected, Lee stopped. Immediately. He was doing what ninety per cent of boys do: seeing how far he could get—completely normal behaviour. But the moment Maia drew a line, he stopped. I'm sure all of you jury members can relate. Think back—it's normal teenage behaviour. It's certainly not criminal.'

AT LUNCHTIME, EVA walked quickly away from the courthouse down towards the lakefront, and, because the spring sun had a real warmth in it, when she'd eaten she lay back on one of the new benches with her feet hanging off the end. She watched the seagulls glide in and out of her field of vision, dark silhouettes against the blue of the cloudless sky, and it reminded her of another day, of lying on a thin lounger mattress alongside her friend Hil, on the stone patio at her gran's, with the smell of lavender and geranium. They were drinking wine that day, and lazily pulling weeds from the cracks in the crazy paving, flicking up sandy soil and ants. Hilary had been her lab partner all through first-year health sci. She was the only one of Eva's friends who'd got into med, and consequently they hadn't seen much of each other for a while, but that year Hil was a house surgeon at Wellington Hospital and Eva was working there as a physio, and so their friendship had been reignited. Hil had very short hennaed red hair then, which Eva still wasn't used to, and she was lying in the shade, long and lanky with her jeans rolled up and her legs pale with translucent blonde hairs. Hil had just been left by the love of her life, so they were discussing relationships and sex. She was lamenting her inexperience—she'd been with the same man since she was nineteen. And Eva, lying fully in the sun in just a pair of khaki shorts and a bikini top, tanned and muscly, was telling Hil how much fun they would have socialising together.

Hil had suggested that they should recount who they'd had sex with. Hil's list was short and all men, and it'd made Eva feel shy, but she'd listed her partners: there was Paora—her high school boyfriend whom she had her first sex with at seventeen; Josh—a friend of her older brother's whom she'd been obsessed with before, after and occasionally during Paora; Simone—a holiday fling at a backpackers in Northland, who'd set her on her bi-path, as she called it. So then Nita—her first real girlfriend; Tasmin—a fling, a cheat, she said, going a little red; Christos, a fellow backpacker in Cambodia . . . Eva paused. 'I missed someone,' she said.

'Well, add them in.'

'There was this guy during Orientation Week at university. I never told you.' Eva stopped. There was a long silence. She poured some more wine; the bottle was hot.

'Was it bad?' The way she asked made Eva think Hil would be a good doctor.

'I just don't think about it.'

'You don't have to say.'

'His name was Greg . . . I was very drunk—I don't really remember, but I ended up sleeping with him.'

'He doesn't count.' Hil said it in a bright neutral tone. A tone which left no room for argument, or even elaboration. 'We don't count that kind when we do this.' Sometimes when Hil used the first person plural like this, it irritated Eva, but now it added weight to her assertion, and Eva had felt so grateful it'd made her laugh.

'Absolutely. He doesn't count.' Hil had looked Eva in the eye and Eva held her look, and then she'd told Hil what a great doctor she would be, and finished her list.

• • •

WHEN ALL THE defence lawyers had done their part, Eva attempted to assess the clarity of the evidence. She knew the defendants' lawyers had deliberately undermined the narrative coherence. They'd brought up evidence the prosecution had barely referred to, discussed girls who were not alleged to be part of the Dice Game, and given differing explanations for how the game originated and about each event. She'd expected them to interlock the evidence into a different shape, some rough pattern to stand in contrast to the prosecution's so the jury had two alternate versions to compare. Instead, the defence lawyers were each entirely focused on their own client's case. Their stories were not only separate, but at times contradictory, so that Eva was not left with one contrasting shape, but with a pile of debris so broken and strewn that she could see no hope for the jury to agree on a lucid account of events.

What's more, two of the lawyers had emphasised that the jurors could not wake up on the weekend and think they'd made a mistake. When they came to consider their verdicts tomorrow, the lawyers said, they needed to be *sure beyond a reasonable doubt*.

'*Sure*,' said Travis's lawyer, 'that the prosecution has proved that Travis was a party to rape—and can you be sure of that? It is not enough that you think Travis might be guilty, or even that he is probably guilty. If you are left with a reasonable doubt as to his guilt, as I believe you will be, then it is your *duty* to acquit.'

• • •

ON THE THURSDAY morning, inevitably, the atmosphere in the jury room was fraught. It was the last day of the trial. They had the judge's summing-up and then the responsibility passed to them, to decide.

Eva had slept poorly after the closings, convinced the evidence was unravelling, and whereas just a few days earlier the jury seemed to have reached an acceptance of each other, she was sure they would splinter when it came to the deliberation. Not for the first time, she wished Fiona was still there. While Fiona had been easily shocked by the teens' behaviour, she'd been insightful. And not prejudiced.

Eva had taken sociology and psychology course at university; she'd completed a postgraduate diploma in neurological physiotherapy. She understood how social norms had set these boys up to act like this, set the girls up to be victims of this behaviour. She could unpick the ways in which the lawyers were claiming that the girls had not acted as 'real' rape victims would, and she could see those claims for the stereotypes they were.

But Mark and Scott—God knows what they thought of these girls. Dave lacked concentration, and Bethany would do whatever she was told by the others. Eva thought Hayley believed the girls, but she barely spoke. One lunchtime Eva had followed her, out of simple curiosity, on an hour-long power walk along the lakefront past Sulphur Point and through the Sanatorium Reserve. She suspected Hayley knew, but neither of them made any move to connect, and Eva was content with that.

Eva had grown up in Wellington, studied in Dunedin, and spent time living in London before she'd returned to Wellington to specialise. She'd moved in circles of young professionals and academics before she accepted the job in Rotorua, excited about the lifestyle—the biking, the lakes and off-road triathlons. Naively, she'd been unprepared for the provincial conservatism and casual racism and sexism she'd encountered since moving here. From someone like Scott or Les it was hardly surprising, but she found Susannah's brand, while not uncommon, particularly irritating. Until today, Eva had remained reserved in conversations with the other jurors, but that final morning, as they waited to be called in to hear the judge's summing-up, Susannah had made an offhand comment condemning Amy's flirtatious behaviour: 'Amy led them on. What did she expect would happen?'

Eva had responded gently at first. 'Amy can flirt and kiss and then withdraw consent at any time, Susannah.'

'Amy was kissing them both. Letting both of them touch her.'

'And that's her call.'

Eva was aware that the others had fallen silent.

'But you admit she was consenting to that,' said Susannah.

'She can still decide at any point she's had enough. She's not on board a train. She can stop when she likes.'

'She must have known where it was going, Eva.'

'You're buying into that conception that boys can't control their sex drive. Just because she was consenting to kissing doesn't mean she was agreeing to intercourse.'

'She knew—' Susannah started, but Eva interrupted, annoyed now: 'Even if someone's actually having sex, Susannah, it doesn't mean they're agreeing to everything, anything. It's just the same as if one of them rolled her over and penetrated her anus or started strangling her.'

Kahu made a reflex noise; Bethany flushed red.

Susannah didn't answer, and Eva was cross that she'd allowed herself to become emotional. She carefully tucked her hair behind her ear and resolved to contain herself.

Les, though, was looking up, intent, considering. 'So, forgive me, Eva, I'm ignorant of the sexual mores of today's generation.

Susannah mentioned how on television now it often appears that couples go straight from kissing to intercourse. I know that's television, but how much of an expectation is it? At that age? Kahu, what do you—?'

Eva jumped in: 'It depends—'

But Dave interrupted them both. Shaking his head, he said, 'Hell, Les, there's not a manual, mate,' and people laughed.

Quietly, Eva said, 'My point is the principle. Susannah's argument is essentially, "Amy was asking for it."'

'Was she?' said Scott, in a tone Eva couldn't grasp, but then Les started again.

'I suppose that's my conundrum. We have to deal in practicalities and realities, not principles. From the prosecution's closing we have to establish what the boys believed with regards to her consent, and then decide if it was reasonable.'

Eva was about to argue, but then she realised he might have a point.

'Bearing in mind the boys were drunk and high too,' said Jake.

'But that's not an excuse,' said Eva.

'You fellas are gonna have to explain this better,' said Chantae.

'Actually, we don't need to think about any of this right now,' Mark interjected. 'We need to wait till after the judge's summing-up. I know from last time I was a juror, that's the most important part.'

Eva felt chastised, and irritated because Mark was right. She glanced at Les and he gave her a small nod, and Eva thought, please let the judge's summing-up guide them through this.

'THIS IS NOT a trial about the sexual morality of young people today,' said the judge. 'You must put aside any feelings of prejudice or sympathy. For example, you may feel sympathetic towards a complainant because she is young or sexually inexperienced, or prejudiced against her because she kissed two boys. Or you might feel sorry for the defendants because they were schoolboys. But you must put aside any feelings like that, of either sympathy or prejudice. Those feelings are irrelevant. This is not a popularity contest. Nor is it about your own moral views.'

Eva stole a glance at the public gallery. She was separated from it only by Jake, so on the days the public were allowed in, she'd identified some of the regulars. There were two sections of seating. On the far side, closer to the dock, sat the boys' parents; on the near side were the girls' families and the police officers. Eva wondered then about the people she couldn't place—who would come to watch this trial if it did not directly affect them?

'As is the case with many trials involving alleged sexual violence, credibility and reliability of the witnesses is a critical issue. In this trial, this is complicated by the number of complainants and defendants and alleged incidents. As I have explained, you will need to deliberate on each defendant for each charge.

'Now, credibility and reliability are different matters. A witness may be credible but unreliable—for example, because of their level of intoxication. And that is a factor for you to consider. How, then, do you determine the credibility of a witness? Members of the jury, you should feel confident about this. Every day, in the course of your lives, you assess people's honesty—as a parent, a friend, a co-worker. Between you, you have considerable life experience as to how people behave.

'One way we do this in everyday life is we look at a person's demeanour. Similarly, here, one factor you can consider is the manner of the witnesses when answering questions. However, in court we need to be careful about judging witnesses in this way. As you yourselves know, being part of a formal court proceeding can be a nerve-racking experience. The court setting may make witnesses anxious and hesitant, especially when they are discussing inherently private matters. So people may be nervous, but still be honest and reliable. It is a matter for you.'

Eva had identified Lee's parents early in the trial. His mother had the same blonde hair and long straight nose, which gave her a haughty expression. Lee's father was older but looked fit; he held his jaw tense. As usual, they were sitting in the front row of the section behind the dock, alongside a bland-looking couple—a short stocky woman and a worried-looking man with thinning, wispy hair—who Eva believed were Travis's parents. As she watched, Lee's father leaned across his wife to whisper to Travis's dad. Lee's mother shook her head vigorously, and Eva wondered if these four would ever believe their boys were culpable whatever they, the jury, decided. She was surprised the couples appeard to still be friendly.

The judge was talking now about Jayz admitting he had lied in the first police interview when he said there was no sex on the trampoline. The judge said if the jury accepted that he had lied they could take it into account, but that just because someone lied it didn't necessarily mean they were guilty. People might lie for many different reasons, he stressed, so they should consider it carefully before attaching significant weight to it. Eva was still considering what exactly the judge meant when he started talking specifically about sexual violence cases.

'I need to address one element which several of the defence counsel raised, and that is the fact that Maia and Amy did not immediately report what they allege to have been sexual violations.

I need to tell you that there are many reasons why a complainant in a sexual offence case may not complain immediately, and it does not necessarily mean that the complaint is untruthful. So that, too, is a matter for you.

'Finally, I would like to disabuse you of any notion that sexual offences require corroboration. This is not the case. Historically, there was a requirement that a sexual complaint must be corroborated by evidence in addition to the complainant's testimony, on the basis that a woman's word on this sort of matter was unreliable. Obviously, society has moved on from that position, and I want to make it clear that you can convict solely on the basis of the testimony of a complainant, but only if you are sure beyond a reasonable doubt that each element of the offence has been proven.'

The morning wore on. The courtroom was cool, and the judge was trying to vary his tone, but Eva felt a heaviness in her eyes despite knowing how integral this summing-up was to the trial. The judge told them he had prepared a question trail in consultation with the lawyers for the jury to follow and that he would now go over the key legal elements of each offence and those questions before summarising the evidence for the prosecution and for each defendant. Suppressing a yawn, Eva wondered if Dave was already asleep.

THE JUDGE WAS talking about the charges relating to Maia and was defining consent: 'A person does not consent if they are asleep or unconscious. A person does not consent if they are so affected by alcohol that they cannot consent or refuse to consent.' The sensation crept over Eva then, like the spread of a blush—a sensation that began as disquiet, but deepened quickly to apprehension. The judge explained that the jury did not need to agree whether Maia was unconscious or so affected by alcohol that she could not consent, if they all agreed that she was one or the other, and that all the other elements of the offence were present.

There was a medical phrase Eva used at work—'impending doom'. Initially, she contained the feeling. To help her stay focused she had been drawing mind maps on her notepad as the judge went through each charge, and she determinedly finished the page relating to Maia before she put down her pen, placed her hands palm down on the pad in front of her and concentrated on steadying her breathing. She could not think about this now. She had to listen to the rest of the judge's talk.

• • •

GREG WAS AT the same university halls of residence but on a different floor. He was good-looking, not the kind of guy who had to work to find a girlfriend. He was part of the group who'd gone to the nightclub, but she hadn't really talked to him. At one point, when Eva was having a boogie with a group of girls, he took her hand and they danced, their bodies fitting together easily. She enjoyed it; it was flirty, sexy even, but then she wandered off, danced with another guy, accepted a drink from Greg and later bought him one in return.

As a group of them were walking back to the halls, Eva stumbled, and Greg caught her arm. She told him he was her hero, and then she meandered over to a bench and sat down to unstrap her high heels. He stayed with her while the others kept walking, and when she got up again, barefoot, he put his arm around her, teasing her about being wobbly. And she was. And she was happy. She gave him a hard time about all the girls who liked him, and mentioned she had a boyfriend in Wellington, just to be straight up, even though the relationship was on the rocks.

At the hostel they found a seat in the corridor near her room and Greg told her to wait, and then came back with a bottle of tequila. She said she'd had enough to drink, but when he gave it to her she took small gulps and swallowed it quickly and he did too. Things blurred and jumped—time was no longer a coherent stream. She remembered them leaning against each other, laughing. Remembered seeing that quarter of the bottle was gone and being surprised. She remembered saying, 'I fear for tomorrow, I fear for tomorrow,' over and over, and him kissing her to stop her saying it, and it becoming a joke, her saying it so he kissed her. She even remembered the kisses; soft, gentle kisses. Teasing kisses. She told him he was trouble, that people had warned her off him, and he liked that.

Remembered at the door of her room saying goodnight. Some more kissing, fumbling. She remembered saying she had to sleep, would see him tomorrow, being excited, thinking this was the beginning of something. Staggering across the room, stumbling over her clothes and shoes, while he leaned against the wooden architrave watching her. She'd asked for a glass of water, and he'd gone to get one, and she remembered knowing as soon as she lay down that she wasn't going to stay awake long enough to drink it.

She woke. The room was spinning. The underwire of her strapless dress was poking into her side. Shifting, she realised he was there next to her, arm around her, and she cuddled into him, facing him. The room was lit a dim black-orange from the streetlight outside because they hadn't let down the blind. She wondered if she was going to vomit, thought about how far it was to the shared bathroom. Rolled over, moved away, too hot. Then nothing again. No recollection of him speaking, or whether he was awake or asleep. No recollection of how she felt that he'd climbed into her bed. Just a drunken acceptance.

Jump cut. Woke. Nauseous. Room spinning, bed moving, he was on top of her, inside her. He had no shirt on; she was still wearing her dress, but it was pushed down, one breast exposed. She tried to move her arm to get him off her, but couldn't seem to lift it. Felt she couldn't move. Nothing.

Woke again; he was gone and she wondered if it was a dream. The room was light enough for her to see the full glass of water by the bed. Her head pounded when she moved.

THAT AFTERNOON SHE went to his door. He gave her a goofy grin, then when she didn't return it, a fake grimace. 'Friggin' tequila.'

The bottle was on the floor by his shoes—only a third left.

'I don't remember stuff,' she said.

'I know, you were trashed. I put you to bed.'

'Did you . . . sex?'

'I'm sure we can do better with practice.'

She didn't look at him as she asked if he'd used a condom.

'We were wasted, eh? Maybe you should get the morning-after pill.'

'Jesus.'

'Hey, hey, takes two to boogie. Two to fuck.'

Under her breath, as she walked away, she'd muttered, 'Apparently not.'

She remembered that now. Those two words. But between then and now she hadn't thought about it like that. She'd dealt with the doctor's disapproving expression when she asked for the morning-after pill, and the vaginal swab for an STD check, and pissing into a plastic carton so they could test because she thought she had cystitis. She'd been cross with herself for getting too drunk to know what she was doing, and for the rest of the year she'd avoided Greg as much as possible and he'd left her alone. She'd regarded it as bad sex. She'd been unreasonably pleased when Hil had told her it didn't count.

• • •

THE JUDGE SUGGESTED they eat an early lunch before beginning deliberations and he told them that today it would be provided for them. He explained that they would deliberate for as long as it took to reach a decision and that, if necessary, they would go home tonight and return tomorrow. There was some mumbling among the jurors then.

While they waited for the lunch to be delivered, Les looked through the transcript and a few people bickered about the judge's comments regarding lies. Mark and Susannah said they had notes, and Jake joked that Les's notes were the definitive ones.

There had been penetration. Greg had told her to get the morning-after pill. She'd felt him inside her. She was not sure, but she thought him pushing into her was what had woken her. Which meant she'd been asleep when he started. Drunk sleep. She hadn't spoken, moved, consented. They'd kissed earlier. She'd agreed to that, had kissed him back, but then she'd told him she had to sleep. She couldn't even remember him coming back with the water or getting into her bed. Back then, she had believed that was the reason she'd become paranoid about locking her door and window. She'd started getting up at night to check. Once or twice a night. Sometimes three times. But she hadn't heard Greg come back that night because it was drunk sleep. And when she'd woken with him having sex with her body and tried to push him away, she'd felt almost stoned—like she couldn't move or speak or act. She'd just lain there. She'd always blamed the tequila—she'd never drunk it again.

But Greg had been drunk too. More so than these boys, she thought.

But he had taken off her knickers. His shirt. She couldn't remember feeling his trousers against her legs.

Remembered him above her. Moving.

Remembered looking at the lightshade. Looking past him. Past his eyes.

Had he not realised she didn't want sex?

She flicked through the stapled papers the court attendant had given them from the judge—the question trail. There were pages of it. She found the sheet with the part at the top before it was broken into factual questions about Amy and Jayz, Amy and Chris. The part that set out the law.

*Person A rapes person B if person A has sexual connection with person B . . .*

She was person B.

*. . . without person B's consent . . .*

She had not consented.

*. . . without believing on reasonable grounds that person B consents . . .*

The judge had explained this—there were two ways it could be rape: if Greg did not believe she was consenting or if no reasonable person in Greg's position would believe she was consenting. Eva tried to think about the difference between them. Either way, when he started, when he pushed inside her, she was asleep or in a drunken bloody coma. No one could think she was consenting. She remembered some discussion about alcohol and the effects on the defendants, that it wasn't a defence, but now she wasn't sure—was it a factor to take into account? Could it affect the reasonable belief of person A? Was it the reasonable drunk person? Was a drunk person reasonable?

Eva turned the pages back to the beginning. Sipped her water.

So she had been raped.

The percentage of women who'd been sexually assaulted in their lives was staggering, she knew that. A recent survey had placed it at over thirty per cent. She also knew that a huge proportion of forced sex was committed by people who knew the victim and that more than ninety per cent of these rapes were never reported to the police. She had not previously considered herself as one of these victims.

Eva looked around. Who else in this room had been sexually assaulted? According to those statistics there might well be others. And then it occurred to her—the corollary: that statistically it was likely that a man in this room had sexually assaulted someone. Not Les. Or Kahu. Or Jake, surely? Dave? Scott? Mark, perhaps? Eva didn't want to look at the world like this. To look at men like this.

IN THE TOILET, while the others were starting to settle down, Eva remembered the quiet, confident way Hil had said, 'It doesn't count.' She wasn't saying it didn't matter. Eva hadn't described the night in any detail, except to say that it was drunken bad sex. But Hil hadn't been trivialising it; she was telling Eva she didn't need to accept it as part of her sexual history. And Eva thought that because she had always conceptualised it as bad sex, not date rape, it had carried less weight in her life. The relief she'd felt when Hil told her it didn't count was that she'd been freed from it having any meaning. She imagined it now as a balloon she'd let go, pictured the two of them lying in her gran's garden, with the heat of the crazy paving radiating up through those thin mattresses as they watched the dark silhouette of that night floating up into the blueness, getting smaller and smaller until you could no longer be sure where it was against the sky, and as Eva washed her hands in the bathroom of the jury room in the courthouse in Rotorua, looking at her own narrow, slightly pointy face in the mirror, she thought, even if she knew now that legally it was rape, why would she reconfigure it in that way? Why should she give it that significance? And while she made herself a tea, she acknowledged that this could be some state of false consciousness, some form of repressing the memory—but for now, at least, it didn't feel like that.

Gradually Eva became aware of the substance of the others' conversation. Slowly, as the cogs of her mind gained purchase, she became engaged again as Susannah said, 'But there's so many versions, how can we decide which is the truth?'

'That's not our role,' said Les. 'We're not trying to find the truth.'

Mark started to object, but Chantae cut him off. 'What do you mean, Les?'

Eva noticed that Chantae sounded afraid and that prompted her to answer, 'He's right, Chantae. We're not trying to decide the true detailed version of every aspect of the Dice Game, nor where we stand on it morally. We simply have to answer the judge's questions.'

She waved the handout at the others. 'And to do that, we have to decide if we believe what the girls told us.'

CHAPTER FIFTEEN

# The deliberation

While they waited for lunch in the jury room, Mark reiterated that they would not start deliberating until they had eaten. Initially there was a subdued air—the solemnity of the summing-up had taken its toll—but gradually, as they realised they were nearing the end, sharing a meal and having an enforced break, the mood lightened. It reminded Kahu of the end of senior year classes, when the jubilation was tempered by the looming exams.

The smokers nipped downstairs, and both Kahu and Hayley followed, just to be outside. Mark cleaned Les's chart off the whiteboard, while Susannah made him a cup of tea. Eva, who'd been flicking through the handout from the judge, went into the toilet.

As they regathered there was a brief discussion about truth, before Mark shut it down. Chantae asked how they would vote and Les showed them pieces of paper he'd cut up, ready. Anaru brought in a platter of sandwiches and another of fruit and brownies. There were comments about this being more like it, compared to their usual single biscuit. Plates were passed around. Bethany had a poke at the sandwiches and announced the fillings—ham and lettuce, cucumber and cream cheese, and tomato and cheese.

Chantae asked Kahu to say a karakia, which he thought was weird because they hadn't used a karakia for anything else; he rushed through it.

Scott quizzed Bethany about her love life, and she said she didn't have a boyfriend and was grateful when Susannah didn't call her out.

With his mouth full of sandwich, Mark asked Kahu about his swimming competition, because Mark had forgotten all about it, what with Ruby and the whole Brayden drama.

'Yeah, I made the qualifying time. For the two hundred, not the hundred, but I'll get to race both.'

There was a chorus of congratulations. Bethany clapped, and Chantae told him she'd have to call him Mako now. There was talk of Hawaii, the Commonwealth Games, of them being able to say they knew him before he became famous. Kahu considered telling them he'd put up a GoFundMe page—he'd already told Eva about it when she asked him on Monday how he'd gone—but he decided against it. Jake asked if he'd celebrated, and Kahu admitted to having a few beers with his brother, because his mates had mainly left town. Mark said he was looking forward to a drink at the end of today, and maybe they should all have one, which made Chantae roll her eyes at Kahu, because Mark was clearly looking at Susannah when he said it.

Eva had the sense this camaraderie would be short-lived once the discussion started, and the feeling was reinforced by Mark's paternalistic tone when he said, 'It's time, people. We need to get down to business. Chantae, Susannah, can we move the plates up to the sink?'

'*We* can,' said Chantae, but Mark didn't notice.

Once they'd resettled, Mark announced they would work through the charges defendant by defendant and would start with Lee. Several jurors agreed.

Lee was Bethany's second-favourite. She liked the blueness of his eyes, especially on the days he wore the navy shirt. He was smaller than her, but she liked his confidence.

'Les?' Mark had to repeat it before the old man responded.

Les had been eating methodically as he checked through the transcript for answers to the seven questions he'd noted down during the closings. It'd taken a while because the judge had told them that on any issue they should not only check the examination and cross-examination, but also the re-examination of each witness. 'One more thing to check, Mark.'

'No.'

Startled, Les looked up.

'We need to begin,' Mark said. 'It's eleven-forty. I want to get out of here before five. I've got business issues to resolve.'

'Too right,' said Dave. He'd been told yesterday he was booked on a flight to Los Angeles on Monday night. He had a lot to get sorted before then.

Les could see that it was important to Mark to establish his authority, so he agreed. It was imperative that Mark lead them to consensus—this was what Les had known he would not be able to do. He gave a curt nod. 'You're right. We should start as soon as Anaru brings the transcripts of the closings.'

Mark and Eva both answered him: 'We don't get them.' 'There aren't any.'

'I beg your pardon?' said Les.

'The judge said. It was the same last time. We don't get the closings or the judge's summing-up—just this.' Mark indicated the judge's question trail booklet.

'Because the closings aren't evidence, Les,' said Eva gently.

There was a silence. A collective pause.

'I need them,' Les said.

Still no one spoke. Mark shrugged.

'I didn't make notes. I relied on us receiving the transcripts.'

'There aren't any,' said Bethany, her tone gleeful.

Carefully, while they all watched, Les turned back the pages of the transcript he was reading, pushed down the clip and shut the folder. He slid it towards the centre of the table, flicked his notepad back to the front page and sat back.

'For goodness' sake,' Susannah whispered to Mark.

'Les?' said Mark.

He didn't answer.

When Mark asked again, Eva noticed his plaintive tone and it made her realise how much he was relying on Les. How much they all were.

Softly, she said, 'Five more minutes, Mark? Perhaps Les could go outside? Chantae, d'you think?'

Mark admired the way Eva bundled Chantae and Les out the door, after knocking and persuading Anaru that Chantae needed one more smoke. She even forbade Dave from following. It was the way Maggie was with the girls—the same reassuring yet completely bossy tone. It was the ability to both deflect and address drama.

DOWNSTAIRS, CHANTAE LIT up, while Les stood stiffly by the wooden gates.

'Didn't you hear the judge say that, Sandwich-man?'

He looked at her for the first time since he'd realised. 'Did he? Did he tell us that?'

He hadn't believed Mark; he'd confirmed again with Anaru that there were no transcripts being hurriedly typed up.

'I'm not sure when,' said Chantae, shaking her head, commiserating. 'But he did. It's all right, though, Les—you've got all your notes, and pages and pages of transcripts already.'

'I thought I didn't need to make notes on the closings. It wasn't like with the witnesses—their truth wasn't dependent on expression or demeanour. The lawyers' tones are mere puffery, distraction. All I needed was the substance.'

'Les, you're the guy who gets it the most. We need your help now.'

'I've made a dreadful mistake,' said Les softly.

Chantae couldn't help but smile; she took a quick drag on the cigarette. 'Those lawyers' korero, their talks, you'll remember what you need.'

'Yes,' said Les suddenly. 'I've a good memory. If we go back right now, Chantae, I can write notes—I can probably recall eighty per cent.'

She caught his arm; she could feel the bones through his shirt-sleeve. 'Les, they talked all yesterday.' She tried a slight laugh. 'We need to start deliberating.'

He didn't reply.

'You've got this.'

She stubbed out the cigarette and, dropping it into the metal container, looked at him expectantly; he returned a precise nod.

'All right, Sandwich-man, let's go sort these turkeys out.'

As they walked back up the stairs, Les said, 'I'll use point form.'

IN THE JURY room, Mark said to Susannah, 'Jeez. Could do without this.'

'It doesn't matter.' She pressed her fingers into the crook of his elbow for just a moment. 'You're the foreman.'

'I've got shit happening at work.' He had an impulse then to confess that he and Maggie were separated, but Jake interrupted.

'We need a method.'

'We've got one,' said Eva. 'We follow the judge's questions.'

'He told us to look at the game, at the charges for each round,' said Hayley.

Eva agreed; she was pleased that Hayley seemed willing to participate. Eva had deliberately sat next to her when they settled for lunch because she'd noticed, in Hayley's rare comments, her respect for the girls.

'True, we have to keep in mind the context of the Dice Game,' said Jake. Tilly had said that to him over breakfast after the radio report on the case. They hadn't discussed the evidence—just exchanged a few opinions.

As Les and Chantae came back in, Mark said, 'Okay, let's try again.'

Mark was a dick, thought Kahu. Chantae was right to call him Mr Big Man—he was a 'look at me', as Kahu's mum would say. Les was shaken, but Chantae had got him back into it, flicking through his notepad, and soon Kahu saw him writing, underlining, circling words; he didn't speak or look up.

'As I said, we'll go through each defendant, starting with Lee. I think he's the easiest,' said Mark.

'Most of Lee's charges are as a party, though,' said Jake.

'Yep,' said Mark.

'So, we can't decide those until we've decided if the principal boy's guilty of the offence,' said Jake.

'Okay,' said Mark, drawing the word out.

Chantae glanced at Les, but he was busy scrawling notes.

'So, matua, the boys can only be guilty as a party if we find the main person guilty of the crime, eh?' asked Kahu; he didn't think Mark had understood Jake's point.

Mark nodded hesitantly, his eyes on Les.

BETHANY WAS TRYING to take off her ring. When she pushed it up towards the knuckle, the flesh on her finger bunched up, so she wriggled it backwards and forwards, and all of a sudden it jerked free. The suddenness of the movement made people stare. She murmured, 'Oops,' and pushed it back onto her finger.

MARK SAID, 'JAKE, why don't you be scribe?' He tossed him the whiteboard marker; Jake fumbled the catch.

Mark flicked through the question trail. The judge had set out each charge almost like a flow diagram. 'So, the only offence Lee is charged with as principal is indecent assault,' he said finally. 'With Maia. Oh yes, remember? On the beanbag at the sixteenth birthday party.'

'That's the very last charge,' said Eva. No one replied, so she continued, 'There are six charges. The charges are each against a principal boy in the first instance and then the others are charged as parties.' Still no one spoke. 'There's Chris indecently assaulting Samara; Chris sexually violating Maia by forced oral sex; then Travis recording it, and he's pleaded guilty—but we have to decide on the others as parties. And then for the last round the rape charges against Jayz and Chris—and, finally, this indecent assault one against Lee.'

'Right,' said Mark. 'So, I'm looking at page seventeen of the question trail.'

'Seventeen!' said Dave.

'The judge set the charges out in the order of the game, so shouldn't we start at the beginning?' said Hayley.

'Yes,' said Eva.

Mark said, 'Jake, there's five questions on this page, so if you can write—'

'All for this one charge?' asked Susannah, still finding the page.

'First, "Are you sure Lee assaulted Maia by putting his hand inside her underwear and touching between her legs?"'

Eva glanced at Hayley; it was easier to let Mark take control for now. They had to pick their battles.

'I'm not going to fit all this,' said Jake, scrawling notes on the whiteboard.

'Once we've decided each charge, we can rub it off.'

'It's hardly an assault,' said Dave.

'Yeah, copping a feel,' said Scott.

'We only have to be sure the physical act happened. Remember, the judge said an assault can be an unwanted kiss,' said Eva. 'And that's the next question—was Maia consenting?'

'She didn't say anything,' said Susannah. 'How was Lee meant to know?'

'The judge covered that. Just because you're silent doesn't mean you're consenting.'

'Yeah, but she didn't push him away or get up.'

'She did. That's why she left,' said Eva irritably.

'Hold on,' said Mark. 'We've got to look at both sides of the story. Lee said he didn't do it. He said he put his arm around her, tried to kiss her, and when he realised it wasn't a go, he moved on. We don't have any actual evidence he put his hand up her skirt.'

'There's what Maia said,' said Hayley.

'Her testimony—that's evidence,' said Eva.

'Yes, but Lee said it didn't happen,' said Susannah.

'Didn't he get with Samara that night?' asked Mark.

'I think Tia,' said Kahu.

'Doesn't mean he didn't do anything with Maia,' said Chantae.

'So, did it actually happen?' said Jake, circling the first question.

Dave, who'd been chewing the end of his pen, tossed it onto the table. 'Jesus, this is only the first charge.'

Mark jumped in then, determined to reassure them. 'Look at the way the judge has written this question trail. We have to answer yes to every question for our verdict to be guilty, so we can also knock it out at any of these questions. As soon as we answer any question with a no, it's not guilty. So, listen—I'm jumping down to the fourth question—"Are you sure that the act of putting his hand inside Maia's underwear and touching between her legs (in the surrounding circumstances) is indecent to right-thinking members of society?" That's us.' He pointed around the table. 'We're the right-thinking people. This was part of the last case I was on. So even if Lee felt Maia up, and I'm not saying he did, in the circumstances it's not indecent, is it? I mean, they were in private. Alone. It wasn't daytime. It was a party, just normal fooling around, kids "hooking up"—that's what you guys call it, isn't it?' He sought buy-in from Kahu, but the boy didn't answer.

'It is about the context,' said Jake.

'So, you're saying if a stranger stuck their hand up your skirt on the bus it's indecent,' said Chantae slowly, 'but at a party . . .'

'You mean, 'cos she'd kissed him and stuff,' said Dave.

'I don't think she did . . .' started Eva.

'It doesn't seem criminal, like something you should go to jail for, eh?' said Chantae.

Dave said, 'Kahu, d'you think that's indecent, like at a party? Would your friends?'

They all looked at him. 'I think it's hard for guys, but . . .'

Susannah interrupted. 'It's not Kahu's friends who decide, it's us, and I think, at a party, it would have to be extreme to be indecent.'

'If he'd forced himself on her, that's different, but seeing as he was just giving it a go,' agreed Dave.

'He wanted to hook up with her, but, I dunno, sticking his hand up her skirt seems . . .' Kahu let the rest of his sentence fall away, as Mark talked over him.

'And look, the next question—he has to have *intended* to act indecently. I just think there's no way. Lee certainly didn't *intend* anything indecent.'

'This charge is more for people jumping out and exposing themselves, isn't it.' Susannah's tone didn't make it sound like a question.

'Wanking in public,' said Dave.

'Something perverse,' said Jake.

'So we're agreed?' said Mark.

'Yep,' said Scott.

'Don't we need to go round and vote?' asked Jake.

Les glanced up from his notepad. 'We need to vote on each question, for each charge, for each defendant.'

'That'll take all afternoon and all night,' said Susannah.

'So be it,' said Les determinedly.

'The thing is,' said Mark, holding up his hand, 'if we get rid of this charge against Lee, then we've got rid of all the party charges on it too. Actually, that's what we should put on the whiteboard, Jake: each charge against each defendant in a table, so we can put ticks or crosses.'

'Like a matrix,' said Jake.

'And after that discussion, I think we can just vote guilty or not guilty on this charge, since it's not serious, can't we?' said Mark. 'And if we don't agree, we can go through and vote question by question like Les suggested.'

No one argued; Les was busy writing.

'So, is everyone agreed Lee is not guilty?'

People said yes. Distractedly, Les glanced up before returning to his notes.

'Don't we need to count?' said Chantae.

'Depends if anyone says no,' said Mark. 'Anyone?'

Eva looked at Hayley. She was staring at her folded hands; they were trembling. This wasn't the time to fight. It was a minor charge.

'Excellent. And if it didn't happen, then the rest of them can't be party to it,' said Mark, and they watched as Jake wrote *Ind Ass Maia* in a column on the left, and then *NG* under each of the defendants' names.

'We're not saying it didn't happen, though, are we?' said Eva.

'LOOK, I THINK we can knock Lee off altogether,' said Mark. 'Because the thing is, he wasn't there when anything else happened.' He spoke quickly, excited now—he had this. He felt as if he was unfolding a map for the whole deliberation.

Dave agreed. 'Can't convict him when he wasn't even friggin' there.'

'He made it up.' Hayley's voice was almost a whisper.

'Made what up?'

'He did,' said Eva. 'The Dice Game—*Lee* started it.'

'They were all over the place about that,' said Scott.

'Lee didn't ever expect anyone to do anything illegal,' said Susannah. 'He said that.'

'Exactly,' said Mark.

'Did we believe him?' asked Kahu.

'We haven't actually decided anyone did anything non-consensual yet,' said Jake, pointing to the lines of empty boxes on his chart. He remembered now that Tilly had told him she took the minutes at school board meetings so she had control over what was recorded.

'Too true,' said Dave.

'Yeah,' said Scott.

Hayley opened her mouth and then shut it again.

'Well, let's put *NG* with a question mark next to all the party ones for Lee,' said Mark.

'We haven't discussed those charges yet,' said Eva, looking around.

No one answered.

'Or voted.' Eva needed Hayley to object now; Les to focus and insist on a proper process; Fiona to be here.

'I'll put question marks by them for now, Eva, all right?' Jake suggested they go next to the other indecent assault charge, Chris with Samara. He wrote it onto the board.

'Yeah, all right,' said Mark. 'So this is on . . . oh, page one.' He felt vindicated. They were on the right track, working as a team.

'Well, if the Maia one isn't illegal, doesn't it mean this one isn't either?' said Kahu. 'Chris was an idiot, but they were just messing round.'

'What's this one?' asked Chantae.

'Undoing her bikini top,' said Dave.

'Pulling down Samara's togs and touching her pubes in the lake—in public,' said Eva. 'Isn't that a factor? Like you said, Chantae?'

'D'you reckon it's a crime, though?'

'Are we sure Chris did touch Samara down there?' asked Kahu.

'Again, it's a he-said, she-said,' said Jake.

'Well, what did Travis say?' asked Dave. 'He witnessed it.'

'At the time Samara wasn't bothered, though, was she? She didn't shout out. The lawyer said she just kept partying and chatting up Lee,' said Jake.

'That was Chris's lawyer, don't forget,' said Eva.

'Yes, and Samara said she was upset,' said Chantae, flicking back through her notepad. 'It's her answers that are the evidence.'

'But as you said, Chantae, it's not a crime, is it? They pulled down Travis's shorts too,' said Susannah.

'They're not charged with that,' said Jake.

'Same difference, though,' said Susannah.

'Travis admitted he was yelling to Chris when he was chasing Samara, but he claimed he didn't see what Chris did to her because he was still on the raft,' said Chantae.

'I agree with Susannah. No one would think kids messing around in a lake was indecent. No "right-minded member of society",' said Mark firmly.

Hayley could visualise Lee's hand groping under Maia's skirt. She could feel the heat of fingers on her thigh. Could imagine Chris grabbing Samara.

'Chris was sleazy,' said Chantae.

'But not intentionally indecent,' said Mark.

'It was just a joke,' said Scott.

'Boys mucking around,' said Jake.

'Boys being boys,' said Dave.

'If it even happened,' said Mark.

'Yeah, true, girls make up this stuff, don't they?' said Dave. 'For attention.'

Hayley tried to imagine these comments as if they were contained within cartoon speech bubbles. In that way the words were held within a black circle. She visualised each bubble breaking away from their mouths and floating off into the room. Congregating up near the cream-painted ceiling.

Soon Jake had marked up all four defendants as not guilty on that charge too.

Eva felt the deliberation was slipping away. It was not that she vehemently disagreed yet; it was more that she couldn't see where in this process she would find any traction when she did want to argue.

'SO NOW WE move to the three serious charges,' said Mark. 'Now, I've thought about the best way to deal with these, because I suspect we won't all be on the same page. In my experience of negotiating, I find it's best if people don't get locked into positions early on, so I don't think we should try an initial vote yet. I think we should work through the judge's questions.'

Jake said, 'So you mean carry on as we have been?'

Kahu and Dave exchanged a smile.

'Exactly,' said Mark; he wasn't sure if Jake was being disingenuous. 'Jake, it's important our process is transparent.' Eva made a 'ha' noise, but Mark continued, 'So, the first serious one is Maia at the barbecue, and the principal charge is against Chris for oral, er, contact between his mouth and her . . . you know. So this would be sexual violation, *if* we think it's true.'

'And we have the video,' said Eva, determined to get in early, to carve out a handhold.

'And we have the video,' Mark repeated.

'So, hard evidence,' said Eva.

'Yes,' said Susannah. 'But we do need to be careful—what does it actually *prove*?'

'It proves it happened,' Mark insisted.

'The act,' said Les, looking up.

'Exactly, Les.' Mark nodded encouragingly, aware that several jurors looked eagerly towards Les because this was his first substantive contribution.

'So, Jake, that's the answer to the first of the judge's questions, the act—he did have sexual relations with that girl.' Mark laughed briefly, but no one responded. He pressed on, 'So, the next question is was she consenting, and the prosecution are saying Maia was inexperienced, hadn't drunk much before, was a virgin . . .'

'Perfect,' muttered Scott.

'The perfect victim?' asked Eva. 'You mean she's more credible because she's like that?'

Scott smirked. 'She was drunk, so she was probably all over it.'

'They got her drunk—Lee and Chris, at least,' said Eva.

'They offered her drinks,' said Mark. The tempering voice—that was more his role.

'Lots of drinks,' said Eva. 'They pushed her to drink.'

'But she didn't have to,' said Susannah. 'She chose to.'

'Susannah's right,' said Dave. 'She went there to get wasted. That's why she stayed over at a friend's.'

Chantae's voice was measured as she said, 'I believe her. From what we saw of Maia, there's just no way she'd have gone along with this unless she was off her face.'

'You mean intoxicated, Chantae?' asked Les seriously.

Susannah and Dave laughed.

'Totally out to it. And she's religious.'

'I believed her when she said, like, she's not even kissed a boy,' said Kahu.

'Yeah,' said Chantae.

'On the other hand, we have to remember she was obsessed with these boys,' said Susannah. 'That's why she went to the barbecue—and like Dave said, she lied to her parents about that, so can we trust her?'

'It certainly shows a propensity,' said Mark.

'She didn't like *Chris*, though,' said Eva. 'Anyway, so what? Even if she went to party with those boys, it doesn't mean she wanted to be violated.'

'She wouldn't have let Chris do *that* with the others watching. It's not . . . I mean, it's not *normal* unless you're so out of it you don't know what's happening,' said Chantae.

'Speaking from experience,' mumbled Scott, but over the top of him, Mark said, 'I agree that Maia was drunk, but remember one of the lawyers talked about the way alcohol makes people become disinhibited. Then they regret their actions when they're sober. Maybe that's what happened.'

Susannah said, 'It could have impacted her judgement. I mean, no disrespect, Chantae, but we don't actually know what Maia thinks is acceptable or normal. You know, you people . . .' She shrugged disarmingly. 'I'm not being racist, but look at, say, the teenage pregnancy rate among Māori girls . . .'

'I don't even know where to start.' Eva tried to keep her voice even. She was wondering how to convince them that just because Maia was drinking it didn't excuse what Chris did. That teenage pregnancy rates didn't necessarily equate with promiscuity. She wanted to say that she, too, had Māori ancestry, even though she didn't identify as Māori. She wanted to dissolve their categories and assumptions. Especially Susannah's. Since Eva had moved into Fiona's seat in the jury box, Susannah had assumed they were friends. Eva wanted this enforced closeness to be over.

Her brain whirred around what to say and how to say it without losing her cool, and then she tuned in again and they'd moved on—they were talking now about whether boys would ever voluntarily go down on a girl who was unconscious. What would be their motivation? This group of strangers were debating this as if it was an intellectual conundrum.

HAYLEY NOTICED THAT the more they spoke, the more the speech bubbles inflated, competing for space in the room, competing for air. And inside Hayley, sitting solid like a stone at the bottom of her stomach, was her own silence.

'AND NEITHER MAIA nor Amy were *actually* hurt. We do need to remember that,' said Mark.

'Yeah, it wasn't like a rape,' said Dave. 'Maia wasn't forced. No one was holding her down. Sexual violation is definitely too extreme. There was no violence.'

'Maia doesn't even remember,' said Susannah.

'She was unconscious,' said Kahu.

'So she says,' said Scott.

'She actually said, "mostly unconscious",' said Mark. 'What does that even mean?'

THE MORE THE words ballooned, the less room there was for Hayley, the less air there was above her, the more compacted she became, and the silence inside her grew.

They were discussing whether Maia was unconscious and the video, and the seconds when they could see her face. They were speaking about how her eyes had opened just for a moment, about a movement of her head as if she were taken aback.

'Shocked,' someone said.

'Conscious,' someone else said.

'If she was conscious, she could have fought or run away.'

Hayley couldn't get a breath. She must have made a noise, because Eva gave her arm a little rub. Hayley froze, muscles tensed.

Eva went to the sink and came back with two glasses of water. Hayley nodded and drank two big gulps before she realised her mistake as she felt the nausea rising. She took small gasps of air and forced herself to swallow back the lump in her throat.

JAKE SAID, 'EVEN if we agree Maia was not consenting, the last question we have to ask is if Chris reasonably believed she was consenting. But how would he know she didn't want it if she said nothing, and took no action to prevent him doing it?'

Chantae, flush-faced, muttered, ''Cos every girl's gonna want to be watched and videoed while some guy's doing that.'

'How can we expect her to take action to prevent it if she was mostly unconscious?' asked Kahu.

Mark thought Jake had jumped ahead. 'We need to prove she wasn't consenting first, and the thing is, if we saw her open her eyes, and her mouth move . . . and we did, didn't we?' He looked around, checking. 'Well, first off, see, it proves she was conscious—doesn't it?' Again, he sought buy-in. 'But look, even if—say you're right, Chantae, and it's shock at what was happening—well then, she could have shouted, "No," and made it clear she didn't want it, but who's to say . . . that look . . .' He shrugged. 'I mean, the thing is she could have been liking it.'

HAYLEY PLACED HER fingertip against her thumb and tried to envisage Lake Waikareiti, tried to hold the smoothness of its surface in her mind, but the picture rippled and warped.

'The big O,' said Scott, raising his eyebrows.

Hayley tried to visualise gradually submerging her body, the cool water on the arches of her feet as she stood on the stony beach. Water lapping her ankle bones, her calves, her thighs as she waded into the lake, about to dive right under, where the coldness would claim her breath. But she couldn't feel that. She could feel only the heavy silence inside her, taking up all the space, as she remembered the movement of Maia's mouth. She'd opened her mouth and it had stayed open, widening. They were discussing it as pleasure or shock, but Hayley could see what it was. Maia had been trying to scream, but her voice had betrayed her. Just as there was the tension of fight in her body without movement, and wild disconnection in her eyes.

'It was a scream.'

They spoke back at once.

Chantae said, 'A scream?'

Gently, Kahu said, 'Hayley, there was no scream on the video.'

Derisively, Mark said, 'No one testified she screamed. Not even Maia herself.'

Hayley couldn't explain, but she knew how that sound could turn back inside you, and reverberate, and fill every moment and stop every thought, so there was only the noiseless sound inside. And the shame.

'LOOK, I THINK we need to take stock,' said Jake. 'In light of the video, we know Chris did that to Maia—that's the judge's first question.' He pointed at the board.

'Agreed,' said Mark. 'Keep going, Jake.'

'Well, the next question is: was Maia consenting? Ultimately that comes down to whether she's credible. Do we believe her?'

Eva watched as Hayley stood up. She assumed Hayley was going to the toilet, but instead Hayley gripped the edge of the table, looking around, as if searching for an escape.

'You all right?' Kahu asked her.

'Hayley?' said Eva, but she didn't respond.

Shakily, Hayley moved to the corner of the room and, to Eva's astonishment, she sat on the floor, her back against one wall, her side against the other, and she turned her face away from them, towards the wall.

Everyone stopped talking. Susannah whispered something

to Mark. Ignoring her, Eva went to Hayley and bent down. She didn't touch her this time. She crouched by her, waiting.

In a voice all tight and scrunched up, Hayley said, 'Just let me be here.'

Eva understood that Hayley was attempting to control her emotions, and so she nodded and slowly returned to her seat, pushing back her chair so she could keep checking on her.

Mark silently gestured to Eva, hands turned up, and Eva responded with a waving-on motion, as she said, 'We all need to respect everyone's opinions, and how difficult this is.'

There was a reassuring chorus then, and Jake said they were all in this waka together, but Susannah's voice trembled. 'No, it's too difficult. We shouldn't be expected to do all this. It's too many charges and the evidence is so . . . graphic. Three weeks of this, it's not surprising if people aren't coping. I haven't had a proper night's sleep—'

'At least it's not murder,' said Dave.

Kahu looked over at Hayley and thought that while they were here trying to find consensus as a team, they were each also alone with this responsibility. 'Do we need to tell the judge?' he asked Eva.

'I don't think so,' she said. 'Not yet anyway.'

'We can't,' Les said. 'With Fiona having been dismissed, there are only eleven of us. I think he'd be forced to declare a mistrial if another juror couldn't continue.'

'Yeah, that'd be right,' said Mark. 'You can have a majority verdict, but it has to be eleven to one, so we can't do that.'

Chantae turned the pages of her pad. 'I thought the judge said we could—'

'So, we have to reach full unanimity?' interrupted Jake.

Mark stumbled over an answer. Susannah said they might as well deal with that if it came to it.

'Let's just keep moving,' said Dave.

Jake said, 'Well, what I was saying is we need to decide if Maia's credible—'

'Hold on,' said Mark. 'I think we should take a vote right now on the Maia and Chris charge as a whole. If we agree, it's all over, red rover.'

'The charge of Chris sexually violating Maia,' said Chantae firmly.

'Like I said.'

'No, what you said made it sound like she did it too.'

'Oh my God,' said Scott.

'Anyways, I thought you said we shouldn't vote?' said Chantae, which made Mark raise his voice.

'I'm foreman. And we're going to vote.'

Chantae and Eva exchanged a glance. Les said, 'I've cut some paper.'

'No,' said Mark firmly. 'Let's just do a show of hands.' He looked around; no one made eye contact. He wasn't sure anymore that he had this in him—there was too much stuff going on in his life. 'At least it'll give us a starting point.' His tone was pleading now.

No one argued.

'Those who think Chris is guilty on this charge, raise their hands.'

'Surely we need to go through each of the judge's questions,' said Les.

'It's just indicative,' said Mark. 'Who thinks guilty?'

'Well, I do. I don't think Maia was consenting, and I think they knew that,' said Eva. She looked around. 'Hayley?'

Hayley lifted her hand. After a moment Chantae raised hers and Kahu followed.

'All right, that's four guilty,' said Mark. 'And those who think not guilty?'

He raised his own hand, and immediately Bethany followed, then Susannah, Scott and Dave.

'Jake?' said Mark, as Les said, 'I abstain. We need to work through the judge's questions systematically with the evidence.'

'I, er, yeah—I agree with Les. I'm thinking probably not guilty, but I need to work through the questions,' said Jake.

'Whatever,' said Mark, and he pushed back his chair and told them they were having a break as he headed for the toilet. He wished he had his phone so he could call Maggie to check on Ruby.

WHILE THE OTHERS settled back down, Mark remained standing at the end of the table. They were all looking up at him, waiting for him to sort out their impasse, and he was sick of it, sick of them, sick of being foreman, CEO, dad. He wanted to go under the radar, set down the load he was carrying. He wished he was in the garden with the girls or making a sheet fort in the living room with them bossing him around. But he would have to sort this mess out first.

'So the question we're stuck on is: was Maia consenting? Eva, why don't you tell us why you're so sure she wasn't?'

Eva looked at Chantae, debating whether to raise Mark's aggressive tone. Instead, she said, 'Well, there's Chantae's point—who would want to do that in front of Jayz and Travis? And there's Maia's testimony. I found her very credible—she was clearly traumatised.'

'On the police interview, eh?' said Kahu.

'Yeah, true, because she wasn't upset when she was testifying live,' said Chantae, remembering the flatness of the girl's answers. 'She was kinda weird then.'

'I thought we weren't meant to take that into account,' said Jake. 'Her demeanour.'

There was bickering and disagreement; people had different recollections of what the judge had said. Eva tried to explain about the effects of trauma.

'I reckon she was hamming it up on the police video—she was just about hysterical,' said Scott. 'And she wouldn't look at the camera.'

'To be fair, that was when she first saw the video, Scott,' said Dave.

Mark called a halt. 'Let's all go round and say what we think happened that night.'

'You mean like in real life, not the law questions?' said Chantae.

'Yes,' said Mark. 'Susannah?'

'Why do I have to start? All right, well, I do think *something* happened. With both Maia and Amy—'

Eva cut her off. '*Something* happened?'

'Yeah, something bad, but—'

'It's so hard, isn't it?' interrupted Jake. 'These cases are just he-said, she-said. I mean, it's different if it's murder—we know what's happened then, someone's dead.'

'It didn't just *happen*,' said Eva. 'If something bad happened, what you're saying is *someone* did *something*. You can't ignore the culprit. And we know what happened and who did it because we saw the video.' Eva was aware that Les was watching her with that eagerness she'd noticed before when something caught his imagination—only, with Les, it wasn't his imagination, it was something far more methodical, banal even.

Les nodded. 'So, what you're saying, Eva, is that Susannah's leaving out the subject?'

'Yes. But a meaningful verb too—what the culprit did. That passive language just takes away the meaning. And the responsibility.'

'So the verb would be—to assault.'

'To assault, to rape, to violate, to force oral sex on her.'

'I don't even know what you two are on about,' said Mark.

'It supposedly started with me,' Susannah said with an outraged laugh.

Eva replied, 'What I'm saying, Susannah, is that when you say, "Something bad happened," you're saying it in a way that's designed to protect the defendant and to pacify me, or Maia, or Amy—all of us. It's a cop-out. What you really mean is you think Chris sexually assaulted Maia, but you don't want to take responsibility for saying that, so instead you're gonna say, "Something bad happened," and rely on this amorphous standard of proof as a way out of attributing criminal responsibility.'

'Whā waho,' said Kahu, stifling a laugh.

'You go, girl,' said Chantae.

'What're you on?' said Scott.

Dave stared.

Bethany had broken the last oval biscuit into little pieces, and was placing it back together like a jigsaw. She didn't like it when they argued. She wanted them all to be clear, so she knew what to do.

Kahu suddenly said, 'Yeah, I get it, Eva. I've got a mate who always starts his stories with, "Something bad's happened." His car got pranged. He got fired from his job at the bakery. Got kicked out of home. I get it now.'

'Get what?' asked Chantae impatiently.

Kahu blushed. 'Like, those things don't just happen—he causes them. Saying it like that just means he doesn't have to . . . take the blame.'

Les was stuck on the last clause of Eva's argument. That 'amorphous standard of proof'. He could see what she meant, but it was an issue. A live and kicking issue. He said, 'Beyond a reasonable doubt—we need to talk about what exactly that means.'

He heard Eva harrumph; she would think he was distracting them from her point.

'For each element we have to be "sure", that's what the judge said. It's not absolute certainty; we can never know the one hundred per cent absolute truth,' said Eva.

'Yes,' said Les. 'But we need to quantify how sure—'

They spoke over the top of each other until Les held up his hand and asked them to talk one at a time. Susannah said reasonable doubt wasn't a mathematical percentage. Mark's point was that 'sure' was enough, but that it highlighted that they needed texts or DNA evidence from Amy, something concrete as proof—they couldn't just rely on someone's word.

'Actually, we can,' said Jake. 'The judge said that. Remember, Mark, when he was talking about credibility.'

'Yes, matua, because he said you didn't need that corroboration thing, eh?' said Kahu.

There was some discussion then, because Les and Mark also remembered the judge saying that one way to test a witness's credibility was if their story was consistent with texts, or other evidence.

Dave yawned. 'We're gonna be here all friggin' night.'

'And so be it,' said Les again.

'I DO THINK they planned it all out,' said Kahu slowly, forty minutes later. 'When Chris threw a one for going down on Maia, he knew how hard that was gonna be, so he wanted to get her drunk, eh? Travis told us Chris said that. And then he and Jayz took her upstairs. Remember the way Travis said they told him to start recording—he knew what he was meant to do.' Kahu glanced around the table. 'It was all pre-planned, don't you think?'

'Yeah,' said Dave. 'That's why it shocked Travis when Chris said it was his turn. That wasn't part of the Dice Game. Travis hadn't thrown a one.'

'I don't think that's why,' said Jake. 'I think Travis was freaked out. He didn't think Chris would be able to do that with Maia.' Jake wondered then how much influence TJ's friends had over him.

'Yes, matua, remember when Travis suggested that going down on them be part of the game, he said it was so someone else would fail too,' said Kahu.

''Cos he didn't know they'd get her coma'd first,' said Chantae.

'I don't think we can prove that. We don't know they did that. Do we? Les?' asked Mark.

Les flicked back through his notes, and for a moment Mark thought he'd drifted into his own analysis again, but then he opened the transcript. He said the page number, even though the other copy was still sitting untouched in the middle of the table. 'Lee admitted giving her at least one drink, although he did say he was pouring drinks for lots of people.' Les turned to his notepad. 'Now, in the defence closing submissions for Jayz and Chris—and this is only my recollection, so correct me if I'm wrong—both lawyers said effectively the boys didn't get her drunk, but . . . there's an answer . . . Yes. I've noted that Maia said Lee poured her drinks—plural.'

'Which isn't what Lee said,' said Kahu, while Dave objected, 'We've finished Lee.'

Les glanced up. 'We haven't decided anything yet.' He went back to his notes. 'And Maia said she thought Chris was nice to begin with, because he *kept* finding her "vodka cruisers" when she refused to drink beer. And if you remember, Caleb said the reason he pulled out of the game was because Chris said they would get the girls drunk if necessary.'

'I thought he pulled out because of his girlfriend,' said Dave.

Eva said, 'Caleb told us Chris said they had to do what they threw on the dice *no matter what*, so he would have been willing to force her.'

'And it was him who took her upstairs,' said Kahu.

'Just being nice again,' said Chantae. 'But you know it was Jayz too. It was the two of them together. Remember, even Travis said that.'

'So, you think it was all a set-up?' asked Susannah.

'Oh my God, yes,' said Eva. 'Of course it was a set-up. We know that they made up the Dice Game to treat girls like crap, to sexually assault them.'

Hayley lifted her head.

'That's a huge overstatement,' said Jake. 'It was teenage boys on a bus being dumb. A mistake. I don't think they foresaw where it could lead. At least, not Lee and Travis. Bad judgement, I agree, but . . .'

'It depends, to some degree, on whether you believe it came from *The Dice Man*,' said Les.

'Is that the book?' asked Kahu. 'Sorry, matua, but I didn't get what the difference was, if they read it in a book or saw it on TV.'

'It was a red herring,' said Mark confidently.

Les disagreed. 'I understood the point to be that because the book talked about raping the woman downstairs, they knew from the beginning they were going to carry out the challenges whether or not the girls consented.'

'It fits with what Caleb said about Chris,' said Eva.

'Chris was definitely the most . . . sleazy,' said Chantae.

'. . . dangerous,' said Susannah at the same time.

Mark felt it was time for some reality-checking. 'I'm concerned that there's a bit of mass hysteria here, because of politics—the Me Too bandwagon and all that. And the judge said we can't allow prejudice to influence us. I just wonder if the way the police interviewed these girls stirred it all up. Maia didn't even complain until after Amy . . . and the prosecution have formulated this elaborate story that everything comes back to the Dice Game. I mean, Maia wanted to be with those boys, she was very drunk, and she doesn't even know what happened. So how *reliable* is she, even if we think she's credible?'

'True,' said Dave, nodding.

'But you're not saying she made it all up?' said Susannah, suddenly annoyed. 'We saw the video. You said that yourself. And the police went to her when they found the video.'

'But she can't remember . . .'

'If she can't remember, how bad can it be?' said Dave.

'So, if someone gets hit over the head with a hammer and they can't remember, it didn't happen?' said Susannah, surprised at her own irritation.

'That's not what we're saying,' said Mark.

'It kinda is,' said Eva, nodding to Susannah.

'If someone gets hit over the head, they've got a bloody great dent,' said Scott. 'Maia just got . . . licked.' He laughed, as Kahu gasped and Chantae glared.

'That's disgusting,' snapped Susannah. 'Scott, these are girls, sixteen-year-old girls.'

'I'm just saying. It's on a bit of a different level, isn't it?'

'They videoed her naked. They put it on their group chat. They humiliated and shamed her.' Chantae's voice was a low growl.

'But she went to the party and got drunk,' said Mark. 'And she went upstairs with Chris . . .'

'To a bedroom. What did she expect?' said Dave, shrugging.

Hayley, still sitting against the wall, drew up her legs and bowed her head.

Eva didn't see that, though. 'Listen,' she said, 'imagine at school there's a kid who keeps hitting other children over the head with a hammer, and imagine if the teacher told the other children to stay away from the woodwork table so they won't get hit, and maybe wear a helmet all day too. That's what you're saying. Girls need to not get drunk or go upstairs with boys, in case they "accidentally" get raped.'

'Or licked,' said Scott.

Dave laughed, shaking his head at him.

'For God's sake,' shouted Eva.

'Yeah, I think that is unnecessary, Scott,' said Mark; Scott was undermining their argument.

Les said, 'Travis admitted Maia didn't move when he came into the bedroom.'

'So she was unconscious,' said Eva.

'Now, what's also interesting—'

'Interesting?' said Chantae.

'—important,' said Les, 'is that there's a conflict in the evidence here, because Maia's parents' testimony was that from the day after the barbecue, she was quiet and withdrawn and didn't want to see her friends or go to school. But Maia's saying she was really drunk, wasn't conscious and doesn't remember anything. That's a significant inconsistency.'

'But what about that sea bit, where Maia thought she was under the water? Remember that, Les?' said Chantae.

Les frowned; Chantae was relying on him, but he'd read so much and he couldn't recall anything about the sea. He gave a shake of his head and started skimming his notes.

Chantae, too, flicked back, wondering how to find that reference in all the pages and pages of notes she'd written.

Mark said, 'What the parents say suggests Maia knew what was happening, so she probably just woke up the next day and regretted her drunk actions of getting it on with Chris in front of the others.'

Eva could hear the triumph in his voice.

'An older guy,' said Jake.

'Bit dodgy,' said Mark.

'And she's religious,' said Dave.

'So she made up being unconscious?' said Susannah, her tone disbelieving.

'As a way of avoiding responsibility for her actions,' Mark explained. 'It's not uncommon.'

'Oh, here we go,' said Chantae.

'You can say that, Chantae, but girls, women, they do make up these kinds of allegations. Everyone knows that,' said Mark.

Jake agreed. 'And as one of the lawyers said, having claimed it was forced, the whole allegation might have got out of control—you know, with the police being called. At that point, it's very hard for the girls to go back on what they said.'

'I s'pose she might have been embarrassed because of the video—one thing to get with him, but doesn't mean you want a video going round,' said Dave.

With a sense of dread, Eva said, 'The not-knowing, it might not be straightforward.'

Kahu, his cheeks reddening, interrupted. 'Remember when her friends took her home and, like, she went to the toilet and realised she had no undies on.'

'I think it was when she woke up,' said Chantae.

'Doesn't mean she wasn't into it,' said Scott.

'Couldn't that explain why she was upset?' Kahu looked at Eva. 'Because she knew they did something to her, but she didn't know what?'

Eva nodded. She couldn't say any more right now.

'That's true, Kahu,' said Jake, frowning. 'So does that explain your inconsistency with her parents' evidence, Les?'

'There is more evidence on Maia's state, here,' said Les, tapping the transcript. 'In cross-examination, the prosecutor asked Travis, "When you saw Maia being taken home by her friends, how did she seem?" And he said, "Wasted," and when the prosecutor asked him to clarify, he said, "She was very drunk—they were practically carrying her."'

In her notes, Chantae had finally found the page number of the quote she wanted. As she started to search for it in the second copy of the transcript, Jake told her there was an index at the back; without looking up, Chantae rolled her eyes.

Les read out the interchanges between the prosecutor and Travis about how Maia had reacted when he videoed her. He changed his voice to help them identify which speaker was which, and that caught Bethany's attention and she stared at Les.

Then Chantae said she'd found Maia's answer that she was looking for, and she read it out to them. '"I couldn't move my arms or legs . . . I couldn't hear what was happening. And then every so often I would burst through . . . back to being there, desperately trying to stay conscious, trying to tell him to leave me alone, but they'd just push me back down and I'd sink under the surface and the noises would be muffled . . . and I couldn't move." So to be going in and out of consciousness like that she must have been really drunk.'

For a moment there was a silence, before Eva said, 'Mark, can we go back to the questions now, one by one?'

Mark nodded, wondering how many other people weren't sure exactly where they were up to. 'Jake?'

Jake stood and pointed at the board. 'We know the act happened, we saw the video. So, the next question is, are we sure Maia wasn't consenting—'

Eva interjected. 'This is where the judge talked about being too intoxicated to consent. It's on page three of the question trail.'

Several people turned to the page.

Eva's voice was strong now. 'I remember this well. So, we don't have to decide if she was conscious or not, because we've heard evidence from various witnesses that she was very intoxicated. So she was incapable of consenting—that's part of the definition. Does everyone agree?'

'I agree, she was totally out of it,' said Kahu.

'Me too,' said Chantae.

Hayley looked up, raising her hand, checking around the room.

'Yep, she was pissed,' said Dave, at the same time as Scott said, 'All right, he had his evil way.'

Mark said, 'Fair enough, guilty, but only Chris.'

He asked Bethany then and she nodded, her eyes on Mark.

Jake said, 'Yes, I agree. Les?'

'I agree that Maia was either unconscious or too intoxicated to consent.'

Eva realised then that most of them had conflated the last two questions. Les knew, but, bizarrely, it seemed to her, he wasn't focusing on their process; he was too busy picking over the details of the evidence. She doubted Hayley would thank her for it, but, wearily, she said, 'That's not the determination of guilt, Mark. We still have to do the last question.'

'Shit,' said Mark.

'Oh, you're right, Eva,' said Jake.

'You forgot me too,' said Susannah. 'But I guess I'm with you so far.'

'Thank fuckin' God,' said Dave. 'Let's have a break.'

'No,' said Jake. 'We have to answer the last question: are we sure that Chris did not believe that Maia was consenting? And his belief has to be reasonable.'

Dave got up. There was barely any room between the backs of people's chairs and the window, but he squeezed through anyway, and stared out past the corner of the brick pub, to the line of trees by the car park and through their foliage to the hills beyond.

Susannah was complaining that because Chris hadn't testified how could they know what he believed? And Les was moaning about not having a transcript of Chris's lawyer's closing. Dave pushed his forehead against the window. On the hill there was a clear line where the native bush had been replaced by the orderly rows of pines.

Les said, 'Of course the closing speeches are just arguments, not evidence, but Chris's lawyer said he and Maia got together *downstairs* in the kitchen. He said it was *Maia* who suggested they go to the bedroom, but that wasn't put to Maia by Chris's lawyer, I checked that before lunch. So it's not very reliable.' Les looked around the table to ensure they'd all understood.

Chantae said, 'You're a bloody legend, Les. Keep going.'

'But Chris's lawyer also argued something like, "It would be unusual for a boy to give oral pleasure to a girl who was not conscious. It wouldn't be physically pleasuring him, so what motivation would he have?" That's how I remember it anyway. So that suggests Chris might have believed she was consenting.'

'Yes, Les. I remember that,' said Mark.

'We've discussed this,' said Dave.

'Because that's what he shook,' said Hayley, her voice muffled because her head was tipped forwards again.

'Yes,' cried Eva.

Dave turned to look at the woman sitting on the ground in the corner and he nodded. 'Hayley's right; there's his motive—that's what he shook.'

Eva said, 'That's why we have to remember the context of what they were doing the whole time. Of the Dice Game.'

Les continued, 'So Chris's lawyer said they were together in the room when Jayz and Travis burst in and started videoing, and Chris said, "Turn it off."'

'But that's not true, matua,' said Kahu, his face getting hot. 'That's a lie. Remember on the video, before he speaks, Chris looks up at them—he's grinning, not cross. He was happy when he realised they were videoing. And he said something else before he said "turn".'

'What d'you mean?'

'On the video, what Chris said was "something turn", and the prosecutor said it was, "Your turn."'

'We could ask to watch it again, I suppose,' said Mark.

'God, no,' said Susannah.

Jake said, 'So I think we've got two versions of events or even three. Either Maia was with Chris consensually, but freaked out when she saw the video, regretted it, and then made up the allegation.' Jake paused; Eva stared. 'Or they got together and Chris didn't realise how intoxicated Maia was and thought she was consenting.' Again, he let that sink in. 'Or—your version, Eva—that Maia was too drunk to consent, but knew afterwards something bad had happened, and Chris knew she wasn't consenting because it was all planned.' When he saw Eva nodding, Jake felt almost excited as he added, 'But remember, the judge said that if different versions are believable, we have to go with the one that makes the boys innocent. That's the presumption of innocence.'

'If the alternatives are reasonable,' said Les.

'They're all reasonably *possible*, aren't they?' said Mark.

'You think? Really? Even with Travis's testimony?' asked Eva. She looked at Chantae. 'Do you?' Then she turned to Susannah, and Kahu.

'I think she might of been embarrassed,' said Bethany.

There was a pause. No one spoke.

'Eh?' said Bethany. 'I reckon she was embarrassed. I would've been.'

Very gently, Les said, 'Embarrassed because she was having consensual sexual relations with Chris and they came in and videoed, or embarrassed because she wasn't consenting and he forced her?'

'Both. I think she was embarrassed 'cos of both,' said Bethany.

'RIGHT,' SAID MARK. 'We vote again now. Could Chris have reasonably believed Maia was consenting?'

Susannah, Mark, Scott, Dave, Bethany, Jake and Les raised their hands.

'And just to be thorough,' said Jake, ignoring Mark's glare, 'who thinks Chris didn't believe she was consenting?'

Eva, Hayley, Kahu and Chantae raised their hands.

Mark said, 'Actually, I'm changing my vote on whether Maia was consenting—I think that's reasonably possible too.'

'Yeah, me too,' said Scott.

'So, we've been going for . . . over three hours,' said Dave. 'And we haven't got any-fucking-where.'

Jake had sat down during the discussion, but now he was back at the whiteboard writing *7NG 4G* under that charge. 'We have. Look, let's just decide about them making the video. So, we know

Travis pleaded guilty—did the others assist or encourage him?' He pointed to the other squares along the line of that charge.

'Can't we have a smoke first?' said Chantae.

'No,' said Mark. He was irritated with Jake for taking the lead. 'We need to decide this while the incident is in our heads.' He turned the pages of the question trail.

'Well, Jayz helped. He went and got Travis and he knew he was videoing. He stepped to the side when he opened the door,' said Eva. When no one argued she carried on. 'And Chris knew. He planned it all.'

'Didn't he say turn it off?' said Scott.

'We've talked about this,' said Dave. 'We're going in circles.'

'Chris was grinning; he wasn't telling them to turn it off,' said Kahu. 'I go guilty.'

'Fine,' said Mark.

Within twenty minutes they'd agreed on guilty verdicts for Chris and Jayz as parties to making the video, but most insisted Lee was not guilty because he wasn't there.

EVA SUGGESTED HAYLEY come downstairs while they had a break, but she shook her head, and she refused a hot drink too. She said she just wanted to stay where she was. Her voice was calm, but Eva felt bad leaving her alone. Surprisingly, it was Dave who came and said he would tag team Eva so she could go outside. Eva couldn't recall having seen Hayley and Dave speaking during the trial, but she supposed she'd had no reason to notice.

Downstairs, Susannah was thinking about transitions. She'd always liked the moment filmmakers paused at. The moment of hesitation before a relationship became sexual. While Jon watched tennis, golf or cricket, Susannah watched films. Films where men kissed women up against walls, or while they were dancing, while they were leaving, while they were saying not to but didn't mean it, because then they kissed them back. She'd watched women touching men's arses, undoing their shirts, holding grabbing clutching crying. She remembered films from her childhood when women slapped men who kissed them, and then kissed them back and married them. And now she watched TV programs where the first kiss was rapidly followed by breathless undressing, by immediate and welcomed penetration.

Now, in the middle of the deliberation, she thought that from her own early sexual fumblings there was another transition—on one side you were doing stuff, wanting the stuff, and on the other side stuff was being done to you. It probably wasn't black and white, a sharply defined door to pass through, but rather a blurring, until suddenly you knew you were on the other side.

Susannah tried to describe this to Eva, who at first wanted only to discuss Hayley, but then she seemed to pick up what Susannah meant.

'Yes, like there's a point when you've lost agency? When you become the object, rather than one of the subjects?'

Susannah hated it when Eva intellectualised the whole thing.

'Of course, sometimes having stuff done to you is sexy,' continued Eva. 'Really, it comes back to what we were arguing about before the summing-up. There has to be consent at the time the act in question is happening—active and ongoing consent—that's the key.'

As they went back inside, Eva started talking about Hayley again, and then she said she wished they still had Fiona.

'I saw her,' said Susannah. 'Did I tell you? Last weekend. She was at a Thai restaurant we went to, with a big group of women.'

Eva asked how she was, but Susannah hadn't actually spoken to her. She had kept watching Fiona, though, watching how she enthralled the ladies around her, how she passed dishes down the table and immediately became engrossed in new conversations, and how she hadn't even noticed Susannah and Jon at the window table, each eating their own curry.

PEOPLE WERE DRAGGING the chain coming back. Mark could understand it, but they had no choice, and the quicker they got on with it the quicker they'd be out of here. He announced that they would approach the Amy charges by discussing what they thought had happened, before they went through the judge's questions, and he launched in while people were still settling themselves. 'It was at the sixteenth party. We know Amy went onto the trampoline of her own accord and she's not claiming she was paralytic, like Maia.'

'Yeah, Amy definitely can't say that because she claims to remember it all,' said Dave.

'I think the boys went to that sixteenth party specifically to carry out their Dice Game challenges on Amy and Maia,' said Eva. 'They didn't know the girl whose birthday it was. And remember, Chris, Jayz and Travis all shook Amy . . .'

'Was that proved?' said Dave.

'Didn't Amy invite them?' asked Jake.

'It was an allegation,' said Les.

'Which Amy denied,' said Chantae.

'It's inconsequential,' said Eva. 'No one's denying Amy wanted to be with Jayz.'

'I think Jayz liked Amy too,' said Kahu.

'Do we know what Travis had to do to Amy? What did he shake, Les?' asked Mark.

'Travis went and got Amy, eh?' asked Chantae, while Les leafed through his notes.

'Yep, and she got on the trampoline by herself with those older boys,' said Susannah.

Something made Jake think about his daughter, Annelyse, then. It was easy to think this was all irrelevant to her because she was only fifteen, but in a few years she would potentially be out there at parties mixing with kids like this.

'And they took something,' said Kahu. 'Ecstasy, right?' Kahu had only ever smoked dope a couple of times—he wasn't gonna stuff up his body.

'Yeah, MDMA. Molly,' said Mark.

'Which Chris brought specifically for Amy,' said Eva.

'What would it do?' asked Kahu.

Mark said, 'Makes you feel happy, relaxed, maybe more into stuff.'

'Stuff?' said Chantae.

Jake hadn't realised schoolkids in Rotorua would have anything but dope. At least, not the ones that weren't gang kids.

'Okay, so she's on the trampoline, and they're drinking, and she's taken the E. What next—that they all agree on?' asked Mark.

'She kissed Jayz and Chris.'

'And they set that up,' said Eva. 'I agree she was consenting at that point, but everything you've described so far was pre-planned. Remember the texts about divide and conquer and the molly?'

'Fair enough,' said Dave, and a few others nodded.

'And those texts from Jayz persuading Amy to send the nude pic—they show how much power he had over her,' said Jake. The idea of Annelyse sexting terrified him.

'She was into it at that point,' said Susannah.

'All over it,' said Scott.

'To begin with,' said Eva. 'But this is what Susannah and I were discussing this morning. She has to be consenting at the point of intercourse. You can stop consenting at any time.'

Susannah nodded. 'So Chris gets them lying down looking at the stars and Amy agreed to that.'

'And that's when they start upping the ante,' said Jake.

'Remember the way she talked about them taking off her bra, together, as if it was all planned? It was so creepy.' Chantae looked around, seeking affirmation.

Mark said, 'I remember what *she* said, but she was high.'

'The problem is, matua, we don't know what they're saying,' said Kahu.

Mark looked blank.

'Because neither Jayz nor Chris testified, eh?'

'We've heard it from their lawyers, though,' said Mark.

'Which is not evidence,' said Les.

'I agree with Kahu,' said Jake. 'I'd rather have heard it from the horse's mouth.'

'Yeah, but we didn't,' said Mark. 'Anyway, they've got her between them, and Jayz starts undoing her jeans. So, from the defence arguments, they're both saying she was into it, and was kissing and touching them both.'

'They said she was wet,' said Scott.

No one spoke.

'She came,' said Scott.

Kahu started to doodle on his pad. Chantae drank out of her cup. Susannah scratched her eyebrow.

Mark sighed. 'That was an allegation.'

'Actually,' said Les, 'remember the judge said the answer is the evidence, not the question. I can check, but I don't think Amy ever said she had an orgasm.'

'I think it was bullshit,' said Eva.

Les frowned. 'There was also the doctor's testimony about arousal non-concordance.'

Mark asked him to remind them, and Les explained as best he could. 'Ultimately, I think the doctor was saying you can have a genital response of arousal without it meaning that you wanted or desired the sexual experience. Like a disconnect between your body and mind. I would never have known that.'

'Isn't this your field, Eva?' asked Susannah.

'Yeah, it sounds right. Physical reactions occur to external stimuli that trigger—'

'Like Pavlov's dog?' blurted Kahu.

'What the . . .' said Dave.

Kahu started to explain, but Mark interrupted. 'Okay, I don't think we need a psychology lesson. We're getting off track. But effectively what we're talking about is the first question: do we agree intercourse between Jayz and Amy took place on the trampoline, and then between Chris and Amy? So what's our *actual* evidence to prove penetration?'

'Yeah, why didn't the pigs do DNA from inside of her?' said Dave.

'They let us down,' said Scott.

'But there are the texts, and messages,' said Kahu.

'Wait, I think there's a misunderstanding,' said Les.

'Yes, I think so,' said Mark.

'They've all agreed that the intercourse took place. We've discussed this. Jayden denied it in the first police interview, but then admitted he'd lied.'

'Which the judge told us not to take into account,' said Mark.

'We just can't assume it means he's definitely guilty—' Eva started, but Les interrupted.

'Nor are we allowed to make an inference from the fact they didn't testify.'

'What does that even mean?' asked Chantae.

'We can't hold it against them that they didn't testify. It's for the prosecutor to prove guilt.'

'But if you were totally innocent, you'd tell your side, wouldn't you?' said Kahu. 'And you wouldn't tell the police you hadn't had sex.'

'Sorry, Kahu, but I think that's exactly what we're not meant to assume,' said Jake. 'Look, Jayz and Chris agree penetration happened, so that's the first question ticked. So the issue is these last two questions—was Amy consenting? And if not, did they reasonably believe she was?'

'Actually, I thought Amy was credible,' said Susannah. She met Eva's gaze. 'For me, it's the difference between her not consenting and her letting them know she wasn't. I do believe that she didn't want intercourse—probably with either of them. I mean, she did want to have sex with Jayz, the texts and everything make it clear she wanted to fuck him.'

Jake did a double-take, and both Dave and Scott laughed—it was the word coming out of Susannah's mouth, in her pink linen shirt and her gold necklace.

Susannah just carried on. 'But I think she was only going to do that if they were by themselves, and maybe not even that night. But with Chris there, she didn't want intercourse with Jayz, and she definitely didn't want it with Chris.'

'So, you're saying she wasn't consenting?' asked Dave.

'Yes,' said Susannah.

'How do we know for sure?' said Dave.

'We have to decide to believe her,' said Eva.

'Amy said she tried to stop them taking off her jeans,' said Les. 'Didn't she laugh?'

Eva said, 'I think she laughed to make it okay. To keep it low-key.'

'I get what Eva means,' said Susannah. 'She laughed because they were older, and she was trying to make it not a big deal, but she meant to stop them. I think she just didn't want to come across as being prudish.'

'We can't win, can we?' said Chantae. 'Don't do it, and you're a tease or a prude; have sex and you're a slut.'

'Ha!' said Susannah. 'Too true.'

'And maybe it's even more than that,' said Eva. 'If she laughed, it could just stop, and not be anything, but if she started shouting, and fighting, and they didn't stop . . .'

'It got really serious,' said Chantae.

'Yes,' said Eva. 'There would be no way to conceive it as anything but an attack.'

'Maybe she didn't want them to think she was overreacting,' said Susannah.

'Either way, she didn't scream or yell out,' said Dave.

'To who?' said Eva.

'Could the drugs have made her laugh?' asked Kahu.

'So, the argument is the boys wouldn't have known she wasn't consenting because of the laughing,' said Mark.

'I agree,' said Susannah.

'You just said it wasn't a genuine laugh,' said Eva.

'But did they know that? They can't read her mind.'

'Well, I don't think there's any suggestion she was laughing when they were having intercourse with her. She told them not to,' said Eva.

'While laughing,' said Scott.

'Amy told Jayz to stop, and they said it was because Travis was watching. Was that when they said Travis left?' asked Kahu.

'Les, what did Travis say?' asked Mark.

'Because he is another witness as to whether Amy wasn't consenting and whether the boys knew,' said Jake.

'If we trust him,' said Kahu.

'I reckon Travis was just trying to weasel out of it all,' said Dave.

'I got the impression he left because of what had happened with Maia,' said Eva. 'He didn't trust Chris and Jayz.'

'I agree. He knew something was going down, eh?' said Kahu. 'Remember he said he was scared of what they were going to do. But I agree with Dave too. Travis said he narked because he wanted to take some responsibility, but he was still a coward because he didn't tell the whole truth—he did know what they were going to do, he knew they'd shaken a six. It's Caleb who did the right thing, testifying against them all, and he said Travis was freaked out when he phoned that last night. I reckon Travis saw them forcing her.'

'Caleb thought Travis was totally freaked out—remember, he told the judge,' said Dave.

'And when Caleb went to see him the next morning, Chris was with Travis smoothing it all out. Chris is so dodgy,' said Chantae.

'And they called Travis a pussy, on the group chat afterwards, so they must have expected him to go along with it,' said Kahu.

'I agree, Travis knew they were forcing her,' said Eva.

'Yes,' said Jake.

'Here it is,' said Les. 'So Travis said: "I wasn't sure what was going to happen. I felt weird, so I left."'

'There's another bit too . . .' said Kahu, reaching for the other transcript folder. 'Where he says he was scared of what they were going to do.'

'Yeah, I reckon,' said Chantae, leafing through her notepad.

They waited. Les found it. 'You're right, Chantae—oh, actually, it's the prosecutor. He asks Travis, "When you decided to leave, was it because of what happened to Maia?" And Travis says, "They weren't trying to have oral sex with Amy." And then the prosecutor says, "Is that why you left?", which doesn't really make sense. Travis says, "I left because they were undressing her." The prosecutor says, "Was Amy helping?" "No." "Was she objecting?" "Amy said, 'Don't,' but then she was laughing."'

'So, that doesn't get us anywhere,' said Susannah.

'Probably not far,' said Mark.

'Didn't Amy say Travis was there the whole time? So he'd be cagey, because that means he watched them rape her,' said Eva.

'It is only her word,' said Mark.

'Yeah, but that's only Travis's word. Why would we believe him over her?'

'The burden of proof,' said Les.

A few people frowned. Eva sighed.

'Don't the "Diced" messages help?' asked Kahu. 'And Jayz put up that photo of Amy.'

Scott picked up his photo booklet and turned to the page. 'This one.' He held up the final photo—the nude of Amy with her head superimposed on it. 'Except for us they blanked out her tits.'

'It's like she's a trophy,' said Eva.

'The lawyer said that was her motive for going to the police with the accusation?' said Dave. 'Because they sent the picture and told everyone she'd had group sex?'

'What if . . .' said Kahu. 'So you know how Travis leaves, and then a bit later someone shouts to them, right? D'you reckon Travis went to get Lee to stop them?'

'There wasn't evidence of that, Kahu,' said Jake.

'And would Lee have stopped it anyway?' asked Eva.

'D'you know what I'm beginning to think?' said Mark, and there was a silence. 'I think the girls knew about the Dice Game—Lee testified to that and so did that girl, Tia. And Samara participated, knowing about the game, so the others would have known too—kids gossip. And then Samara got annoyed because Lee didn't want to get with her, and the "Diced" messages and that photo annoyed them all—Sacha said that too. I think the girls whipped up this whole thing.'

'You mean they colluded?' said Jake doubtfully; he didn't believe the girls were outright lying.

'The thing is, it's pretty easy to make up this stuff, but it's hard to throw it off,' said Mark.

'Yeah, these kinda allegations could ruin someone's life,' said Dave.

'If the girls started it to get back at the boys for their texts, and then got trapped into the story they'd created'—Mark made a circular motion with his hand as he spoke—'they might even have started to believe it, like children whose parents whip up a hysteria of child abuse claims.'

Les, who was working through his asterisked notes, looked up. 'That's why the prosecution have to prove it beyond a reasonable doubt. We have to be certain.'

'Sure,' murmured Eva.

'Yes,' said Mark. 'That's our duty, remember, people: the boys are innocent until proven guilty. Proven.'

'One hundred per cent certain,' said Dave.

'How can we be when we weren't there?' asked Scott.

'How can anyone ever be in these cases?' asked Dave.

Eva noticed then that Hayley's hands were covering her face. 'The test is beyond a reasonable doubt,' said Eva slowly. 'We have to be sure. Not absolutely certain.'

'Agreed,' said Les. 'But I'd still like an indication of the percentage . . .'

Jake was thinking about a comment Tilly sometimes made about society needing to protect girls from sexual abuse, not boys from false claims.

'If it was all true, why didn't Amy go straight home and tell her parents?' asked Mark. 'Then the police could have got proper forensic evidence.'

'That doesn't mean she was lying necessarily,' said Les. 'Remember the judge talked about people delaying complaining.'

'Yes. She might have been too shocked and traumatised. Or it's possible she didn't even understand that it was rape that night,' said Eva.

'Do girls actually make this stuff up?' asked Jake.

'Rarely,' said Eva, at the same time as Mark said, 'All the time.'

'What gets to me, though, is Amy's actions straight after. She couldn't explain that, not to the prosecutor or when she was cross-examined,' said Susannah.

'You mean when she got in the car with Jayz? Yeah, that was weird,' said Chantae.

'And she put on his top,' said Susannah.

Les said, 'Those are important points which go to her credibility. The lawyer said that in his closing: she wouldn't get in the car with her rapist.'

'And why did she get in the back seat?' asked Chantae.

'That does undermine her credibility,' said Jake.

'And another thing: she had no injuries except, like, one bruise,' said Dave. 'So it can't really have been rape.'

'Actually, the doctor addressed that, Dave,' said Les. 'She explained that just because she found no internal injuries on Amy that wasn't conclusive either way on whether she was raped. Remember, she talked about the nature of vaginal tissue—its stretchability. A girl can be raped without injuries. The problem is, it explains the dearth of physical evidence rather than providing any, which leaves us back relying on her word.'

'Maybe she was consenting with Jayz but not Chris?' said Jake.

TWENTY MINUTES LATER, Mark sighed and leaned back, hands behind his head. 'Look, it's unfortunate. It was a dumb thing to do, but teenagers make mistakes, especially with social media—don't you think, Kahu? The idea we'd put these boys in jail for, like, ten to twenty years for a drunken mistake . . . I think that's what we're talking.'

'Seven, isn't it?' said Jake.

'Well, that's their futures ruined. You know, while their friends are off living . . . They're Kahu's age and look at him.'

'They're not like Kahu,' said Eva firmly.

'Of course, we can't take the sentence into account,' said Les.

'But it's a factor,' said Mark.

'That's irrelevant to us,' said Les.

'I can believe Chris did it,' said Jake suddenly. 'Raped Amy. I think he'd do that.'

It was Tilly who'd brought up the blog Jake had read back when the boys were first charged. It wasn't intentional. She'd said, 'So it was Chris, the oldest one, who had sex with the thirteen-year-old? Which complainant is she?'

Jake had been evasive, flustered by the daily warnings from the judge not to discuss the case with family members, but then in the night he'd woken to a door banging shut. TJ coming home from Melissa's, he supposed; he wasn't allowed to stay at her house on weeknights. Lying there, Jake thought that was the difference between TJ and the defendants. TJ had been in a relationship with Melissa for a year now—he respected girls.

Jake remembered then the day he'd read the blog online, the day Liam had killed the dog. He picked up his phone and searched for it. He assiduously ignored all the reports that covered the trial and went back to before the charges were laid. He couldn't find it, but saw a reference in an early news article that said the oldest of the Dice Bros was being investigated as a result of separate allegations that he'd had sex with a thirteen-year-old. Jake was surprised they hadn't been told about it; surely it was too much of a coincidence—no smoke without fire. If Chris had had sex with someone so young, it suggested there was a pattern to his behaviour. There might be another whole trial against just him after this one. Jake could remember cases which had sparked media debate about whether jurors should be told about defendants' prior convictions or other charges against them. Perhaps Chris had already been acquitted of that one and that's why he was so disdainful in court.

Mark and Les had remonstrated with Jake before when he'd tried to mention the thirteen-year-old, so he knew better than to bring it up, but it certainly made you think.

OVER HALF AN hour later Mark called for a vote on the charges relating to Amy. He knew already who was for and who against, and sure enough, he, Susannah, Bethany, Dave, Scott and Les voted not guilty. Eva, Kahu and Hayley voted guilty. Chantae said she hadn't decided and the other surprise was Jake, who said he was heading towards guilty for Chris on this one, but seeing as the vote was split he wouldn't make a final call yet.

'So, what do we do now?' said Dave. 'We've achieved absolutely sweet FA.'

'Actually, that's not true. In fact, I think we've gone as far as we can,' said Mark. 'We've agreed not guilty on both the indecent assaults. We've agreed guilty as parties to making the video of Maia.'

'Except for Lee, because he wasn't there,' said Jake.

'And I think it's time to admit that we're a hung jury for the three sexual violation charges. We're almost evenly split—that's not going to change.'

There was a silence as they considered this.

'I don't believe we are going to reach consensus. We're not making any further progress. Isn't that the rule, Les?' said Mark.

'We have to keep trying,' said Eva.

'Let's be done with it,' said Scott.

'Too right,' said Dave.

'You fellas thought through the consequences of us not deciding?' asked Chantae.

'It's not our responsibility to think about the consequences, you said that before,' said Dave. 'I need to go. I've been confirmed; I'm going to California in a few days.' To make the point he looked at his watch.

'California?' Susannah was surprised; his job was cutting down trees.

'Firefighting,' said Kahu. 'He volunteers, whaea.'

'Yeah,' said Dave. 'Wildfires.'

Bethany wasn't sure what a hung jury was, but she understood that it meant they could leave, and all she wanted now was to go home to Carly and to go to work tomorrow.

'It was me who said it's not our responsibility to think about what the sentence might be,' said Les, 'but we are charged with attempting to reach a unanimous verdict.'

'What alternative do we have?' asked Susannah. 'We can't force anyone to go against their moral convictions.'

'Too right,' said Scott.

Susannah was aware that Scott was staring at her then, and as she met his gaze she experienced an instinctive shudder of revulsion, even though he'd never been anything but polite towards her.

Jake was thinking if it was a hung jury he could fudge which side he was on when he explained it to Tilly. 'We can't force anyone to go against what they believe,' he said.

'Although you didn't actually decide what you do believe,' said Mark.

'We are talking about teenagers. Just boys. And they made some awful mistakes, but they're not criminals,' said Susannah.

'Actually,' said Les, 'if they broke the law, they are.'

'Christ, Les, do we always have to talk in literals?' said Mark.

'They're charged as adults, so isn't it kind of emotive to say they're teenagers?' said Eva. 'They're eighteen and nineteen—maybe Chris is twenty now.'

'I just hope the girls get some counselling,' said Susannah.

'Why would they need it if you've decided nothing happened?' said Hayley from down on the floor.

'That's not what we've decided, Hayley,' said Mark angrily. 'We've decided we can't reach a decision on three of the charges, and I think it's unfair for you to complain when you've effectively opted out of the whole deliberation.'

There were murmurings then, and Mark was aware he might have taken it too far.

'So? We're a hung jury on all the sexual violation counts?'

Into the silence, Dave said, 'Yep, let's stop going round in friggin' circles, mate. Let's tell the judge.'

CHAPTER SIXTEEN

# The verdict

'Defendants, please stand. On count one, Chris, you are charged with the indecent assault of Samara at Blue Lake. How does the jury find?'

'Not guilty.'

Chantae watched as Chris's face broke into a smile. Jayz whispered something to Lee, who didn't look relieved, he looked smug. Chantae felt anger rise in her that Lee had got away with so much, and she shifted slightly in the jury box so her arm rested against Hayley, who didn't pull away. Chantae could hear the tiny catches in Hayley's breathing.

As the registrar turned to the second charge, Eva saw that Chris was looking straight at Mark expectantly, and she was surprised to feel only sadness as she sat watching, anticipating his expression.

'On count two, Chris, you are charged with sexual violation through unlawful sexual connection. This is the allegation that you performed oral sex on Maia without her consent. How does the jury find?'

Mark shot a look at the front row of jurors. Too late for him to see, Eva gave a small nod.

'Guilty.' Mark's voice was louder than normal.

Chris's face transformed. The noise level in the public gallery rose. The jurors exchanged glances. The other defendants started to whisper.

Chantae saw the look Chris threw Travis, and thought she wouldn't be in his shoes now for anything.

Mark kept his eyes fixed on the judge while he answered that Jayz and Travis were also guilty as parties to the oral sex charge, but that Lee was not guilty.

There was so much movement and whispering from the public gallery that the judge had to quieten them down. Scott shook his head slightly; Kahu dropped his eyes. Dave watched the boys' shocked faces and he thought their lawyers or their parents must have told them they would get off. He felt a sense of dread inside that he was partly responsible for this outcome, as he thought back to the jury room, to his own comment that the boys had gone too far and crossed a line that night.

The registrar explained that Travis had already pleaded guilty to making the video of Maia, then she said, 'Jayden, you are charged as a party to making that intimate visual recording. How does the jury find?'

Mark said, 'Guilty.' His voice caught slightly, so when he said the same for Chris he spoke forcefully, and with the same force he said, 'Not guilty,' to Lee on that charge.

It was complicated. The people watching were trying to take it all in, to clarify. The judge asked for silence again.

The registrar read out count four. 'Jayden, you are charged with the sexual violation by rape of Amy. How does the jury find?'

Utter silence. A collective bated breath. Jayz and Chris looked terrified now, Eva thought.

'Not guilty,' Mark said.

Through her tears, Hayley glanced down at her hands, but made no move to connect a finger with a thumb.

The registrar boxed on, over the noise. 'On count five, Chris, you are charged with the sexual violation by rape of Amy. How does the jury find?'

'Not guilty,' said Mark.

The noise level rose again, and this time the judge spoke harshly, threatening to clear the court. Kahu wondered if his tone meant that he thought they were wrong. He wondered if they *were* wrong.

'On count six, Lee, you are charged with the indecent assault of Maia. How does the jury—'

Mark had spat out the 'not guilty' before the question was even completed.

Lee bowed his head, but the smile was obvious to Susannah, and she resented him for it, even though she was confident, as the jurors confirmed their agreement with the verdicts, that they had reached an appropriate compromise.

## CHAPTER SEVENTEEN

# Dave

They were driving north towards Base 8, through an area the wildfire had swept over so fast the trees were left standing, blackened leaves on the branches. Dave knew this species would survive as long as the flames had passed rapidly enough.

Ted, the driver, told him he'd worked wildfires for years.

'You from here then?' asked Dave.

'Nah, Montana. I come here, though, once our season's calmed down.'

'I've not been to America before. Been to Canada and Aussie a bunch of times.'

Ted talked about last season being up by Yosemite. Dave listened, staring out the window. There were more areas now where the ground was smoking. They passed the charred remains of a house with twisted metal gates, another still partly standing.

'Be a while before they can even check the houses out here,' said Ted.

'Yeah, could flare up easy.'

They were back in among stands of burnt trees, and there were flashes of orange now and then in the undergrowth.

'There'll be a crew heading here to do some dousing.'

'Montana,' said Dave. 'Don't know much about it.'

'Big Sky Country. Beautiful.'

'Land of the Long White Cloud—that's us,' said Dave, but Ted wasn't listening. He'd slowed the truck.

'Look.'

'Holy . . .'

Ted pulled over. They both got out.

'Got your phone, dude?'

'You seen this before?' asked Dave.

'Once. You?'

'Nah—heard of it, though.'

They looked up at the tree. It was a ponderosa pine, still partly green, but its trunk was split where maybe a branch had fallen away, and the inside seemed to be hollow. The split part of the trunk was glowing orange with yellow flames licking at the spike of wood. Further down, where the trunk appeared whole, there were fist-sized gaps in the bark and each was lit from within by fire.

Dave was videoing with his phone, watching the flames climb inside the hollow tree, when Ted said, 'We should move. It'll go soon.'

There was the first whooshing sound of the branches catching alight as they were getting into the truck. Dave fumbled his phone back on in time to video the flaring yellow flames engulfing the crown of the tree.

Inside the truck, and over the noise of the engine, they heard the final cracking and the low *harrumph* as the burning tree collapsed.

Fastidiously, Dave put his phone back into the waterproof pouch he'd used since his second Aussie trip, and put it inside his heavy firefighter's jacket down by his feet. Soon the jacket would reek of smoke and sweat from twelve-hour shifts. He would only get to shower every few days. At night they would sleep in tents. In Canada, he'd kept his clothes on so he was ready, and his socks had started to smell like vinegar, and in the mornings they were stiff with dried sweat.

Dave took a long drink from his water canister, screwed the lid back on and then undid Ted's bottle and passed it to him. Ted drove fast, chugging down the water, before passing it back. He told Dave they were close to the base now. Dave was thinking he needed a slash, and how much he'd like a cold drink and some time to get the lay of the land. He knew that wouldn't happen, and he knew it even more when Ted started telling a story about a fire engine—a converted military truck—that had broken down when the driver was making a mobile attack from in the green.

'He couldn't get the truck going, and before anyone could help, the fire closed in. Flames shooting out the truck windows. Tyres exploded—totally burned out. Three minutes, they reckon, from when he reported it down.'

'Hell,' said Dave, shaking his head. 'The driver?'

'Yeah, went into the black to save himself.'

Dave could feel the fear inside as he pictured the man running into the burned-out area. It would settle, though, once he was working.

They had come out into the open. The smoke-filled sky glowed a heavy orange-brown, and ahead, on the hills, the forest was burning.

Dave thought again about the ponderosa pine—he wanted to check the video.

'I was on a jury just before I came here,' he said.

'No shit,' said Ted. 'Murder?'

'Nah, rape. But not like a normal rape, not an attack—it was a group of kids—they all knew each other. Days and days inside a courtroom with no windows, listening to kids talk teenage crap.'

'So you acquitted?'

Dave heard a plane passing overhead.

'It was complicated. The boys had done dumb shit. We were going hung jury. Then this one juror persuaded us we couldn't do that.'

Now Dave could see an air tanker flying the line between the forest that was burning and the green. He watched it let loose a billowing red stream of retardant. Imagined, at least, that he could smell its acridity, even from here.

A second plane was following the first. As it released its retardant, Dave said, 'This one juror, mate. She told us stuff about her life. She was full-on . . . like, *fierce*.'

The older man laughed.

It was the ponderosa, Dave thought.

They were approaching a compound with a barn and some RV trailers. People were readying vehicles.

'They all are,' said Ted. 'All these times when one girl says something happened with some big shot, and then before you know it, ten more jump on the bandwagon and say it happened to them too.'

Dave was quiet. What Ted was talking about was different. Finally he said, 'I guess,' and then he added, 'Like wildfire,' and they both laughed.

Dave felt almost hyped up then. There were firefighters gearing up. He would be out there soon, saving the forest and homes and lives. Real work.

As he parked, Ted said, 'It makes me sad, you know. We should all be able to get along. I mean, where's it heading?'

'Too true—it's outta control,' said Dave. But when they were unloading the gear, he added, 'You know, those boys needed to pull their heads in though. They took it too far, for sure.'

CHAPTER EIGHTEEN

# Hayley

They are running through the Redwood Grove—she and Phil and Tyler. The ground is thick with the rust-orange fallen foliage. In every direction she sees the straight red-brown trunks, some thin enough to circle with your hands, some so wide it would take five people, arms outstretched, to reach around them. Overhead, their crowns form a green whispering ceiling. The sounds of people—calling out, children laughing, the occasional car—fade as they head deeper into the forest, until they are alone in the quiet of the trees.

In her consciousness now, Hayley hears only the steady drawn-out exhale of their breaths and the soft thud of their feet on the track; sees only the vertical lines of the tree trunks; feels the lightness of her limbs, the energy firing her muscles. She knows the bend of the path ahead, where the tree roots cross it, the unevenness of the boardwalk over the stream, the place where the wire mesh is lifted, the white-glazed look of the vegetation preserved in the sulphurous water.

She is utterly in the moment for the first time in more than a month.

• • •

THE DAY AFTER the trial finished, Hayley woke early to a curved shimmer of light at the edge of her vision. Within an hour she was reacquainted with the throbbing pain behind her left eye and up into her skull. At eight, Phil called her boss to explain she had a migraine and was vomiting and wouldn't be able to work that day. It was Saturday afternoon before she felt her head clear fully, and even then she fell asleep on the couch while they watched the Black Ferns game.

On Sunday afternoon, though, she insisted on running in the forest, just as she and Phil had done four times a week for six years now, just as the three of them had done each Sunday afternoon since she moved in with him and Tyler. Back in the early days, Tyler used to sprint ahead through the redwoods towards the thermal pool with its surreal turquoise water, his footsteps muffled by the thick layer of redwood needles, so that when he called back to them it was almost like he was shouting in a church. But by the time they'd reach the spring-green ponga track, Tyler would be dragging his feet and whining about having a stitch. Once he started playing rugby, though, Phil sat him down and explained how to pace himself, and since then he ran between them and matched their strides, and the three of them were a unit.

But that Sunday Hayley was unable to find a rhythm, felt out of breath and taunted by the tight jabbing pain of a stitch. She left Phil and Tyler to run the usual track up to the lookout and down past the mud pools, and she walked the shorter loop back through the grove towards the car park. She could hear the people around the visitor centre and the Treewalk—the tourists and locals, mountain bikers and walkers; further down the road there would be horse floats. She tried to imagine cantering on a horse along these trails, but it was too far removed from her experience.

She sat on one of the wide sculpted benches in among the redwoods and, leaning back, tilted her face up towards the canopy. The pole-like lines of the towering trunks gave the illusion that she was encircled by trees. High above, their thin branches reached blackly out towards each other, but the spray of each tree's foliage left between it and the next a space where the pale grey light seeped through.

MONDAY NIGHT WITH their running group was not much better. Hayley ran the whole way but trailed at the back with the newbies and the older man. She kept needing to take extra breaths and had a jangly pain in her lower back.

On Wednesday she opted out.

Work, though, all week, was a pleasure. She was weeding in the Government Gardens—not the ornamental rectangular beds of tulips and salvia, but in the wilder part around the gazebo and the ponds, and the effects of her work were obvious and immediate. She cleaned the interpretation signs, line-trimmed the base of the fences around the thermal mud pools and sprayed the box hedge-edged path between the bowling greens that led up to the earthquake-prone museum with its mock-Tudor facade.

ON THURSDAY MORNING Hayley had a message from a 'Dave Watkins'. She was about to delete it, when she recognised, from the tiny profile pic, the scraggly beard and Swanndri. The message said, *This made me think of you. Hope you're doing ok.* There was a video of a tree burning from the inside out.

That afternoon, a week after the end of the trial, she said to Phil, 'I need to walk not run today, but with you. I need to tell you what happened to me at the trial,' and he nodded and said, 'I'm ready.'

They drove out to the lake for a change. With daylight saving, the afternoon sun was still on the track. As they walked down the hill through the tree tunnel, Hayley remembered that when she'd first moved here these trees were knee-high seedlings.

On the boardwalk, she started to explain the dynamics of the deliberation. Paused when they spotted a spoonbill, and then another, watched the relentless scything of their beaks sweeping in an arc, snapping shut as they found their prey, and then the tilt of their heads as they let the food slide down their throats.

When they set off again, Hayley said, 'They were talking in circles, there was no progress. Some thought the girls had made it up and some that it was exaggerated or that it didn't matter. I couldn't join in or explain. I felt weighted down. Like I couldn't breathe.'

'Weighted down?' said Phil.

• • •

AT THE BEGINNING of the deliberation, Hayley had suggested they follow the judge's instructions and look at the charges for each round of the Dice Game. Then she'd tried to articulate Maia's truth, but they ignored her or spoke over her and they turned the talk away from Maia's words. As they sparred and pontificated, Hayley felt her silence solidify inside her, and the longer they talked the more the silence grew and there was less and less room for air. She tried to distance herself from their comments so they could not cut at her, and finally—weakly, she knew—she attempted to distract herself through her visualisation exercise, as if she were a child picking up a favoured cuddly toy or blanket.

For years she'd trained her mind to respond so she merely had to place her index finger against her thumb and, like a reflex, she was swimming in Lake Waikareiti. Her second finger was the sound of her and her friend laughing and laughing, her friend saying, 'You're such an egg,' because it was the time in the changing room at the gym with the cloying smell of spray-on deodorant, when Hayley had realised the lump in the back of her jeans was yesterday's bunched-up undies. And her third finger was touch. The psychologist had suggested imagining sand or water running through her fingers, the softness of velvet or the warm fur of a pet. Without admitting it to her, Hayley had chosen the feeling of trailing her fingertips down the line of Phil's trapezius from his skull to the dip before his deltoid. She loved to feel, below his skin, the latent power of his muscles. For six years she'd practised these sensory memories again and again, until they were as second nature to her as tumbling had been years before. Back when she was eleven and twelve, back when tumbling through space was her favourite sensation—the momentum, the power, the rush, as she turned her body over and over in handsprings, round-offs and aerials.

But in the jury room, during the deliberation, her mind let her down and she could not find the lake when they were discussing Maia on the video. She tried to envisage it, to hold its smooth surface in her mind, but the picture became distorted as if by a migraine's aura, and then Scott had made his foul comments and she had to speak and tell them that Maia was trying to scream, but they didn't listen, and when she tried to hear her friend's laughter all she could hear was her own reverberating silence. In desperation, she thought of the touch of her fingers on Phil's shoulder, but what she felt instead was the pressing hands of another man. She was twelve again. Sitting on the spring floor of the gym, legs open in a V, stretching forwards with her arms, forehead against the ground, as the new coach pushed down on her back, palms either side of her spine. She could feel the pressure on her back as she sat there at the table in the jury room.

Her hamstrings had burned as he pressed, and then the relief of release, but one of his hands had stayed, resting gently there. And then his fingers had slipped down her vertebrae, one bony ridge at a time, moving slowly over her leotard. Right down, between her bum cheeks, pressing, pressing, lower. Right there. And her whole body had flushed with shame and she hadn't moved, and then his hand was gone, and he was straightening, promising, 'We'll work on this,' and that was the first time.

Sitting there in the jury room as they debated why Maia had stayed silent, Hayley asked herself why she had not let the sound of her own fear and disgust come out back then. Why she hadn't shouted in her coach's face, pulled away, run away; why she hadn't told her mum or a teacher or the police; why she'd continued to go to gymnastics five times a week; why she hadn't spoken when he brushed past her, leaned against her, whispered. Why she'd frozen every time he stood behind her, his hands on her hips, thumbs on her sacrum as he pushed her into a forward bend, her head to her knees as he moved closer, until her bum was against his thighs. And she knew that the other girls had seen. And they said nothing. And the older girls who helped the coach said nothing. And she was so ashamed that she'd said nothing. Ashamed that her body made him touch her. That her widening hips filled his hands, that her buttocks curved against his thighs. She hated that her small breasts in the sparkly leotard held his eyes. That her legs had goosebumped up at a competition just before her turn on the high beam, so that he, sitting next to her on the bench and reminding her to hold the arabesque before the dismount, saw the invitation of the goosebumps on her thin pale legs and rubbed her puckering skin, slowed to a stroke and then let his fingers travel slowly up the inside of her thigh even as she'd tried to push her legs together as tightly as possible to eliminate any gap. But his hand had been unrelenting, so that on the beam, as she turned her body in a walkover and then stopped in the centre, right leg trembling as her left arched behind her, up so high she could grasp her toe behind her head, all she could feel was the burning left by his hand against the crotch of her leotard.

In utter shame in the jury room, Hayley stood up and went to the place where the walls met, and she sat on the ground with her back against one, her side against the other, where they couldn't see her face, where they couldn't see her shame for what she had let him do in that echoing vaulted room. Her shame that she had not spoken out, that she had not stopped him touching her, touching her friend, touching the girl with the pale skin and the dark hair in the group below.

And when Hayley sat on the ground, the other jurors stopped talking. There was a whisper. Eva came and bent down, but Hayley said, 'Just let me be here,' and she was surprised to hear her own suppressed anger, but she shouldn't have been surprised, because she was angry. Angry she couldn't be part of this, that she couldn't speak up for Maia, or for Amy, or Samara, or the girl with the dark hair, or even for her thirteen-year-old self. And she had tried. Tried to stay with the roaming discussion of the deliberation, tried to speak up, but it was only when they were talking about being a hung jury that the bitterness sparked inside her, so that when Susannah said the girls needed counselling, she couldn't help but spit out, 'Why would they need it if you've decided nothing happened?'

It was Mark, though, who gave her the final prompt.

He said, 'That's not what we've decided, Hayley. We've decided we can't reach a decision on three of the charges, and I think it's unfair for you to complain when you've effectively opted out of the whole deliberation.' Finally he said, 'So? We're a hung jury on all the sexual violation counts?'

Hayley stood then, and as she moved from the corner of the jury room to the table, she knew they would see her as the weird, shaky, too-thin juror whom Chantae called Jumpstart. She had to lean her hands on the tabletop to steady herself. She spoke softly. 'If we go back and say we can't decide, then all of this has been for nothing. The girls telling the police, and testifying, all that time being cross-examined, it's for nothing. If we're a hung jury, they have to do it all over again.'

'Or, even worse, they won't,' said Eva, her tone high-pitched and urgent. 'And the boys will just get off. And they'll think it doesn't matter. It doesn't mean anything. The boys'll think they can do it again.'

In a voice still hesitant and faltering, Hayley told them, 'I know how hard it is to speak up. When I was young, my gymnastics coach abused me for . . . nearly two years. He came from overseas, when I was twelve. He'd coached Olympians. We all worked so hard for him and we thought the touching was just . . . his way. You talked about Amy laughing—we sort of laughed at him. Not because it was okay . . . but to defuse it, to make it not matter.

'And then it got so much worse. It wasn't just me. It was three of us, and people saw stuff, but no one asked him what he was doing. And those of us he did it to, we tried to avoid sitting in the front seat of the van or being alone with him in the gear shed, but it didn't stop. I told a school friend, and she told me I had to tell or give up gymnastics, but it was my whole life. It was who I was. I'd started as a preschooler, running in and out of a rainbow parachute and doing roly-polies. By thirteen I was training fifteen hours a week.' Hayley glanced at Kahu then and whispered, 'Can you imagine? Your coach?' She didn't wait for him to answer, but Kahu gave a slow shake of his head.

'So I kept going, until it got really bad, and finally I worked up the courage and told the assistant coach. He put his face so close to mine it was as if he thought he could climb into my head and take back everything I'd said. He told me the coach was a professional, that he would never do that, and if I ever told stories again he'd expel me from the club. I still don't know why the coach left in the end, but I know that guy told people it was my fault, and I left too.

'I've tried to work out what I did to make him choose me. And I've hated myself that he could be out there, doing it to other girls, because I was afraid to report it properly.'

'It wasn't your fault—you tried,' said Eva, and her voice sounded like it was going to split open.

'I'm sorry,' said Susannah. 'Sorry for you. And look, it's very brave to tell us. But, honestly, Hayley, this is a totally different situation. With respect, this trial is just not the same as child abuse . . .'

'Yeah,' said Scott. 'Stuff happens when you're a kid, but it doesn't mean—'

'Let her finish,' said Chantae, in her low growl.

And then something happened.

It was as if the years of silence inside Hayley rose up and she did not want to be silent, she simply did not want to be silent any longer, and her words became fierce, and by the end there was a mana about her that they couldn't ignore.

'It's so easy,' Hayley said, 'not to hear us. Believe us. It's so much easier to say Amy should never have got onto the trampoline, or taken the E. That she shouldn't have led them on by kissing them—what a slut.' There was such hatred in her voice then, that some of the jurors glanced at each other in confusion.

'And Maia shouldn't have drunk so much. Shouldn't have been at that barbecue, if she couldn't handle herself. Shouldn't have big breasts, or shaved pubes . . .' She caught Scott's eye. 'I heard you. It's much easier to find a reason to make it their fault. Or to say it wasn't as bad as if someone attacked you in your house or grabbed you at night on the street.

'I know they liked those boys. I know they wanted to get with them. But they didn't want to be raped or violated by them. I know they are just boys. I know all that.' Hayley looked at Jake and saw an expression of openness that she had not expected.

'But I believe those girls. Do you know how hard it would be to go through this? To tell the police and to say it over and over here in court with everyone watching? With those boys watching?'

Hayley turned to Dave. 'If it's a stranger, you can distrust strangers. Install a burglar alarm. Avoid walking alone at night. But if it's someone you know, then who is safe? Who can you trust? For years I panicked whenever I was near men. Any men. Teachers. At work. In a cafe. I tried to be someone people didn't even see, so no one would ever pick me again. It took Phil more than a year to persuade me even to go for a drink with him. I've had counselling and medication and I'm still screwed up. Say what you like about the effect on those boys' lives, but they've already irreparably damaged the girls, even if Maia doesn't remember it all.'

Around her now, she could feel their support sustaining her courage. Dave nodded. Kahu's and Eva's eyes were locked on to her. Chantae was murmuring agreement. Hayley said, 'You all know they planned the whole thing. They made up the Dice Game and they didn't care whether the girls wanted to be part of it or not. They didn't care whether they were consenting or not. They did what they shook on the dice with the girls they shook. It wasn't random hook-ups. They did what the dice told them, whether or not the girls wanted it. They told us they chose

Amy and Maia because they were young and inexperienced . . . We have to take responsibility now and make decisions.'

And, like a wave breaking, they spoke up.

'Yeah, too right,' said Chantae.

'I agree with Hayley—I think it is an abdication of our duty if we accept being a hung jury,' said Les. 'We have to strive to find common ground.'

'Hayley's right,' said Kahu. 'We know they decided to carry on even if the girls didn't agree. They said that in their messages.'

'We know they planned to get Maia drunk and Amy high. That's assisting and encouraging,' said Eva.

'I think Hayley's got a point. Maybe the boys went too far, crossed a line,' said Dave.

'But if we can't reach consensus . . .' said Susannah, and Hayley could hear the whine in her voice. 'We can't force people . . .'

Mark spoke up. 'No, but we could compromise.'

'Okay,' said Les slowly, considering.

'I agree. Now Hayley's explained more about the context, we need to rethink,' said Jake. 'My wife once told me it's girls that need protecting, not boys.'

'Let's start with Chris, what he did to Maia,' said Eva. They had been so close on that one.

'The video is hard evidence,' said Jake.

'She was coma'd, and they knew it,' said Kahu.

'It's true she didn't look startled when they burst in,' said Susannah. 'And with Maia there weren't mixed messages like with Amy.'

Mark looked at Susannah and then nodded. 'I can live with that.'

There was a pause, then a rash of agreement, although from Scott it was an almost sulky, 'S'pose.'

'Are we meant to do it like this?' asked Eva. 'What about the judge's questions?'

'I think this is progress,' said Chantae.

'So, we go guilty for Chris on the charge of . . . "sexual violation by unlawful sexual connection",' Jake read from the question trail. 'What about the others as parties?'

Mark said, 'I could go guilty for the lot on that one charge.'

'Even Lee? I thought we'd decided Lee,' said Susannah.

'Well, perhaps not Lee, but the rest.'

Eva wanted to slow it down. 'So, Jayz helped get Maia up the stairs. Several of the kids at the barbecue said that, and Maia remembered them, one each side of her. And that's why I said yes to Chris too—if you can't walk, you can't consent, and they both knew it.'

'And Jayz went to get Travis, so he knew what was going on,' said Susannah.

'Yes, and Travis has admitted videoing it, so that was encouraging Chris, don't you think?' said Kahu.

'I think to be guilty, Travis had to know she was so intoxicated she couldn't be consenting,' said Jake.

'He knew,' said Kahu, and Hayley was surprised at the confidence in his voice now.

Chantae said, 'If she'd been okay, she'd've looked at him when he came in. If you were doing that and someone came in . . .'

'Yeah, good point, Chantae,' said Kahu.

'Travis did see her eyes open, though—he saw what we saw on the video,' said Jake.

'Bah,' said Chantae. 'She looked out of it.'

'Yeah, he'd surely expect Maia to say something,' Kahu added.

'Does everyone agree?' asked Mark.

'I agree,' said Les. 'I think they could see the oral sex was non-consensual.'

'Yeah,' said Dave. 'I thought maybe it didn't mean so much if Maia couldn't remember it, but from what Hayley's said . . .' His voice trailed away.

'I think it's the fact we've got the hard evidence for this one, the video. I mean, how dumb were they? But Lee wasn't there, so he's not guilty,' said Mark. 'Everyone agree? Scott?'

'You're telling the story.'

Mark jumped in fast. 'So we do that. We go guilty on the lesser sexual connection charges. That's not going to stuff up the boys' whole lives, but it teaches them a lesson. Not Lee, though; he wasn't involved—he wasn't in the bedroom.'

'And the trampoline ones?' asked Susannah.

'Nah. Rape's seven to ten years, isn't it? We can't honestly think—' said Mark.

'Yeah, you can't have both,' said Scott, looking at Hayley and then at Eva.

'We're not having anything—they did both,' said Eva.

'If this is what we're doing, we go guilty on the Maia oral sex ones, and not guilty on the rapes,' said Mark. 'Otherwise it's off.'

'Yep,' said Scott.

'All right,' said Susannah.

'Not guilty on the rapes on the basis, I presume, that we're not sure the boys knew there was no consent?' asked Les. 'I mean, we don't actually think she was consenting?'

'Exactly,' said Mark.

'You think they didn't know?' said Chantae, at the same time as Hayley said, 'But what does that do to Amy?'

'We can't take that into account,' said Mark. 'That's irrelevant.'

'Yep, Hayley, there's just not proper evidence with Amy,' said Jake. 'With Maia there's the video.'

'Amy had no injuries, Hayley. At the end of the day, there's nothing to back her up,' said Dave, shrugging.

'Yes, it's just he-said, she-said,' agreed Susannah.

'In fact,' said Les, 'Chris never said anything, and Jayz barely.'

'Yeah, we can't just go on her word,' said Mark.

'We can if we believe her,' said Hayley.

'If we're sure,' said Eva.

'How can we be sure without hard evidence?' said Mark.

*They head down the stairs as a pack. Almost all are talking, someone laughs. There is a collective release of tension. In the courtyard, Dave raises his hand in a generalised farewell, but he nods specifically to Hayley, whose eyes are still puffy. He sets off with Kahu towards his ute, and as they part he says, 'Thank Christ we're finally out of there.' Kahu smiles back, 'Stay safe, matua.'*

*As Hayley follows Dave and Kahu out of the gate onto the road, she sees her man sitting on the wall by the pub. He is wearing his faded black running shorts and the army green jersey his dad used to wear when he went dragnetting, its sleeves ragged. He's been to the barber today and his black hair is shorter than usual, and it makes Hayley look at him anew. He looks tough because of that, because of that and his muscly thighs there in the early evening sun, and she wonders how she ever came to trust him. And she wonders how these others would see him and who they would think he was. And for just a moment she feels inside her again that fierceness, that now would defend him against a single withering look or careless comment from Mark or Susannah.*

*He is here waiting for her, without them arranging that he would be here, without him knowing what time she would finish. He is here waiting in the place she told him nearly three weeks ago was the gate the jury used. He is sitting here smiling at her, in his running gear, because he knows that is what she will need now, and he holds out his hand to her and she comes and stands in front of him with the breeze catching the bottom of her cardigan and blowing it out behind her. And as she takes his hand she knows she deserves this—him and his son, her work, all of it—and he jumps down from the wall and without mentioning her tear-stained face, nor the relief that it is over, they walk together to the car.*

IT IS ONLY *when Bethany is about to cross the road that she realises she won't see any of these people again. She turns back, but can see through the open gate that the group, standing together in a semi-circle, are busy talking. She watches for a moment, returns Eva's wave, and then, seeing Scott break away and come towards her, she turns her back and walks hurriedly towards the bus stop by the library.*

WHEN SCOTT AND *Bethany have left, Mark suggests a drink at the Pig. Susannah and Jake agree immediately. Jake says he'll invite his wife to join them—he believes she'll be proud of their decision. Susannah looks at her Fitbit and thinks she'll just tell Jon it took them longer to reach a verdict.*

*Les catches Chantae's eye and waits to see if she will come to the pub, but she has to go to work. She steps forwards and hugs him, a brief awkward gesture which makes them both laugh, as she says,*

*'Goodbye, Sandwich-man.' Les wants to say something more but he can't articulate it, and even when he goes, a few months later, to the MexTex restaurant for dinner with his daughter and her partner, and asks if Chantae is working, and she comes out in her black-and-white-checked trousers and her black shirt and apron and agrees to sit for just a minute, still he can't think how to say what he wants to, and instead settles only for: 'Good luck.'*

AND SO THEY *leave, on foot, by bus or car, back to their own lives, and they may pass in the supermarket or on the street and for a while they will acknowledge each other; some will even stop to chat.*

*Eva will see Les and Scott again at the sentencing hearing. In the time between the trial and the hearing she has repeatedly worried that she failed the girls. She will continue to grapple with this recurring thought for many years.*

*At the hearing she sits next to Les, in the row behind Maia's parents, and they listen to Maia read her victim impact statement in a hurried, toneless voice. It is brief and factual. She has kept her feelings separate.*

*Samara and her family are not there.*

*Amy is not there.*

# Amy

She feels blurry. Lines are indistinct. The light from the deck is dim; everything is grey and shadowy. Jayz is lying facing her. Hands are touching her. Some hands are his hands. Some hands are not. When it's his hands her body responds, her mind responds. When it is not, her mind tries hard not to connect.

The lights on the deck are a string of old-fashioned globes—red, blue, yellow and green. While Jayz kisses her neck and shoulder, Amy gazes at those lights through the mesh of the trampoline, her fingers in his hair. Now he lifts his head to kiss her, his face super close, shadows below his cheekbones. Eyes deep-set. Large, brown, beautiful eyes. She can't believe he is with her—is touching her, kissing her, stroking her. But she can feel Chris's stubble against the back of her neck too. She doesn't understand why he doesn't leave them alone, why he doesn't find someone of his own. She tries to lose herself again in the touching. Jayz's touching. His hand on her hip, undoing her shirt, his thigh pushing against her leg.

Somewhere by her feet, Travis is sitting silent in the darkness, playing the music, watching through the dim light, and she is not sure what he can make out.

She whispers again into Jayz's ear, 'Let's go somewhere, just you and me.'

'Stay here,' he whispers back, and his voice is hoarse and wanting.

'Stay here,' mutters Chris, moving closer against her back.

Jayz has undone her shirt and she feels hands on her back; her bra is unclasped and immediately Jayz pushes the fabric up over her left breast and his hand is there. She catches her breath as her nipple hardens, and his tongue is in her mouth again.

Now his hand slides down her rib cage, and Chris's hand reaches over from behind to touch her breast; she pushes it off, but Jayz takes her hand with his and puts it on his back and Chris's hand returns.

'Don't,' she says with a little giggle as she prises it off again.

Chris laughs too, and she feels his leg against hers. His hand moves now to her back.

She holds Jayz's shoulders as he lazily strokes her waist. Even in the darkness she pulls her stomach in and holds it tight so that as he runs his fingers lightly across her belly he feels the dips and curves of her abs. Then his hand slips down the side of her hipbone below the waistband of her jeans, just the pads of his finger skating down, and she inhales, holding her breath with anticipation, with trepidation.

'Easy,' he whispers. His mouth finds hers again even as his other hand finds the button of her jeans. She twists, trying to move away, but Chris's body is right against hers now, keeping her there, pinning her there, between the two of them, and now both Jayz's hands work to undo the button and zip on her jeans.

'Don't,' she whispers, and hears Travis moving. Earlier his foot was touching hers and she hadn't minded that, because he was harmless and funny, and she knew he had a crush on her, but now, although he is still there in the darkness, he has shifted away from her, from all of them.

Jayz has undone her jeans and he pushes her onto her back and whispers to her, 'Relax, babe, it's all right,' and she can't feel Chris next to her and she's relieved, as Jayz strokes and manoeuvres and slips his fingers into her undies, and he is kissing her as he touches her and she's wet and she wants him to touch her, his hand moving teasing stroking, and the repetition and the anticipation make her lift her hips to his hand, but then suddenly Chris has his hand under her, cupping her butt, and she doesn't want him to. She doesn't want him on the trampoline with them. She doesn't want to be on the trampoline. She doesn't want to be high and drunk; she wants to be in control. But Jayz's fingers are inside her and then stroking over her clitoris and inside her, and she moans, and his mouth is on her breast, and as his hand keeps moving, she is coming, as his fingers push deep inside her Jayz is kissing her, which means that it is Chris's mouth on her breast and his hand in her hair.

As she comes down from that moment she is washed in shame. The shame of what she has let them do, of what she has liked them doing. And she scrambles to leave and get away from Chris, from Jayz, from both of them—all of them. She struggles away from Jayz's hands, from his body. 'I need to go . . .'

But as she twists away from him it brings her up against Chris, and he holds her still, his hands on her shoulders, pushing her back down.

'Whoa, whoa, whoa—slow down, babe.' His voice is lazy.

'I don't want to . . .' she says.

'No. No, you can't go now,' says Chris. 'We've only just got going.'

The words break through the blur. The words are clear and immediate.

'Please,' she whispers, and there is a flush of fear through her.

'More like it,' says Chris, still holding her shoulders, while Jayz is easing her jeans down over her hipbones, leaning over her, trying to kiss her again.

She wriggles, turns her face away.

'Take them right off,' says Chris, and his tone is light and playful, and she notices that incongruity.

'Don't, Jayz,' she says, as Jayz says, 'Come on, Ames,' softly, pleadingly, with a laughing lightness.

So when she says it again, she responds in kind, she laughs to deflect, to distract, to disarm, but she means the words.

They are working together, the boys, and she is still saying, 'Don't,' and she is still trying to keep that line blurred by a half-laugh, by a pleading, 'Jayz, stop . . . I don't want you to,' as they each caressingly hold an arm and push down her jeans with their other hand, one on either side, while she twists and wriggles. Jayz kneels over her, leans down and kisses her hard, his tongue pushing into her mouth, and then he is twisting, stripping her jeans over her feet, pulling down her undies, while Chris holds her shoulders firm, leaning over to suck her nipple. She is struggling more now, almost kicking at Jayz, her body shaking. She is not laughing now, but Chris is. Laughing as her hips buck and fight.

She can't hear Travis, even when Jayz swears and then says, 'Hold her leg.' She is afraid to call out to Travis. Afraid he will become one of them.

Her jeans and undies are off and Jayz pushes her legs apart, forcing his knee between them, holding one of her arms above the elbow, his other hand on the trampoline as he lies down on top of her. Chris holds her other arm and shoulder. She tries to move her bottom, her hips, away from him, but Jayz guides himself into her. Grunts.

Jayz's weight. Chris's grip. Travis's silence. It all makes her still as Jayz pushes into her again and again.

She is limp, lost in the greyness, her body moving with his motion, her hearing muffled, but when Jayz pulls away, lies between her legs for a moment more, she hears clearly Chris's voice, thick and harsh. 'My go,' he says. 'Move.'

And Jayz does. And even after what he has done to her, she is shocked that he does. And because he does, she has become nothing—as if the real her is not even there, only her body. So when Chris moves onto her, she lies still—she doesn't fight or scratch or bite, she doesn't push or scream or run—the only movement her body makes is the sobbing. She lies motionless even though Jayz is not bothering to hold her down, even when Chris pushes deeper, and gasps, inside her.

Travis has not moved. The whole time he has been still. Silent.

Chris says, 'Your go, Travis.'

He doesn't move.

'Don't be a fuckin' pussy, bro.'

Chris moves off her and she lies there—shirt undone, bra pushed up, naked from the waist down—Chris's semen inside her; Jayz's on the black polypropylene surface of the trampoline between her legs.

'Travis? Fuck's sake, mate—now's your chance.'

There's a shout then from the deck.

'Don't be a homo,' says Chris.

Amy has lost track of Jayz.

Another shout. Travis scrambles for the zipper of the trampoline. He is making a noise, and it is only after the trial that Amy realises he was crying. He was crying while they were raping her. He wasn't shouting, running for help, beating them off—he was crying.

WHEN THEY LEAVE, she lies curled up, until gradually she becomes aware of her teeth chattering; her heart beating. Her breathing. A morepork in the bush. The music. The sound of laughter, guys yelling, voices. A car on the drive.

When Jayz comes back, she's done up her shirt, and has her knickers on, but not her jeans. When he first climbs back into the trampoline, she backs away, even though part of her is pleased he's come back. Wants to find a way for it not to be him that did this. She wanted him so much.

'Come on, Ames,' he says. 'Why aren't you dressed?'

He has to repeat it before she answers. 'Can't find my jeans.'

He laughs, feels around in the dark, gets out of the trampoline and finds them on the grass, damp now.

He gives them to her, and she struggles into them.

'Come on. I'll take you home.'

She doesn't move.

He repeats, 'Amy, I'll drive you home.'

Her body keeps shuddering, so he puts his hoodie over her head, and she lets him push her arms through the sleeves. He tries to help her out of the trampoline, but now she won't let him touch her. He carries her sneakers, and she follows him barefoot out onto the road. She won't get in the front seat of his car. She sits in the back. On the way, he keeps looking at her in the mirror.

'Talk to me.'

She doesn't.

'Amy, I'm sorry if you're hurt. I do like you, babe, but I don't want to be your boyfriend, you know?'

And after another silence, 'Look, I know Chris is a bit pushy, but he's okay, honest.'

When he turns into her street, he says, 'You're all right, Amy. Just be chill, you know?'

At her house, he gets out and opens the car door.

'You'll be all good once you've warmed up.' He leans over and kisses her on the cheek and she lets him. Then she walks around the side of the house to the back door so she won't wake her parents, and it is not until Tuesday in maths that she starts to cry, because a boy she doesn't know well sends her a Snapchat of the nude pic she'd sent Jayz, her head from the other photo superimposed onto it. The caption says: *Done and Diced—Chris and Jayz. Travis u pussy. wtf???*

Reading the caption, Amy understands for the first time that everything happened because of the Dice Game. She is sure now that they came to the party and got her alone, gave her drinks and the E, made her body respond, and then raped her, because of a game.

## ACKNOWLEDGEMENTS

Given the setting of *Dice*, I would like first to acknowledge the district of Rotorua, Lake Rotorua, and the people of the waka of Te Arawa.

*Dice* began as part of a PhD in Creative Writing at the International Institute of Modern Letters at Victoria University of Wellington/Te Herenga Waka. Thank you to Damien Wilkins and Yvette Tinsley, both of whom provided motivating, challenging and inspiring supervision. While the novel is entirely a work of fiction, it was informed by the jury research component of my doctorate, which analysed some of the juror responses from the New Zealand sexual violence trials from the Trans-Tasman Jury Project—thanks to Professor Yvette Tinsley, Dr Warren Young, Professor Jonathan Clough, Professor James Ogloff and Dr Benjamin Spivak for allowing me to use this data.

In Chapter One, the song referred to is 'Lyk Dis' from the album *Yes Lawd!* (2016) by NxWorries. In Chapter Seven, when

Fiona takes her heart in her hands, I drew on the concept from Grace Paley's story 'My Father Addresses Me on the Facts of Old Age', published in *The New Yorker* on 9 June 2002. In Chapter Eight, the song referred to is 'Lost' from the album *Channel Orange* (2012) by Frank Ocean. In Chapter Fourteen, the survey Eva refers to is the New Zealand Crime & Victims Survey (NCVS), the results of which are available on the NZ Ministry of Justice website. In Chapter Eighteen, I drew inspiration from David Whyte's poem 'The Truelove', *The House of Belonging* (Many Rivers Press, 1997). A short story based on an early draft of Chapter Eleven was published as 'Fly' in the anthology *Horizons 4* (NZSA Top of the South Branch, 2019).

I have read the work of many jury researchers, legal academics and sexual violence survivors—too numerous to mention here—as well as many court transcripts, all of which provided background research. When writing the courtroom scenes, I found the book *Rape Myths as Barriers to Fair Trial Process* by Elisabeth McDonald with Paulette Benton-Greig, Sandra Dickson and Rachel Souness (Canterbury University Press, 2020) and Alison Young's article 'The Waste Land of the Law, the Wordless Song of the Rape Victim' from the *Melbourne University Law Review* (vol. 22, 1998) particularly useful.

I am grateful to have been awarded a Michael King Writers Centre Emerging Writers Residency, and a Surrey Hotel writers residency in association with The Spinoff, while writing *Dice*. I also appreciate receiving a Graduate Women New Zealand Postgraduate Fellowship and scholarship support from Victoria University of Wellington.

Thanks to Allen & Unwin—to Jane Palfreyman for publishing me, to Jane and Ali Lavau for their insightful and stimulating editorial input, to Melanie Laville-Moore, Angela Handley, Clara Finlay and Lisa White.

For providing feedback on drafts, discussing craft, challenging my thinking and/or bestowing wise advice—huge thanks to Kate Tokeley, Paddy Baylis, Stella Weston, Maire Vieth, Cate Mills, Sam Elworthy, Lisa Reynolds, Manawa Cox, Caren Wilton and my writing group from back in the day. I appreciated the support and feedback from my PhD cohort, especially Mikaela Nyman, Roxane Gajadhar, Anahera Gildea, Holly Walker, Justine Jungersen-Smith, Johanna Knox and Maraea Rakuraku. Thanks also to Catherine Chidgey and Vanessa Munro.

I appreciate the many people who willingly contributed their professional and personal expertise as I researched this novel; however, any mistakes or inaccuracies are my own. Thanks to all those who patiently answered my questions or provided feedback on specific characters or aspects of *Dice*. As well as those already mentioned, these include Anahera Gildea, Bill Lawson, Averil Herbert, John Herbert, Jeremy Cox, Tom Sladden and Katrina Weblin.

My close friends and my Baylis, Weston and Prebble families have been incredible over many years supporting me as a writer—thank you all. Thanks to my parents, Linda and Geoff Baylis, for their encouragement, and for instilling in me a love of stories and questions. My children joke that I am an author in spite of them, but in reality I would not be the person nor the writer I am without my family—Henry, Jack, Paddy and Stella. They have believed in me, critiqued my work with rigour, love, care and insight, commiserated and celebrated with me. And without Henry's constant support and unshakeable faith in my writing I would not have written *Dice*.

## ABOUT THE AUTHOR

Claire Baylis was born in England and moved to New Zealand before her final year of high school. She worked as a legal academic at Victoria University of Wellington/Te Herenga Waka for twelve years before moving to Rotorua with her family. There, she wrote, brought up her three children and worked as a jury researcher, before completing a PhD in Creative Writing from the International Institute of Modern Letters. Her fiction has appeared in *Landfall*, *Sport*, *Takahē* and *Turbine/Kapohau* and has been read on Radio New Zealand.